Whatever it Takes

Whatever it Takes

PAUL CLEAVE

upstart press

A catalogue record for this book is available from the National Library of New Zealand

ISBN 978-1-988516-90-5

An Upstart Press Book
First published in North America in 2020 by Upstart Press
Level 6, BDO Tower, 19–21 Como St, Takapuna 0622
Auckland, New Zealand

Designed by www.CVDgraphics.nz
Printed by Times Offset (Malaysia) Sdn Bhd

For my cousin, Katrina Cox — one of the strongest and most positive people I've been lucky enough to know.

One

"You're going to kill him," Drew says.

I rest my forehead against the wall and stare at the floor. I try to get my breathing under control. There's a half-flattened cockroach down there, along with a cigarette butt tossed at the garbage bin that's missed. There's something in my mind that hurts. I pinch the bridge of my nose and squeeze my eyes shut and will the pain away, but it holds on tight. It's like a splinter buried deep that's gotten infected, and the only way to dull the pain is by punching the guy tied up in the chair. Which is what I do. I hit him so hard I hear something crack and I don't know if it's one of my fingers or his cheek. I've hit him so many times already my fingers hurt bad, but his face has to hurt more. His left eye is swollen and purple, his nose is broke and his bottom lip split and there's plenty of blood and torn skin. But despite all that the son of a bitch still looks up at me with a grin, the kind of grin anybody would want to wipe off his face, only so far nothing has worked. The

9

only thing I can wipe are my knuckles on my shirt, which is already plenty messy.

Drew puts a hand on my shoulder and I shrug it off.

"Don't," I tell him.

He puts his hand back on my shoulder and looks me right in the eye. Drew and me, we've been best friends since we were kids. Growing up, we chased girls across playgrounds and climbed trees and went fishing. When we were older we joined the police together and played the role of best man at the other's wedding. If he doesn't remove his hand in the next two seconds, I'm going to break it.

"This isn't you, Noah. This isn't the way we do things."

He's right. This isn't me. Yet here we are. He takes his hand off my shoulder.

"Goddamn it, Noah, I can't let you beat him to death."

Drew has a look on his face that's a mixture of confusion and panic, mixed in with an overwhelming look of wanting to pretend this isn't happening. I feel the same way.

"You should leave."

"I . . ."

I take another swing at the guy in the chair before Drew can say whatever it is he thought he could say that would stop me. Blood and sweat mist the dry air and the punch echoes in the room. I can smell wood and blood and sweat. The guy spits a glob of blood on the floor and shakes his head. His smile comes back and I feel something in my stomach roll.

"My dad is going to put you in a box," he says. His name is Conrad, and the same way me and Drew grew up together, so did me and Conrad, only everything was opposite. We never hung out. Conrad isn't a hanging out kind of guy. He's a selfish son of a bitch. He's a bully without an ounce of decency in him. The kind of guy women warn their friends about and cross the road to avoid.

He's also the sheriff's son.

"You should be spending time thinking about your future, not mine," I tell him.

He spits again. "I told you already," he says. "I don't know where she is."

I pace the office. The windows are closed and the air isn't just hot, but sticky hot. My clothes are damp. They cling to my skin and stretch when I move. The wooden floors are worn smooth by the years of anxious foremen pacing them the same way I'm pacing them now, and they creak a little under my weight. Conrad is the current foreman. The furniture in here is so old everything could be a prototype. The first desk ever built, the first filing cabinet assembled — hell, even the computer is so big it looks like its first job was cracking the Enigma code. There's a TV bolted on the wall with a screen as round as a fishbowl. The ceiling is pitted with fly crap and the in-out trays on the desk have paperwork spilling out of them. My headache is starting to rage and the thing turning in my stomach turns some more. I don't like where this is going. I wish there were a way to take it all back.

There isn't.

I have to carry on.

For the girl. Alyssa.

I stop pacing in front of him. "Where is she?"

"I want my lawyer," he says.

Drew steps between us. He puts his hand on my chest and the other is on the butt of his gun that's still holstered and I wonder whether he'd use it, whether he even knows if he would. I shouldn't have gotten him mixed up in this. "Let's have a word outside," he says.

I stare at him, unblinking. Then I relent. We head into the factory. I put my hands on the iron railing. A few lights are on, but they're not doing a great job, the vastness of the factory is sucking the enthusiasm out of them. I can only see twenty yards in front of me. There are rows of lumber stretching out into the dark, long beams running as straight as train tracks. The night is pressing hard up against the dusty windows. I lean against the railing so I can face Drew as he closes the door. I can see Conrad through the window, looking out at us.

Drew keeps his voice low when he says, "Even if he does have her, he's not going to talk."

I undo the top button of my shirt. There are streaks of blood on it. The air in here is thick. The factory's powered down for the night, which means no air conditioning.

"He will," I say, for Alyssa's sake, and for mine too. There's no going back from this. "He has to."

Drew shakes his head. "We can't keep beating on him. Especially when we don't know for a fact he has her."

"He has her," I say. "I know he has her."

"You don't. Not for a fact. You think he does, and you want to believe he does, because if you're wrong, then we've messed up here big time." He exhales loudly and looks up at the roof as if answers or escape are up there. "Ah, hell, Noah," he says. "Even if we're right we're still in a world of trouble. Even if he confesses right now he's going to walk away from this. You gotta know no attorney in the world would prosecute him after what we've done."

"We'll deal with that later. Right now we have to find Alyssa. We've come this far. We can't have done all this for nothing."

"I wish I could say I let you talk me into this, but that would be naïve."

"I can make him talk."

He shakes his head. "We're done. We have to take him in. We have to do this properly. Best we can hope for is we don't end up in jail alongside of him."

"If we take him in he'll never talk. It's like you said, nobody would prosecute him. We wouldn't even be able to charge him. The only way we find her is if we keep doing what we're doing. There's no other way now."

"We can't keep doing this," Drew says.

I nod. Then I shake my head. I exhale slowly and loudly as if my body is deflating. The headache stays. It pounds against the walls of my head. I pinch the top of my nose and close my eyes. "Jesus, Drew, I've messed up. I've really messed up."

He puts a hand on my shoulder. "Maybe there's a way we can fix it, but we need to call the sheriff. He ain't gonna be happy, but . . ."

I slap one handcuff on his wrist and the other one onto the railing.

"What the hell, Noah?"

I take my gun out and point it at him. There's no need for both of us to throw away our careers. *We* can't keep doing this. But I can. "I'll say it was my fault. I'll say you tried to stop me."

"Noah . . ."

"I'm going to need your gun and your keys."

"Don't do this, buddy."

"Hand them over."

"And if I don't?"

I don't answer him. I won't shoot him, he knows that. He sighs. It's hard seeing the disappointment in my best friend's eyes. He takes his gun out and lowers it carefully, kicks it over, then tosses me his keys. I kick the gun over the edge of the landing and it hits the floor below but doesn't go off. Guns don't do that. I send the keys after it. I ask for his phone and he tosses it to me. I put it into my pocket.

"It can only go badly for you," he says.

"I know."

I head back into the office. I close the door. Conrad smiles at me. "Tick tock," he says.

"What the hell is that supposed to mean?"

He spits on the floor where his blood is forming all sorts of patterns of the type a psychiatrist might find interesting. "It means there's only so long you can keep this up before my dad gets here. You know what he's going to do to you. I'd bet the farm he's going to put you in the ground."

"Tell me where she is."

14

"You're a broken record, man."

"We found her headband."

"What headband?"

"The one that fell off her when she was abducted. It has your fingerprints on it. That's what put me on to you, Conrad."

He doesn't say anything.

"I took a look in your car out in the parking lot before we came up here. Her school bag is in the trunk."

"You're lying, and if you're not lying it's because you put it there."

I stretch out my fingers. They need patching up. They need ice. They need splints.

"You going to hit me again?" he asks. "You always were a pussy, Noah. Why don't—"

"I know the kind of guy you are, Conrad. And you *know* that I know."

His laughter makes me cringe. "Finally, the truth as to why we're really here. That missing kid has nothing to do with any of this," he says. "We're here because you're still holding a grudge, even after all these years. You're pathetic."

I take my gun out and shove it into his stomach. His grin disappears. "Listen to me, Conrad. I know you took her. She's seven years old. Just an innocent kid. Tell me where she is, and this all ends." I push the gun in tighter. "You don't tell me, this still ends, only in a much messier way. My partner out there, he wants me to stop, but he's cuffed to the railing and can't do anything to help you. There's nobody else coming. Your whole tick-tock thing, that's really about me shooting you if you don't tell me where she is. Could be in the arm. Could be in the leg. Maybe I'll shoot you in the dick. You really want a life where you only have a tube to piss out of and legs that don't work?"

"You don't have the balls," he says.

I grab a pair of invoices from the in-out tray and ball them into his mouth. Even when I shoot him in the leg it takes his mind a second to catch up. He thrashes around and spits out the invoices and they're bloody and wet and stick to the floor. Drew is yelling at me to stop, and on this side of the door Conrad is screaming and my ears are ringing from the shot and the thing in my stomach is turning and turning and the thing in my head is banging and banging. Blood is pouring out of Conrad's leg to join all the other blood on the floor. I can see a butterfly. I can see a pair of women's shoes. I can see a missing girl, and I can see death.

"Where is she?" I yell.

"Go to hell."

I think of Alyssa, scared and alone and tied up somewhere. I know Alyssa. She's had a rough few years, first losing her dad, then earlier this year losing her mom. She's a tough kid fighting a mean world. She's gone through so much I refuse to let her go through anything else. The ringing in my ears starts to subside. I can hear blood dripping on the floor. I can hear my own heartbeat.

I jam the gun into the wound. I feel sick. I can't do this for much longer. I need him to tell me. I need this to stop. He screams. "I'm not kidding, Conrad, I swear to God, I'm not kidding."

"Please, Noah, please, don't, please don't."

"Where is she?"

"Wait," he says, and he's caught between hyperventilating and crying. "Just a second, just . . . just wait."

I wait, giving him the chance to compose what needs composing. It won't be an insult. It won't be a denial.

"What if . . . what if I didn't take her, but I know who did?"

Relief floods my body. I can work with that. "And how would you know that?"

"What if — I mean, Jesus, my leg . . . it hurts, man, it really hurts. I need an ambulance."

"Where is she?"

"You're crazy, you know that? You're a psychopath."

"Where is she?"

"What if . . ." His eyes roll and he looks pale. I shake him. He looks right at me. "I don't feel so good."

"Tell me where she is and I call an ambulance."

"An ambulance," he says, and he starts to pass out again. I slap him.

"What?"

"Alyssa."

"Yeah, Alyssa, Alyssa . . . I overheard a couple of guys, right? They were talking at the bar last night. What if I told you what they said?"

"If what they said finds her, then I don't have to shoot you no more."

"They were search and rescue guys," he says, "from out of town, here looking for that hiker who got lost recently. I've never seen them before, I swear."

Search and rescue guys. The town of Acacia Pines is surrounded by an endless sea of forests and lakes that out-of-towners get lost in. Locals refer to that vast wilderness as The Pines. Search and rescue refer to it as the Green Hole — black holes absorb light, but the Green Hole absorbs hikers and campers. We'll send out search parties, and sometimes search parties will come in from other cities to help, and most of the time we'll find the missing campers, but sometimes we don't. "You didn't think of picking up the phone and calling your dad? You figured you'd do nothing and let a seven-year-old girl you knew was missing stay missing?"

His head droops. I put my finger into the bullet wound and he screams and I take my finger back out and wipe it on my shirt.

"Why didn't you tell somebody?"

He grits his teeth. "I didn't want to get involved."

I should shoot him anyway. Instead, I say, "Tell me what they said."

He sniffs up another gob of blood and lets it fly into the puddle. "They said they were looking at selling her, that she was . . ." he says, and he grimaces as a wave of pain rips through him. "They said she was cute and ticked all the boxes. They were going to move her offshore in the next few days."

"Doesn't explain how her bag got into your car."

"If you didn't put it in there, then I don't know how it got there."

"And your fingerprints on her headband?"

18

His voice takes on a whiny quality and he says, "There's a million ways that could have happened. Maybe I picked it up thinking it was something else. Maybe it's been somewhere else other than on her. I don't know. Maybe your tests are wrong. It's your job to figure that shit out."

"What about the ski mask I found in your glove compartment?"

He doesn't say anything.

"You want to explain it to me?"

"It's . . . it's not what you think," he says.

"Yeah? And what do I think?"

"It's just a ski mask," he says. "I wear it when I'm out hunting when it's cold. That's why shops sell them and why people buy them. Come on, Noah, I'm bleeding to death here."

"Where is she, Conrad? You overheard them — where'd they say they had her?"

"I don't know," he says, and he's crying now. "I swear I don't know."

I push my finger back into the wound. I fight the urge to gag. His body strains against the rope as he leans forward. His veins stick out and his face is as red as a face can get before something hemorrhages, usually in the eyes.

"Wait," he says. I take my finger back out and I wait. "They mentioned the old Kelly place," he says, and he's blubbering tears and snot and it's mixing with the blood and making a disgusting mess over his shirt.

"The Kelly place," I say.

"The Kelly place," he repeats.

19

I holster my gun and walk out of the office.

He yells out at me through the open door. "You're dead, Noah. You hear me? You're dead."

"What the hell did you do to him?" Drew asks me.

I don't answer him. I can't. I hand Drew back his phone, head down the stairs and I don't look back.

Two

Most of the trees in the few miles that surround the sawmill have been logged, regrown, and logged again. Various areas are in various states of regrowth, but the trees bordering the mill are young and fresh-looking and not much taller than me. The road out to the highway is a mile long and none of it straight. I take it quick. The air conditioning is running at full strength. The sawdust on my skin itches. I head north toward town. The nearest building to the sawmill is Earl's Gas Station, the forecourt and highway out front all lit up like a football field. The owner is one Earl Winters, and he calls us every month or two when somebody puts buckshot into those lights, and every month or two we get no closer to figuring out who's doing it. Could be one person. Could be lots of different people, since the lights are offensively bright. I blow past the gas station so fast I expect to see it dragging behind me, caught in my wake.

There are no lights on the highway. No signs of life. Out

in this part of the country the world could have ended and unless somebody sent word to Acacia Pines none of us would know. The highway is the only road in and out of town. It cuts a swath through The Pines, where the ghosts of missing hikers are still out there walking in circles.

Every half-mile or so I pass ninety-degree turnoffs that lead to small farms and big farms and animal farms and vegetable farms. I pass barns painted red that during the day look like they're floating on seas of wheat, but at night look like black holes on the horizon. It's a ten-minute drive that I do in six. I take the turnoff to the Kelly farm. The large *For Sale* sign staked into the ground out front has faded as it baked and froze over the last three years' worth of seasons. The road goes from asphalt to dirt and gravel and the back of the car fishtails and bits of stone flick up into the undercarriage. The house is on the other side of a set of oak trees that keep it hidden from the road. I drive around them and point the car at the front door and leave the lights on and get out. Plumes of dirt float up from the driveway and fog the air. The land out here is dry. Only stuff that grows is stinging nettle and gorse and patchy clumps of grass.

The house has lots of red wood and white trim, and an A-frame roof sharp enough to prick the sky. There's a shed with no front wall next to it, a car and tractor in there with eight flat tires between them, the walls lined with hay bales. I send the beam of my flashlight looping around the porch and over twisted floorboards. There are cobwebs as long as summer evenings over all of it. Something scuttles across the porch and disappears. The headlights from the car and moonlight reflect off the windows. The door is locked, but it's also old and neglected and doesn't put up a fight. I figure in all the years the Kellys lived here this door was probably always unlocked. It's that kind of town.

The house smells of dust and the air tastes of mold. The last time I was out here was three years ago when Jasmine Kelly called Drew from the other side of the country to say she hadn't heard from her folks in a week. I flick the light switch but there's no power. I follow the footprints in the dust. Floorboards creak under my weight. I can feel the heat coming up through the floor. Shadows move across walls as my flashlight lights everything up, and there are a lot of everythings — couches, a dining table, beds, kitchen utilities, a coffee table with magazines and a TV that can't be any older than five years. There are paintings and photographs on walls and shelves. It feels like the house is waiting for somebody to return. I look into the bedroom where three years ago Ed and Leah Kelly took handfuls of sleeping pills and didn't leave a note to say why. The farm was heavily in debt and their daughter used to say her dad thought the land was cursed because only the weeds knew how to grow.

I head to the basement. Basements are where men like Conrad Haggerty keep girls like Alyssa Stone. I open the door. It smells like something crawled out of the grave, died all over again, then crawled back in. I hold my breath and light up the steps. They groan as I move down them. The walls are gray cinderblock. There are tools hanging on them. There's an

23

old chest freezer big enough for a body, that I hope is empty. There are piles of blankets and an old dining suite with chairs stacked on top and boxes of junk beneath it. I can no longer hold my breath. The smell doesn't improve any. There's an old heater, a couple of bicycles, an old TV. There are shelves full of Christmas lights that could only be ready in time if the untangling started at Easter. The same dust that coated everything upstairs coats everything down here too, even the floor, but the floor also has footprints going back and forth across it.

I follow them.

I don't have to follow them for long.

If anybody grows up being allowed to believe in curses, then it's Alyssa. Her father gave his life to the sawmill in more ways than one. He started working there when he was sixteen, gave the place eighteen years of his life, then bled out on the factory floor after a spinning blade snapped, flew thirty feet through the air, and severed an artery in his leg. Alyssa was six months old. Three months ago a car accident took Alyssa's mother out of the world. Her uncle took her in after that. I can only pray that this is the last bad thing ever to happen to her.

Right now, Alyssa is trying her hardest to blend into the mixture of paint cans and old board games in the corner. She's shying away from my flashlight as if she's lived in the dark her entire life. She looks gaunt and scared and she has a black eye from where somebody hit her. She's looking out at me from behind black hair that is matted with grime and her face is streaked with tears. Looking at her makes me want to cry. It breaks my heart. I want to hug her and protect her and never let her go. I want to make the world okay for her, because so far for her the world has been a harrowing one. There's an iron shackle around her ankle with a padlock on it. A chain connects it to the wall, welded onto the shackle at one end and bolted on the other. Her ankle is scuffed and puffy and the thing that hasn't turned in my stomach in some time turns again. When I'm done here, I'm going to have another conversation with Conrad Haggerty.

"Alyssa," I say, "it's Deputy Harper." I point the flashlight at myself. Here I am. Deputy Noah Harper, all lit up in the basement of a dead couple's house on the final night of his career.

She tries to back away some more but there's nowhere to go. She stops moving. She stares at me and doesn't say anything. I can't tell if she recognizes me or not from the day her mother died.

"You're going to be okay." I sit the flashlight upright on the floor so the beam hits the ceiling. I keep my voice light. Nice and friendly. "It's going to be okay," I tell her again, because it *is* going to be okay. "He's not coming back."

She keeps staring at me. Her fingertips are bleeding from where she's tried to loosen the bolts from the wall.

"I'm going to find something to take this chain off you, okay? I bet I can find something among all these tools that'll get it off you right quick."

She says nothing.

"I'm taking you out of here, Alyssa, and back home to your uncle."

Three

I find a pair of bolt cutters on the wall, but the blades look like they were used to cut bricks before being left out in the rain for a winter. I focus on the other end of the chain. It's bolted to the wall next to the mattress Alyssa has been sleeping on. I find a socket set and get the right-size piece lined up with the first of the bolts holding the chain. My fingers are so sore from torturing Conrad Haggerty that I have to kick at the handle to get the first one to turn, but it does, and then I'm able to spin it free. I get no less resistance from the remaining three bolts.

I'm expecting her to run once the chain is loose from the wall, but she stays where she is. "Uncle Frank misses you, and he's worried about you. Everybody is worried about you. The man that did this to you, we arrested him. He can't hurt you anymore."

She has her arms folded and her knees pulled against her chest.

26

"It's time to go home, Alyssa. Now, you have a very important decision to make. I can either carry you, or you can walk with me. Which would you like to do?"

Slowly she puts out her hand. It's shaking. I reach out and take it and we stand up together. She doesn't go anywhere for a few moments, then she lets me lead her to the stairs. I carry the chain so she doesn't have to. It's heavy, and it feels grimy. We get to the top and the dust and the mold smell pretty good compared to the basement where Alyssa's toilet was a bucket. Outside we stand on the porch and Alyssa looks up at the sky and I look out over the fields and we both suck in some fresh air.

We reach the car. The dirt floating in the air earlier has settled. There's a warm breeze rippling across the paddocks, bending the blades of grass toward us. The thing about small towns is they give you large skies. Right now, the view is spectacular, not a single star lost to light pollution. The big sky makes me feel small, and makes Alyssa seem even smaller. By becoming a monster I've given her a chance at a big life. I don't know what's next for each of us — whether she'll bounce back like she did after her mom died or if she'll want to hide from the world. Whether I'll end up in a jail cell next to Conrad Haggerty or if I'll be put in the ground by his father. Big skies, big questions.

I get Alyssa seated and put the chain on the floor and ask her if that's okay, or if it's pulling at her ankle, and she stares at me and says nothing. I strap the seatbelt across her. There are no sirens or lights in the distance. Maybe Drew didn't call. Maybe he couldn't get a signal. Maybe he did call but Conrad

PAUL CLEAVE

hasn't told them about the Kelly farm. Maybe Conrad bled out.

I pop the trunk and toss my bloody shirt in there. It leaves me with my uniform pants and a white t-shirt that looks clean enough. I get into the car and I flick the lever that sprays water over the windscreen. The wipers cut arcs through the dirt, streaky at first, then finally clearing. We drive into town. Alyssa stares out the window. I dial back the air conditioning and crack open the window. I think about calling Alyssa's uncle. I think about calling Sheriff Haggerty. I think about calling my wife. In the end I call Dan Peterson, and ask him to meet me out front of the hospital in fifteen. I tell him to bring his work van. He says sure thing, but before he can ask why the signal cuts out. Out here where the lights don't reach the sky, cellphone reception comes and goes like the tide.

The farmhouses are closer to the road now and soon they're closer to each other too. Cellphone reception comes back. The paddocks fall away and make room for family houses on family-sized plots as we hit the edge of town. We drive over a bridge, giant metal trusses freshly painted red bolted together over a river forty feet wide and endlessly long, sweeping into town from the forest before sweeping back out. We hit Main Street. We pass stores and park benches and bars with plenty of neon and mercury. A quarter-mile up and a right will take us to the police station, and into the heart of Acacia Pines, population twenty thousand, but we go left instead, passing a cinema and a school and a park before hitting Acacia Hospital.

The hospital is three stories of white brick with a flat roof lined with satellite dishes. Square windows without any light behind them look out over the parking lot where there are a dozen cars, most of them belonging to staff. The hospital has three ambulances parked by the main door, but right now one is missing. It's a small-town hospital with sixty beds. The surgeons and doctors can mend bones and insert stents and pacemakers and put you on dialysis, but they're not going to give you an organ transplant. I know that, because Drew got sick a few years ago and needed a new kidney and had to travel for it.

I park out front next to Dan Peterson's van. The back of it is dark with exhaust fumes. Somebody has written *I wish your wife was this dirty* with their finger through the dirt. He's leaning against the side with his hands in his pockets and his stomach overhanging his belt and a cigarette overhanging his lip. Peterson is the local jack-of-all-trades and five years past retirement age. The sawmill and the quarry beyond and all the farms may provide heartbeats to the town, but when Dan finally retires, the rest of us are going to have to figure out how to build birdfeeders and shingle roofs and dig graves at the cemetery.

I open the passenger door of my car. I help Alyssa turn to the side so her legs dangle outside. Dan stares at her, recognizing her from the news.

"You can pick the lock?" I ask him.

"In under a minute."

It takes him three.

"You want to tell me who had her?" he asks.

"It'll be in the news tomorrow," I tell him.

"Well, I'm glad she's back safe," he says, and he glances at my raw and puffy hands and gives me a casual salute before driving away.

I pile the chain onto the passenger seat and wipe my hands on my trousers, then I lead Alyssa into the hospital the same way I led her out of the Kelly house, with her little hand in mine. Doctors and nurses are waiting near the door. My guess is the missing ambulance is out getting Conrad. Alyssa has been in the news and they all recognize her, but they don't make a big deal out of it, not wanting to scare her.

A nurse in her forties, slim and pale with gray streaks in her hair, comes over. Alyssa tightens her grip on my hand. The nurse gives me a slight nod, then smiles at Alyssa and crouches to get to her eye level. "How are you feeling, honey?" she asks. Alyssa hides behind my leg. "My name is Nurse Rosie, but you can call me Rose, if you like. How about we get you all cleaned up, huh?"

I look down at Alyssa. "You can go with her," I tell her. "I'll be out here to make sure everything goes okay."

She waves her fingers to indicate she wants to tell me something. She lets go of my leg and I take a knee and she leans forward and cups her hand over my ear so she can whisper. "Is Uncle Frank mad at me?"

"Mad?"

"Mad I didn't get away from the man. They tell us in school never to get into . . . into a car with . . . with strangers. I tried

30

to fight him, I really did."

"I know you did, Honey."

"Did the man rob a bank?"

"Why do you think that?"

"He wore a mask like bank robbers do."

The ski mask we found in Conrad's car. It means he didn't want her to be able to identify him. It means he was planning on letting her go at some point.

"He wasn't a bank robber," I say. "He was just a really bad man."

"A really bad man," she says. She wraps her arms around me and hugs me tight. I hug her back.

"Now go with Rose. She'll clean you right up and we'll get your uncle here. How's that sound?"

She keeps hugging me. "Will the bad man come for me again?"

"No."

"If he does, will you save me?"

"Of course. I'll do whatever it takes."

She pulls back so she can look at me. "Cross your heart?"

I cross my heart.

The nurse leads Alyssa to the bathroom. Another nurse comes over, this one in her mid-twenties, her blonde hair cut short and swept back, her glasses looking more cosmetic than medical. Her name is Victoria, and Victoria is my sister-in-law.

She puts her hand on my arm. "Jesus, Noah, where did you find her?"

"Locked up in the basement at the old Kelly place."

31

Her glasses shift a little on her face as she frowns. Her jaw tightens. "Who took her?"

"Conrad Haggerty."

She says nothing for a few seconds. I suspect somewhere in her imagination she's hunting down Conrad to do bad things to him. "That piece of trash," she says, all the words coming out on an exhale. "You sure it was him?"

"I'm sure."

"This is going to be bad," she says.

I shake my head. "Bad doesn't even begin to sum things up."

Four

The parking lot lights up blue and red, first from the ambulance and then from the single patrol car that pulls in behind it. A ring of six-foot trees separates the parking lot from the road, and interlocking branches capture the light and don't reflect any back. I watch from the window of a doctor's office on the top floor as a pair of paramedics roll Conrad out from the back of the ambulance. They must have shot some painkillers into him because he looks in a better mood than when I left him. Drew spills out of one side of the patrol car and Sheriff Haggerty spills out the other. There isn't much of a physical difference between Sheriff Haggerty and his son, other than the quantity of wrinkles and the color of hair, and of course the sheriff's horseshoe mustache that, legend has it, was fully formed in the womb.

I stand at the window adjusting the ice pack on my hands. Victoria offered to x-ray them and clean them up, but I told her it could wait. There are posters on the wall of the human body, close-up drawings of shoulder joints and ankle joints and finger joints, the kinds of images that remind me how fragile we are. There's a fake skeleton in the corner and cupboards and drawers full of latex gloves and bandages and syringes. I can smell disinfectant. Sheriff Haggerty is yelling at somebody outside the main entrance but I can't see who. Then he hitches his thumbs into his belt and looks up at the window and finds me. We stare at each other for a few seconds before he follows his son into the hospital.

I wait for him.

He doesn't come.

I give it a little longer.

He still doesn't come.

After ten minutes I'm at the point where I just want this over.

I flinch when the door opens. It's not the sheriff. It's Maggie, my wife, and she's all sharp angles and anger. Her eyes are dark, her face red and tight, her dark hair tied into a fast and messy ponytail. She closes the door and I push myself away from the window. She focuses on my hands.

"So it's true," she says.

I step toward her and she puts her hand on my chest. The anger is coming off her in waves. She isn't here as my wife. She's here as a lawyer, and not my lawyer.

"So how bad is it?" I ask.

"Let's sit," she says.

We take the two chairs in front of the desk and sit with our knees almost touching. I adjust the ice pack. None of the swelling has disappeared.

She holds up a finger and she says, "You beat him."

"It was the only way."

She holds up a second finger. "And you shot him."

"He took her, Maggie."

A third finger goes up. "You handcuffed Drew and pulled a gun on him."

"He had her chained up like a rabid dog."

She holds up another finger, and she says, "And you planted evidence and framed him."

I fight the urge to jump up. "You're kidding, right? Is that what he's saying?"

"No, but he will. You said what you did was the only way, but it wasn't, Noah, not by a long shot. You could have brought him in. I could have made a deal with him. We could have gotten Alyssa back and put Conrad away for a long time."

"That's bullshit. His dad might not like him much, but he sure as hell would have given him a pass. You know that better than anybody."

She leans back as if slapped.

My hands are shaking. I tell myself to calm down. "Look, I'm sorry," I say. "I shouldn't have said that."

"Is that why you beat him so bad? Because of what happened when we were kids?"

"Of course not," I say, but I can't claim what he did back then wasn't on my mind when my fists were flying. Anyway, we weren't kids — we were teenagers. She makes it sound like it was just childhood antics. "It's like Newton's third law —

for every action there's an equal and opposite reaction. It's possible you *could* have gotten Alyssa back, like you say, but it's equally possible you *couldn't* have."

"You should have trusted me," she says. "You should have trusted Drew and Sheriff Haggerty, and trusted yourself too. You should have trusted the system, but instead you broke the law and—"

"I couldn't risk not getting her back. I know him, Maggie. He wouldn't have—"

She puts her hand up. "Let me finish, Noah."

"Conrad would have let her die."

"I asked you to let me finish."

I get up. I walk back to the window and stare into the parking lot. Moths not much smaller than the palm of my hand slap at the streetlamps. The sky doesn't have the same sparkle it had out at the Kelly farm, most of the stars hidden now behind the curtain of light coming from the town. "You're right. I'm sorry."

"We can't prosecute him," she says, and I don't turn to face her because I can't look at the disappointment in her face. "I know you think you did the right thing, and I understand why you think you had to do it, but what you did makes it impossible for us to get a conviction. You violated his rights, and now he's going to walk. And the worst thing is the fact you couldn't see that makes you — and it hurts to say this, it really does — it makes you a bad cop."

I did see it, and seeing it and ignoring it makes me an even worse cop.

"He can come after you, legally. You tied him up and beat him and you shot him. There'll be an endless line of lawyers eager to represent him. They'll be calling from all across the country to take his case, and for the first day or two the media everywhere are going to love you, and then they're going to hate you."

I adjust the ice pack. My knuckles look like ball bearings that grew skin.

"You've messed up, Noah, and there's nothing you can do to fix it."

"I did what I had to do," I say, and there's no strength behind my words. No conviction. Not now, now that I know Conrad is going to walk free.

She shakes her head. "You did what you've been wanting to do to Conrad for the last ten years."

"That had nothing to do with this."

"I wish I could believe you. Despite what you think, we could have made a deal, found her safe, and Conrad would be going to jail and you'd be keeping your job."

"His father would have made sure that didn't happen."

She stands up and moves behind the chair and puts her hands on the back of it. "Listen to yourself, Noah. Sheriff Haggerty isn't the enemy here. He's been good to you all these years. He would have done the right thing, but you let your anger cloud your judgment. You let the past take over."

She's right. "I'm sorry."

"You know, despite everything, I don't think you are."

My headache is coming back. "So what happens now?"

"Now we figure out if we can keep you out of jail."

I rub my temples. It doesn't help. "That's not what I meant."

"No?"

"No. I mean what about us?"

She takes some of the strands that didn't make it into the ponytail and tucks them behind her ear. Some of the anger slips from her features, replaced with sadness. "I wish you'd given that some thought earlier," she says. She turns and a few paces later she's at the door.

"Meaning?"

"Meaning you almost killed somebody, Noah. You tortured somebody, and I don't see any remorse, I don't see contrition, and given the chance to do it all over knowing the outcome you'd do the same damn thing."

"Maggie . . ."

"What it means, Noah, is you're not the person I married. I have to go."

"Please don't," I say, but she's already gone.

Five

Downstairs the surgeons are operating on Conrad and I'm told by a doctor they're confident he'll be okay. She tells me the bullet hit bone but missed vital arteries and I act like that was the point. Victoria x-rays my hands and tells me I have a couple of fractures in my right they can't do much about, other than taping my fingers together with a splint.

"Ice and painkillers are your friends for the next few days," she says.

"They'll heal up okay?"

"They will. For now, just think of them as spoils of war. How mad is Maggie?"

"About as mad as anybody can get."

"She'll be okay," she says.

"I don't think she will. How's Alyssa?"

"Banged up, but doing okay. She's a tough kid."

"They run a rape kit?" I ask, and my stomach tightens in anticipation of the answer.

She nods. "He didn't touch her. Whatever he was planning on doing, he didn't get to do it."

Her answer makes me feel better about the way tonight has played out. She leaves to get me some painkillers. I stare at the doorway wondering who will come in next, and that turns out to be Father Frank Davidson. He comes into the room looking taller than when I saw him earlier today, the good news of getting his niece back alive not only lifting him emotionally, but physically too. He hasn't shaved in days and his dark hair is going in all directions. He comes in with a big smile and his hand extended. I figure this guy more than anybody must be truly committed to his faith, especially after what he's just gone through. Then again, he probably thinks God is why his niece came back to him in one piece, but I'm not sure how he'd equate that with her being taken in the first place. His hand crushes mine and I bite down on the pain and he doesn't notice the splint. Until yesterday the last time I spoke with him was to tell him a logging truck had rolled onto his sister's car.

"Thank you," he says. "Thank you, thank you, thank you."

"You're welcome."

"I couldn't have lost her," he says. "Not as well."

"I know."

He lets go my hand. "And you? How about you, Noah? Are you going to be okay? I heard what you did."

"I think you'll need to do some praying on my behalf, Father."

"What you did — that kind of thing weighs heavily on good men. It might not feel like it right now, but you'll question what you've done. I'm thankful you got my little girl back, I truly am. I just . . ." But whatever it is he wants to say he doesn't have the words. He fiddles with his clerical collar, trying to get it sitting right. He keeps looking at me and I keep looking at him, and then he shrugs. "I'll be here for you, Noah. Whatever happens."

He asks me to come and see him tomorrow. I smile and tell him I'm not in a place where I can make plans. He pats me on the shoulder, nods solemnly, and thanks me again for getting Alyssa back. He gets to the door at the same time Victoria is coming back through. She hands me a small plastic container full of painkillers.

"Only take them when you need them, and don't take them when you don't."

It's good advice, especially since we've both seen what can happen when people misuse them. I take two now.

"And Maggie, she'll come around," she says. "I know she's mad now, she just needs some time."

"I hope you're right."

"Sheriff Haggerty told me to let you know he's waiting out in the parking lot."

"Okay. Thanks," I say.

"You want me to come with you? Mightn't hurt to have some witnesses in case he decides to shoot you."

"I'll be fine," I say. "Maybe have the surgeons on standby, just in case?"

I slip the pills into my pocket and head out. Doctors and nurses turn to watch me as I go. It makes me feel like a condemned man walking the final piece of real estate between jail cell and noose. The main doors slide open and the night outside is just how I left it, warm and glowing from the parking lot lights and buzzing with energy. Sheriff Haggerty is leaning against his car with his arms folded and his big shoulders bursting at his shirt. I have no idea where Drew is. He's either been fired or sent home or both.

"Noah," he says, nodding in my direction, then his eyes flick to the hospital behind me, faces are pressed to the windows. Hopefully that means he won't shoot me.

"Sheriff."

"You shot my son."

"I did."

"You shouldn't have done that."

"Your son shouldn't have kidnapped Alyssa Stone," I say. "Your son shouldn't have chained her to a basement wall to do whatever it was he was going to do."

He shakes his head. "According to him he overheard those two guys in the bar and he gave you their location."

"And you believe him?"

"He's my son."

It's what I expected. Everything I did felt justified while I was doing it, and feels twice as justified right now. If I'd brought Conrad in for questioning, we'd never have gotten a word out of him. Alyssa would have died out there.

"There were no two guys in the bar," I say, "and if there had been, he might have done himself a favor by coming to you earlier."

He unfolds his arms and hitches his thumbs over his belt. "You know as well as I do Conrad doesn't think much outside of himself. His neighbor's house could burn down and he wouldn't pull himself away from the TV to give a damn. I'm not saying it's right, him not helping that girl when he overheard those boys, I'm saying that's how he is. The thing that grates on my nerves the most, son, is that *you* know that's the way he is."

"He took her," I tell him. "If he hadn't, he'd have told me when I first questioned him about his story."

"You mean when you started torturing him."

"Look, let's pretend for one second he was telling me the truth. If so, then his sitting there taking everything I did to him makes him the dumbest guy in the world. He would have told me right away what he'd overheard. He wouldn't have waited till I shot him."

"He ain't dumb," Sheriff Haggerty says, "but he ain't bright either," he says, but surely he can't believe what he's trying to sell me. He knows anybody in their right mind would have given up those two search and rescue guys the moment I showed up.

"We found her bag in his truck."

"He says somebody else put it there."

"And his fingerprints are on her headband," I say.

"There's a thousand ways that could have happened."

"That's what he said."

He says nothing. I say nothing. We stare at each other for a few moments. Then I break the silence. "Come on, Sheriff, you know it didn't take a beating to fire up Conrad's memory."

"You should have brought him in."

"You wouldn't have been objective."

I see it coming, and he knows I see it coming, this big lumbering right hook that he winds into, but I don't try to avoid it. It catches me in the jaw and makes my teeth ring and numbs my entire face, and I drop to the ground.

"Don't get up," he says, and I don't. He stands over me, a light creating a halo effect around his head as he looks down. "Here's what's going to happen. You hurt my son and you shouldn't have. You crossed the line so goddamn far there's no coming back for you. I've always liked you, son. Back when I was throwing your dad into the drunk tank every second day, I was happy to help you out because you were a good kid who didn't deserve the father he got. I was proud of you when you entered law enforcement. Hell, you've been more like a son to me over the years than my own son. We have history, you and me, and right now that history is the only thing keeping me from throwing your ass in jail. You're going to hand me your badge and your gun and the keys to the car, then you're going to get the hell out of Dodge and you ain't ever going to come back. If I see your face in this town again, I swear to God I'm going to lock you up and leave you to rot."

Twelve Years Later

Six

It's a big-city bar with neon in the windows and big-screen TVs on the walls. There's a lot of blonde-colored wood around the bar, darker stuff on the walls, and a lot of character knocked and chipped and worn into all of it. There's a jukebox in the corner that doesn't play anything recorded either side of the seventies and a pool table that needs new felt after somebody spilled their drink on it a few weeks ago. We serve thirty different kinds of beer, thirty different kinds of wine, and spirits from all different countries. Friday nights we have a live band, Tuesday night is ladies' night, and Sunday night — so it seems — is armed robbery night. I've been working here for the last twelve years and have been part owner for the last ten, and in that time we've been robbed twice and the guy in front of me is amping to make that a third, and every time it's been a Sunday. His floppy hair is dirty and his face is covered in acne and he's skinny and jacked, and if the gun accidentally goes off it could hit me or maybe it could hit something a mile to my left.

"This isn't a bank," I tell him, and my hands are out to my sides in a nice peaceful gesture because I'm a peaceful gesture kind of guy. "Why don't you put the gun down and walk on out of here and we all go about putting this behind us?"

He looks left, then he looks right, and whatever he's looking for he doesn't see it. Or maybe he does. Pink Floyd is coming from the jukebox, the band singing about being comfortably numb, which sums up half of what I'm feeling.

"Just give me what you have."

"I have some advice," I tell him.

"I don't want your advice."

"It's free. That and the peanuts, those are two things in here you don't have to pay for, though if you're going to have the peanuts it's understood you're going to have bought yourself a drink. We give away peanuts to everybody who doesn't buy a drink, well, we'd end up not being able to afford peanuts anymore."

He looks confused. He looks left and right again, and this time it's only his eyes that move. The gun wavers a little.

I carry on. "And if we couldn't afford peanuts, then we couldn't afford a lot of other stuff too. You'd be wasting your time coming in here waving your gun around because there'd be nothing to steal."

"Seriously? Dude? Seriously? Do you want to die?"

I shrug, as if it's no big deal, but of course it's a big deal. My heart is hammering but guys like this are like dogs — you show fear around them, they'll use it against you. He'll

47

take the cash out of the till, then take my wallet, take wallets and phones and jewelry from everybody here, maybe take a hostage, maybe kill somebody. Of course guys like this are also unpredictable, so if you don't show fear they're equally likely to put you down for disrespecting them. The gun might be unloaded, or it might be he's itching to shoot somebody today, or maybe it's loaded and he thinks it isn't. There's no right or wrong. There just *is*.

I open the till. There are a dozen people in the bar, some of them watching and some unaware of what's going on. Sunday-night crowds are generally low key. It's why an hour ago I gave the other bartender the rest of the night off.

Pink Floyd ends and The Doors take over, playing something also recorded just in time to make the cut. The thing about small towns is I got used to dealing with small-town assholes — now living in a big city I have to deal with guys who asshole things up on a bigger scale. I rake out the cash and put it on the counter. There can't be more than four hundred bucks. It's not worth dying for. Then again, no amount is.

"The coins, man, the coins too," he says.

"You catching the bus?"

"You want to catch a bullet?"

I scoop out the coins and put them on the bar and a couple roll off and land on the floor on my side and I go to bend down for them and he tells me to stop, which is a real shame because there's a gun down there and it's why I let a couple of nickels roll off the bar.

"Put them in a bag."

"I don't have a bag," I tell him.

"Why not?"

"Do you have one?"

"No."

"Then don't give me a hard time for not having one. You're the one who had all this planned out, not me."

He grabs the notes and stuffs them into his pocket. "Give me your phone too."

"I don't have a phone."

"What?"

"I don't have a phone. Look, buddy, you've got what you came for, so how about you leave while things are still good?"

"Just . . . just give me your phone, your phone, man, just . . . just hand it over without all your grief about, about not owning one, because everybody has one."

"Not me," I say, and then, right on cue my phone rings. Of course it does. Why wouldn't it? "That's not mine."

He puts both hands on the gun to steady it. It rocks back and forth as he tries to draw a bead on my face. It's unnerving as hell. "I can shoot you and take it from you," he says.

I put the phone on the counter. It's still ringing. Caller ID says it's Maggie.

"You lied," he says.

"Please, I'm begging you, don't take my phone. I need it," I say, looking at the display. I haven't spoken to Maggie in ten years.

The door to the bar opens behind him and my robber for

the evening spins and around and takes a shot, the bullet lodging into the doorframe between a man and a woman walking in. They stare in our direction looking at the gun, then the man dives to the floor and the woman turns and runs back outside. I grab at the shooter's arm but I'm not quick enough. He points the gun at my face.

"Don't," I tell him.

He pulls the trigger. The gun clicks and nothing happens, and he looks at the gun then looks at his hand and tries to figure out what the problem is, and whatever answer he comes up with he doesn't share, because he grabs my phone off the counter and bolts for the door. I watch him go, unable to move, listening to the sound that gun made over and over inside my head, not just listening to it, but *feeling* it, the same way you feel a dentist drill you hear operating on another patient. I put both hands on the bar to keep myself from falling over. All the strength has drained out of my legs. He pulled the trigger. He tried to kill me. In another timeline right now another version of me is lying on the floor with a head that doesn't look like a head anymore.

"You okay?" A guy has come up to the bar, but I can barely hear him because my ears are ringing loudly. I can't answer him. The guy who dived for the floor a few moments ago gets up and dusts down his suit. He's completely pale. His color and look reflect my own. In that other timeline he's lying dead on the floor too.

"Hey, hey, man, you okay?"

I look at the man at the bar talking to me. Feeling comes

back into my legs. I let go of the alternate timeline and focus on this one. "I'm fine," I tell him, my voice low.

"You don't look fine."

"I'm fine," I say, louder this time, then to prove just how fine I am, I say, "Drinks are on the house." I say it loud enough for everybody to hear. I'm expecting everybody to woohoo, but nobody does.

Suit Guy looks at me, and says, "Okay," either to this entire situation or to the free drinks. He looks confused. He jams a finger into his ear and waggles it back and forth as if he can pry out the ringing sound. I don't see him being a repeat customer. "Did that . . . did that just happen?"

"It did."

"I should . . . I should go find my girlfriend."

We talk with loud voices so we can be heard. "That sounds like a good idea," I tell him.

"I . . . I'm not so sure we'll come back," he says.

"I won't hold it against you."

He heads out in the direction his girlfriend went. I can see her across the street, standing in the doorway of a restaurant. She's on the phone, no doubt to the police. The guy who approached me asks again if I'm okay. I tell him that I am. And I am. Now.

With the danger over and the police on the way, people go back to the business of drinking. Nobody leaves. Plenty of them have their cellphones out making calls. The ringing in my ears fades. I pour some beers as if what just happened is no big deal. I answer some questions about how scared /

51

nervous / kickass I was, and then the police show up. They don't come in guns blazing which means they know the perp has long since gone. It's a pair of patrol officers, a guy and a woman, who look like they could be brother and sister. Not charismatic, but both nice enough, the kind of people you forget you ever met about fifteen minutes after they've gone. I offer them a drink and neither of them look tempted.

I go over the sequence of events. There isn't much to say. A guy came in, he pointed a gun, and he left with money that wasn't his. What did he look like? He was thin, wiry, ugly, he looked like he was high, he looked like an asshole, he looked like the kind of guy who'd say things like *meth is the breakfast of champions*. Could I be more specific? Yeah, he was *really* ugly. He *really* looked like an asshole. He was wearing blue jeans and a gray hoodie. Nothing more? No characteristics? How old was he? Did he have tattoos? Scars? I tell them everything happened so quickly and all I really saw was the gun. I tell them that the gun seemed like the biggest thing in the room. It had its own gravity. It was a black hole I couldn't see beyond.

What about the security cameras? I shake my head. I tell them they haven't worked in eighteen months. They tell me I should get them fixed. I tell them that's the plan. They interview others at the bar and ninety minutes later they leave, telling me they'll update me if they find anything.

I call final drinks and nobody complains because everybody is figuring I deserve an early night. Thirty minutes later I'm locking up the bar. In the office I watch the security footage I told the police I didn't have and get another good look at the guy. Then I fire up the computer and log in to my phone account and a minute later there's a blue dot on a map telling me where my phone is. It's a mile away from here. A fifteen-minute walk, maybe twenty. The dot isn't moving. I write down the address and grab the gun from under the counter and lock up the bar.

Seven

It's midnight when I get home. I live on the top floor of an apartment building that's six stories high, giving me a nice view out over the city. It's a nice place. It has two bedrooms and an open-plan kitchen flowing into the dining room and lounge. I used the money from the sale of our house back in Acacia Pines to invest in the bar ten years ago, and since then business has been good. There's a set of French doors that open onto a balcony, the one on the right with a cat door cut into it. My cat, Legolas, a rescue tabby who lost one of his back legs when he was a kitten, spends his days out there, jumping from the balcony onto the oak tree that reaches our floor, coming inside when he's hungry or tired or wants cuddles. He comes in now and follows me into the bathroom and watches me wash up.

"You hungry, Lego?"

He meows. Yes. He's hungry.

I fill his bowl and freshen up his water and sit down on

the couch with a beer. I use a tea towel to wipe the blood off my cellphone. Then I have a drink and dial the number that reaches out over a thousand miles and takes me back twelve years to the last time I saw her. In the beginning we'd talk on the phone a little. Then she asked for a divorce. Then we sold the house. Then we stopped talking. In a way it was like she had died.

"Hello, Noah," she says.

The line is so clear it sounds like she's sitting next to me. I picture her on the couch we used to own in the house we used to own in the life we used to share. How have I let ten years go by without reaching out?

"Hey," I say. "I hope I didn't wake you."

"I was still awake," she says. "I'm glad you called. I . . . I wasn't sure you would."

"Your message sounded important." I had listened to it outside the apartment complex where the man who'd stolen my phone lived. Maggie had asked me to call her back as soon as I could, day or night. "I mean . . . I would have called you back even if it hadn't."

"It's good to hear your voice," she says.

"It's good to hear yours," I say, and it is. It really is.

"I've often thought of calling you," she says, and I know that this isn't a social call. She's ringing to tell me something. Somebody has died. Either her mom, or her dad, or maybe it's Sheriff Haggerty, or Drew, or any one of a number of people I used to know. Maybe it's all of them. Maybe a tornado came and swept everybody from my old life out to sea. "I've always hated the way things ended between us."

"None of it was your fault," I say, and it's true. For years I blamed Conrad Haggerty. He was the reason I had to leave town, the reason my marriage fell apart, and it took time to admit the reason for those things wasn't him, but me. It was never Maggie.

"Still . . . I've often thought of calling you to tell you how sorry I am about the way things turned out."

"I'm sorry too."

"Can you believe it's been twelve years?" she asks.

"Feels like eleven."

She laughs. It's a little forced. Whatever is wrong, I want her to get to it on her own. I wonder if she's been drinking. I hope so. I hope this is a melancholy call and nothing more. Legolas jumps up on the couch next to me and stretches out.

"I'm . . . I'm married," she says.

My chest tightens. "I'm happy for you."

"I have children too. Two boys. Seven and five. My husband . . .his name is Stephen. You'd like him."

"I'm sure I would," I say, sure that I wouldn't. Why would I?

"You?" she asks. "Are you with anybody? Do you have a family?"

"No," I tell her, and I don't elaborate because there's nothing to elaborate on. I could tell her about my apartment, the nice view, the three-legged cat I adopted from a shelter when I moved in here since the place already came with a cat door. I could tell her that I just put a dent in somebody's skull so I could get my phone back to hear the message she left me.

I could tell her that the man I became twelve years ago didn't stick around — that it took a man trying to kill me in my bar to bring him back.

"Are you happy?"

"Yeah, I am," I tell her, because I am. I've had a few relationships that have ended amicably. Every couple of years I try to visit another small corner of the world. I like my bar, my apartment, my cat. I like my life. "Really happy."

"I'm sorry," she says. "I'm sorry about the way everything went down. I'm sorry I didn't do more for you back then. I'm sorry . . . I'm sorry I didn't go with you."

"It's okay," I tell her. "It's all in the past."

"I thought . . . I thought you were going to come back, you know? After a few weeks or so, or maybe a month. I thought everybody would cool off and things would go back to normal, even though I knew they couldn't."

She'd made it clear before I left that she never wanted to see me again. I had no reason to come back. "Maggie, why are you calling me? It's great to hear from you, it really is, but there's a reason you're calling me now, and as much as I love the idea of catching up, something must have happened."

"It's Alyssa," she says. "Alyssa Stone."

I'm back in the basement, walking down the stairs with my flashlight. I can smell the room and feel how warm the house is and I can see Alyssa huddled in the corner. I can see her swollen ankle, her black eye. My ex-wife isn't ringing me to give me good news. She's not ringing to tell me Alyssa graduated college or wrote a novel or won the lottery. I tighten

57

my grip on the phone, take my feet off the coffee table and sit up straight. Legolas, who was dozing, can sense the change in atmosphere. He looks at me, concerned.

"She's missing," she says. "She's been missing since Thursday, and I . . . I guess . . . I guess I thought you'd want to know. I . . . I guess . . . I don't know," she says, only she does know, and I know too. I was the one who found Alyssa all those years ago because I was willing to do whatever it took. Maggie is reaching out to ask me if I'm willing to do it all over.

Eight

I book a flight online for 6am and ring Scott, my buddy I bought the bar with, and tell him I'm going to need a few days off. I call my next-door neighbor to ask if she can look after Legolas and water my plants. She's done it before when I've been away. She loves Legolas as much as I do. I try to get a few hours' sleep, but can't, my mind racing with thoughts of Alyssa and thoughts of the past.

I get a taxi to the airport earlier than I need to. The airport is geared toward self-service to make things feel futuristic, but the staff in the security line are still surly, so I guess some things will never change. I finish a quick breakfast just as the boarding call for my flight is announced. The gate ends up being so far away they ought to have people handing out cups of water along the way. I have a window seat, which isn't so bad, but I'm next to a guy who doesn't feel the need to wear shoes or socks, which isn't so good. He smells like cigarette smoke and he's carrying a notepad on which he's scrawling a random selection of numbers. He'll stop every now and then, look up at the roof of the cabin for thirty seconds or more, then go back to his scrawling. I wonder if he's a mad scientist or just mad. I text Maggie and tell her what time I'm flying in and then switch off my phone.

The flight is two hours. I stare out the window the entire time. When we land there's a text from Maggie to tell me she's in the pick-up zone out front. I have only carry-on luggage, so walk off the plane and head for the door. It's hot outside, and glary, the sun bouncing off the cars in the long line of pick-ups and drop-offs. I turn right and there she is, a few spaces down, leaning against a dark blue sedan.

She's smiling at me. I'm smiling. She pushes off from the car and we meet halfway. There's a moment of hesitation when we try to figure out whether we're going to shake hands or kiss each other on the cheek or hug, and we go with the latter, and the awkwardness that was there a moment ago melts away. It doesn't feel like it's been twelve years. I want to tell her I've missed her, but I don't. I want to tell her that part of me still loves her, but I don't. I want to tell her so many things and say none of them. She smells like shampoo and body wash and perfume, none of them the same scents that I remember.

"It's really good to see you," she says, once she's pulled back to look at me. Her hands are warm on my arms. I like feeling them on me.

"You look the same," I tell her. She's wearing her hair shorter than she used to, and she looks too thin, like something has worried the weight away. I know what that worry is.

"And you never were a good liar," she says. "But you look good too," she says, and I laugh. "What?"

"You're the one who's the bad liar," I tell her. This conversation is played out a million times by a million people at airports every year. Maggie *is* lying, though. I didn't hit the gym or go running as much as I should have in my thirties. Now I'm a year into my forties, and no matter what I do the following morning I hurt from it. Creaky joints, stiff knees, skin that was tight that isn't tight anymore — none of that was on the horizon when I was with Maggie.

I put my bag in the trunk and climb into the passenger seat. There's a child's seat in the back and toys scattered across the floor.

"The kids are in school," she says. "You'll meet them later."

"And Steve?"

"Stephen. He hates being called Steve. He's at work, but you'll meet him tonight."

"He doesn't mind me being here?"

She indicates and looks over her shoulder, spins the wheel and applies a little gas and pulls out from the curb. She adjusts the mirror, as if between driving out here and now she's gotten taller or shorter and the angles have changed.

"Maggie?"

"Well . . . I haven't told him yet."

"He doesn't know I'm here?"

"I think he'd struggle with it. He can get . . . a little jealous. Otherwise I'd offer for you to stay with us."

Cars coming out from the parking lot exits are merging like

a closing zip fastener. Windows are open and arms are dangling out and people are looking hot and frustrated and tired.

"There are some really good motels," she says. "Acacia has gotten bigger since you've been gone." She looks over and smiles for a moment. "It's good to have you back, Noah. I know it's only for a little while, and I wish it were under better circumstances, but it's still good to have you back."

Nine

It's a ninety-minute drive to Acacia Pines with the sun in our faces. The town was named after two of the three most common trees surrounding it, the third being Douglas fir, but locals normally refer to it only as Acacia. It sprang up a hundred and fifty years ago, the sawmill the heart of the town with the town expanding around it, but then sixty years ago the sawmill got shifted twenty minutes south and the town kept growing. Acacia is like a cul-de-sac, with one road in and that same road out. Behind it is nothing but trees and lakes and beside it nothing but trees and lakes, and in front of it with the road splitting it right down the middle are more trees and lakes. The nearest town is an hour away. We drive past big hills and bigger mountains, there are long rivers and giant lakes, and the highway curves and straightens and curves some more, all of it under a wide blue sky, all of it shimmering in the heat. We have the windows down and the air is fresh and I feel like I'm being detoxed.

We start off talking about the town. About the people I used to know. About her children. Damian is seven and he's going through a Superman phase. He sleeps in Superman pajamas and takes his lunch to school in a Superman lunch box and he has Superman figures scattered all through his room. Her younger son, Harry, is heavily into a group of superheroes I never heard of before, each with different powers ranging from whatever it is that superheroes have to whatever it is the rest of us wish we had. I figure if any of these people were real, they'd have found Alyssa Stone within minutes of her going missing. I figure they'd have stopped it from happening.

Maggie tells me Sheriff Haggerty retired a year ago after he had a stroke. He still has a presence in town, but is a shadow of the man I used to know. In the twelve years since I left town, he's never mentioned my name once, not after those first couple of days. It was only a few days after I left town that I learned no charges were going to be laid against Conrad Haggerty, and that there wouldn't be any charges against me either. The investigation was closed, which told me Sheriff Haggerty knew his son had been responsible. Drew was lucky to hang on to his job, though I've always suspected it wasn't just luck, but the town being unable to lose two of its deputies at the same time. Now Maggie tells me there are some who believe Conrad's story about overhearing the two men at the bar, and some who don't, and over the years the town has let those events fade from its collective consciousness. Conrad, like me, now works behind a bar. It makes me cringe to hear we're doing the same thing in life. Then she tells me that I sound different, that I've replaced my small-town accent with a big-city accent. She doesn't say if she likes it or not.

She's still practicing law. Mostly it's dealing with property boundary issues and prosecuting drunk drivers and wife beaters and people for theft. Her parents are still alive, and I'm glad to hear it. My own parents passed away when I was in my twenties. My dad drank himself into an early grave, and all that drinking broke my mother's heart and she joined him the following year. Drew is sheriff now. She says he's a good man and people love him. We go through all sorts of names and the road winds on and Acacia Pines gets closer. We reach the turnoff to the sawmill. I can hear machinery from a mile away. I remember on summer days when the breeze was just right you could hear the mill from town. She tells me a new sawmill has just finished being built, one double the size of the original. She says they're in the process of transferring machinery and stock from one building to the other, and as she says it, we catch up to a truck turning into a new turnoff a few miles past the old one, a turnoff that back in my time didn't exist. She says the old building will be left empty for nature to reclaim.

Then she tells me a similar thing is happening to the quarries we passed a little further back up the highway, that they're expanding out into the forests. She says there are days when the road we're on is full of trucks.

We pass the gas station. Earl Winters is out front patching up gunshot in the store sign, collateral damage from where somebody has shot out his lights. He's probably so used to it that it doesn't bother him anymore. He looks as old as he did back when I knew him, but Winters has been an old man ever since I was a kid. Something out in these hills stops him from aging. Could be the fresh air. Could be the occult. Whatever it is, it keeps his mind sharp. He has this thing he can do with numbers. You can throw any combination of numbers at him and he can add or divide or multiply them in his head as fast as a calculator. He can see how things work. He can tell you what's wrong with your car by listening to it. He also has a memory for grudges. He's an almanac for who pissed off who and when.

I tell Maggie about Lego, about the countries I've seen, about the bar, about how Scott and I are looking at opening a second bar. She asks if I've ever thought about getting married again, and I tell her it's not something I really think about, and she asks what I'm waiting for, and I shrug off the question because I don't really know.

We catch up to an overloaded SUV, plastered with bumper stickers faded beyond recognition. Tents and backpacks have the windows bulging. Maggie can't get past it. Sometimes these SUVs and cars will come into Acacia and refuel on gas and food, the occupants getting one decent meal into them before heading out to go hiking and camping. Thankfully this one doesn't. It takes the turnoff to the hiking tracks. I wonder if people get lost out in the Green Hole like they used to, or if technology and GPS have made that a thing of the past. I guess GPS can't help you out against bad luck, or running into a bear, or falling down a slope, or getting caught in a surge of water when crossing a stream. I remember begging my dad to take me camping when I was a kid. For months on end I wouldn't shut up about it, and finally he gave in. I was ten years old. We got two miles down the track when he leaned against a boulder and said he needed a drink. Turned out he needed more than one. We ended up camping in that spot and the following morning I begged for us to go back.

As we get closer to town, a ball of apprehension tightens in my stomach. We pass big farms and large fields that merge into smaller farms with smaller fields. We pass the Kelly farm, where I found Alyssa. The *For Sale* sign out front is at an angle because one of the wooden legs is rotting. Fifteen years of sun and wind and rain have stripped away the words. The paddocks are overrun with weed. I can't see the house behind the big oak trees, but assume it's been swallowed into the earth.

"There's never been any interest in the place," Maggie says. "People say it's priced too high."

"What about the daughter? What's her name again — Julie?"

"Jasmine," Maggie says. "She hasn't been here since you left. I couldn't tell you where she is these days, or what she's doing. My guess is she's hoping the town will keep expanding and one day the land will be worth something again."

The farms end and the houses start earlier than the last time I was here. Maggie tells me the population has grown from twenty thousand to thirty thousand. People move to Acacia for the lifestyle. They move here for the peace and quiet. There are new schools, a new swimming pool complex, new movie theaters and gyms, and the town library is now twice the size it used to be. The supermarkets are bigger and there are more of them. The sheriff's department is bigger too. A few years ago Acacia got featured on a travel show as the place to go to get away from it all, and now summers see tourism booming, and motels and bed and breakfasts have sprung up all across town.

"There are more restaurants and bars too," she says. "There's a lot you'll recognize, and some you won't."

We come to the bridge over the river that separates Acacia from the world. Red paint is flaking off the metal trusses. Slivers of it form metal puddles in the weeds alongside. Maggie says it hasn't been repainted because it's going to be replaced within the next year, that it'll be wider and stronger. The banks of the river are wide and the water is dark and when I was a kid I used to come here with Drew and we'd go fishing, and never once did we catch anything. We go over the bridge. It's Acacia Pines, but it's not Acacia Pines. There are bigger buildings, new facilities, more people on the streets. We pass a car dealership that wasn't there when I was here, and Maggie tells me that's where her husband works. I take it all in. Some of the shops are the same. Other people too. The roads. The skyline. The big blue sky.

"It feels the same," I say. "It might look a little different, but it feels the same."

"How does it feel?"

"Like coming home."

"That's good," she says, and she smiles at me.

I smile back. Then the smile disappears. "Tell me about Alyssa," I say.

"Drew," she says, "well, Drew thinks she up and left. People do that — Acacia is proof of that, right? People are up and leaving other towns and cities to move here, only makes sense the opposite is true too, and Alyssa is certainly of that age where people want to flee the nest. At least that's what people seem to think."

"So the police haven't classified her as missing?"

"No," she says.

"But you think she is."

"She's a good kid. We know her pretty well. She used to babysit Damian for us," she says.

"But not Harry?"

"By the time Harry came along she was too busy with school and exams."

"So why do you think she's missing as opposed to having left town? Drew's a good cop, and I can't imagine him taking this lightly."

"She wouldn't have left without saying goodbye."

"What about her phone? Her handbag? Her car? Were those things gone?"

"Yes, and before you say anything, you know as well as I do that doesn't mean anything. The person who took her could easily have taken those things too."

"Any clothes missing?" I ask. "A suitcase?"

"They were gone too," she says. "But she just wouldn't leave like that."

I twist in my seat so I can get a better look at her. She keeps looking ahead. She knows what I'm about to say. "Look, Maggie, unless you have something more than that, you might as well turn the car around and take me back to the airport. People aren't going to be thrilled to see me here, and unless—"

"Father Frank said you'd help."

"Father Frank?"

"He said for a few years after her abduction she used to have nightmares. There was a figure in her dreams she called The Bad Man. She said she was scared, but she always knew things would be okay because Deputy Harper would save her. She says Deputy Harper promised her in the hospital that he'd find The Bad Man if he ever came back."

I remember. I crossed my heart and told her I'd do whatever it takes to keep her safe.

"What makes you so sure there's a bad man?"

"It's probably easier if I show you," she says, and we carry on driving into town and into the memories I have of this place, most of them good, worried there's a whole fresh set of bad ones on the way.

Ten

Saint John's isn't the only church in town, but it is the original — at least in spirit. When the town was built, the church was in the center, a hundred yards from the original sawmill, the founders of the town figuring if it was good enough for the Roman Empire to have all roads leading to Rome, then it was good enough to have all roads in Acacia Pines leading to Saint John's. Which it was, up until it burned down a hundred years ago. Perhaps that was something else the Roman Empire taught the founders.

The church was rebuilt half a mile away. The rebuild allowed for a bigger cemetery, one that would need to expand as the town expanded, and as the town grew bigger in various directions, the church became more and more off-center.

The new church is white weatherboard and in need of painting, one end of the building low and flat, the other peaking three stories high like a rocket ship, with a cross on the top. The gardens surrounding it are beautiful but overgrown, stretching out into the adjoining cemetery. The church can seat two hundred people, though I'm not sure how many go on a Sunday to feel closer to God. I've only ever been for weddings and funerals.

The parking lot between the church and the road is empty. We drive through it and around the church to the residence out back, a rustic-looking home with a low roof and wide eaves that also needs painting. I remember Father Frank Davidson being meticulous. When he wasn't preaching, he was painting, or mowing, or trimming. The last time I came here was to tell him his sister had been killed. Maggie parks the car and we step out into the sun. The heat of the gravel comes through my shoes. Out here summers always feel like they're going to burn the town to ash. I'd forgotten days could be like this.

The residence has two bedrooms and a kitchen and a lounge and not a lot else. That I remember. There's an apple tree next to it with branches so heavy with fruit they're at breaking point. There's a wooden porch out front that at this time of the day is half shaded by the eaves. We climb the steps and Maggie doesn't knock. We step inside and the smell tells me everything I need to know. It tells me why she thinks Alyssa never ran away, but it also tells me that Alyssa had good reason to.

The décor is out of date and unlikely to ever swing back into fashion. The carpet is worn to the point I'm not sure it can still legally be called carpet. The first bedroom is Alyssa's. The bed has been made, but everything else looks slightly askew. The next bedroom has Frank in it. He's lying on the bed in a pair of shorts and a thin white top. There's a fan on and the windows are open but it doesn't help with the heat, doesn't help with the smell. A tube runs from under Father Frank's nose to an oxygen machine that's plugged into the wall.

There are sores on Frank's skin and blisters in various states of erupting. There's bruising on his arms and legs, a side effect of the medication. His eyes have sunk into his skull. He's lost most of his hair, most of his color, most of his life. It's like looking at a poorly made showroom mannequin. There's a clock on the wall, and I can hear it ticking. If I were dying, I'd want that clock in a different room. Or out of the house. The oxygen machine hisses and the fan whirrs. The mystery of his missing niece is keeping him alive. Perhaps that's why she's run away. Father Frank has declined permanent care, just as strongly as he declined to spend his final days in a hospice. A nurse, Maggie's sister Victoria, comes in every morning to check on him, and a doctor every evening.

I don't know where Father Frank is, but this isn't him. This is only half of him. Whatever is eating him has worked away at the muscle and is now working away at the bone. I think back to the last time I saw him, at the hospital the night I found Alyssa. He told me what I had done was the kind of thing that would weigh heavily on good men. He said I would come to question my actions. He was right. When I left Acacia Pines, I left knowing I would never be a cop again. I couldn't risk being in a situation where I lost myself the way I had lost myself that night.

His eyes flicker open. He smiles, and for the briefest of

moments the disease is beaten back and the man he used to be is out on display. "You came," he says. His voice has a whistling effect to it, like there's a hole in his throat.

There's a chair by the bed. I take it. Maggie stays standing in the doorway. My clothes are sticking to me.

"It's good to see you, Frank," I say.

He laughs, and the laugh turns into a cackle, turns into a cough, then ends with a spasm. Something rattles in his lungs. He reaches for a small bowl and coughs phlegm into it. I hand him a glass of water. He sips slowly, and hangs on to it.

"Two pieces of advice," he says. "Number one. Don't get old. Number two. Don't get cancer."

"How long?" I ask.

"I should be dead already, but I'm sure as hell not dying without . . ." he says, and he closes his eyes and turns his head away as something — a bolt of pain or nausea — fires through his body. He holds on, grits his teeth and turns back to me. "I'm not dying without answers." He smiles at me, and it's the saddest smile I've ever seen. "It's . . . it's a funny thing to describe, Noah, it really is. I can feel it coming, this death of mine, I can feel it coming and yet I've been taught my whole life not to fear it — don't fear it, Frankie, don't fear it — and I've told others not to fear it too. But I must confess that I'm scared, Noah. I'm scared of dying without knowing what's happened to my daughter."

His daughter. I wonder when the switch happened, when she went from being his niece to becoming his daughter. I like the way it sounds. I look at the window and see it can't get any wider. I look at the fan and see it can't spin any faster. I look at Father Frank and see he can't hold on much longer.

He coughs into his hand. There are flecks of blood on it. The original Frank that peeked out from under the cancer with that smile has slipped back under the surface. "She wouldn't have left me, not at the end. I need for you to understand that. To believe that."

"Isn't it possible it all became too much for her? I know you don't want to think so, but—"

He puts his hand up for me to stop talking. "Drew, that's what he thinks. It's what others think."

"But not you."

He reaches out and grabs my hand. His grip is strong. "Sometimes people know things. How many times on the force did you rely on instinct? How many times did you trust your gut? This isn't any different. I've raised her most of her life, Noah. The last time she called me Uncle Frank was the same night you got her back for me. Since then she's called me Dad. She's gone from being my niece to being my daughter, and I know my daughter. I know her better than you know her, better than the sheriff knows her, better than anybody in this town knows her." He closes his eyes. He grimaces. Something in his body — or perhaps everything in his body — is hurting. He keeps his eyes closed as he talks, a thin line of tears coming from them. "I get that kids keep secrets. I know they have boyfriends and girlfriends and they smoke and they shoplift and they sneak out at night and fool around. I know teenagers have secret lives and they hold back from us, but she wouldn't have left without saying goodbye." He says it again. "She wouldn't have left without saying goodbye."

I let that sink in. He sips some more water. Droplets spill down his chin. He wipes at it, his fingers rasping across his unshaven skin. He looks tired, like he could close his eyes and never open them again. It's time to ask what needs asking. "Has she ever spoken of leaving?"

He says nothing for a bit. His head sinks into the pillow and he stares at the ceiling. He lets go of my hand. "Yes," he says. "After I've gone, there's nothing here for her. Her friends are moving on, she's got no more family. She's applying for universities. I know that makes it sound like maybe she couldn't wait, but she was waiting. The thing is, Noah, I should have died months ago. She was there for me then thinking every day could be the last, so whatever notion you're building up that she left because she got scared — well, you go ahead and scrap it." He rolls onto his side to face me. It's an effort for him. "Trust me, Noah. Something happened. I'm not . . . I'm not saying somebody kidnapped her, but something happened. She wouldn't have left like that." He reaches out and takes my hand again, and uses what strength the cancer hasn't finished eking away to squeeze it tighter than he squeezed it before. He tries to sit up further, but can't manage it. "You have to believe me. You have to find my daughter."

"I'll find her," I tell him. "I promise."

He takes me at my word, and he relaxes and lets go of my hand and settles back into the position he was in when we first arrived.

"She used to have nightmares," he says. "About The Bad Man."

"Maggie told me," I say.

"She used to say back then you'd always save her."

"Let me get my bearings," I tell him, "and I'll come back in a few hours. I'll want to look through Alyssa's room and go through her things, get the names of her friends from you. And I'll talk to Drew, see what he says."

"Anything you need." Then he looks at me and goes to say something else, but doesn't.

"What is it?" I ask him.

"It's nothing."

"Tell me."

"I can't . . . I can't have you doing what you did last time," he says. "I can't have that on my conscience, but . . . but at the same time I need you to do what it takes."

"And if what it takes is more than your soul is willing to bear?"

He doesn't answer right away. This is a question he's been grappling with ever since he decided I was the man who could help. "I don't know," he says. "Forgiveness is a big thing in my faith, Noah."

"I'm going to find her," I say. "I hope I won't have to break any bones along the way, but if I have to, then I'm okay with you forgiving me."

"That's not what I'm saying."

"You'd rather forgive whoever did something to her?"

"I'm not saying that either."

"So what are you saying?"

He exhales loudly, and it worries me because it sounds like it could be his last one ever, but then he sucks in a breath that rattles in his chest. "I'm saying . . . I'm saying do what it takes, I'll do my best to square things up for the both of us when I'm on the other side."

Eleven

Maggie gets Father Frank some fresh water and asks him if there's anything else we can do to make him comfortable. He tells us that he's fine, and promises he'll have more energy when I come back later this afternoon.

We step outside and the day has gotten hotter. I listen to the porch timbers straining against the nails. It was hot back when I used to live here, but this is something different. This feels like somebody drilled for oil and went too far, venting heat out from the planet's core.

There's another car in the parking lot now. It's shimmering in the heat, and the man leaning against it is shimmering too. He's no longer in uniform, but he's wearing the same hat he always used to wear. He has the same horseshoe mustache and the same gun strapped to his waist. He's wearing a pair of aviators. He's lost weight, and a lot of what's left has been redistributed. His hair has gone gray, but it's still thick, and the smile lines have turned to frown lines and the frown lines he had back then have turned to furrows deep enough to slot a dime into. He has his arms folded across his chest and a cigarette hanging out of his mouth. There's a chipped red portable oxygen tank next to him, parked up on a couple of wheels, a tube running from it to over his ears and under his nose. I've been back in town for thirty minutes, and other than Maggie everybody I've seen so far is on oxygen. Maybe the town is so hot the air here burns your lungs. I'd have thought that mixing smoking with oxygen was one seriously bad idea, but it doesn't seem to bother him. Maybe he likes the idea of going out in a ball of fire.

I walk down the steps and my feet crunch into the shingle. I put my sunglasses on before my eyes catch fire. I stand a few feet away from Sheriff Haggerty who is no longer Sheriff Haggerty, but Walt Haggerty, a man I've known most of my life, a man who, under different circumstances, I'd be shaking his hand and telling him how good it is to see him. He stays leaning against the car and keeps his arms folded and I can't see his eyes behind his glasses.

"Noah," he says.

"Sheriff."

"It ain't Sheriff anymore, son."

"I heard," I tell him. "I'm sorry about your stroke."

"That's not the thing you need to be sorry about."

I stare at him and he stares at me and the temperature gets a little hotter and the sun gets a little higher and the shadow he's casting gets a little smaller.

"You shouldn't have come here," he says, and then he looks

at Maggie. "You shouldn't have called him. Frank . . . you know Frank's not in his right mind."

"Come on, Sheriff," she says, putting on her lawyer voice. "Father Frank asked me for Noah's help, and I wasn't going to let him down. You have every reason to just leave us be."

Haggerty's face tightens. He looks from Maggie back to me. "Listen to me very carefully, Noah," he says. "There's nothing for you here. There's no case here. What I said to you twelve years ago still stands, only given the circumstances I'm going to let things slide a little. I'm going to give you the chance to let Maggie drive you to wherever you came from. You do that, and we don't have a problem."

"And if I don't?"

He turns to adjust something on his oxygen tank. There's a faded sticker on it. Only two words I can make out are *Property of*. His left arm hangs without much purpose. Looking at Father Frank, I thought only half of him was there. Looking at Haggerty, it's like the stroke took away a third of him. Time has made these men smaller. He leans back into the position he was in earlier, only now his left arm is hanging and his right hand is on the butt of his gun. The stroke wasn't kind to him, but strokes aren't known for decency.

"That's not something you want to find out, son."

"Only thing I want to find is Alyssa," I tell him.

He pushes himself off from his car. It's takes more effort than it should. "Like I told you, there's no case here. I'm giving you an hour's grace here, son, and that's only because of our history. You're still here in an hour, then I can't stop what's coming your way."

"And what's that?"

He takes the cigarette out of his mouth, tosses it onto the ground, and grinds it out with the heel of his boot. He looks at me for a bit, and then climbs into his car, dragging his oxygen tank with him. We watch him pull away.

The dust from his car hangs in the air, then starts to settle on my damp clothes and skin. There's no wind to shift it.

"He's just trying to throw his weight around," Maggie says. "It's not like he's actually going to come after you to drag you out of town. He has no authority here. Still, I knew he'd be mad, but I didn't realize he'd still be that mad."

I tortured his son. Then I shot him, and tortured him some more. It's not something you stop being mad about. "He's taking me being here better than I thought. What do you think he meant when he said there was no case here?"

"Doesn't matter what he meant," she says. "He's not investigating it. He doesn't know what's going on."

"He might be retired, but I don't doubt he knows what's going on."

"So now what? You're not going to let him run you off, are you?"

"No," I say. "Of course not. He's an old man," I say, "trying to throw his weight around like you said."

"One with a gun," she says.

"And an oxygen tank," I say. "The wheels on that tank are so old I'll hear them squeaking a mile away. I doubt he can even shoot straight. You saw the way his arm was hanging."

"He's right-handed," she says. "The stroke affected his left. Don't forget his son has a grudge too."

"They don't scare me."

"They scared you enough twelve years ago," she says.

"Twelve years ago was a different story. Back then it wasn't about being scared, it was about being sensible." I turn to look at her. "You must have known before you called me this was going to happen."

She nods. "You're right. But Frank . . . he was insistent."

"These two cars," I say, nodding toward the two other cars parked here. "One of them belong to Father Frank?"

"The Toyota," she says. The beaten-up Toyota looks like it should be buried in the graveyard out back. It reminds me of my car. "Keys should be in the ignition."

I look at my watch. Haggerty said he'd give me an hour. "I'll go talk to Drew, see what he says."

"Should I come with you?"

"No. There's no reason to make trouble for you with Haggerty."

"Okay," she says. She gets into her car. "You'll call me soon?"

"Of course. Despite everything, it's good seeing you again, Maggie. I've missed you."

She blushes. She's unsure what to say, and I don't need her to say anything. She drives off, putting more gravel dust into the air. I check out the Toyota. It's old and well used and looks like it would double in value if I hosed it down. Keys are inside it, like Maggie said. Could be because nobody would steal a car from a priest. Or because nobody would steal *this* car from anybody. The steering wheel is hot. The engine complains when I try to start it, and for a while it could go either way, life or death. It chooses life. For now. There's a grinding sound when I try to wind the windows down, and none of them budge. When I try again I can't even get the grinding sound. I turn the air conditioning on. The air is warm and stale. I turn it back off.

I drive out of the parking lot with fifty minutes of freedom left.

Twelve

I feel like I'm in a Bruce Springsteen song as I drive the streets where I grew up. Fragments of different memories play out like a parade. I can see the last time I drove out of here, my splinted fingers making it painful to drive. I can see myself heading inside The Big Bar at my mom's behest to tell my dad it was time to come home. It was a dark sticky-floored sports bar with pool tables and dart boards and TVs showing horse racing or football, and people drinking at the bar looking like they slept there too. I can see us with a Christmas tree strapped to the roof of the car, my dad braking quickly for a dog and the tree snapping its bindings and hitting the pavement, and us leaving it in the street and never getting another one again. I see myself walking the streets as a kid, walking them with Maggie, walking them as a cop. Some buildings have seemingly been put into a time capsule the day I left to be brought back out on my return. Some of the faded shop fronts haven't faded any more, or maybe they were replaced and faded all over again. The cars are more modern, clothes are more modern, people are on cellphones that twelve years ago nobody would have thought possible.

Father Frank's car chugs along, the engine hiccupping every now and then, and something from the front clicks loudly when I make left-hand turns. I pass by a couple of bars unsure which one has Conrad Haggerty working in it. I pass The Big Bar, its name now up in neon. I pass a shop where I bought my first and only suit. I pass the barber my dad always took me to. I drive through my history, pangs of regret for having to leave coming from everywhere I look.

I reach the police station. It's a flat building with brownstone walls stained by small-town life, exhaust fumes and bird crap and dirt swept in from forest and quarry. The front has floor-to-ceiling windows with closed blinds on the other side, big letters painted in gold across them saying *Acacia Pines Sheriff Office*. Maggie was right — it is bigger than it used to be, the front closer to the road, the right-hand side extending further into the parking lot. There are seven patrol cars out front, fairly new models. Back in the day there only ever used to be four.

If driving into Acacia Pines was like coming home, then walking into the sheriff's office is like coming to work. There are notice boards with messages and photographs and wanted signs, large filing cabinets scattered around the walls, maps of the town, of the forest, of the country, ring binders and lamps and computers covering the desks, people sitting behind them tapping on keyboards, or talking on phones.

Some people I recognize, some I don't. The air conditioning is working overtime.

Drew, or Sheriff Drew Brooks as he's now officially known, is pouring himself a coffee from the same machine we were looking at replacing all those years ago. He's aged better than I have. He's lost weight and gained muscle and those two things make him look taller and younger. He looks thirty instead of forty. He's grown a horseshoe mustache to match the one his predecessor had. He glances at me, looks back at the coffee, then glances back at me again. He straightens up and has a look about him of a man who thinks he might be dreaming.

I offer him my hand. He looks at it without any expression and doesn't move. Coming here was a mistake. He puts his coffee down, and then he smiles, and he steps forward and puts his arms around me and smacks me on the back a couple of times and I do the same to him.

"Jesus, Noah, Jesus, it's good to see you." He pulls back and keeps smiling. "It's great to see you."

"Out of everybody in this town," I say, "they made *you* the sheriff?"

"I'm the only one who could read and shoot straight."

He goes about pouring me a coffee. He remembers how I take it. Black, and in a cup. The machine has either been serviced or blessed by the church because it doesn't jam up halfway through the pour like it often used to.

"You learned to read while I was away?"

"Picture books, mostly." He hands me a cup. It says *World's Sexiest Sheriff* on the side. "What's it been? Ten years?"

"Twelve."

"Twelve." Slowly he nods as that night comes back to him. We've never spoken a word to each other since then. "Yeah, twelve. Of course, of course. That was messed up, what you did to me back then, Noah," he says, and then he shakes his head. "Sorry, I didn't mean to say that."

"You have every right to say it," I say, and I can't defend it. He has every right to be mad. I need to let him tell me, take what's coming, and hope we can move on. "I've always wanted to apologize, but never quite knew how."

"By picking up the phone," he says. "I was willing to listen."

It sounds so simple, the way he puts it. "You're right. For what it's worth, I'm sorry."

He thinks on that. "You ever wonder where we'd be if things had gone different?"

"Every day," I tell him.

"Every day." And then the big smile from a few moments ago comes back. "Well, hell, it's all water under the bridge now," he says, even though it isn't. He slaps me on the shoulder.

"Can we talk? I have about forty minutes before Old Man Haggerty straps me to the front of a tractor and drives me into the sunset."

"Old Man Haggerty. You know, we actually call him that here at the station when he's not around. If he heard he'd strap us to that same damn tractor."

I follow him through to his office, which is Old Man Haggerty's old office, which is along the back wall next to a fire exit that Haggerty often propped open so he could sit out on the step to have a cigarette. The office looks the same, and Drew hasn't put his touch on it. The same painting of horses in a landscape that Haggerty hung up a hundred years ago is still there. Same aerial photograph of the town. Same map on a wooden board of the town framed by the forest. The way the town has expanded, the map must be for nostalgia, not as a reference. The only things in here that have been updated are the calendar on the wall and the computer on the desk. We sit down either side of the desk. I think about the questions I need to ask. *When was the last time anybody saw Alyssa? Has she used her bank account? Has she made large withdrawals of money? Who are her friends?*

"So how have you been?" he asks. "You married? Got children? What have you been up to?"

"I never got married again," I tell him. "No kids. And I own a bar."

"You own a bar?"

"Yeah, with a buddy of mine. We own it fifty-fifty. It's a good bar. And I have a cat."

"Cats are good," he says. "So are bars. You sound happy, and you look good," he says.

"And you? What's new with you, other than the promotion?"

"Leigh's good. She's still selling houses. We have a couple of more kids since you were last here. Three in total now. So, Father Frank called you, huh?"

I take a sip of my drink. If the machine has been blessed to get it up and running, the effects don't extend to making the result taste any better. "In a roundabout way."

"Maggie?"

"Maggie."

"And I take it you didn't need much convincing," he says. "Because you figured without you here, the rest of us don't know what we're doing. You figured you'd come here and save the day, while the rest of us keep rescuing cats out of trees and writing up tickets.'

His response hurts, but it's not unexpected. "I don't think that at all."

"No? Then why did you come?"

"Because Maggie asked me to."

He sips at his coffee. I'm in no hurry to take another sip of mine. "You know she's married now, right?"

"She told me."

"Has a couple of kids and everything."

"I didn't come here searching for my old life, Drew. I've moved on. I came back for Alyssa. That night I found her, I promised her I'd make sure nothing bad ever happened to her again."

"And then you left," he says.

"And then I left."

"And now you're back." He fiddles with a pen between his fingers. He used to do this a lot when he was questioning people. It always made him look casual, and that, combined with his easy-going nature, made him the kind of guy you could open up to. Of course, out here career criminals are sheep stealers and tractor joyriders, not serial killers or

90

assassins. Now he looks like he could flex his way out of his shirt and pick somebody up by their ears.

He carries on. "The thing is, Noah, we don't need your help. I appreciate you coming all this way, and I know it was an effort and it's sure great seeing you, but there's no case here. I know what you're thinking, that Alyssa wouldn't run out on her dad like that at the end, but that's exactly what she did."

"You sure about that?"

He sighs, puts down the pen, and forms his fingers into steeples, tapping the front two against his lips. Then he points those front two at me, the rest folding down, so he's now making the shape of a gun. "Yes, I'm sure, because I know how to do my job."

"I didn't mean—"

"Look, I get you made Alyssa this promise, but the thing is, it's a wasted trip. If Maggie had come to me first before calling you, I could have saved you both a whole lot of time. Alyssa . . . well, Alyssa didn't disappear."

"No?"

He starts rotating his cup on the spot, ninety degrees clockwise, then ninety degrees anti-clockwise and so on. "No," he says. "She left town four days ago for personal reasons."

"Personal reasons? You're going to need to give me more than that," I say.

"No, I don't, Noah. I don't have to give you anything."

"Come on, Drew, I'm not trying to be a pain here, I'm just trying to help out. I owe her that."

"You think we need your help?"

"I'm not saying that."

"She left town to have an abortion."

What he's saying doesn't make sense, not at first, and that's because this whole time I've been keeping my promise to the Alyssa whose hand barely fit in mine. Not once have I seen her as the girl she might be today.

"Is that personal enough for you?" Before I can answer, he carries on. "Something like that, well, she's not going to be advertising the fact on her way out of here, is she?"

"Why hasn't she come back?"

He picks up his coffee. He takes another sip. "Says she can't face Father Frank."

"You've spoken to her?"

"Several times."

"What, you just rang her? She answered, and that solved the case?"

"Actually no," he says. "I spoke to her friends. A couple of them said she was struggling, and that after her dad died she was going to leave. Which made sense. Which made me think maybe she wasn't going to wait. We treated this as a missing person case even though we figured it likely she'd run away, but still, we treated it like a missing persons. It wasn't until yesterday her best friend told me they were still in touch. She'd been sworn to secrecy, but she could see how serious things had become. Her best friend told me there was more to it, but wouldn't say what, and had texted Alyssa to tell her she needed to talk to me. After that, Alyssa started taking my calls. Look, Noah, I've tried convincing her to come back, hand on heart," he says, and puts his hand over his heart. "I've said everything humanly possible to get her to return. The thing is she thinks her uncle will see it in her somehow. She thinks she'd rather he die disappointed that she isn't here than be ashamed of what she did. And to be clear here, those are her words, not mine."

"And you let people think she's missing?"

"Yeah, I knew you were going to say that," he says. "Goes to show you have no faith in what we do around here."

"That's not what I meant."

"No? We told Father Frank yesterday she was okay, but she couldn't deal with watching him die. He didn't believe us. You see him already?"

"Before I came here."

"Did he tell you we found her?"

"No. He didn't."

"My guess is he didn't tell Maggie either. Like I said, if she had spoken to me first you wouldn't have needed to come here."

"You tell Frank about the abortion?"

"Are you kidding?"

"He deserves to know the truth."

"Actually, Noah, he doesn't. This is Father Frank here. He's probably the nicest guy in Acacia, but let's not forget he's a Catholic priest. Alyssa thinks this would devastate him, and I'm inclined to agree."

"I'm not so sure it would. Frank's a liberal guy, and I think more than anything he wants to know she's safe."

"Could be you're right," he says, "but it doesn't much matter. This isn't about what you think, or what I think, this is Alyssa's decision, and I have to respect that. You, you're seeing Alyssa as a kid who makes kid decisions, and you think Father Frank still has the mental capacity of the Father Frank you knew. Look, it's easy for you to ride in here and think you know what to do, but it's not so easy when you're on this side of the desk. But you know what? I think it's more than Alyssa not wanting to face him or talk to him because she feels she's let him down. You've seen him, you know this is a man who isn't close to death, but is halfway on the other side of it. It's all over the house too. You can feel it. Alyssa, well, she lost both her parents when she was young, and now she's losing him too, and it's not pretty. It's too much for her to handle. She might not be seven anymore, but she's still a kid. If I were nineteen and that were my dad, hell, I'd want to run away too. Tell you what, if you think I'm wrong, if you think Father Frank really deserves to know, then by all means head on over to the church and tell him the girl he considers his daughter got pregnant, and compounded that sin by having it taken care of. Could be you telling him that is what he needs so he can let go and go see his Maker."

He's right. Of course he's right. I've come into town and weighed up an hour's worth of facts, and who am I to think I know what's right here? I think of my own mother wasting away the year after my dad wasted away. They were different kinds of wasting, and both were ugly, but neither looked as bad as Father Frank. If they had, I might have driven away too until it was all over.

"I'm sorry," I say.

"Sorry for thinking we'd dropped the ball?"

"Sorry for being a jerk," I tell him. "Sorry for everything."

He brightens up. "Never apologize for being a jerk. You start doing that, nobody else is going to get a word in." He starts rotating his coffee cup again. "So — you going to stick around for a bit, or let Old Man Haggerty run you out of town?"

"I'm not sure."

"Come on, man, you can't up and leave — you just got here. Stay a while. Come stay the night with me and the family. Leigh would love to see you and I'd love for you to meet the kids. You can tell me more about what you've been doing the last twelve years. I can provide you around the clock protective custody against Old Man Haggerty and Leigh can provide around the clock protection against my cooking. What do you say?"

"It's tempting," I tell him.

He glances at something on his computer, then writes down a number on a piece of paper and slides it across to me. "It's Alyssa's. You're about to ask for it. I know you're thinking you're not done here until you speak to her yourself. Keep in mind she might not answer, I don't know. You could leave a message maybe. I think . . . I think considering what you did for her, she'll talk to you. Just . . . just go easy on her."

I fold the piece of paper into my pocket. He was right about me not being done here until I've spoken to her myself. "Has she had the procedure done?"

"She has." He stares at me for a few seconds. "After you call her, you're leaving, I guess. You're not going to come by and see us, are you?"

"I really should get going." I stand up. He does the same. We reach out over the desk and shake hands.

"So this is it," he says.

"Yeah. I think it is."

"I'm still in the same place," he says. "I'll be firing up the barbecue around seven, but I promised Leigh I'd be home around four to help out with the kids. Seriously, drop by. Old Man Haggerty — screw him. If he tries anything, I'll arrest him."

"No, you won't," I say.

He smiles. "No, I won't."

He walks me to the car. Once I drive out of town I have no need to ever drive back, not unless Alyssa goes missing in another twelve years. Neither of us say it, but I can tell he's thinking it too. I've missed Drew over the years, but I didn't realize how much until seeing him again.

"It really was good to see you, Noah. I mean that. I wish . . . I wish things had worked out different. You were like a brother to me."

"Likewise," I say, and we part ways and this man who was my best man, my best friend, this person I grew up with, I watch him walk back into the station knowing I'll never see him again.

Thirteen

Compared to the mammoth-killing temperatures inside the police station, getting back into the car is like catching a rocket ship to the sun. I pilot it out of the parking lot and into the shade of a large elm tree over the road. I dial Alyssa's number. She doesn't answer and I leave a message.

I drive back to Saint John's. I pass an outdoor swimming pool that only has a few people using it, but will fill up with kids when school is out. The one I used to go to when I was younger has closed. Every summer me and Drew would win medals at that pool, at least until we started competing in state championships where we'd be up against guys who were bigger and faster. I pass a supermarket where, when I was fourteen years old, I got my first job packing groceries. I drive past the bowling alley where I once dropped a ball on my foot and broke my toe, all while Maggie couldn't stop laughing.

I call Maggie. I tell her I'm heading back to the church, and she tells me she's heading to the school. She says Damian isn't feeling well and she's on her way to pick him up. She asks how I got on with Drew, and I tell her everything he told me.

"Frank didn't tell me Drew had been to see him," she says. "I wouldn't have called you if he had."

"That's probably why he didn't tell you."

"Did Drew say who the father was?"

"I didn't ask," I say. "It doesn't change anything."

"I'm glad we have an answer," she says. "But you've come all this way and . . . and for that I'm sorry. It feels like I've wasted your time."

Up ahead a brand-new building is replacing an old one. I can't remember what used to be there. People in brightly colored vests are scurrying around, cutting and nailing and bolting. I think about the town having expanded, and how it will expand some more. At some point it will double, and then over time it will double again. In a hundred years this new building will be pulled down to make way for another one. That's what progress is — pulling apart the past and making it better.

"I'm glad you called," I tell her. "It was good coming back here."

"You mean that?"

"Of course. Even somewhat cathartic."

"I'm glad," she says. "So what are you going to do now?"

It's a tough question, and one I've been asking myself on the drive from the station. "Do you think we should tell Father Frank the truth?" I ask her.

"I don't know," she finally says. "I . . . I guess not."

"That's my feeling too. Let's tell him what Drew told us, that she's safe but everything going on here is too much for her to handle. I'll talk to her, and see if I can convince her to return home."

"Are you going to head back home today?"

"Yes."

"It's just . . ." she says, but then doesn't say what. I stay silent as she formulates her thoughts. "It's silly, you know? You coming all the way out here and going right back."

"I have no reason to stay."

"I . . . I guess I can see that," she says. "I have to pick up Harry after school. How about I come and get you from the church after that, and drive you back out to the airport?"

"I'd appreciate it," I say, trying to imagine how I'm going to spend the next few hours. Maybe I should go back to the pool.

She goes quiet again. More silence on my end and more thoughts being formulated on hers. "You . . . you should stay," she says.

I don't say anything.

"At least for a night. We could have breakfast tomorrow morning after I've dropped the kids off at school. Catch up some before I take you to the airport. It'll be easier for me to do that, because it means I won't have to get home late tonight."

Seeing Maggie has sparked up emotions I haven't felt in a long time. I wasn't kidding when I told Drew earlier I'd moved on — I have — but I also can't deny that the reason

I've let my relationships since then peter out is because none of those women were Maggie. So maybe I haven't moved on as much as I thought. After all, I beat a man unconscious so I could get my phone back to be able to return Maggie's call.

"Noah?"

"I'd like to stay, except for the fact Old Man Haggerty is probably putting together some kind of lynching party." I make the turnoff into the church. I park the Toyota where I found it earlier. The engine sighs with thoughts of retirement when I shut it off.

"How about I meet you at the church in forty-five minutes? Maybe we can figure something out. Then if you want to go, I'll take you out to the airport."

"Okay. Thanks, Maggie."

I find shade beside the porch where the lawn is greener and longer than anywhere else. I lean up against the apple tree and decide to help out its overweight branches by lessening the load. I polish my apple up against my shirt and carry it inside. The air is thicker and I can hear the oxygen machine and the fan and Father Frank's chest singing out its death rattle. I'm a couple of steps in when I hear a creaking floorboard behind me. I don't manage to turn all the way before something hard and heavy smacks me in the side of my head. I hit the ground in a heap and stare at a pair of feet in a pair of cowboy boots.

Fourteen

I can smell dust on the floor. I can hear the clock in Father Frank's room ticking. I can hear the oxygen machine. The apple I was holding has come to a stop against the wall. I can see jigsaw puzzle pieces of dirt that have fallen out of the soles of somebody's shoes — maybe out of the cowboy boots I'm staring at. One of those boots swings back, and then swings forward, and I barely manage to get my arm in front of my face to take the impact. I can't stop the second one; it's aimed at my stomach, and it punches the air out of me. I'm grabbed around my ankles and dragged outside. The boards of the porch are hot. Nails snag at my shirt and scratch at my back. My head, already spinning, bounces up and down. I'm pulled off the porch into the sun and my spine digs into the edge of the step before slamming into the shingle, my head getting the same result. Then shade as the person doing this crouches over me. My cellphone is ringing.

Conrad Haggerty's face is full of anger, and something

else too, a certain sense of smug satisfaction. "I always hoped you'd come back," he says, spitting the words at me. "Every day I prayed for it, and now here you are." He punches me in the side of the face, and there isn't anything I can do, except bleed on his fist and hope one of his fingers breaks. I roll onto my side and push my hands into the ground and try to get onto my knees. Small stones dig into the palms of my hands. Conrad swings in a kick that I try to turn away from. His foot covers my eye and cheek and part of my nose. Maybe something breaks, maybe it doesn't. I don't know. He kicks me again and my teeth loosen and the impact puts me on my back again.

"I used to say to myself, *Conrad, if you could do anything to that prick who hurt you, what would you do? Would you cut off his fingers?*" he says, and he's holding a knife in front of my face now. "And I'd say to myself, *You know what, Conrad? I think that's a good idea.*"

He rolls me onto my stomach and zip ties my hands behind me, then drags me toward Father Frank's car. He gets the trunk open, gets my head and shoulders into it, and then stops when somebody yells out at us. He lets me go and I fall back to the ground, my shoulder taking the impact.

A man is walking across the parking lot from the church. I blink rapidly until my vision sharpens. It hits me then that Father Frank may have a replacement. It's probably who the second car in the parking lot belongs to. People still need to get married and still need to die and still need to confess and ask why God does this or that without reason, and this is the guy who's getting all that asking.

"This ain't any of your business, Father," Conrad says.

"I may not know what's going on here, son," he says, "but I can certainly tell you that it is my business."

My protector is wearing a black shirt with a white clerical collar. It's hard to guess his age. Could be forty, could be fifty-five. He's completely bald, and balances that baldness out with a beard that's white in the front and black around the sides. He's six foot and two-hundred-plus pounds. He looks like he could tie Conrad into a knot. His voice is deep and authoritative.

"Why don't you piss off inside, Father, and mind yourself?"

"I could do that," the priest says. "I could go in there and call the police. Maybe get you arrested, maybe have you spend a few nights in jail before getting charged with assault and spending even longer."

"Phone them if you want, old man, there's no way in hell they're sending me to jail."

"You sure about that? Whatever beating you've come to administer, well, you've administered it. Anything else you had in mind, you best let that go, then come back tomorrow and thank me for not taking the other option."

"Which is . . .?"

"Which is me kicking your ass."

Conrad isn't sure how to respond. What he came to do clearly isn't going to get done.

"Seriously, son, walk away before anything else has to happen. Or you spend tonight in a hospital. Choice is yours."

Conrad sniffs as much phlegm as he can, then spits it out. It lands on my shoulder and makes my shirt one I no longer want to own. "This isn't over," he says. He glares at me, then at Father Kick Ass, then at me again. When he's all out of glaring, he heads to the road without looking back.

Father Kick Ass helps me up. "You must be Noah Harper," he says. He leans me up against the car. "I'm Father Barrett. Father Frank said you'd be coming by, though I can't say I was expecting to meet you under these circumstances."

"I wasn't expecting to be under these circumstances," I say.

"Is that you thanking me?"

"Sorry," I say. "Thank you."

"You're welcome. Let's go inside and get you cleaned up."

"It's nothing a new shirt can't fix."

"We'll see."

My ribs hurt and my kidneys hurt, as does my chest and head. My shoulders are under strain from the zip tie. My feet are okay. I walk slowly on the only parts of my body that don't ache, and I start to question if this is a con. Father Barrett uses a bully to beat people up, only to save them so he can patch them up inside his church and sell them the Catholic lifestyle. We step inside and it's cold in here, but churches often are. It's like the heat from hell can't make it past the front door.

In his office there are diplomas on the wall and photographs of people in various degrees of smiling. There's a photograph of Father Barrett as a much younger man with lots of hair standing in front of a much bigger church. The church has lots of windows compared to this one, and I wonder if he did something to be demoted and sent here. Maybe he beat the crap out of somebody in a parking lot. The office has modern furniture, a nice bookcase, a computer that looks like it just came out of the box. It looks like the office of an architect, not of a Catholic priest. He takes a pair of scissors from a desk drawer and snips the zip tie holding my wrists together. There's a couch against the wall, and I sit down on it, and everything sways a little.

"Here," he says, handing me a bottle of water from a small fridge in the corner. I swallow half of it in one go. Being face down in gravel is thirsty work. Then he hands me a first-aid kit from a drawer under his desk. His readiness adds another tick to the column that this is all a set-up to convert the unconvertible. He hands me a mirror. "I can help clean you up," he says, "or you can do it."

I grab the mirror. There's blood trickling out of my nose. My bottom lip has been split. My face is puffy and there are scuff marks and scrapes, but it looks worse than it is. In a couple of days I'll be as good as new.

"You got a bathroom?"

"Down the hall, first door on the right."

I take the first-aid kit and head down the hall. I rinse the blood off my face and things look better but feel about the same. Most of the bleeding has stopped, and I apply some salves to stem the rest, my hands still shaking a little. It all hurts now, but it's going to hurt even more tomorrow. Father Barrett hands me a fresh shirt through the doorway.

105

"You can keep it," he says.

I get changed and ball up the old one and take it back to the office where he's now sitting behind his desk. "Much better," he says.

"I didn't think priests were allowed to lie."

"There's always an exception to the rule," he says. "I know that was Conrad Haggerty out there. I know what you did to him the night you found Alyssa Stone. You want to talk about it?"

"No."

"You want to at least tell me how long you're back for?"

"Not long."

"Long enough to find Alyssa? That is why you're back, isn't it?"

I lean against the doorframe. "What's your take on it?"

"Can't really say she seems the sort to run out on her uncle right when he needs her the most. But then again she's only nineteen, and nineteen-year-olds are apt to do whatever they please without much thought for other people. Anyway, it's a moot point," he says. "I was here when Drew came to talk to him. Best as I can tell, she's doing okay."

"I heard the same thing," I tell him.

"And yet you're still here," he says. "There some other reason you're sticking around?" He laughs, then smiles. "I'm sorry. I heard how that sounded. It sounds like I'm trying to get rid of you, but I promise that's not the case at all. I'm curious." He pauses for a few seconds. "Tell me if I'm being too curious."

"It's okay," I tell him. "I'm used to it. I only came back to tell Father Frank what he's already been told, and to drop his car off. Most likely I'll be on my way later today."

"You won't stay?"

"No," I tell him. I push myself off the doorframe.

"It's a shame," he says. "It's difficult to put the past behind you when you're always running from it."

"Thanks for the shirt," I tell him. "And thanks for saving me back there."

He looks disappointed the conversation is over. We walk out to the parking lot. We shake hands. His grip is firm and he's smiling at me and everything about this man makes me like him.

"I don't know how he's hanging on," he says, nodding in the direction of the house. "Every day I think is going to be his final one. He told me how you saved Alyssa. He thanks God every day for you getting her back, but he's conflicted over the way you did it."

"Why is he here? Why isn't he in hospital? Or in a hospice?"

"We've tried convincing him, but you know what he's like — he's stubborn. This is his church, his home. He's lived here and he wants to die here, and he'll be buried here, and he's okay with that. Now here you are twelve years later, and it's his turn to be saved. He's suffering, God knows how he's suffering. If you can convince Alyssa to come back here, he'll finally be able to let go and find the peace he deserves."

Fifteen

I toss my shirt into the back of the car. There's no sign of Conrad. No sign of Conrad's father. My day is improving. I get out my phone. There's a crack across the screen from the rough and tumble of earlier, but it still works well enough. I check who called me. It was Alyssa. If Conrad hadn't shown up when he did, this could all be over by now. Father Frank could blissfully fall asleep one last time.

I move into the shadow of the apple tree. I don't pluck one. My new shirt is already feeling damp and my body is seizing up. One of my teeth is throbbing and I'm worried it might have been cracked.

I call Alyssa.

"Hello?"

I was so sure the phone was about to go to voicemail that when I hear her voice it takes me a few seconds to answer. "Hey, Alyssa. Thanks for calling me back."

"It's been a long time," she says, and she doesn't sound

happy that I've reached out to her.

"Twelve years."

"Twelve years. A lot has changed."

"For all of us."

"I know why you're calling," she says, "and I wish you hadn't. You're ringing about my dad. You're ringing to ask me to come back home."

"Something like that."

"How's he doing?" she asks. She sounds distant, like she's asking a question she already knows the answer to.

"He's hanging on. He just wants to know you're okay."

"You can tell him that I'm doing fine. Where are you? Not back in Acacia?"

"I am."

"You came there looking for me?"

"I did."

"I'm sorry you've wasted your time, Noah, and I'm sorry the folks there thought the best way of convincing me to come home was to reach out to you."

"Your dad reached out because he thinks you're missing."

"I know. I know I should at the very least call him . . . but, but I can't, just like I can't come home. The thing is, things are complicated. I don't really want to get into it, but there are reasons I can't come back."

"I spoke to Sheriff Brooks," I say.

She doesn't answer. I picture her on the other end of the phone, pacing a room as I talk to her, looking at her feet while she walks, trying to get the balance right between saying what needs saying and hiding what needs hiding.

"He told me why you left," I say.

"He shouldn't have done that. I asked him not to."

"And he didn't want to. I had to fight it out of him because I needed to know you were okay."

"I'm just . . . I'm just so ashamed. Dad . . . I mean Uncle Frank . . . he'd be so disappointed in me." She's crying. "Are you going to tell him? You can't," she says. "Please, you can't."

"I won't," I say. "He loves you and he wants to see you. You can come back and he doesn't even have to know why you were gone."

"I can't risk it," she says. "This is about protecting him. I can't have him know, and I can't . . . I can't be, you know, the priest's daughter who got herself knocked up and had an abortion. I can't hurt him like that, and I can't hurt his reputation either."

"His reputation will be fine," I tell her. "This isn't nineteen fifty."

"You say that because you don't get it," she says. "For a lot of people it still is nineteen fifty. You have no idea what it's like, because you're a man, and you get to choose what you want to do with your body, but as a woman I have men making those decisions for me. The day I went into the clinic, I had to walk past people holding up signs and screaming at me, calling me a baby killer, and telling me I was going to rot in hell. Six months ago one of the nurses at that clinic was murdered. Two pro-life people ended hers by stabbing her to death. When you say this isn't ninety fifty anymore, all that does is tell me you don't know what it's like, and that you'll never know what it's like. There were people, Noah, people I don't know, people I'll never see again, screaming so much hate at me, so much hate. Now imagine that happening in a town where these are people I know. Imagine being the Catholic priest's daughter, and having to go through that."

I look down at my feet. I feel like a real asshole. "You're right," I say, struggling to find my voice. "Of course you're right, I can't know what it's like, and I'm sorry you had to go through that, but your dad, he doesn't have to know. You can come back and give him another reason why you left."

"You want me to lie to him."

"That's not how I would have put it."

"Listen, I appreciate you coming back to look for me, but like I said, you don't get it. I can't come back, not just for him, but for me too. I can't come back and have people find out what happened. Drew knows, and you know, and . . . have you told anybody?"

I can feel myself turning red. "I told my ex-wife," I say.

"See? See how easy it will happen? Look, you made a promise and you kept it, and I'll always be thankful for what you did for me. You saved my life. Those twelve years, each of them I've had because of you. I owe you everything. But don't ask me to come home and tell my dad what happened, and don't ask me to come home and lie to him. I've gone through all of this with Sheriff Brooks. He's called me a hundred times telling me the same thing you're telling me, and I've told him a hundred times the same thing I've told you. I can't. I can't face my dad, and . . . and if I'm honest I don't even know if I can come back when he's died. Acacia . . . Acacia was mean to me, Noah. Meaner than any town ought to be. My mom, my dad, what happened to me when I was a kid . . . when you think about it, it's a miracle I stayed there as long as I did."

"Can I come and see you? Can you at least tell me where you are?"

She's crying harder now. "You're not listening. I'm telling you everything, I'm pouring my heart out here, and you're still not listening. I know what it cost you to save me, I get that, I really do, but my dad, that place, all those bad things that happened back then and the good things too — I have to say goodbye to it, let it all go. I'm sorry if that makes me sound petty, or selfish, or like I don't care about my dad, it's just the way I feel."

"It doesn't make you sound any of those things," I say.

"Will I regret it once he's gone? I'll probably wake one day and hate myself, but that's for me to live with. I'm going to hang up now, Noah. I love my dad, I really do, but I can't come back. I can't put him, or myself, through that. One day . . . one day I hope you can understand that. Tell him I'm safe. Tell him I love him. Tell him . . . tell him I'll pray for him."

"I will."

"Goodbye, Noah."

And just like that, she's gone. I stay in the shade, listening to a disconnected line, with Father Frank dying inside a handful of yards away. I feel shame and embarrassment. She's right — I wasn't listening. And I can't imagine what it's like to go through what she went through, to have people screaming abuse, to have others tell you what you can or can't do with your body. I slip my phone back into my pocket. My hands have stopped shaking. I take a few beats for myself, deciding what the best course of action is.

But really, what I'm doing is putting off what I need to do next.

I can't put it off anymore.

I take the creaky step onto the creaky porch and step into the house. It's time to tell Father Frank it's okay to let go.

Sixteen

Father Frank is asleep. I remember the day his sister, Alyssa's mother, died. When a logging truck tips over on you, you usually come out of it in more pieces than you did going in. The truck was turning out of the sawmill. The driver had twenty years' experience on the job and he was sober and alert, but sometimes none of that matters. Forty tons of logs landed on that car. Even so, Alyssa's mother was alive when I got there, pinned in such a way the very car crushing and killing her was also keeping her from bleeding out. I held her hand. She cried. She begged for me to keep her alive. I told her I would. Then she thought I was her husband. She called me Brett. She begged me to look after their little girl if she didn't make it. I told her I would. Then she asked me to come closer, and I leaned in and she asked if I would do one more favor for her, and I said I would, and she died before she could ask it. It was the most traumatic thing I'd ever seen. When the rescue workers got her free, we found both her legs had been severed.

I cried that night. The truck driver cried too, and four days later he took his own life.

I watch Father Frank's chest as it rises and falls. I take his hand. It's hot. His eyes flicker open and he turns his face toward me. There are all sorts of things in the way he's looking at me. First, there's a moment of confusion, then it comes back to him. There's the look of a dying man who suddenly remembers he's dying, and wishes for it not to be true. There's the look of a man who's scared for his daughter. It breaks my heart to look at him. Breaks my heart to have to lie to him.

"Alyssa is okay," I tell him. "I've spoken to her."

"Where is she?" His mouth sounds dry. His voice is scratchy. I offer him some water, but he doesn't want any.

"She wouldn't tell me. We spoke on the phone. She left because she's struggling. She left because she's lost so much in this town, her parents, her sense of innocence, and now she's losing you. She said she loves you but can't be here for you."

"She wouldn't leave me," he says.

"She says she can't stand to see you like this. It hurts her so much."

Slowly he shakes his head. "You're telling me the same thing Sheriff Brooks told me yesterday." He looks at the ceiling, tears in his eyes. The oxygen machine keeps pumping air into him while the clock keeps ticking his life away. "I really am alone."

"You have friends here. You have people that care about you."

He turns to face me. "I'm alone in knowing something bad

happened to her. Somebody took her away from me. Last time you fought to bring her back and you did. This time you're giving up."

He coughs. Now he accepts the glass of water. He sips at it then hands it back. There are flecks of blood in it. His head sinks into the pillow and he closes his eyes. "Are we alone?"

"Yes."

"Where's Maggie?"

"She's picking up one of her kids from school."

"Good." He opens his eyes again. "Good. Whatever you think you know, you're wrong. Whoever told you she's fine is lying to you."

"I spoke to her myself."

"Then somebody is forcing her to tell you she's okay. She wouldn't do this to me. She wouldn't have up and left like that.

Will the truth bring him peace? Or more anguish? I promised Alyssa I wouldn't say anything, and I still feel ashamed I told Maggie. Alyssa was right — it's the kind of secret that won't stay secret for long. There is so much pain in Frank's eyes I want to say something that can help — but what is there?

"There are things . . ." he says, and his face twitches as he constructs what it is he wants to say. "Conrad Haggerty," he says.

"You think Conrad took her again?"

He shakes his head. "Not Conrad," he says, then he reaches out and takes my hand. "Never Conrad. What would you do if . . ." he says, and again his words run out. He's crying now.

"Not even by omission," he says, as he slowly shakes his head.

"You're not making any sense."

"Even now on my deathbed, not even by omission." He tightens his grip on my hand. "Somebody took her. I know somebody took her."

"Nobody took her," I tell him.

"Promise me you'll find her. Not just talk to her, but find her."

"I promise." It's easy to say.

"You don't mean it," he says, "but I'm going to hold you to it. You can't break a promise to a priest," he says, and he tries to smile, but can't get there. "Promise me one more thing."

"What's that?"

"Promise me you won't tell anybody. You have to find her by yourself." I don't say anything, and he can see he needs to elaborate. "I mean it," he says. "Friends, family, you can't tell them. You can't involve them. The police, you can't go to them, not until you know."

What he's saying sounds crazy. "What about Drew?"

"Not Drew. He . . . he has a family. Anybody who helps you, you put in danger."

Despite the room feeling like it's being microwaved, a chill runs down the back of my neck. "Danger?"

"Even Maggie knows too much. You can't let her help you any more. Nobody can." He gets up onto his elbow. The amount of pain and effort involved is obvious. He reaches out and takes my hand like he did earlier, and there's a strength to his grip I wouldn't have thought possible. "The people you love, the people you're close to, you risk them all."

"What do you mean, I'll risk them? Are they—"

"You think I've lost my mind," he says. "You think I'm a crazy old man, but I'm not messing around, Noah. The people you love, they're in danger. You're in danger. I'm sorry, Noah, I'm so sorry, but I didn't know what else to do. You can't tell anybody."

"What is it you're not telling me?"

"Promise me," he says, and there's fear in his eyes, genuine fear, and now I'm doubting everything Alyssa has told me. "Promise me you'll do this alone."

"I'll do it alone," I tell him, and I mean it now. "I promise."

He squeezes my hand so tight I'm in fear it will break. "Please find her," he says. "Please, you have to find her."

I ask him again what it is he isn't telling me, but he's exhausted now. He falls away and lies on his back, our conversation over. After a while he falls asleep.

A car pulls up outside. Father Frank's words stay with me as I head outside. *Promise me you won't tell anybody.* But there are two other words that are keeping me cold, two words that are heavy and try to pull me into the earth as I walk.

Two words.

Never Conrad.

Seventeen

As I straighten out my sunglasses that got bent when Conrad was kicking me earlier, Damian stares at me through the open window of the car the way seven-year-old kids stare at things. He's wearing a t-shirt with the Superman symbol on it. He has blond hair with a fringe that comes close to his eyes and a fading black eye where an older kid on their street hit him in the face with a hockey puck. When Maggie tells me what happened to him, he speaks up, and tells me he's going to be the greatest hockey player in the world. Then he tells us his sore stomach is still sore, and the one thing he believes, that he really, genuinely believes, is that ice cream will fix it. When Maggie tells him that isn't going to happen, he looks so mad it makes me worry for the kid who fired the hockey puck into his face.

Maggie stares at me the same way her son stares at me. She's looking at the swelling and the cuts and scrapes that weren't there when we last spoke. The sun has peaked but the day hasn't lost any of its heat. I get my sunglasses on but they sit at an angle and I go about straightening them some more. Old Man Haggerty's One-Hour Get-Out-Of-Town-Free card has long expired and it's time to decide whether I'm staying or leaving.

Never Conrad.

"Father Frank," I say. "All the things he's saying, is he getting confused? Is he saying things that aren't right?"

She shakes her head. "He's so consistent with what he's saying, it's hard to doubt him. You believe him? That somebody took Alyssa?"

"He's convinced."

"That's not what I asked."

"Twelve years ago, what happened with Conrad?"

The change in subject throws her for a second. "In what way?"

"He was never charged with a crime," I say, "even though he confessed to it."

She looks mad at me. "You know the answer to that," she says. "We couldn't charge him with anything because of the way you got his confession."

"Do you think he did it?"

She goes quiet. I put my sunglasses on and they fit okay and I no longer have to strain to see anything in the bright light.

"Conrad's a mean son of a bitch, Noah, but to think he would have kidnapped Alyssa? I always struggled to buy it."

"You believe he's innocent."

"I'm not saying that."

"So what are you saying?"

"That I don't know."

Twelve years ago when Maggie told me on the phone that all the charges were being dropped against me, she also told me that all the things I did to Conrad, Conrad said I didn't do. He says he fell over hunting, hit his face into a tree and shot himself in the leg. A deal was worked out to balance the scales. Conrad wouldn't be charged, I wouldn't be charged, and in a small town where secrets are hard to keep, everybody would have an opinion on whether or not I did the right thing.

"If Haggerty believed somebody else was responsible, why would he close the investigation?"

"You'd have to ask him," she says. "What I do know is Sheriff Haggerty did his best to protect both of you after what happened, and whatever that was it cost him his relationship with his son. They've never spoken since then."

"They haven't?"

She gives me a hardened look. "Father Frank said something else to you, didn't he, something that's making you think you might have made a mistake."

"He said a few things," I tell her.

"And you're not going to tell me."

"I want to think about it for a bit first."

"Do you think Alyssa is safe?"

"Yes."

"Then that's what's important," she says. "All that other stuff can stay in the past."

"I don't think it wants to. Something isn't right here."

"The kind of something that you don't want to tell me about."

"I don't want to throw around theories without knowing anything for a fact. You know how badly that can turn out," I say, but that's not why. I can't tell her because of what Father Frank made me promise. Anybody I tell I put in danger.

"So you're staying?" she asks.

"I'm staying."

Eighteen

I grab my bag from Maggie's car before she leaves. I'm going to keep using Father Frank's car, at least until it dies. I suspect there's some symbiotic link between the two of them, that when one dies so will the other. Only thing I know about cars is how to count the tires and doors, so it's possible all this thing needs is a flux capacitor to get it running smooth. The apple I dropped earlier is dented and bruised and now sitting in the backseat.

It's a five-minute drive to The Local Spirit, a store I sometimes went to when I was a younger man, one who'd sometimes unwind from the day with a shot of something that burned on the way down. There are bottles of spirits for sale in the window, and a sign saying there's a great deal inside on a new local beer. I step inside and the whiskey is in the same place it always used to be. I grab a bottle, and I grab a six-pack of the local craft beer being promoted. I also grab a fifteen-dollar bottle of wine because I'm a big spender. The guy behind the checkout looks me up and down while scanning my purchases. He has a bumped nose from a past break and a painful-looking shaving rash. The top of a tattoo pokes up from under his t-shirt and climbs his neck. He looks bored, like he'd rather be drinking the merchandise than selling it.

"It's Noah, right?" he says.

"Hey, Sam," I say. I used to go to school with Sam. We were in the same class together. We were on the same baseball team, the same football team, the same everything team. We even lived on the same street.

"I thought you'd died," he says.

"Nope. I'm very much alive."

"Huh," he says. "So you're saying these guys were wrong, then? The guys who said you were dead?"

"Yeah, Sam. They were wrong."

He sniffs loudly, and it's the kind of sniff that makes me want to leave my purchases on the counter and walk out.

"You seem disappointed," I tell him.

"I shouldn't seem anything," he says. "Means nothing to me either way."

"What do I owe you?"

He gives me the amount and it's higher than it ought to be, but then again Sam never was good at math. Or baseball. Or football. Only thing he was really good at was living on our street, and even that was only for a few years before his family moved across town.

"You got any kind of painkillers here?"

"Planning for the hangover already?" he asks.

"Something like that."

"We have some aspirin," he says. "Sort of stuff you'll find in supermarkets. Nothing stronger than that."

"I'll take some."

He puts them into a bag, and I buy a bottle of water too. I take a couple of pills when I'm back in the car in the hope they'll stop my tooth from hurting.

It takes me thirty minutes to drive to Drew's house because I zigzag through different neighborhoods to see how much has changed and how much hasn't. My talk with Sam has put me into a nostalgic frame of mind. I pass the old place I grew up in. It's a two-story bungalow with windows that were always too small and seemed to never get any sun. It wasn't all bad. My dad drank a lot, sure, but there were days when he didn't, sometimes he could go weeks without a drop, sometimes he'd come home from work with a present for me that he'd bought on the way, a book, or a magazine, or a toy, or he'd come home eager to take us to the cinema to see something his workmates had been talking about that day. There were summer nights where we'd stand out in the street throwing a baseball back and forth, mom watching us as she sat on the porch looking up from her book. My dad could be a mean drunk, but he also had the greatest laugh in the world. He would tell me he loved me, and that everything was going to be okay.

Things were never as okay as they should have been. Back then the place was falling apart, and back when I was a deputy the place was empty. I'm expecting the neighbors to have uprooted it and dumped it beyond the town limits, but instead

I find it looking better than it ever did, to the point where I suspect the only original thing about it is the address. Black roof, gray walls and lots of white trim, the small windows replaced with bigger ones, it looks well cared for. The gardens look nice enough to host a small wedding. My mom would be embarrassed that they'd never had it look so good. My dad would either laugh it off or be too drunk to care.

It's a little after five when I get to Drew's house. The big tree in his front yard has gotten even bigger. There's a swing hanging from it on ropes that look brand new. It's the same house he grew up in, a single-story brick home with a low roof with twice as many downpipes as needed. I open the screen door and press the buzzer. A girl half my height appears. She's wearing a baseball cap backward with a ponytail coming out from beneath it, and a yellow dress with flowers on that's got smears of dirt from playing outside. There are dirt marks on her face too. She has a big smile.

"Hi," she says. "Who are you?"

"My name is Noah," I tell her. "I'm a friend of your mom and dad. What's your name?"

"Julia," she says. "J. U. L. I. A. And you're N.O.E.R."

"And you're a fantastic speller," I say. "What are you, ten years old?"

"I'm five," she says.

"Five? You're way more grown up than five."

"Did you get in a fight?" she asks.

"I did."

"Mommy and daddy say fighting is bad."

126

"It is bad," I say.

"Daddy's a policeman, and he arrests bad people. He could arrest the people who did that to you, if you asked him."

"I might just ask him to do that then."

"Is that beer?" she asks.

"It is."

"I'm not allowed beer."

"The beer is for your dad."

"What did you get me?"

"How about I get you something next time?"

"You promise?"

"I promise. Can you get your mom or dad for me?"

"Okay," she says, and she shuts the door and disappears.

The heat is leaving the day, but it won't disappear completely. The pain in my tooth has faded. Birds are shifting around in the trees and making a real song and dance about it. Leigh opens the door. She looks great — but she always has. She always used to do yoga three times a week and ate better than the rest of us to stay in shape. Perhaps she's the one who got Drew into hitting the gym. She's wearing a flannel shirt and cut-off jeans and her long legs are tanned. Her blonde hair is tied back into a ponytail just like her daughter's, and passes through the back of her baseball cap. Her face lights up when she sees me. A big smile that could solve any problem. She leans in and I put the drinks on the step so we can hug.

"Noah," she says, and she pulls back to look me up and down, the way people are doing today. "Drew told me you were back."

"For a day or so," I say.

"You look like shit," she says.

"Mummy swore," I hear Julia say, from not far away.

"Then I look like I feel. You look great," I say, "like you haven't aged a day."

"Then I don't look how I feel. I can't believe you're here," she says. I pick up the drinks and she grabs my hand and leads me through the house. The house is comfortable, well lived in, knick-knack souvenirs covering most flat surfaces. There's a wedding photo in the dining room, and I'm in it, standing next to Drew, and a bridesmaid by the name of Gloria next to Leigh. I can smell coffee. I can hear a TV going, the sing-song voices of cartoon characters. We come out onto a deck that eats up a quarter of the backyard. Drew is crouching over a small paddling pool, laughing and splashing water with his three-year-old. I feel like I've stepped into an alternate reality.

"Hey, stranger," he says. "I knew you wouldn't be able to stay away."

Leigh leans on my shoulder. "Other than the last twelve years?"

"Well, yeah, other than those."

Drew picks up the boy and throws him into the air, then does a double take and looks back at me. "Old Man Haggerty did that to you?"

"Young Man Haggerty," I say.

"Goddamn it." Drew plucks the small boy out of the pool and places him on the lawn to play, but instead of playing the boy stands staring up at me. Drew looks mad. "I'm going to throw his ass in jail."

"Let it go," I tell him.

"Let it go? Are you kidding me?"

"I'm still walking and talking," I tell him, "so yeah, just let it go."

I tell him what happened, that Conrad ambushed me and Father Barrett saved the day.

"He's definitely not the kind of priest you want to mess with," Drew says. He's calmed down a little. "Seems the kinda guy who can go door to door selling his faith and not take no for an answer. You sure you don't want me to pick up Conrad?"

"I'm sure."

"Then we're going to need to get those beers you're carrying open."

We do just that, along with a bottle of wine. I sit with Leigh and we watch the kids while Drew messes with the barbecue until flames shoot out of the burners and almost take his eyebrows off.

"I'm telling you, this thing is alive," he says, "and it hates me."

"He's not lying," Leigh says. "How about I call Charlotte and get her to come look after the kids?" she asks.

"Charlotte?" I ask.

"The babysitter," Drew says, and he tastes the beer, then studies the can and shakes his head a little. "Where the hell did you find this?"

"The Spirit," I say.

"Let me guess, it was on sale? It tastes like it was on sale."

He takes mine off me before I can try it, then goes inside to get us different ones.

"What about Glen?" I ask Leigh, Glen being my godson, and a teenager of sixteen now. "He doesn't babysit?"

"Glen is a teenager now, Noah. He won't do anything, other than spend all his free time in his room on his computer," Leigh says. "If we let him babysit, the kids would starve and the house would burn down. I'll call Charlotte, I'm sure she won't mind."

Drew comes back out and hands me an open beer. "I'm sure Noah won't mind hanging out with our rug rats and one adolescent teenager who probably won't talk to him for just the one evening," he says.

"You okay with that, Noah?" Leigh asks.

"I couldn't think of anything better."

Leigh tells me that Charlotte is Antony Bauer's daughter. We went to school with Antony. He was one of those guys who was good at any sport he ever tried. I remember being jealous of him. Leigh tells me Charlotte isn't long for this town, that it's only a matter of time before she finds her way to a big city, where she wants to study drama or get into modeling. Already she's approaching agents. Leigh tells me she'll get one too, that in the next few years we're going to see her on the big screen and on billboards.

"You should see this kid. Nineteen years old and a real heartbreaker, don't you think so, honey?" she asks, looking at Drew.

"It's probably why Glen refuses to babysit, just so she'll come around," he says.

Drew disappears inside, and when he comes back out he's wearing an apron that says *Don't shoot the Sheriff, I just work here*, and he's carrying a tray full of ribs. Last thing I ate was airport food, and watching the ribs cooking makes my mouth water. It's nice hearing about people I once knew, and how their lives have branched in different directions, some leaving town, some moving into the family business, others getting married and making small versions of themselves. The ribs sizzle and my mouth waters and my stomach grumbles. Leigh tells me she's still selling houses. With the population increasing, new houses are constantly being built. The sun is arcing toward the horizon and the ribs smell great and the air is warm and the beer is cold and this, all of this, could have been my life.

When dinner is ready, Leigh goes inside to fetch Glen. He's a taller and skinnier version of his dad and looks like his only experience with sunlight is adjusting the curtains in his bedroom to block it out. He says hi in a way that sounds like he doesn't mean it. Drew takes his apron off and we all sit down at a picnic table and use our fingers to eat the ribs. Out in the edges of the yard a cricket starts to wind up. Others hear it and join in. Leigh picks the meat off the bone for the younger kids first. Drew tells Glen to put his phone away, and Glen tells us he's done anyway and asks to be excused. The rest of us keep eating. There's laughter as we all make a hell of a mess. There's salad and fries and more beer. Both Drew and I are on to our third. Leigh is still on her first glass of wine. We finish dinner and Leigh takes the kids inside for bath time and I sit on the deck with Drew and we watch the sun filter through the trees as it sinks. The back boundary of Drew's house used to border the forest, but now there are new streets and new houses in between. Moths start flying out of the shadows.

"You speak to Alyssa?" he asks.

"I did."

"You ask her to come back?"

"I did."

"Were you more convincing than I was?"

"She's not coming back. Fact is, I don't think she's ever going to set foot in Acacia again. In a way I can't blame her. There's been a lot of pain here for her."

"Ain't that a fact. I'll call and try to change her mind, but . . ."

"But it's only going to upset her."

"My sentiments exactly. Soon she won't even take my calls, I'm sure of it. What did you decide about telling Father Frank the truth? You gonna do it? Or you've done it already?"

"I couldn't tell him," I say, and he looks relieved. "I told him she was safe, that she loved him, and that she was too sad to come back."

"Let me guess, he didn't believe you?"

He said not to tell anybody. He said people I cared about were in danger. "He's upset, but I think he's starting to finally get it."

"At least now he can . . . I mean, this sounds mean, and I'm not saying it right, but at least now he can let go, right? He knows she's safe." Drew finishes off his beer and opens another. "Want one?"

"I'm good," I tell him. "I still have to drive."

"Why don't you sleep here?"

"I can't."

"Because?"

"Because Old Man Haggerty would find a way to take your badge off you if he found out I was staying the night."

He laughs at that. "So what's the plan now? You heading back tomorrow?"

"I'm not sure when I'm heading back."

He looks confused. "You're staying?"

"I have a favor to ask. It's to do with Alyssa's abduction twelve years ago."

He looks surprised, but before he can say anything Leigh comes out with the two kids in their pajamas. She's carrying Lenard, the small one. Both of them wish me a good night, and Julia asks if she can hug me, and I tell her that she can. She puts her little arms around me and she smells like soap and shampoo and she tells me I smell like beer and barbecue. She hugs me tight, tells me not to get into any more fights, then Drew takes the kids inside to read them a story and put them to bed, while Leigh tops up her wine and sits with me as the last of the light dies away.

"So what about you, Noah? You have any kids?"

"No," I tell her.

133

"You got somebody in your life? You're seeing somebody?"

"Nobody at the moment."

"That's a real shame," she says.

"I'm okay with it."

"Don't tell me you're still carrying a torch for Maggie, are you?"

I sip at my beer. "No," I tell her.

"You sure?"

"Not really."

She shakes her head. "You need to move on."

"I thought I had."

I drink my beer. She drinks her wine. The crickets get louder.

"You really think I still look the same? Or you're bullshitting a middle-aged woman?"

"I'm bullshitting you," I say, and she punches me in the arm and we both laugh.

"Christ, am I going to have to write my own wife up for assault?" Drew asks, coming out onto the deck. He's carrying another beer. "By the time you leave here half the town's going to have taken a swing at you."

"Only half?"

"Town's bigger than you remember," he says. "Only half the people here know you. You sure you don't want another beer?"

"I'm sure."

We talk for a while. Some reminiscing. Some ribbing. Some catching up on life. Leigh doesn't ask about Alyssa at all, even though Drew must have told her that's why I came back. Drew turns on the outdoor lights and it doesn't take long for moths and beetles to target them. Leigh finishes her wine and wishes me a good night and tells me not to be a stranger before disappearing inside.

"I think it's time we open this," Drew says, and grabs the bottle of whiskey I brought with me. He pours us each a glass. "So what's this favor you're after?" He's had four beers now and his words are a little slower.

"I want to go over the case files from twelve years ago, that's all."

"That's all," he says, and laughs. "That the best you can come up with? How about you tell me what's going on."

"I'm not sure yet."

"Not sure yet. So you do think something has happened to Alyssa."

"No, it's not that," I tell him, "and I'm not looking for a connection between what happened back then and her leaving now. It's just that . . .well, Father Frank said something about Conrad being innocent back then."

Drew sips at his drink. He looks annoyed.

"And if Conrad was innocent back then, then I screwed up."

"You did screw up," he says. "We both did. We let things get out of hand. But Conrad . . . Conrad did it. We found stuff of Alyssa's in his car, and his fingerprints on her headband, and there was a ski mask in his glove compartment — and that's nothing compared to the fact he knew where she was.

That story he gave about overhearing people, that was pure fantasy."

"But was it?"

"Of course it was. Conrad . . . he's trash. You know it, I know it, everybody knows it. After what he did to Maggie back in high school . . .hell, I'm surprised you didn't kill him then."

"I often think that if he hadn't hurt Maggie, then what happened twelve years ago would have played out differently."

"You wouldn't have shot him?"

"I don't know. I think, you know, that I used what was happening as an excuse to do to him what I'd been wanting to do for a long time."

"You were," he says. "I thought it then and I still think it now, but he was guilty, buddy, and you got Alyssa back. Father Frank . . . it's like I've been saying, Father Frank isn't Father Frank anymore."

"If it's all the same, I'd still like to take a look at everything, especially whatever you got from the Kelly farm. I need to make sure I had the right guy. For my own peace of mind."

He sips his whiskey and grimaces. "Well, I'd help you out if I could, I really would, but I don't have it."

"What do you mean you don't have it?"

"All that stuff, Sheriff Haggerty got rid of it. He told us the case was closed and if any of us spoke about it anymore we'd be fired. We went out there, you know, out to the farm. Me and Hutch and Logan. You remember them?"

"Yeah, I saw them earlier today," I say, and Logan and

Hutch had joined the department not long before I left it.

"Well, we went out there along with the sheriff. He wouldn't let us in. We had to wait around outside while he did whatever the hell it was he was doing inside — investigating, obviously, because he took a bunch of photos and dusted for prints and collected some evidence. He brought all the stuff back to the station in a box. The whole time I kept thinking, this is some kind of conflict of interest, right? Haggerty isn't going to want to find anything to suggest his son was ever there. Anyway, he gets all this evidence, and the next day it's gone, and that's when he warns us that if any of us . . . hell, I remember what he said now, he said, *If any of you talk about this again, you may as well pack your shit up and follow Noah.* I don't know what he found, but then Conrad changed his story to where he shot himself by accident while hunting. Whatever Sheriff Haggerty found, it's gone. I'm sorry, Noah, but I've got nothing for you, because there's nothing to give."

"There's no backup of anything?"

"There's nothing."

Drew knocks back his whiskey and pours himself another. I still haven't touched mine. "So now what? You going to go around opening up old wounds to try and make a guilty man look innocent? He did it, Noah, and you know he did it. You beat the absolute hell out of him because you knew he did it."

"I need it to sit straight," I tell him. "I need to know."

He wipes his mouth. "So you're going to poke your nose into things and stir everything up, is that it? After all this time you've come back here thinking you know best."

"It's not like that."

"The hell it ain't." He stands up and swats at a moth that tries to land on his face. "Noah, I know you think I always used to follow you around like a puppy dog. You were the leader and I was the follower and we always pretended things were equal. Best friends, always best friends, but the truth is I always resented you a little. Things came easy for you, and I actually hated how you always made decisions for the both of us, and then you do this one really bad thing that gets you driven out of town, and still people talk about you like you're some kind of hero." He grabs an empty beer can, crushes it and tosses it far out into the yard. "Even all these years later I still hear how the sheriff's job would have been yours if you'd stayed." He laughs, but there's no humor in it. "Well, I guess you'll do what you have to do," he says, "and play the hero, but I'm going to do what I have to do, and that's run you out of town or throw you in jail once you put one foot out of place."

"Drew . . ."

"Good night, Noah. You can sleep on the deck if you want."

He walks inside, switches off the light, and leaves me in the dark.

Nineteen

I don't sleep on the deck. I walk around the side of the house, out through the gate and across the front yard where something small is rustling in the bushes. The moon is a day or two away from being full, but even so it's bright and offers as much light as the streetlights out front. Father Frank's car remains blessed as the engine turns over first time.

I'm shaken by Drew's words. Shaken by the fact he's felt this way a long time, and what's worse is he's right. One more thing I need to do now before leaving town — fix my relationship with him.

I pull into the first motel I see, a place called Forest Nights, a long L-shaped building two stories high with a continuous concrete balcony linking all the upstairs rooms that overlook the parking lot. It wasn't here the last time I was. There's a sign out front that says *Vacancy* and a vending machine by the door that says *Out of order*. I need a shower. I need to change into some fresh clothes. I grab my bag and step into

139

an air-conditioned lobby where fifty percent of the floor space is taken up by potted plants. Makes me think I might need search and rescue just to find my room. The woman behind the counter gives me a big smile and flicks at her hair and asks how I'm doing. She's late twenties, a real girl-next-door look, if the girl next door was the prom queen. She's holding a pencil and working away at a sketch of a horse. I can see smudged lead on the side of her hand.

"I'm doing fine," I tell her, and her smile is infectious. If her name badge can be trusted, her name is Zoey.

She sees me looking at the sketch. She blushes and turns it over. "It's just something I do to pass the time," she says.

"You're very good," I say.

"And you're very kind. You're after a room?"

"I am."

"A single?"

"It is."

"How many nights?"

"I'm not sure," I tell her, and her smile wavers a little.

"What's your name?" she asks.

"Noah Harper"

The smile she was trying to hang on to falls away completely. "I thought as much. You used to live here, right?"

"That's right," I tell her.

She looks embarrassed. It takes everything she has to look me in the eye. "Umm . . . you seem like a really nice guy and all, and I mean like, *really* nice," she says, flicking her hair back behind her ear again, "especially with what you did for that little girl and all, but, umm, this is kinda hard for me to say because it's not fair, but . . . but you can't stay here."

"There aren't any rooms?" I ask, knowing that's not what she's getting at.

"I wish I'd said that right up front but I didn't know you was you when you came in."

"Plus the sign out front says you have a vacancy."

"It does," she says. "You'd have gotten me there."

"So what is it then?"

She looks down at the pencil, then looks back up. "We had Sheriff Haggerty come by here earlier today."

"He's not the sheriff anymore," I tell her.

"That doesn't stop him acting like it," she says. "You know what he's like. You don't want to cross him."

"He told you I can't stay here?"

"He didn't say what he'd do to us if we let you stay, but it'd be something, right? He's that kind of guy. We'd get shut down for something. I want to help you out, mister, I really do, but . . . but I can't. My boss would kill me."

"Can you recommend anywhere else?"

Now she looks even more embarrassed. Now when she looks down at her pencil she can't pull her eyes off it. "See, that's the thing. There is nowhere else. He's been everywhere. You've been blacklisted."

She's upset. "It's not your fault," I tell her.

"I wish I could help. I have a spare room at my house. I guess . . . I guess if you didn't tell nobody, you could stay there," she says, and that's one of the great things about this town — there's this thing built into people that makes them want to help.

"I appreciate the offer," I tell her, "but I don't want to get anybody into trouble."

"You sure?" she asks, and she sounds relieved.

"I'm sure."

There are a few other motels I can try, but I have no reason not to take Zoey at her word — I've been blacklisted.

I drive through town, and soon I'm taking the same path out of town I took the night I left twelve years ago. I cross the bridge, the car bouncing up over the small lip where the pavement meets the thick wooden beams, lights from the town making small orange orbs in the slowly moving water. Houses become small farms. Small farms become big farms, and the highway winds on, lots of curves and lots of trees and lots of darkness. I pull into the Kelly farm. Gravel crunches beneath the car as I drive past the oak trees. The house comes into view. It's still standing, just like Drew said. But it's faded more over the years, the sun leaching the color from the weatherboard while the rain pelts at it. I think of Father Frank's words, and the reason I'm clinging to them so hard is because there's always been something about that night twelve years ago that hasn't sat right with me. That night moved quickly, quicker than any other, and there's something I overlooked, or a feeling, or something I saw that was out of place. I know it, I've always felt it, but I've never been able to identity what. Whatever it is, maybe it's the kind of thing Sheriff Haggerty got rid of. I haven't come here to look for it now. I've come here because it gives me somewhere to sleep.

Last time I was out here I kicked down the door and busted plenty of woodwork in the process. It's been patched up since then, a new door and new frame put in place, a new lock too. The door handle has sucked up the day's heat, and I feel it ebb into my palm. The door doesn't budge. I try the windows and they're locked too. I figure it's cheaper to replace a piece of glass than a wooden door, so I break one using a piece of firewood from a pile stacked up against the house. The shattering glass echoes into the night.

I unlatch the window and get it open. I clear away the broken glass and climb inside. I use the light from my cellphone to guide the way. The window being opened and my movements bring dust up into the air. It triggers my sinuses and I start sneezing. The air smells old. I find a light switch and flick it up and down for zero reward. I rummage through the kitchen drawers and find candles and matches. They crackle in the still air as they burn. I leave them on various shelves as I walk through the place. All the same furniture is here, but time and sunlight have faded it. There are photographs on the walls so washed out it's like looking at snow. There are cracks in the walls and patches of mold on the ceiling and empty spider webs up high in corners. The basement door is closed and this crazy thought enters my head. What if Alyssa is down there now? What if she never left town? Would Drew even have come out here and checked? I open the door.

"Alyssa?"

Alyssa doesn't answer. I go down the stairs and the candle

lights the way, and one of the first things I see is a shelf with a lantern on it. I light the lantern and the basement shakes off the darkness, and it allows me to spot her right away, Alyssa, seven years old and hiding herself in the corner where she's chained up like a badly treated animal.

She fades from view. The sensation makes me shiver. I'm alone down here.

I'm about to turn away when I notice it. Alyssa has faded from view, but the chain hasn't. I crouch next to it but don't touch it. It's the same kind of chain as last time — and could even be the very same one. Same goes for the bolts I took out of the wall. The mattress is still here too, as is the bucket. The bucket has been hosed out, and the mattress is even old and more stained. There are empty plastic drink bottles on the floor next to it. I roll one of them with the tip of my finger until I can see an expiry date. It's a year away. Water bottles normally have an expiry date of up to two years, so this thing has been here for a year at the most.

Somebody has been kept here recently.

The question is, was that person Alyssa? Or somebody else?

Twenty

I move my car behind the house in case whoever was last here chooses tonight to come back. Then I choose which bed to lie on, going for the one that used to belong to Jasmine since nobody died on it. I put a baseball bat I found in the basement on the floor within reach. I switch off the lantern, switch off my cellphone to save power, and stare out at the dark. It only takes a few moments for my eyes to adjust. I can hear the house settling. I can hear wildlife outside, small creatures burrowing into the dirt and running through the weeds, some hunting, others being hunted, some doing both.

The chains. The mattress. The water bottles. Is Conrad involved in this too?

It's a little after 7am when I wake to the sunlight coming through the window. I head into the bathroom, cross my fingers and hold my breath and hope that the plumbing still works, and it does. I run the shower and let rust drain from the pipes. When the water is clear I take a cold shower since cold is the only option. I look in the mirror at the beating I took yesterday. The swelling has gone down and the cuts don't look as raw. I probe at my tooth and the pain is a quarter of what it was yesterday. Maybe it isn't cracked after all.

In the basement I use my phone to take photographs of the chain and the mattress and the drink bottle. The rusted tools hanging from pegboards have rusted some more since that night I tried using the bolt cutters. If it wasn't Alyssa who was kept here, then who? Then I do what I didn't think to do last night. I look at the other water bottles. There are eight of them, with eight dates that cover the last ten years.

Were there eight different people here?

No, because if people had gone missing, the police would know. Everybody would know. I'd have heard about it by now.

So what in the hell is going on?

Outside the temperature is rising steadily. I check out the nearby shed in the hope the Kelly car will be better than the Frankmobile, that maybe all it'll need is the battery and wheels switched over. The tractor and car that were parked in there all those years ago are still here. The tires on the tractor have perished and left the tractor to sit on its rims. The wind has carried seeds to it, and straw is growing out of holes in the seat. The car is in even worse condition.

I get Father Frank's car started. I check the glove compartment in the hope he has a car charger for my phone. There's a Bible and a box of tissues, a fold-up umbrella, a flashlight, and no charger.

Dirt fills the air as I drive out to the road. It gets caught in my slipstream and washes over the car at the top of the driveway where I wait for a pickup to drive by, the guy lifting his hand to tap two fingers against his cowboy hat to acknowledge me. I wave at him, and then the dirt can't keep up with me when I accelerate onto the highway. I call Maggie on my way into town. She sounds tired. She asks if I've found out anything I feel like sharing.

The chain. The mattress. The water bottles. "Not yet. You still want to meet for breakfast?"

"I can't," she says. "Whatever bug Damian picked up at school, he's given it to the rest of us. We've all spent the night throwing up and today we're staying home, and I don't want to pass it on to you. We're so sick I wouldn't be surprised if the CDC quarantines our house."

"I'm sorry to hear that."

"And I'm sorry to have said it. It's been so long, Noah, and now you're here and we're hardly going to get to spend any time together. Hopefully tomorrow we'll all be cleared up. I feel really awful, I don't mean from being sick, I mean because I really wanted to see you this morning. You'll stay another night? Please?"

"I'll try."

"I guess that's the best I can ask for. Did you stay at Drew's last night?"

"I stayed out at the Kelly farm."

"What? Are you serious?"

I reach the edge of town. A couple of old guys are sitting in camping chairs a few yards down from the bridge, fishing poles in the water, hats pulled down low to avoid the sun. They both wave at me as I pass. I tap two fingers against my forehead to salute back to them like the guy I saw earlier did, liking the symmetry of it.

"It's still abandoned."

"I know," she says. "Does the place even have power?"

"No, but it has plumbing."

"Geez, Noah, why didn't you stay with Drew?"

"I didn't want to make things awkward between him and Old Man Haggerty."

"You're insane," she says. I almost say *That's why you married me*, but of course that's not why she married me. But it is why we divorced.

I tell her that I'll check in with her later today and we hang up. I find a park half a block down from Andy's, a diner that always makes me feel like I'm stepping back in time to the sixties. The diner is short and wide, with air-conditioning vents snaking across the roof, an old building next to a brand-new one, the new one being a gym that was built a year ago to replace the aging movie theater, the theater being rebuilt bigger and better only a hundred yards away. There's lots of chrome and glass, booths with curved edges next to large rectangular windows, a jukebox in the corner set to silent, a black-and-white tile floor leading to a counter that can sit a dozen. There are fans of different shapes and sizes hanging from the ceiling that look like propellers from old war planes.

I sit in a booth and order bacon and eggs and hash browns, wanting to bathe in the smells coming from the kitchen. There are posters on the walls of old cars and old buildings the way they used to be here back when time in Acacia Pines began. It turns the waiting into a history lesson. Out the window town is coming to life. Lights come on behind windows, awnings go up and shop owners open their doors, exchanging *good mornings* with people wandering by.

My food arrives. The bacon tastes great and so do the eggs and hash browns. I fight the temptation to order a second helping. When I'm done I leave a tip healthier than the meal and wander down to a bakery in the same block. It's called Bear Claw County and it's on the shady side of the street, which keeps the goodies in the window out of the sun. The store has been around forever. My mom worked here part time for a few years after I started school. She used to call it The Sugar Shop. My mouth waters when I see what's on display in the window. Different types of pastries and pies and cream buns behind spotless glass barriers that make my cholesterol level spike just being near them. A teenager with acne and messy hair uses tongs to put into a cardboard box whatever it is I point at. He doesn't ask how my day is going, and I don't ask about his. It's like being back in the big city.

I head to the police station. It's a two-minute drive. The blacktop in the police parking lot is shimmering. The elm tree over the road already has a car under it, so I park in the lot in the sun near the main entrance. I leave the doors open and I carry the box of donuts inside where a couple of guys on a couple of ladders are tinkering with the air-conditioning system, which right from the get-go obviously isn't working.

They're swearing at it and cursing it. There are fans on desks and papers and files being held down by weights. There are open cans of soda and open bottles of water everywhere. They should shut their doors for the day. It's too hot to fight crime, but it's too hot to commit crime too.

I knock on Drew's open door and head in and take a seat and put the donuts on his desk.

"I'm sorry about last night," I tell him. "I'm sorry about everything."

"You think you can fix everything with donuts?"

"I was hoping I could."

He smiles. "You'd be right." He leans over and opens them. "You've got enough here for everybody."

"I bet they don't last you an hour."

He laughs and picks up a bear claw. It has a frosting of icing sugar over it. "That's the old Drew. He'd have probably finished them by now. Still . . ." He takes a bite. "They're pretty good."

He asks while chewing if I'm not going to have one, and I tell him I just ate.

"More for the rest of us," he says.

"Sure. The rest of us."

He laughs, and takes another bite. "Listen, Noah, I'm sorry about last night. All that stuff I said—"

"You were right."

He shakes his head. "No, I wasn't. I don't know where it was coming from. I—"

"You had every right to say it," I say. "I'm sorry for being an asshole all these years."

"I'm not saying you're an asshole."

"I've acted like one on occasion," I say.

"Well, I'm not saying you're *not* an asshole. I know your heart is in the right place, it's just the rest of you that's often somewhere it shouldn't be." His smile disappears. "Look, I don't want to walk back on what you're saying, but I shouldn't have said what I said. It's been a while since I've had that much to drink, and the truth is, with the kids and the job, sometimes things get to me, you know? Things . . . well, things are more stressful than they look. I wake up sometimes and wonder if I'm becoming like Old Man Haggerty."

"You grew his mustache," I say.

"For which I don't have any defense."

"I really mean it when I say I'm sorry," I tell him.

"So do I. So, where'd you end up staying last night?"

"The Kelly farm."

He almost coughs out his donut. "You're kidding, right? You couldn't find anywhere else?"

"Old Man Haggerty had me blacklisted from all the motels."

He laughs so hard he almost chokes. He bangs himself on his chest and I'm getting ready to help him when he gets himself under control. "I don't know why I'm laughing," he says. "It's not even funny, but . . . but, man, can you picture him dragging his oxygen tank from motel to motel to tell them you couldn't stay?"

"He probably called most of them."

"Probably," he says, "but that's not as comical. I don't think anybody's been out at that farm in years. You know Leigh has the listing for it, right? I can't even remember the last time we spoke about it. What was it like? Must be getting close to falling down."

"It was comfortable enough," I tell him.

"But not that comfortable, huh? Does it have power or running water?"

"Running water."

"And weeds coming up through the floor, I bet. Any families of raccoons living in it? Squirrels?"

"I need to ask you something," I tell him.

"Why do I get the feeling I'm not going to like where this is going?"

"How many people over the years here have gone missing?"

He's confused by the question. "Say again?"

"How many missing persons reports have you fielded?"

"Missing? You mean like *missing* missing?"

"Yeah. Like they've disappeared off the face of the earth."

He wipes his fingers on his shirt, then rolls his eyes like he can't believe he just did that. He grabs a napkin from the box and wipes at the fresh stain. Then he leans back. "Well, sure, I mean, people leave town without telling us, and sometimes we'll get a call trying to track them down, and a few years back we had a woman who owed tens of thousands of dollars to the tax department and she skipped town, and nobody has seen her since — at least nobody around here. But nobody's gone missing in the way I think you're getting at."

"You're sure?"

Now he goes from looking confused to looking annoyed. "Of course I'm sure. If people were disappearing, trust me, you'd have heard it from everybody you've come into contact with since being here. You ate somewhere this morning, right? There isn't a diner or restaurant in town where gossip like that wouldn't be flying. Why do you ask?"

The chain. The mattress. The bottles.

Before I can answer, his phone rings. He looks at the display, then takes it. He says okay a few times, and slowly nods, then he spins his seat slightly off to the side and looks out the window into the parking lot. He says okay a few more times, and then tells the person on the other end of the phone that he'll be right over. He hangs up. He looks up at me. Despite his attempt to clean it away, there's still icing sugar on his shirt.

"That was Father Barrett," he says. "Father Frank died during the night."

"Ah, that's a goddamn shame," I say.

"A guy like that, everything he's done for this town, for the church, he deserved a better exit."

"I couldn't agree more."

"This thing about missing people — you want to fill me in on your thinking?"

"Not yet," I tell him.

"Goddamn it, Noah."

"It's probably nothing."

He stares at me for a few seconds. He's annoyed. "Like I

said, if people were disappearing, we'd all know about it." He gets out from behind his desk and moves toward the door.

"Can I come with you? To the church?"

"If you want to," he says. "If we're lucky, Father Frank will look down on us from wherever he is and get the air conditioning up and running while we're gone."

Twenty-one

Drew gets into his modern car that has modern air conditioning and I get into my car that isn't and hasn't. I turn on the air conditioning in the hope it won't smell so bad anymore. A spider the size of a quarter crawls out of the air vent. I turn the air conditioning off because it makes me feel like I'm driving through the Mojave. The spider crawls back in. I try the windows again. I figure if Father Frank is going to fix the police station's air conditioning from Heaven, he might fix his car windows too.

They still don't work. I guess some miracles take longer than others.

We reach the church, the rocket-ship steeple coming into view well before the rest of it. It's only a five-minute drive, but that's the thing about small towns — unless you're living on a farm, everywhere is only five or ten minutes away. Father Barrett is waiting in the doorway. He shakes hands with us, as if this is a formal occasion, which I guess it is. We follow him into the bedroom. Father Frank is lying on the bed. The oxygen machine has been switched off and the tube that went to Father Frank's nose has been wound up and is hanging over the handle. The bed has been recently made, and Father Frank has been dressed in fresh clothes. His hands are neatly folded over his chest. His hair has been combed and his eyes are closed and he looks more hollowed out than he did yesterday. Father Barrett has sprayed air freshener in the room and the window is wide open.

"I cleaned him up," Father Barrett says, and he looks at Drew to see if he's going to challenge that decision, but he doesn't. Instead Drew asks if the doctor has been yet.

"On her way," Father Barrett says.

There isn't much for us to do except stand around and wait. It doesn't take long to feel weird making small talk with a dead guy in the room, especially when that room still smells like said dead guy. So we head outside. Right away we all agree it's too hot out there, so Father Barrett asks us if he can fix us some iced tea, and we tell him he can, and we follow him into the church. We wait in the chapel while he disappears into the kitchen. There are stained glass windows of Jesus and other folks from Jesus times, there's a big wooden crucifix with attached Jesus looking not in the greatest of moods, and lots of wooden pews. Pretty much it's wood and glass in all directions.

"Father Frank buried both of my parents," Drew says.

"Were they dead first?"

He stares at me for a few seconds, his face expressionless, then he smiles, and then he laughs, which starts me laughing, which gets him laughing even harder. We get caught in a loop neither of us can escape, and when Father Barrett comes in carrying a tray with a pitcher and glasses on it, we're sitting in the pews wiping tears from our eyes. The embarrassment makes the situation even funnier, by which point I don't even know what we're laughing at. Father Barrett smiles, shakes his head, and watches us until we're able to calm down.

"He was a good man," Father Barrett says, when we're back to normal. He pours us some drinks, and I bet he says that about most people who die. He was a good man or she was a good woman. People who die often are good people. "Guy like Frank, he didn't deserve to go out this way."

"And others do?" I ask, without really meaning to.

"Yes," he says, without hesitation. "I don't know why things are the way they are. I can't pretend to understand the way God works. Why do good people die young, why do good people die painfully, when awful people, serial killers and rapists and pedophiles, can live to a hundred?" He looks at us for a few seconds. "What?"

"I wasn't expecting you to say that," I tell him. The drink is icy cold and I'm tempted to pour it down the back of my neck. "I don't think either of us were."

"Father Frank wouldn't have said it, that's for sure. I have some big shoes to fill."

A woman calls out from down the hallway. "That'll be Doctor Osborne," Father Barrett says, and Drew puts his drink down and tells us he'll take care of things. That leaves me and Father Barrett. I sip at my ice tea and he sips at his.

"You look like hell," he says.

"Thanks."

"But not as bad as yesterday. Did you talk to Alyssa?"

"I did."

"How is she? Is she on her way back?"

"She's fine," I tell him, "but she's not coming back. She made that clear."

"She will now," he says, "for the funeral."

"I wouldn't be so sure."

"Do you know why she left?"

"She has her reasons."

He nods. He can tell I'm not going to elaborate. "When you talk to her again, tell her she's always welcome here." I say nothing, and he says nothing while he sips his drink. He stares at me. Then he says, "What is it?"

"It's just that Father Frank is convinced something bad happened to her. Even after I spoke to her, he didn't believe she was okay. He thinks . . . I guess I should say he thought . . . he thought she was being coerced somehow."

"Is that what you think too? That she's being coerced?"

The chains. The mattress. The water bottles. "Frank was convincing," I tell him. "And I can't shake the feeling he was holding out on me."

Father Barrett doesn't say anything. He stares at me, and he sips his iced tea, and then he glances to the right and then stares at me again. I look where he looked, at the confessional booth. I feel foolish for not making the connection earlier.

Not even by omission.

"Somebody confessed something to him?"

"I'm not saying that," he says.

"What are you saying?"

"I'm not saying anything. I don't know what it is he knew, but yes, it's possible somebody confessed something to him. It could explain why he was so steadfast in his beliefs."

Never Conrad.

Is Conrad innocent of abducting Alyssa twelve years ago? Did her real abductor confess to Father Frank?

"He was a good man," Father Barrett says. "A good priest, and the role of a priest is to not tell. The confessional seal, that's some serious stuff we're talking about here, Noah. Real serious. No priest is ever going to break it."

"So somebody could have abducted Alyssa, and gone and told him about it, and he'd say nothing?"

"In theory, yes, only Frank hasn't taken confession in months."

"But somebody could have told him while on his deathbed."

"That's true," he says, "but in that case Frank could have told him the confessional seal didn't extend that far, and therefore he could tell us."

"Surely if he knew Alyssa had been abducted, he'd break the seal, wouldn't he? He would suffer the consequences of the church, of his God, to make sure she was okay."

"You can't say anything," he says. "You never can, no matter what the circumstances."

I shake my head. "I get what you're saying, but I think he would have told me if he knew."

159

"And yet he didn't."

"I don't think that's what was confessed to him. I think it's something else. I think it goes back to when Alyssa was taken twelve years ago. He said *Not even by omission.* What did he mean by that?"

He exhales loudly, and nods slowly, and takes a little time working on an answer. "Let's say somebody in town did something bad. Let's say, as an example, you knew that person had confessed to a priest. The priest is never going to tell you who, and you can't go ask was it this person, was it that person, and have them go no, no, no, it wasn't him, it wasn't her, then say nothing when you hit on the right name. You can't rule things out by elimination. You can't use negatives to prove a positive."

I think on that. I focus on the two words I focused on yesterday after we spoke that second time. *Never Conrad.* After finding the water bottles last night, my first thought was maybe Conrad was involved. I was thinking that today I was going to have to find him, but now I don't think so.

"If somebody did confess to him twelve years ago," I say, "it's possible whatever that thing was, it's having an effect on what's happening now. It's why he thinks Alyssa is being coerced."

I try to imagine the impossible situation that would have put him in. His daughter is kidnapped, and he knows who did it, and can't do anything about it. All these years he's had to face this person at church, or out and about in daily life, and has to pretend like it didn't happen. He has to know this person might strike again and can't stop them. I think about our conversations yesterday, everything from telling me that Alyssa was in danger, to Conrad being innocent, to needing to be careful because I would be putting those close to me at risk.

The person who took Alyssa twelve years ago — the *Never Conrad* — did Father Frank know who that was?

The chain. The mattress. The water bottles.

Did Father Frank know what was going on here?

Twenty-two

Drew comes back into the church. I look at him, and I think, should I trust you? Are you the person who confessed to Father Frank? Are you the one who put the chains in the basement at the Kelly farm? You'd have the keys because, after all, Leigh is the one who listed the property. Doctor Mary Osborne is with him, and I look at her, and I think, does she have the strength to drag somebody down a flight of stairs? Father Barrett certainly does. The last town he worked in, did he leave because the church frowned upon him tying people up?

Doctor Osborne smiles at me, then gives me a brief hug and says it's nice to see me. I've known her most of my life. In her sixties, her hair is losing the war to the grays, with some blonde ones holding strong. She has a casual smile and an easy manner, eyes behind a pair of glasses a little too big for her, as if she's trying to see more of the world than the rest of us. She was my family doctor growing up. She's the one who

162

told my dad if he didn't give up drinking it would kill him. She confirms what we already know, and what she legally has to confirm, which is that Father Frank passed away during the night due to his illness. She tells us it's a miracle he held on as long as he did. Nobody suggests we take a moment of silence, but it's what ends up happening, all of us with our hands clasped in front of us as we take time to think of Father Frank's passing. It's like Father Barrett said — Frank was a good man.

We all shuffle a little on our feet, then Doctor Osborne asks me what happened to my face.

"I walked into something I shouldn't have," I tell her.

"Drop by my office today and I'll check your eyes. Maybe you're not seeing what you ought to be seeing."

"I'm fine," I tell her.

"You're fine, until you're not fine," she says, and she holds my gaze while saying it. "Those cuts look bad. Let's not have you risk an infection, huh?" She looks at her watch, which makes all of us look at our own watches. It's eleven o'clock. "Make it twelve," she says. "You remember how to get there?"

"Do I have a choice in the matter?"

She turns to Drew. "You'll arrest him if he tries to resist?"

"Yes, ma'am."

She leaves, and Father Barrett excuses himself and heads to his office to make a series of calls, the first one being to an undertaker. Drew starts pacing the church, preparing himself for his phone call to Alyssa. I finish my drink and start rattling the ice cubes. Drew makes the call. The phone rings a while, and I think it's gone to voicemail when Drew introduces himself, but he says nothing for a few seconds.

Then he says, "No, it's not about that." He stops walking. "I have some bad news."

He goes quiet then, and no doubt Alyssa is guessing what the news is. I wonder if she's crying. I wonder if she's regretting not coming back. I wonder if the choices she is making are her choices. Drew says nothing for half a minute, and then tells Alyssa that Father Frank was a good man, and that he will be missed.

"I'm not sure," he says. "It could be later this week, maybe Thursday or Friday. Yes, of course, I'll keep you updated. I hope you can make it along."

He listens to her for a little bit, and then he says, "I'm truly sorry for your loss, Alyssa. Like I said, Father Frank was a good man."

He hangs up. He slips his phone into his pocket and comes over and sits on the pew opposite me on the other side of the aisle and his body slumps and he sighs and even though it's only eleven in the morning he looks as though it's been a long day. "That was tough," he says.

"You think she'll come to the funeral?"

He shrugs.

"How'd she sound?" I ask.

"How do you think she sounded?"

I think she might have sounded scared, but I don't want to say that. "Guilty? Relieved?"

"Just sad. Like she knew the call was coming, but still

couldn't believe it. I think the rest will come later. Can you believe what Father Barrett was saying earlier, about some people deserving to die the way Father Frank died?"

"I think he has a point."

"I guess I do too, but man, I wasn't expecting to hear it from him. I like to think we can all be forgiven, but Father Barrett, I'm not so sure he thinks that way. What do you think, you think that makes him a good priest? Or a bad one?"

"I think you'll get the chance to find out."

"Yeah, I think so too." He picks his drink up. The ice cubes have halved in size. "Despite the things he says, I gotta say, I really like the guy. I think he could be good for Acacia. You want to elaborate on what you were asking before, back in my office?"

"It really was nothing," I say, "other than me wondering how many people skip out of here without letting anybody know."

"Bullshit," he says. "You're thinking something, and whatever that something is, you need to take a deep breath before it leads you down a path like last time."

"It's nothing like that," I tell him.

"I ought to either arrest you, or drive you out of town, because something's going on with you."

"It really is nothing," I tell him.

"I don't believe you," he says, and he stands up and walks out of the church, leaving me alone with Father Frank's ghost and a large wooden Jesus.

Twenty-three

The doctor's surgery is in a hundred-year-old house that got converted sixty years ago, long weatherboards painted white, a wheelchair ramp running up the side to the entrance, a black shingle roof that looks new, lots of dark green ivy climbing through the garden. I'm in the waiting room less than a minute before Doctor Osborne comes out and gets me. We head into her office where there are ceramic body parts on shelves, knee joints and back joints and arm joints and certificates on the wall to remind us she knows the hip bone is connected to the backbone. She pulls on latex gloves and leans forward to study the wounds.

"Exactly how did this happen?" she asks. "And tell me the truth."

"I took a beating."

"Should I see the other guy too?"

"I didn't. I was on the floor before I even knew he was there."

"You know who did it?"

"Will it change the diagnosis if I tell you?"

"No," she says. "There's nothing more I can do than you've already done. You did a good job of cleaning it up. I can give you some painkillers if you need them."

"I might have cracked a tooth too," I say.

"Let me see."

I open my mouth and she uses a light to take a look. "I can't see anything," she says, "but you ought to go see a dentist to be sure."

"I will. So you want to tell me why you really wanted me to come here?"

She leans back. She peels her gloves off and drops them into a bin. "It's Maggie," she says, and her answer makes no sense. I had thought she was going to want to tell me something about Father Frank, or Alyssa, or something about chains and water bottles and mattresses. "Can I be candid with you?"

"Of course."

"You've seen her since you've been back?"

"Yes."

"How does she seem?"

"What are you getting at?"

"Her son has a black eye."

I don't answer for a few seconds. There can only be one place she's going with this. "He got hit in the face with a hockey puck," I tell her.

"The same hockey puck that hit Maggie in the eye last year? The same one that hit her other son before then? The same one that has hit her in the stomach, the neck, the arm, the shoulders, the back?"

I grind my teeth back and forth. "Tell me."

"Her husband is beating them."

I want to get up. I want to pace the room. I want to go and find Maggie's husband and tie him into a chair and do to him what I did to Conrad.

"How long?"

"A couple of years, at least."

"She's told you?"

She shakes her head. "She hasn't told me anything, but I've seen the way she is around him, and I've examined some of those bruises and heard her excuses, and lately I've seen the way she tries to hide the marks. When I asked her about it, she said I was wrong, and she changed doctors."

"Did you report it to the police?"

"I told Drew about it."

"He didn't say anything to me."

"He offered to help her, and she said she didn't need any, that nothing was going on. She's scared, Noah, I know it, and I'm scared for her. But Drew said without her wanting to press charges, there was nothing he could do, except keep an eye on her, and if he saw evidence of it he'd throw her husband's ass into jail."

"That's not good enough."

"I agree, and he agreed too. But you know what it's like, Noah. Cops and doctors see it all the time. Some women can't leave the situation. They can't fight it. It's never as easy as others on the outside think. What about the children? Will the husband abuse them more if you try to leave? Will he come looking for you? It's always easy, especially for men, to look at the situation and say *She should just leave*, but it's seldom that easy. Women get so frightened they become paralyzed. They're frightened for themselves, frightened for their children, frightened that if they speak out they won't be believed, frightened if they speak out their husbands will come back and kill them."

"The boy, when I saw him yesterday, he said the same thing that Maggie said. She'd just picked him up from school. He went with the same story about being hit with a puck."

"Then maybe what he said happened actually happened. I can't imagine Maggie sending the kids to school with bruises, otherwise the teachers would ask questions. Or maybe he knows better than to tell the truth. What I know is that they're being abused."

"Why are you telling me this? Surely you're breaking all sorts of rules or regulations and even the law by telling me this."

She straightens herself up in her chair. "When I was twenty-two I moved to New York. It was a big wide world out there, and I wanted to grab a slice of it. You know what it's like, small-town people with big-city dreams. I made a best friend there. Nancy. We became inseparable. She fell in love and she got married, and I was maid of honor at her wedding. Nancy was vibrant and cool and all sorts of outgoing, and her husband was one of the nicest people you could ever meet. Only he wasn't. Soon after the wedding we all stopped hearing from Nancy. See, that's one of the first things that happens — you get isolated. You lose your friends. Then one day she agreed to come out for lunch. None of us had seen her in a few months, and she'd lost so much weight she looked awful. We all knew something was wrong. We begged her to tell us, but she kept saying everything was okay. A month later I ran into her. I barely recognized her. She was wearing sunglasses. I asked her to take them off, and she refused. I asked her to confirm what I suspected, that Will was beating her. She said no, she was fine. Two weeks later he hit her so hard her brain switched off. Every year I spend a weekend in New York to be with her. She's in a care home. She has no idea about what's going on around her. This cool and vibrant and amazing person now sits in a chair and stares out the window and has people feed her and people put her to bed and that's her life, Noah. Will, on the other hand — well, Will went to jail for three years and got released after two and God knows where he is now, or who else he's hurt."

What was it I thought yesterday when Maggie got me from the airport? I thought she looked thin, like something had worried the weight away. I'd put that down to whatever had happened to Alyssa.

"If Maggie doesn't leave her husband, she's going to end up like Nancy, and this world has too many Nancys as it is."

"I'm really sorry for your friend, and for you."

"Thank you," she says. "I miss her so much, you know? She's alive, but she's not alive, and she's not dead either."

"You still haven't answered my question."

"What question?"

"The one where I asked why you're telling me this."

"Right," she says. "Well, honestly, I'm not real sure. I wasn't expecting to see you at the church — I didn't even know you were back. But then there you were, and . . . and maybe I shouldn't have told you. I regret not being able to do anything for Nancy, and I'm always going to hate myself for that. It wasn't my fault, but I could have done more. I'm telling you this because when Stephen hurts Maggie in such a bad way that it can't be undone, I need somebody else to wonder if there's something more they could have done."

"You've told Drew," I say. "The responsibility goes to him."

"Only it doesn't, because I'm always going to think I could have done something more."

I stare at her. I say nothing.

"I can't get through to Maggie, and nor can others — I'm hoping that you might be able to."

I say nothing.

"I'm not asking you to hurt Stephen," she says.

"Aren't you?"

She doesn't answer me for a while. "Something has to be done."

"Do no harm. Isn't that your motto?"

"What was your motto when you were beating Conrad Haggerty all those years ago?"

Twenty-four

Doctor Osborne gives me Maggie's address. I drive there keeping my anger in check, but it's difficult. I knock on the door and she doesn't answer. She told me earlier she was sick, but after what Doctor Osborne told me, I'm not so sure that's true.

"Maggie, it's Noah. I know you're home. Father Frank died," I say. "Can you open up?"

Nothing.

The house is in a street that got added to the expanding town five years ago. All the houses have manicured lawns and trees still too young to look overgrown. Maggie's house has lots of windows and lots of color and an A-frame roof that looks like it would be fun to toboggan down in the winter. There are door chimes hanging next to my head made out of shells, and a welcome mat that says *Welcome*.

"Come on, Maggie, I know you're home. Please, it's important."

"I can't," she says, and she's on the other side of the door. "I'm sorry about Father Frank, but I can't open up because I don't want to risk you getting sick."

"I'll be fine."

"I'm sure you think that's the case," she says, "because I thought the same thing yesterday, but it's—"

"Please, Maggie. I wouldn't have come here if it weren't important."

"I think . . . I think tomorrow will be better," she says, her voice catching. "I'll be better by then, I'm sure of it."

I wait a beat. I exhale slowly, inhale slowly, and then I say, "I spoke to Doctor Osborne."

She doesn't say anything.

"I know Stephen has been hurting you. The kids too."

"Don't do this," she says, and I can barely hear her through the door.

"Please, Maggie, open the door."

"Please, Noah, I'm begging you, please just leave. You're wrong about Stephen. You should go now. Alyssa is okay and you have no reason to stay here."

"I can't, Maggie, you know I can't. Everything Stephen has been doing, it's not your fault, but it needs to stop."

"And you're the person to make that happen? You sound angry, Noah. You sound angry and the last thing I need right now is you coming here and telling me what I need to do."

"I care about you, Maggie."

"If you cared about me you wouldn't be doing this. If you cared about me, you'd listen to what I'm saying. You think

173

you can help, and maybe you can for a day or two, but then what? What happens after you leave?"

"Talk to Drew about it. For the sake of your kids, you need to talk to him."

"Don't do that," she says. "Don't make me sound like I'm a bad mother putting my kids in danger."

"That's not what I meant. Please, Maggie," I say, and my voice is low and calm, because anger is the last thing Maggie needs to hear. I shouldn't be here, I'm only making it worse, yet I can't bring myself to walk away. "Please talk to me. Tell me what I can do."

"You'll really help me?"

"Yes. Anything."

"Then you can help by leaving like I've already asked."

I take a few breaths. I close my eyes and try to focus my thoughts, but all I can see is a stranger hitting the woman I used to love. "Okay, I will, I promise, but please open the door first. I just want to make sure you're okay."

"Then you'll leave?"

"Yes."

She unlocks the door. Slowly it opens. I can only see one half of her face.

I keep my voice low and gentle. "Can you show me?"

She doesn't, not at first. There are tears on her face, and more are getting ready to fall. When she turns, something in my chest catches. Her lip and cheek have swollen and match how mine looked yesterday, and her black eye matches the black eye her son has.

Stay calm. This isn't about you, this is about Maggie.

"Is he at work?"

"Why? You want to ride into town and use violence to save the day, is that it?"

"You're an intelligent woman, Maggie. It's one of the reasons I fell in love with you. You're the smartest person I've ever met. You know where this is going because you've seen it before. You know what he's going to end up doing, if not to you, then to the kids."

She doesn't say anything.

"Black eyes and broken arms heal, Maggie, but it's only a matter of time before he does something that can't."

She starts to cry. I've never seen her cry before.

"This isn't right, Maggie. I know you know this."

"It's not that simple," she says, "and despite what you think, he loves us."

I think about how the town has changed. How the people have changed. How Father Frank isn't the Father Frank I once knew. That Alyssa is all grown up and not the seven-year-old I saved. I think about Drew, muscled and lean and running things around here, and Old Man Haggerty always with an oxygen machine in tow. And Maggie . . . Maggie has changed too. The woman I once knew would never have tolerated this. That Maggie would have left her husband the first time he raised his fist. "This isn't love," I say. I take her hands in mine, but that isn't enough, so I wrap my arms around her. She sobs into my neck. "It needs to stop. Please, I'm begging you, talk to Drew about it. Talk to Doctor Osborne. You don't have to be in this alone."

"Stephen, he . . . he doesn't mean to hurt us." She pulls back so she can look at me. I keep hold of her hands. "It's just that sometimes, you know, sometimes with the pressure of the job, and sometimes the kids keep him awake and he gets stressed and he doesn't mean to do it. I know how that sounds," she says, and she looks down at her feet and doesn't look back up. "Trust me, I know how it sounds. I've convicted wife beaters in the past, and I get it, I totally get it, but this is different. Stephen is different."

"He's not different," I tell her.

"You don't know him the way I know him." She finally looks back up at me. "I appreciate your concern, but things are going to get better. I know they are."

"You really believe that?"

"Yes."

"I don't. I'm going to talk to him," I say, because the red mist is there, painting the world in a shade of blood.

She pulls her hands out of mine. "Noah . . . You'll only make it worse."

"I'm going to help you."

"I'm not asking for your help."

"You never needed to."

"You're not listening to me," she says, and she's right. I turn around and walk off the porch. "Noah," she calls out to me. "Noah, don't do anything. Please, I'm begging you, don't do anything."

"How can I not?"

"You talk to him, and we're done. I swear to God I'll never talk to you again."

"I'm used to it."

Twenty-five

*T*he chain. *The mattress. The water bottles.*

None of them matter. Not in this moment.

Missing people. Alyssa being coerced. Father Frank dying.

They all take a backseat to the red mist.

The used car sales lot that Maggie pointed out yesterday where her husband works has shiny SUVs and sedans and coupes all parked in rows, windscreens and headlights and sales stickers facing the street. Synthetic triangles of colors hang from lines crisscrossing all of it. It looks like there should be clowns here. It looks like the kind of place to have a good time. Signs offer finance deals and cash deals and trade-in deals. Every car has a window sticker with the price crossed out, and a second one below. Every car you can see is on special. I drive onto the lot and I get out of the car and a guy with a name badge that says *Stephen* with the words *Sales Manager* underneath comes out and his smile is so big and his teeth so bright he could use them to lead people out of a mine.

He's wearing jeans and a shirt and tie, and he fiddles with the tie as he approaches me, getting the knot straight and then flattening it with his hand.

"How's it going there, partner?" he says, and then he looks at the car I'm driving. I can see him thinking two things — first, I need a new car and I've come to the right place, and second, if that's the car I'm driving, then I'm not going to be able to afford much. "Ouch, looks like you've been in the wars. Hope that beating wasn't from another car dealer?"

"Something like that," I say.

"Looking at trading up?"

I picture the bruise on Maggie's face. I picture the bruise on her son's face. I think about Doctor Osborne's story, about Nancy wasting away in a care home. I picture where I'll be in two years when I get the phone call that Maggie has been beaten to death.

"You okay, mister?"

"I'm fine," I tell him. "I'm just thinking."

"Sure got a lot to think about," he says. "What kind of thing are you looking for?"

Well, I'm in a biblical mood, so I'm looking for revenge. I'm looking for justice. An eye for an eye. Crossing lines. Doing bad things for good reasons. Pissing my ex-wife off more than I ever have. "I'm not sure."

Stephen is a good-looking guy. Tall. Handsome. Good hair. The quarterback next door. He could be an anchorman. He's the guy who got the girl. The guy who can act like he's your best friend. Easy to see why Maggie would fall for him.

Easy to see why people wouldn't believe this guy could hurt you. He's so friendly I want to beat the hell out of him and still buy a car.

"That's good," he says. "Gives you a lot more options. You have a family?"

I shake my head.

He grins. Like he has the perfect solution for me. "So how about something sporty?"

Maggie told me I was going to make things worse. It was an act of violence twelve years ago on my part that ended our marriage. What will an act of violence do now?

"How about that?" I ask, pointing to a black two-door coupe.

"I'll grab the key."

He walks into the office. I stretch my shoulders back and loosen my neck. He comes back out. He tosses me the key. He asks if I need to answer my cellphone, which is ringing, to which I tell him no, it can wait. It can wait because it's Maggie.

We get in the car. His aftershave is strong. He tells me about the Nissan. It has a V6 three-point-something-liter engine that can get the car up to sixty miles an hour in just over five seconds. He keeps talking. It goes in one ear and out the other. It's like he's speaking in Klingon. The only thing I'll remember about this car when this is all over is the color.

We get out on the road. I put my foot down.

"She sure is quick," Stephen says, "but tell you what, instead of you getting us a speeding ticket, how about we head out to the highway?"

"I was about to suggest the same thing."

I head for the highway. We go over the bridge and the same two guys fishing earlier are still fishing now. They wave, one with a beer in his hand, the other one between drinks. The windows work and so does the air conditioning. The motor purrs. I can feel the power of it under my foot. The dashboard is lit up like the cockpit of a plane. There's a display saying it's ninety-eight degrees outside. My phone keeps ringing and I keep not answering it. Houses become small farms. Small farms become big farms. Stephen is holding on to the handle above his shoulder and I'm going fast enough to have made him stop spouting statistics. I pull up a mile from the Kelly farm.

"So, what do you think?" Stephen asks.

There are no other cars in sight. Haven't been since we left town. High above us are twin white lines in the sky left behind by a plane, but I can't see any plane. A ditch runs the length of the road. During the winter that ditch can fill with water, but right now it's dry and full of cracks. There are weeds growing out of it. I kill the engine and pop the hood and get out of the car and walk around it the way car guys do. I open the hood and the engine is in the front, like I knew — well, hoped — it would be. Stephen joins me and whistles while taking a look at the engine as if he's never seen anything quite so pretty.

Maggie's black eye. The split lip. The boy's black eye.

I could force Stephen into the woods. He wouldn't be the first to die out there, and certainly won't be the last.

"If you think the engine is cool, let me show you something

that will have you reaching for your credit card," he says. "Back in a second."

He disappears. I keep staring at the engine.

Black eyes. Split lips. And in a year, or two years, Maggie's funeral.

Coming here was wrong. Coming here has gone against what Maggie begged me to do. She was right about me trying to solve violence with violence — about making it worse. She was right about me not listening. Shame begins to outweigh the anger. I've gone against Maggie's wishes where the result would only make matters worse. This isn't about me. It's not about how I feel. It's about Maggie.

I'll drive this son of a bitch back and I'll calm down some and talk to Drew and see what we can do. I'll talk to Doctor Osborne and ask her to take another run at Maggie to see if she can change her mind. Maggie has always had plenty of friends, but it's like Doctor Osborne said — people in these situations get isolated. Even so, we can talk to the friends she used to have. There must be support groups. Getting hit by your husband isn't just a big-city problem.

I close the hood. Stephen is standing staring at me, holding the tire iron. The way he's holding it, the way he's staring at me, this guy either really needs a sale, or he knows who I am.

"I looked you up," he says, reading my mind. "When Maggie told me you were here, I went online. I read all about you. That bitch shouldn't have sent you."

"Three things," I tell him. I keep my hands by my sides. "One, she didn't send me. Two, you shouldn't have hit her.

Three, you call her that again and I'm going to take that tire iron off you and put it through your skull."

He smiles and slowly nods in a way that tells me he can't imagine a world in which that could happen. "You don't know her the way I know her," he says. "I've been married to her longer than you were. She's hard work. The kids . . . the kids are hard work. You think I like having to keep her in line? You think I like the fact she can't do a goddamn thing right?"

"I think you like hitting her. I think that makes you feel like you're king of the world."

His face goes red. Veins stick out around his neck. His jaw tenses up, and he says, "It's not my fault."

"It's Maggie's?"

"You bet your ass it is."

"And last night, that was her fault too?"

"That was your fault," he says. "My kid saw you with her. Maggie, she hadn't told me you were going to be here, and then my kid mentions you and she has to explain what's going on, and she didn't have any right to contact you without asking me, and she did it that way because she knew I'd never have let her. She lied to me, and she made me look like a fool in front of my kids."

"You need to give your kids more credit. Why don't you leave her?"

He laughs. It's all fun and games out here on the highway. "I've put in too much time with her to walk away, but something tells me after today she's going to be easier to deal with."

He switches the tire iron into his other hand and comes

for me. He swings hard and I move back and it misses me by over a foot. He grunts with the effort. I figure he's used to swinging his fists and can't judge the right distance. He readjusts. I move toward the car and he swings hard and this time he misses by only a few inches, which makes him a quick learner, but it also puts him in the doghouse with his boss because he hits the side of the car, smashing off the wing mirror. He comes at me again. Instead of stepping back, I step forward into the arc of his swing and put my arm up to block his forearm. I punch him in the throat and he stumbles back and falls down. Both his hands go to where I hit him, but he's still holding the tire iron so he ends up hitting himself in the side of the face with it hard enough to make his eyes roll, at which point the tire iron falls out of his hand.

I stand over him at an angle where the sun still shines in his eyes. It was a mistake coming out here. I bend down and pick up the tire iron.

"Either leave her, or get help," I tell him, not sure if men like Stephen can get help, but who knows.

He doesn't say anything. He can't say anything. I pick the wing mirror up and drop it onto his lap. "Use it to take a good long look at yourself," I tell him.

I leave him sitting on the side of the road getting smaller the further away I get, then the road curves, and then he's gone.

Twenty-six

I don't buy the Nissan. I wish I could, partly for the novelty of having a car I'm not going to spontaneously combust in. I drop it off at the yard and get back into Father Frank's car. Compared to the Nissan it feels like I'm driving a horse and buggy.

I have five missed calls from Maggie. When I call her back, she doesn't answer. I need to warn her about what happened. I see it going one of two ways. Stephen is too embarrassed to tell what happened, so he says nothing. But most likely it will go the second way, where he comes home and takes his anger out on her. In fact, thinking about it, I should have known this before I even went to see him. Isn't that what Maggie was telling me? Isn't that what Doctor Osborne warned me about? My guess is he's going to get home and he's going to say I jumped him and he's going to make her pay for it. I leave her a message to ring me as soon as she can. I tell her it's urgent.

It's three o'clock. The sun is arcing back toward the

horizon. Shadows are getting longer. I drive to Maggie's house. I knock on the door and nobody answers. I walk around the house wondering if any of the neighbors are going to call the police. I look through the windows. I call her phone and leave another message.

It's possible Stephen called her. He has to call somebody to ask them to come and get him. I jump back into the car and it takes me twenty minutes to get out to where I left him without passing him on the way. He isn't out here. I pull over in the place where we fought. I open the door to get some air. I call Doctor Osborne. The receptionist tells me she's with a patient, and I tell her it's urgent. She puts me through.

"Doctor Osborne," Doctor Osborne says.

"It's Noah."

She lowers the phone. "Excuse me for a few minutes," she says, and the microphone is muffled as she keeps it covered. I hear a door close. "You've spoken to her?" she asks.

"I tried," I tell her. "She didn't want to hear it."

"I thought as much."

"So I went to see him."

"Tell me you're joking."

"Tell me you didn't think I would."

I tell her what happened. I tell her that I can't find Maggie. She says nothing. She's upset. I picture her holding the phone, her face pale, memories of Nancy going around in her head. "We messed up. I messed up," she says finally. "I shouldn't have said anything. I was . . . honestly, I don't know what I was thinking. Now we've made it worse." She sounds like she's about to have a nervous breakdown. "I've made it worse."

A four-wheel drive loaded up with camping equipment drives past me, hikers and campers on their way out to the trails.

"What did you think was going to happen? You thought I would kill him?"

"No," she says. "I . . . I thought somehow you could fix it. I thought maybe you'd get through to Maggie. I didn't think it would go this far. All I knew for sure was I couldn't keep ignoring what was happening."

I exhale slowly. "No, of course you couldn't," I say. "You did the right thing by telling me. I'm the one who messed up."

"Look, Sheriff Haggerty is in my office right now. I know he's not the sheriff, but he still pulls a lot of weight in this town. Let me bring him in on this."

"I can't imagine him wanting to help me out," I say.

"But it's not you he'll be helping," she says. "It's Maggie. It's the children."

"Okay," I tell her, and then an idea comes to me. "Listen, Doctor, I need you to do something for me. Whatever this conversation is you're about to have with him, I need you to make it go on as long as possible."

"For what reason?"

"I can't tell you that."

"If you want me to delay him, then you need to tell me why."

"It's to do with Alyssa Stone. Father Frank was convinced

186

she needed my help, and you delaying Haggerty will help me do that. Please, I'm asking you to help me help her."

"It's a day of falling down rabbit holes," she says. "I'll do my best."

"Then text me when he leaves," I say.

"Okay," she says. "You'll tell me more later?"

"Yes."

We hang up. I call Drew. He answers after a few rings. It sounds like he's eating. I tell him about seeing Maggie's bruises. I tell him about my altercation with Stephen.

"Goddamn it, Noah."

"It just got out of control," I tell him. "Don't tell me you wouldn't have done the same thing if it'd been you and Leigh."

"I'll find her," he says. "I promise."

I turn the car around. The clicking from the front left of the car sounds like a time bomb ready to go off. I drive into town. Forest, big farms, little farms, houses, then more specifically Old Man Haggerty's house. He lives in a two-story place his parents built back when this town had a population of less than a thousand. Haggerty always was a keen tinkerer and a keen gardener, keeping the house in great shape and the yard too. It's not that way now, which I put down to the stroke. The bushes are overgrown and the lawns are long and paint is flaking from the weatherboards and the roof is twice as heavy as it should be due to all the lichen up there. He lives alone too, his wife having left twenty years ago. She was always happy enough, until one day she wasn't.

I can remember the last time I was here. It was a week or

two before Alyssa disappeared. Old Man Haggerty had invited a bunch of us over for a barbecue. I was there with Maggie, and Drew had Leigh there, along with their son, and the other deputies were there too. During the summer Haggerty would do that kind of thing a couple of times a month. Often he'd show off his new project, whether he was extending a room or building a deck or working on the old Trans Am he bought when he was twenty-five. The only thing that worked on that Trans Am was its ability to absorb money and time, but Haggerty loved that thing. Now everything here is run down, like Haggerty himself.

I park a block away. I walk to Haggerty's property and I move down the side of the house, past the woodpile and the garden shed to the back door which, sadly, is locked. I guess that's a sign of the times — ten years ago it wouldn't have been. Or it's a sign that the owner is more security conscious than most because of the job he used to do. I try the windows. All locked.

I climb the woodpile. It gives me access to the second floor. I try the windows, and find the bathroom one open. It's a small window, but I manage to wiggle inside and crash on the floor. So far so good.

The house smells of cigarette smoke. Haggerty never used to smoke inside. I guess these days he doesn't care so much. I head to the office. It's upstairs, with the sun coming in from the front during the morning, and coming through the side in the afternoon. The carpet has faded all along one side against the wall. The window is open in here too, and would have been easier to climb through. There's a desk with a computer on it. I switch it on. It doesn't ask for a password. There are filing cabinets lining two of the walls. That's the thing about Haggerty — he always brought his work home with him, and I'm betting he brought those case files from twelve years ago home with him too.

I go through the filing cabinets. I don't find any mention of Alyssa or Conrad or of myself. I try the computer. The display has fallen asleep, and comes to life when I tap the keyboard. There's a photograph of Haggerty and his ex-wife as the backdrop. It makes me feel bad for the guy. There's a folder called *Case Files*. I click on it. There are plenty of reports but nothing involved with what happened twelve years ago. I go to the boxes lining the wall. They're labeled. They cover various crimes he's worked on, but again nothing that relates to Alyssa, and nothing that mentions missing people.

A door downstairs opens.

I look at my phone. There's no text from Doctor Osborne because it's flat. It hasn't been charged in over a day. I look at my watch. It's quarter after five. I've been here an hour. I turn the computer off and climb through the window onto the roof. I can hear Old Man Haggerty coming up the stairs. I move to the side of the window and look out over the backyard into the neighboring properties. It's only a matter of time before I'm spotted. I can hear Haggerty moving around in the office. I take a peek. He's staring at the computer. I pull back from the window and hold my breath for a few moments, and then I peek again. He's no longer staring at the computer, but at the filing cabinets. He opens them and flicks through. He looks at the boxes on the floor. He taps them with his foot, and then he turns toward the wardrobe. He suddenly looks anxious. He knows somebody has been here. He opens the wardrobe door. He starts pulling out clothes that are hanging in there. He wheezes heavily while doing it. When the space is empty he pushes at a panel at the back of the wardrobe half the size of a door. It opens up, revealing a cavity behind it. He reaches inside and pulls out a single box. He opens it and looks inside but doesn't touch the contents. If he does suspect somebody has been inside his house, he seems satisfied that that particular box wasn't found. I wonder if he suspects I'm the one who broke in. Probably. Given the timing, who else would it be? Now he's asking himself why I would do that.

I move carefully around the house until I reach the woodpile. I lower myself down. I stay where I am, trying to sense if I'm being watched, and where from, but there's nothing.

There's nobody around as I walk out onto the street. I don't rush. I can't risk drawing attention to myself. I head up the block to Father Frank's car. The engine is slow to turn over, then it catches, and then I'm pulling out.

I'll have to come back.

I need to see what's inside that box.

Twenty-seven

I order coffee while a waitress charges my phone out the back. It's six o'clock and the diner is nearly full. A guy wider than the counter sits next to me, squeezing himself between it and the chair and ordering a Slow Death. When he talks he sounds like a vacuum cleaner struggling for air. He plays games on his cellphone with thumbs and fingers that seem too big for it while he waits.

I look at the menu and see a Slow Death is a bacon and chicken burger with fries and an extra large soda. I order it, and ask for my phone back. I promise myself when all of this is over, I'm going to start running regularly. At the very least I'll buy some nice running shoes and sit them where I can see them.

The waitress brings my phone over. I have two missed calls, as well as a message from Doctor Osborne, that says *He's leaving now.*

Two messages are from Drew. The first is to ask me to

call him back, and the second one tells me he's gotten hold of Maggie, and that she and the kids are staying with her sister, and that Stephen is going to cool off, probably at a bar somewhere in town.

There are no messages from Maggie.

My Slow Death arrives. By seven o'clock I can feel how the burger got its name. The diner has filled up. Nobody makes conversation with me, other than the waitress who, when I first showed up, said, "Tough day, hon?"

I get out to the car, breathing hard on the way, and walking slow too. It's been a long day. I haven't slept well the last few nights, and exhaustion is catching up. I go to turn on the stereo, thinking loud music will help keep me awake, but the power knob falls off. I drive out to the Kelly farm, and whenever the hum of the engine threatens to lull me to sleep, something will misfire and focus my attention on the road. The blue is being leached out of the sky. Birds fly overhead in V formations toward the lowering sun.

At the Kelly farm I park behind the house. I climb through the window and take a look around to see if anybody else has been out here today, but don't see any signs of it. I take a cold shower, the baseball bat always within reach. I've forgotten to bring my bag in from the car, and don't feel like climbing back out the window for it, so I put the same clothes back on and will change in the morning. I go into the basement and stare at all the things I stared at last night, with all the same questions and all the same answers eluding me. The feeling I had earlier that I've missed something is still with me. I'm staring at something right in front of me, but can't see it. I'm sure of it.

Despite what Father Frank said, it's time to bring Drew in on this. Whatever it is I'm missing, he might be able to see it. It will be just like old times, working together again — at least it will be if he doesn't run me out of town. I grab my phone. There's no reception. I think about heading back to the car so I can drive closer to town to get some bars on my phone, then decide it can wait till tomorrow. I'm tired, and maybe I'll see things differently in the morning.

I sit by the window in the lounge, staring out at the sky, and watch the purples darken.

Twenty-eight

"Batter up!"

My first thought is I'm dreaming. I don't know where the voice is coming from, or what it means. That's as far as my thought process goes before something comes crashing through the bedroom window, the sound amplified by the still night. A bright light arcs across the room, and a moment later that arc collides with the wall, flames bursting out of it. Outside somebody is laughing.

I leap to my feet. A piece of glass goes into my heel. Whoever threw the Molotov cocktail is on the other side of the window, and probably not just the one person.

I grab the baseball bat and snatch up my clothes and my shoes and my phone and head for the door, the piece of glass I stood on coming with me. The flames are already spreading across the ceiling. I step into the hallway where I can still hear them roaring. I can choose left or right, and I choose left because one is as good — or bad — as the other. In the next

194

bedroom I drop to my knees and crawl to the window, and I'm in time to see somebody throwing something. I duck as the window above me explodes. Behind me the shelves with books and expired pot plants and the knick-knacks of life go up in flames. I head into the hallway. I pass the basement. I have to get outside. I sit on the floor and lean against the wall and dig at the piece of glass in my foot. It's shaped like a shark's tooth, and the blood makes it slippery and it takes me two attempts to wiggle it free. The pain immediately eases. I tug on my pants and my shoes and check my phone. Still no signal. Smoke is coming into the hallway. I hold my t-shirt over my mouth. I go to the front door just as a Molotov cocktail hits the other side of it. Somebody out there hoots and somebody else hollers and somebody else says, "Another, another!"

Another one crashes somewhere else inside the house. Smoke is filling the hallway faster now. Everything in the house is so old and sunbaked it's going up in flames fast. I reach the kitchen and shut the door behind me. The room is lit up with moonlight. For now it's a safe space. From here I have access to the laundry, and from the laundry there's the back door. Perfect. I turn the handle. The door opens a couple of inches inward but no more. A chain has been placed around the handle and bolted to the frame. I swing at it with the baseball bat but it's useless.

There's a crash from the kitchen as a bottle of fire is thrown through the window. Flames climb the walls. I take a deep breath. Back when I used to swim competitively, I could hold my breath for two minutes underwater. I head into the kitchen. It's blazing. So much for my safe space. I get into the hallway. There's so much smoke I can barely see. The flames sound like rapids in a river. There is popping and grinding from all over the house as things get ready to collapse. I can't hold my breath any longer. Out with the old, and in with the new, but the new is tainted and hot and gets me coughing.

I stay low. I go into another bedroom. This one has been firebombed too, but more recently as the flames haven't grown as much in here yet. I pull my t-shirt on and I drag the blankets off the bed and wrap them around myself and can't see any other alternative than what I'm about to do.

I run at the bed, put my foot up onto it to launch myself, and dive through the broken window, praying I'll land okay, praying I won't get sliced up, praying I won't come to a stop at the feet of whatever asshole or assholes are doing this. The glass hanging into the frame sprays out into the night but doesn't cut me. I'm instantly winded as I land heavily on the porch outside, but I manage to hold on to the bat. I get onto my knees but before I can go anywhere I'm racked by a coughing fit so violent I can't get to my feet. My eyes are watering.

"Over here," somebody yells.

Still coughing, I get up and head toward the shed. I only make it a few paces before I'm tackled. I lose the baseball bat. We roll in the dirt and separate, and I take a swing at the guy and get him square in his face. He drops to his knees. He reaches out and grabs my feet and holds on, but before I can stomp on his hand something big and dark comes out of the night, knocking me down. I throw my fists and elbows into the wild and don't make any contact. Somebody punches me in the jaw and then in the neck and then in the stomach and then somebody kicks me in the kidneys.

"He 'oke 'y 'ose," somebody says, and he's holding his nose and there's blood seeping through his fingers.

"It'll fix," somebody else says, and that somebody else's voice I recognize. It's Stephen. "Who's the bitch now?" he asks. He kicks me hard in the head and the world fades, but not completely. I watch the Kelly house burn.

Two of them flip me over onto my front. They try to drag me back toward the house by my feet and my shoes come off. I try to get away but they jump back on me and go about dragging me again. Dry grass and weeds scrape at my stomach. I claw at it all but nothing slows us down. They get me up to the porch. The heat is singeing the hair on my arms. Any strength I have left has been kicked and punched and coughed away. Two of them get my arms and two of them get my legs and they swing me toward the house, away from the house, toward the house, away, and then they start counting.

"One," somebody says, and they swing me.

"Two," they all say, and they swing me again.

"Three!"

They swing me toward the flames, but they don't let go, not until I'm swinging back the other way. They launch me off the porch onto the ground. I hand heavily on my back, the wind knocked out of me.

Stephen crouches over me. He has a bruise on the side of

his head from where he hit himself earlier with the tire iron. I can't believe Maggie fell in love with this guy. Can't believe that somebody who is capable of doing what he's doing is also capable of love — or even of faking it.

"Throwing you back in there would be too easy," he says. "You're going somewhere you ain't ever gonna be seen again."

Twenty-nine

They'd left their pickup out on the road so it wouldn't wake me, and now they bring it up the driveway. They bind my hands behind me with duct tape and toss me in the back of it. It's the same pickup I waited for this morning when pulling out of the drive, and one of these assholes is the guy who saluted me a good morning. That's how they knew I was out here.

Stephen and some asshole buddy get into the back with me. Broken Nose gets into the cab and Good Morning gets into Father Frank's car. Stephen and his buddy smell like cheap alcohol. Stephen hands out more cans of beer and Broken Nose spins the wheels up and dirt and shingle spray out the back. The guys start yahooing and Stephen spills beer on his shirt and hangs on to the side of the cab and there's a big smile on his face as the pickup fishtails its way down the driveway. This is as close to Disneyland as these guys are ever going to get.

Broken Nose hangs a left onto the highway. He's got one hand on his beer and one on the steering wheel. The yahooing stops and the car behind us falls into line. We head north, toward the hiking trails and Earl's Gas Station and the new sawmill and the old sawmill.

"Where are you taking me?" I ask.

Stephen upends his beer and drinks the whole lot. He crushes the can and throws it at me. It bounces off my forehead. "There's something that feels really good about crushing a can," he says. "Why do you think that is?"

"You don't have to do this," I tell him. "Whatever you're planning on doing, it's a big step up from hitting your wife."

He nods slowly, like he's really taking in my words, like they could actually change whatever it is he's planning. "You know, if you'd kept yourself to yourself, none of this would be happening," he says.

"Let me ask you something," I say. "If Maggie hit you back, would you also have needed your three buddies here to back you up?"

He goes red. He punches me in the face. I've lost count of how many times that's happened since coming back to Acacia. Maybe they should put it on the town sign. *Welcome to Acacia — don't walk into any doors.* The other guy is pointing a rifle at me while still managing to hold on to his beer. The pickup keeps racing along, bouncing every now and then and making me worry this guy is going to accidentally pull the trigger. Father Frank's car is right behind us, the headlights picking out all the details back here. Broken Nose bangs on the roof and Stephen pops open another beer and hands it to him.

"You recognize me, asshole?" the guy with the rifle asks.

"Should I?"

"I've been wanting to use this on you for a long time," he says. "You and me go back some ways," he says. "Hey, Stevie, bang on the roof, would ya?"

Stephen bangs on the roof and we slow down. I don't have any angle to see anything other than trees, but the guy with the gun points it out into the night. Then it's not night anymore, because it's like the sun is coming out. The forest lights up. He takes a shot and the light goes out and the pickup lurches forward and I catch a glimpse of Earl's gas station sign as we race by. At least I'll die knowing who keeps shooting Earl's light out. The guy points the gun back at me.

"Figured it out yet, asshole?"

"You're the blind guy," I tell him.

His name is Anderson Veich. When he was twenty-one years old he had a car accident that left him blind. Doctors thought it was only going to be a temporary thing, but it became permanent. Only it wasn't permanent. Anderson got his sight back within a week, but pretended to be blind for two more years before anybody caught on to him. He'd run his hands over women's faces so he could see who he was talking to, he'd grope and paw at them and they felt sorry enough for him to let him do it. He was getting disability checks every week and getting his meals delivered. Then one day his TV broke and he ordered a new one on the Internet and his neighbor saw it being delivered, and thought to himself, why would Anderson need a new TV, especially when nobody else ever seems to come over? Once the seed was planted the neighbor kept a close eye on him. We arrested him once we found out and he had to pay back all the money. He was lucky he didn't go to jail. The community that helped him after the accident now shunned him. Well, most of the community anyway.

"And who's that guy?" I ask, and I nod toward the car behind us.

Both Stephen and Anderson look to where I'm nodding, and when they do, I push both my feet up into Anderson's chest. The rifle, pointing out into the trees from him turning, goes off and he drops it. He can't do anything to stop the momentum and he goes flying off the back of the pickup. I don't see whether he hits the car behind us or goes under it. Stephen picks up the rifle, right as I'm adjusting my weight to try and kick him off too. Broken Nose slams on the brakes and Stephen falls forward and I miss with my kick. He recovers faster than I do, and as the butt of the rifle comes toward me, I just have time to turn my face. It helps with the impact, but it doesn't help enough. This time, when the world fades out, it doesn't fade back.

Thirty

At least it doesn't fade back right away. I can't move. Can't see. Can't figure out what's going on. My arms are locked in place. My head feels broken. My memories are jumbled. I remember going in to work. Some asshole pulled a gun on me and stole my phone. He pulled the trigger and the gun didn't go off, not in this world anyway, but in an alternate world alternate Noah Harper ended up dead on the barroom floor and the guy who shot him didn't end up in traction. Then there's the phone call, the flight, driving down Main Street and reliving the past. Father Frank. Stephen. The fire.

Shit.

A light comes on as the car door is opened. I'm in Father Frank's car, and the reason I can't move is because my wrists have duct tape wrapped twice, maybe three times, round them and the steering wheel. Stephen is crouching down next to me.

"Hey, Sleeping Beauty's awake," he says. My head hurts so

bad I want to throw up. "Want to see something fun?"

He reaches in and turns on the headlights. All I can see ahead is the front of the car and a whole lot of night. There's nothing in the distance. It's like the car is pointing up at the sky.

"He can't see it," Anderson says. "If he could, he'd be a whole lot more scared."

The car rocks a little as it's pushed forward. The front dips and the angle changes and headlights light up a rock wall a hundred yards away. I'm on the edge of a cliff looking out at an opposite one.

"Where the hell are we?"

"We're out at the quarry," Stephen says.

The quarry. It extends over several miles, each section mined beyond use before another section is opened. My guess is we're in an area long since moved on from. When that happens, groundwater is allowed to seep back into the pit and rain takes care of the rest and over time you have a manmade lake. I can't see it yet, but it'll be down there, the kind of place you sink to the bottom of never to be seen again. Just like Stephen said.

"Sheriff Brooks knows about you," I say to Stephen. "You kill me, he'll come looking for you."

"You're wrong about that," he says. "You left town once, no reason to think you haven't left again."

I shake my head. The movement hurts. "No, you're wrong. He knows you're a wife beater. He knows what happened today. He'll know it's you. He'll see you burned the farm down. He'll figure it all out. You're signing away your freedom, but it's not too late. You let me out of here and we all walk away, no harm, no foul."

"You disrespected me," he says. "You almost killed Anderson, and that's disrespecting him, which is the same as disrespecting me. You broke Cliff's nose, which is disrespecting him, and again that's the same as disrespecting me. And Terry — well, hell, you've disrespected him just by being around him, and that—"

"Each and every one of you are going to go to jail for the rest of your lives," I say. "Drew will figure it out."

"Don't worry about us," he says. "We'll be fine."

"Killing is easy," I tell him, "but walking away from it is hard." I look at Stephen, then beyond Stephen at the others. They're all staring at me. "This is on every one of you. Every. Single. One of you."

Nobody says anything.

"You let me go, and I let this go," I say. "You still have a chance here."

"Do you ever shut up?" Stephen asks.

"The rest of you married? Got children? You're happy to never see them again? You're happy for your kids to grow up in a small town where everybody knows their fathers took down a man four on one, knocked him out and tied him up and murdered him in cold blood? You want your kids knowing none of you had the courage to stop this?"

"That's enough," Stephen says.

"I 'nk 'aybe we 'uld—" Broken Nose says.

"Shut it," Stephen says, turning toward him.

"—talk a'out it some."

"I said shut it."

Broken Nose lowers his voice. "This i'n't what we ag'eed oh."

"Either shut it or get in the car with him."

He doesn't get in the car with me.

"Okay, let's get this done," Anderson says, taking another swig of beer.

Good Morning says nothing. Just watches, a look on his face like all of this is amusing to him.

"You're all drunk," I say. "When you sober up, you'll regret this. All of you."

"That ain't gonna happen," Stephen says. "As the water fills your lungs, I want you to think about the fact that I won. I want you to think about how I'll get away with this, and over the years I'll look back on this moment and smile. Hang on a second," he says, and he steps back, and he kicks the wing mirror hard and it comes off, attached by a cable he then wrenches free. He puts the broken wing mirror onto my lap, the same way I did with him earlier with the mirror from the Nissan. "Take a good long look at yourself when you're going over the edge," he says.

He laughs and slams the door shut and the light goes out. Then all four of them get behind the car and push. The car moves forward. It tips a little more. It grinds out when the front wheels go over and the chassis hits the edge. I look at the mirror, at the cracked casing and the broken glass, seeing two of me looking back. The headlights reaching out over the canyon to the opposite wall slide south as the men push and lift. I wait to see if it's going to be a prank, like throwing me into the fire was, if it's only going to be a one-foot drop, or if it's going to be a hundred, or somewhere in between.

The lights keep moving. They hit where the water meets the wall. It has to be a twenty-foot drop. Maybe twenty-five.

The car tips the rest of the way and the water rushes up at me.

Thirty-one

One moment I'm dropping and the next moment an airbag is stopping my chest cracking open on the steering wheel. The same miracle that allowed Father Frank's car to still work extends to keeping me alive. Maybe all priests' cars are blessed in this way. My wrists are taped to the wheel in a way that means I'm now hugging the airbag that just saved me. I'm not wearing a seatbelt. The momentum of the car kept me in my seat as it went down, and the airbag kept me in my seat when it went off. The front of the car sinks into the water, holds there for a few seconds, then pops back up like a cork. The airbag is already deflating. The windows I was cursing earlier for not winding down I'm now grateful for. It will give me more time, but already some of that time has ticked away. The impact from the fall, the airbag punching me, all that sensory overload has made me pass out for a few seconds.

I pull at the tape but it won't budge. Water is steadily pouring into the car. Already it's up around my ankles. It's warm. The car is sinking at the front. If the lake is deep enough, the weight of the engine is going to flip it. Everything will be upside down and back to front and even if I can get out I won't know which way to swim. I need to get out before that happens.

The headlights are still on, making the water and the inside of the car glow. The water is now up to my calves. The glove compartment has popped open and all of Father Frank's shit has jumped out of it. The flashlight is floating around the bottom of the seat. The water reaches my thighs. The car tilts further forward. The apple from earlier keeps nudging against me. The broken wing mirror is still in my lap. The airbag is hanging limply from the steering wheel and I get my legs on this side of it so it's not in the way. Then I jiggle the mirror closer to my knees. Then I ram it hard up into the bottom of the steering wheel, expanding the crack in the casing. One half of the broken piece of glass stays jammed in there, but the other half comes loose.

I lift it with my knees and stretch down and grab the loose piece of glass with my mouth by the smooth rounded edge. The piece is an inch wide, a couple of inches long, bigger than the piece of glass that got buried in my foot earlier but shaped the same. I get it into my fingers, turn it back on itself, and cut at the tape, ignoring the pressure on my wrists. The mirror picks and pokes at it.

The water splashes around my waist, lifting the airbag.

I keep working the broken mirror. I form a cut in the edge of the tape. It grows. I put more pressure on it and it grows some more. Then it's through and my hand is free. I slice my other hand free, then wrap tape around the piece of glass so I won't cut myself on the edges and jam it into my pocket. I'm going to need it once I get out of here. I pull the handle of the door and the damn thing won't open. It won't even budge. The car has sunk too far and the outside pressure of the water makes opening the door impossible. There are two options now. Find something to break the glass, or wait for the car to fill with enough water to equalize the pressure. I pound the casing of the broken side mirror against the windscreen. Nothing happens.

The water is lapping at the front windscreen. The headlights cut through it, but without any point of reference I can't tell how far I can see. I expect something big to swim past. It's an uphill climb into the backseat. I try the doors back there. It's no good. I lie on my back and pound my bare feet at the side window, ignoring the pain where I got cut earlier. No result. Same goes for every window I kick at. People who don't wear seatbelts fly through these things all the time. People smash them to steal stereos and handbags. Why are they so damn impossible to break when your life depends on it?

Water is halfway up the backseat. The angles are shifting quicker. They shift some more. The water gets up around my chest. I press myself as far into the back of the car as I can. The car reaches the point where it's hanging in the water straight up and down. The water reaches my face. The flashlight hits me in the chin. I grab at it in the hope that it works, and it does.

My face is up against the back windscreen. High above me, I can see the flashlights of men who did this. I suck the last of the air into my lungs, and the car hangs, it hangs . . .

It drops.

It slices smoothly through the water. The headlights wash over something rectangular on the floor of the quarry. With distance hard to gauge through water, I can't tell if it's twenty feet away or fifty. But I get a fairly good look at it just as the Toyota rolls.

It's another car.

Then I'm heading toward it, upside down and sinking fast.

Thirty-two

Stay calm. Stay calm. You have to stay calm.
      I panic.

Five seconds in and my lungs are burning.

Ten seconds in and they want to explode.

Holding your breath inside a sinking car is nothing like holding it in the pool. I'm going to drown and Stephen is going to beat Maggie to death and he's never going to have to answer for it.

Stay calm. You're a swimmer, goddamn it. You used to compete. You used to be good. You once held your breath for three minutes underwater.

True. But that was over twenty years ago.

The car hits the other car. It rests upside down on its roof. I can hear metal grinding against metal. The Toyota slides off, falls and hits the ground on its side, then comes to a stop leaning up against the other car. The water inside is swirling. The shirt that Conrad spat on floats onto my face and sticks there, making everything go dark. I grab hold of it. I can't tell where the door handle is. Nothing is where it should be. When I do find it, I have to tug at it a few times until I get it right. I have to push upwards, like opening the hatch on a submarine. It opens slowly. Because the headlights are still on I have a bearing as to which way is up. I kick myself upwards off the car, pushing harder than I ever did when I swam competitively, and if I'd ever kicked this hard back then I'd have qualified for the Olympics. Problem is I must be a hundred feet down. Nobody can survive that. Not a hundred feet. I kick anyway. I point my arms ahead and use every muscle to drive myself forward. My lungs are bursting. I need air. Need it now. The hundred feet may as well be a thousand. I can't hold on. Can't. Hold. On.

My mouth opens and I breathe in water just as I break the surface. From up above flashlights are still pointing down at me. I hear shouting, and then there's a gunshot, and all I can do is float in the water and cough. A shot hits the water only inches from me. I suck in a breath and kill the flashlight and dive back under the water and focus on coughing only out and not in. The car isn't a hundred feet down like I thought. Of course it's not. I'd never have made it. It's forty feet, maybe, give or take. The headlights are still going strong. I dive toward it as bullets whiz through the water next to me. Something tugs at my side and I've been hit but there's no pain. I tuck the flashlight into the band of my pants and the t-shirt I grabbed into my pocket and swim.

I swim as long as I can and when I come up for air the men are no longer shooting at me, but I can see them scanning the surface looking. I take another breath and swim slowly toward the rock wall, making little in the way of splashing. When I reach the wall I hug it for a few moments and try to get my breathing under control. I pat the side of my body where the bullet hit. There's no pain. I find a hole in my shirt, but no hole in my body. I can hear the men up there but I can't hear what they're saying. It's only a matter of time before they make their way down here. I need to find the road the quarriers used to get in and out of this pit.

I make my way along the wall. There are footholds and straight edges and chunks of rock to stand on but nothing I can scale. The water is still rippling from my swimming, breaking up the reflection of the moon into white slices. I can see the flashlights moving across the top of the pit to the north. The path has to be that way.

I cut long strides through the water. Muscle memory kicks in and my body feels good. It's like I'm fifteen again. It feels that way for all of ten seconds and then my chest burns and I can't get my breathing under control. It's a race to the finish line, only I don't know where it is. I keep the road above my left shoulder. I draw in ragged breaths and exhale into the water, arms lifting, legs propelling, and up ahead the pit starts to curve to the right. I stop swimming. I float in the water, and now I can see the road, further around the curve, coming right out of the water and up to salvation. I can swim a straight line for it, whereas the men above me still have to take the curve. What's even better is it goes in the same direction I'm swimming. That means once I hit the road I get to run away from where the others are coming.

Which is what I do thirty seconds later. I get out of the water and my feet hit the ground hard and they hurt, stones digging into them, cutting and bruising and keeping me from running as fast as I'd like as I make the ascent.

Two more gunshots. Two more misses. I cling to the fact these men have all been drinking. Their aim is off, and hopefully the beer will keep them from running as fast as they'd like. Then I'm at the top with barely twenty yards on them. I cut across the road and into the trees where there are no longer stones underfoot, but roots and pine cones instead. It's cooler by a few degrees. My eyes had adjusted to the quarry light, but that's different from forest light, and I don't see branches until they're right in front of me. I take big strides and keep my feet kicking high so as not to trip on anything. The guys behind me get to use their flashlights and at this rate it's only a matter of time before they catch me. But then my eyes adjust. I'm able to run faster, but I can't keep running. I'm gulping down oxygen and there's a sharp pain in the side of my abs and my feet can't continue to take the punishment, and nor can my lungs, and running isn't going to help me, not when they're closing the distance.

I take the piece of broken mirror out of my pocket as I run. I peel away the duct tape and wrap it around the smooth edge of the glass to make more of a handle.

The next big tree I see I turn in and hide behind it.
They're only five seconds behind me.
I wait.
I listen.
Three seconds.
Two.
I swing out into view and thrust the piece of glass forward.

Thirty-three

I don't hang around to see who I've hit or what damage I've done. All I know is that I've buried the glass deep in somebody's neck. Somebody fires a shot and there's the thud of a bullet hitting a tree next to me. Splinters hit my face. I'm running again. Lungs screaming and feet screaming and my body leaking energy fast.

They don't come after me. They will, but not right now. Right now they're checking on the condition of their buddy. Right now they're determining if there's anything they can do for him, and they're weighing that up against whatever story they have to tell the police. Could be they get him back to the pickup and race him into town. Could be they leave him to bleed out and they'll throw him into the quarry next to the two cars already down there.

I run for another thirty seconds, bearing left to take me further from the pit. Getting lost in these woods is even easier at night. For the first time I realize I'm shivering. For the first time I realize it's not only these assholes out here that I'm battling, but Mother Nature and biology. At this time of the year hypothermia would take three months to catch. Still, getting colder is going to slow me down. The quarry is a few miles from the old sawmill, and on the same road. I just don't know what direction that road is.

I stop running.

I rest behind a tree and catch my breath. My phone is still in my pocket. I get it out and hit the button and it doesn't turn on. It's dead. With everything I went through the other night to get it back, it annoys me that these assholes have broken it. It probably wouldn't have been any good anyway, unless the reception out here has improved in the years I've been gone. I pull off my t-shirt, wrap it around my foot and tie it off, and do the same with my other foot with the t-shirt I grabbed from the car.

I hear them coming for me. They're more cautious now. The pickup starts up and moves along the edge of the pit. There are flashlights in the trees behind me. They've been trailing me pretty well, helped, I imagine, by the footprints and broken twigs everywhere. I reach around for something I can throw and my hand settles on a rock that fits nicely in my hand. I hurl it into the trees toward the road in the hope it will send my followers in that direction, only it ends up hitting a tree about two feet away from me and bouncing back.

Goddamn it.

The lights come toward me. There's a gunshot and I run. My makeshift shoes aren't comfortable, but better than a forest floor. They won't last long, but I'm able to open up some distance. I hide behind another tree and hurl a heavy pine cone deeper into the forest, and then send a second one right after it. I hold my breath and watch two beams of light approach, then two men go jogging toward the road in the direction I threw the pine cones. I can see their flashlights between the trees.

Slowly I circle back in the direction I came. I can see much better now. The moonlight is bright enough that I can see broken fronds and bent branches and that means the others are soon going to figure out they're *not* seeing broken fronds and bent branches . . . or maybe they won't. Maybe they don't even know what to look for. I've been involved in search and rescue efforts and all these guys have ever been involved in is getting drunk and shooting out gas station lights.

And attempted murder.

Perhaps murder too. I need to get a better look at the other car that was underwater.

I find the man I stabbed, propped up against a tree. It's Anderson. He's pulled out the piece of glass, a mistake that's led to him bleeding out quicker. Blood is smeared all over his neck where he's tried holding it in. I check for a pulse. There's nothing. I don't feel good about killing him. But I don't feel bad either. He's the first person I've ever killed. I'll think on this later, no doubt, but right now I take his shoes and put them on. They're the right size for me.

I can run faster now that my feet aren't getting torn up. I get to the road. I follow it. I run past the road ramping down into the pit. A little while later I find a scattering of beer cans. This is where I got pushed into the lake. The road makes a ninety-degree turn to the right here, toward more pits and the exit. This could be one in a line of half a dozen pits or more.

I think about the advice I would give anybody who got lost in the woods. *Stay where you are*. People who get lost often start circling back by accident. They think they can walk in straight lines when they're lost but they can't. It's impossible to do unless you have training or a fixed location you can keep looking at. Best thing I can do is find somewhere off the track and wait until daylight, then in the morning follow the sound of machinery.

That's the plan.

A good, solid plan.

The plan changes when the pickup comes toward me.

Thirty-four

I scavenge through the forest floor for a good-sized branch. Something that's going to feel like the baseball bat I had earlier. Some are too heavy to work with. Some are way too short. The Goldilocks moment comes soon enough, a piece that's five feet long with a nice beefy end to it.

I stay hidden, ten yards in from the edge of the road. Out to the left flashlights are flickering between the trees, coming back in my direction. Also to my left the pickup has turned around and is doing five miles an hour in my direction. It will get here before the two men on foot.

I hold the branch like a javelin, only I keep both hands on it. I start weaving through the trees between me and the road as the pickup gets closer. I build up pace, and hit the road just as the pickup crosses right in front of me.

"Hey!"

Good Morning is behind the wheel. He has a look on his face of absolute horror. I push the branch through the open

221

window. I don't see where it hits him, but I feel the impact. Because he's already pulled the steering wheel, his fate is sealed, and either he's too dazed to scream or I just don't hear him over the revving engine as the pickup goes over the side of the road and into the lake. I figure if I can survive, then he can survive too, so good luck to him.

The rifle opens up again but I'm already back in the trees. They don't follow me in. They're cautious now. They come to a stop where the pickup went over the edge. Ten minutes ago there were four of them and they were drinking and hollering and watching me sink. Now half of them are dead. Stephen and Broken Nose stand out on the road, only ten feet from me. They don't know what to do. I'm surprised they can't sense me watching. Stephen pulls out a cellphone.

"A'e sig'al?" Broken Nose asks. He's the one with the rifle.

"Nothing," Stephen says, and he shifts the phone around and points it into the sky as if it'll make a difference, but it doesn't. "Goddamn useless phone."

It's disturbing there are people he could call who would help. Signals can come and go out here, and if he gets that phone to connect then I'm not getting out of here alive.

I run at them then, a heavy pine cone in each hand. I throw the first one at the guy with the gun as he's turning it toward me, and it misses him, so I throw the second one, and that one misses too, and he fires a shot at me that, like my pine cones, also misses, and on a different occasion maybe we'd all sit down and laugh at that. I get inside the angle of the gun and I know Stephen is taking a swing at me and I brace myself to take it, because right now Stephen isn't my biggest problem. Broken Nose is. I drive the palm of my hand up into his nose and the gun goes off, and at the same time Stephen's fist hits me in the jaw and makes my teeth rattle and my ears ring. I let Stephen's second punch come in, but there's no strength behind it. I send a second punch at Broken Nose who's still reeling from the first, and this one also gets him in the nose, and the way I'm moving, the way my arms are swinging, it's like I'm back swimming through the lake. I jump on Broken Nose and ride him to the ground. I grab his head in both hands and pound it down hard and it's enough to stop him from moving. Stephen kicks at me as I'm rolling off, but again there's no strength in it. I'm up on my feet and now it's one on one.

One on one with a guy who's been drinking.

One on one with a guy who only hits women, or who hits men when he has the support of his friends.

Also one on one with a guy who's been shot. He's holding the side of his abdomen where his shirt is dark.

The rifle is on the ground, halfway between us. He takes a step toward it, but his leg gives out, and he staggers toward the edge of the cliff, sees where he's going, and lets his legs collapse under him rather than tipping over. He lands on his ass, one leg tucked under him, the other out straight, both hands hanging on to the wound. He's a foot from the edge. He turns to face me.

"Why couldn't you have let everything alone?" he asks. He sounds angry and upset and it's hard to tell which he feels more.

"Who owns the other car?"

"What car?"

"The other one you and your asshole friends tipped into the lake."

"They're not assholes," he says. He's puffing. He doesn't look good at all. "My friends, they're good people. Really good people, and you've killed all of them."

"Good people don't tie other people to a car and tip them into quarries."

"They do when that person is you."

"They made their choices," I say. "Who's in the other car?"

"What other car? What the hell are you talking about?"

"Like I said, the one you and your asshole friends tipped into the lake."

"There is no other car."

"Don't lie to me," I tell him. "We've come too far for you to lie to me."

"I have no idea what you're talking about," he says.

"There's another car in the lake."

"Terry's pickup. You made it go in there."

"Not that one," I say. "Another one. It's been down there longer."

He looks confused. He didn't put the car down there.

"You the one who put the chain in the basement?"

"What basement? What chain?" he asks. His words are slowing down. He lifts his hand and looks at the blood on it then presses it back on the wound.

"You really don't know?"

"Don't know what?"

I watch him closely. He truly has no idea what I'm talking about. Blood continues to seep through his fingers. I'm watching a man die who is not only Maggie's husband, but also the father of her children. No matter what the circumstances, she will never forgive me for not trying to help him.

"Take your shirt off," I tell him. "We can press it against the wound and use your belt to apply more pressure."

"You killed my friends," he says.

"You got them killed, not me. You're a bad friend and they're dead because of you. Come on, give me your shirt."

He shakes his head. "It's because of you," he says.

"Don't give me that shit," I tell him. "This started with you, and I gave you a chance to walk away from it. If we can slow the bleeding I can try and get help."

"I can't go to jail," he says.

"You'll be going there for the rest of your life," I tell him.

"I really do love her," he says, and then he has to catch his breath before carrying on. "She can be a real bitch, and she drives me crazy at how stupid she can be, but I really do love her."

"No, you don't," I say. "Whatever you feel for her isn't love."

Tears roll down his face. He holds up a hand and takes another look at the blood. "I thought it would hurt more," he says. "Truth is I can hardly feel it." His words are slowing even more. His features are drooping. "Mostly I . . . I just feel tired."

I don't say anything.

"We should have thrown you back into the fire," he says.

"You should have."

"Or shot you in the head before tipping you in the lake."

"You should have done that too."

He laughs, there's no humor in it, and then it turns into a cough. "Maybe next time, huh?"

"Maybe."

"Do you think my—" he says, but he doesn't finish. A shudder rolls through his body. He's still sitting there in front of me, but he's gone. His body goes slack and his hands fall away, and then he tilts backward. I watch it happen in slow motion. His head and his shoulders and his upper back hang out into space over the edge, and then he does what the car I was in did earlier, there's a tipping point, and then he's gone.

Thirty-five

I move to the edge of the cliff. I can see the pickup down there, or at least the light from the headlights. The headlights of Father Frank's car are also still going. I sweep the flashlight across the surface and spot Stephen floating face down. I can't see anybody else. I take it all in, the water ahead, behind me the turn in the road, the men who brought me here choosing this point to tip me over the edge because it was the easiest, rather than drive further around.

I walk over to Broken Nose. I look at him, and I think, what kind of person is he? He's wearing a wedding ring. So he has a wife, or a husband, and maybe he has kids, and maybe he has parents, and maybe he goes to church every weekend and plays poker on Friday nights and takes his daughter to the park on Saturday mornings. Maybe he watches her play soccer, or they throw a Frisbee, and maybe he buys her ice cream on the way home or they'll catch a movie in the afternoon.

I drag him to the edge of the cliff.

Maybe he stays late after work and helps his buddies out and maybe Monday night is date night with his wife and his dad's in hospital getting a hip operation and his mom needs new glasses so he goes around there when he can to mow their lawns and get their groceries and they'll babysit his kids and they'll have big Thanksgiving dinners together and Christmas dinners together and at Halloween they'll all dress up as ghosts. Could be he has a dog, or a cat. Could be he reads his son stories at night and makes his kids smile and makes his wife smile and makes a whole lot of people smile.

I crouch next to him, and take his wallet out of his pocket. Cliff Clarkson. Thirty-six. Organ donor. I can't think of anybody who'd want his organs, not if they knew that aside from being a nice guy with a nice family who does nice things, he was also a cold-blooded killer — or at least he was trying to be. I can drag him back from the edge and tie him up, and he can do his time in jail, and one day the courts will decide he's paid his debt, and he'll repent and people will forgive him and he'll try to be better. He'll get new friends, and maybe one day those friends will be pissed off at somebody, somebody who cut them off in traffic, or looked at one of their wives funny, or bumped into them in a bar and made them spill their beer. And maybe they'll get a posse together and Cliff here will get his gun and this time he might hit what he's aiming at.

So maybe this guy has a wife and he beats her too. Maybe he goes to church every weekend and steals money from the collection plate and on Friday nights he cheats at poker.

Maybe he doesn't stay after work on Mondays to help his buddies, but meets somebody he's having an affair with, and maybe date night is rape night. Could be he stomps on his cat or his dog. Could be he reads his kids scary stories because he likes to hear them cry and he hits his daughter if she talks during the movie.

I look at the bullet hole in my t-shirt. I picture the next guy he's shooting at. Somebody whose wife wakes up every day alone because her husband is in the ground. Somebody whose kids cry at night, asking where their dad is, because they're too young to get it. I picture a family in crisis.

The same kind of crisis this guy's family will be in if I push him off the cliff.

But, all things considered, whose family am I better off looking out for?

The answer is simple.

I use my foot to roll Cliff off the edge. I figure his name alone means he was destined for this. He doesn't make a sound until he hits the water.

Thirty-six

My hands are shaking. Adrenaline is coursing through my body. I take the cash out of Cliff's wallet before throwing it into the water after him, a small slap as it breaks the surface. There are no lights showing beneath the water now. I unload the rifle and send it and the bullets the way of Cliff, and I send the empty beer cans in after them. I head to the road that leads into the pit. There's nothing to indicate Good Morning made it out. No wet footprints anywhere. He'll still be in the cab. I go through the trees and find Anderson. I pat him down and find his cellphone. I take it, along with the t-shirts I used as shoes earlier. I add his cash to Cliff's cash, and then slip it into my wallet, which, surprisingly, is still in my back pocket. I wring the t-shirts out as much as I can and put one of them on. Anderson's phone has GPS, and a minute later I have a signal and a way out of here. I take a screenshot of the coordinates of where I'm at. The lake is three miles from the highway. I leave Anderson where he is.

I have a lot going through my head as I make the walk. I think about what just happened, and what it means for me. Jail, I guess. I'll need a good lawyer, and I don't reckon Maggie will be putting her hand up to volunteer. In fact, she'd probably be asking to prosecute me. I think about Father Frank, and him telling me he would try to square the bad things away with God. I wonder if any of that squaring will cover what just happened. I walk at a good pace, jogging when I can, trying to keep my body temperature up. Away from the water it feels warmer. I take the wet t-shirt off and carry it. It's a little after four o'clock when I reach the highway. I go left. I walk an hour before passing the turnoff to the sawmill, and I don't see a single car. It's another fifteen minutes to the new sawmill. I realize I still haven't seen it yet. Fifteen minutes after that I reach Earl's Gas Station. He's already replaced the lights that got shot out, and it's all lit up like an alien spacecraft about to land. Earl is sitting inside the shop drinking coffee, a flat-screen TV up on the wall behind him playing an infomercial for a piece of gym equipment promising the best results for the least amount of work. Earl is wearing overalls with grease and oil stained into them, the kind that look out of place if they aren't dirty, the kind of overalls that look like they come right out of the packet looking used. His name is stitched carefully above the pocket on his chest. There's a red oily rag hanging out the pocket by his hip. If you chose a great American artist to depict the great American small-town mechanic and gas pumper, they'd draw this guy. His hair is completely white, but the horseshoe mustache hiding his lips is stained nicotine yellow.

"Well, I'll be," he says, when I walk inside, and he doesn't elaborate on that. He puts his hand out and I shake it. "Deputy Harper," he says.

"No longer a deputy," I tell him. I can smell cigarette smoke on his clothes, on his skin, and I figure psychics could see it in his aura.

"Well, no shit," he says. "I guessed I'd be seeing you on account of seeing you drive by a few days back, but not at this time in the morning, and certainly not looking like this," he says, looking me up and down. "They don't wear shirts where you live?"

"You got one I can borrow?"

"I got one you can buy," he says. "Real cheap too."

"People buy shirts here?"

"No," he says. "That's why they're cheap."

He walks around the counter. He has a slight limp, and when he sees me notice, he says, "It's arthritis. Can I give you some advice, son?"

"Is the advice don't get old?"

"You heard that one already, huh?"

"It's one of the last things Father Frank said to me."

"Poor Frank," he says. "What kind of world is it where shitty things happen to good people?"

"The only one we have," I say.

I follow him to the back of the store. A magazine rack against one wall displays flashy covers with cars. There are bags of chips and bags of peanuts but nothing beyond that in the food department. There are automotive supplies, batteries, oils, fluids and belts and bulbs, and then there's the t-shirts, folded up on a bottom shelf almost out of sight. He picks one out and shakes it and holds it up and seems satisfied it's the right size. It has *Acacia Pines* written across the front, the words spelled out in tree trunks, a forest of green behind them. "Tourists sometimes buy them," he says, handing it to me. I pull it on. It fits. "It's five bucks," he says, as he makes his way back to the counter. "Don't suppose you're back in town trying to figure out who keeps shooting out my lights?"

There's something reassuring about talking to Earl. Nuclear war could break out and this guy would still be here day after day pumping gas for the survivors.

"Actually, I may have taken care of that problem for you."

"Just now?"

"Just now."

He strokes his mustache, thinking on what I've just said. "Is that so?"

"Yes."

"That why you look like shit?"

"People keep telling me that."

"People are right to."

"So you always open at this time of night?"

"I do when people shoot my lights out and I can't get back to sleep after fixing them. What can I do you for other than the t-shirt?"

"Don't suppose you sell shoes too?"

"Doesn't look like you need them."

"I don't like these ones," I say.

"They don't fit?"

"They fit," I say, "they just don't feel right."

"Can't help you with the shoes. Can help you with gas, though."

"Gas is good," I say, "but I'm going to need more than that."

"Yeah? What kind of more?"

"I need to borrow a car."

"A car? You don't have one?"

"It died," I tell him.

"Want me to take a look at it?"

"I doubt there's much you can do for it."

"I wouldn't be so sure," he says.

"I would. Please, it's important."

"You really think you put a stop to my lights getting shot out?"

"Yes," I say, which may or may not be true. The lights are so offensively bright anybody driving by would want to take a shot at them.

He reaches under the register and comes up with a set of keys. "There's an old Ford out the back. She needs new tires, and I've been meaning to give her a bit of a tune-up, but she'll get you where you need to go, especially if that going ain't too far."

"I'll get it back to you."

"I suppose you want me to start a tab for you? Starting with the t-shirt?"

I hand him five dollars. The good ol' boys out in the quarry can pay for it.

"So tell me, what are you doing back in our neck of the woods?"

"I'm here looking for Father Frank's daughter, Alyssa."

"Didn't know she was missing."

"Let me ask you something," I say. "That thing about you having the best memory in town, is that true?"

"I don't know. Can't tell you what other folks can and can't remember."

"You notice anything not right these days?"

"Not right how?"

"Just, you know, not right."

He shakes his head. "Can't rightly say I've noticed anything like that at all."

"What about folks going missing?"

"Like Alyssa?"

"Yeah, like Alyssa."

He gives it some thought. Shakes his head. "No, nothing like that either. But why don't you ask me a different question?"

The way he says that tells me he knows something. "What kind of question?"

"Why don't you ask me if I noticed if anything was off when Alyssa went missing twelve years back?"

A shiver runs down my spine. "Did you notice anything was off back then?"

"Yep. Even told Sheriff Haggerty about it."

"Tell me."

"Twelve years is a long time," he says, "but this I remember like it just happened. Because it's the night you found the girl."

My heart starts to race and the shiver spreads out across the rest of my body. Whatever it is he's about to tell me, I know it's going to be important. Just know it.

"I remember you speeding past here like the Devil himself was chasing you," he says. "I remember you making your way back much later, some time before dawn. I don't sleep much these days, never have. My parents used to tell me I was stubborn that way, that I'd lay awake all night without sleeping a wink. They said my staying awake would put them early into their graves, but they're still alive," he says, which must mean his parents have to be in their hundreds. "I saw you leave town and I never saw you come back and I've always known those things were all related."

"You know everything that happened that night?" I ask.

"I heard the rumors," he says. "The day after, Sheriff Haggerty came by to ask if I'd seen a couple of guys coming into town, you know, on account of the fact my lights light up the entire highway out here. He came by hoping I'd seen something, or better yet, that some strangers had dropped in for gas, on account of mine being the last station for a hundred miles."

Not only is Earl's the last station for a hundred miles, he's gotten a lot of business from folks who misjudge exactly how far away from anywhere they are and run out of gas. A big part of Earl's income comes from towing these people in when something has gone wrong with their car, or heading out to them with enough gas to get them on their way. He'll also get plenty of callouts to help folks coming off the hiking trails whose car batteries have died while they were gone.

"And?"

"And people I don't know get gas all the time on their way into town. So there ain't nothing unusual about serving people I've never seen before. The thing is, there were a couple of guys back then, a couple of fellas who rocked into town and then rocked back out that same night. See, that's what made it different. Others come, they stay a bit. They're going camping or visiting friends or family or coming here for a wedding or whatever. These guys, these guys weren't like that. Nobody comes to town just to turn around and head back out, not unless their car is full of camping or hiking equipment and they're driving in for supplies or to file a plan, and these guys didn't have camping supplies and they sure as hell weren't dressed as hikers. They came by and got gas on their way in, can't be much more than twenty minutes after I saw you speed by to save that girl. One stood outside pumping gas and the other one made small talk with me inside while he paid."

"So what happened?"

"Nothing happened. He paid and they got into their car, but then an hour later I saw them heading back the way they came. Like I say, that doesn't happen here. No need to, unless you've driven all this way and realized you've forgotten something. But that's not the weird bit."

"No?"

"No, that's coming up. See, when Sheriff Haggerty came around asking me those questions, I told him all that. Gave him descriptions of the car, of the two men, and he took it all down. A couple of weeks later when I saw him again, I asked him about it. He told me he checked it out, but it didn't lead anywhere. He thanked me for being diligent, and that was it."

"Don't suppose you remember their license plate?"

"Is that a joke?"

"Not really."

"My memory is good, but it ain't that good."

I think about everything he's told me. I try to think about what any of it means.

"You see Alyssa leave town this time?"

"No," he says. "But she could have left when I was asleep, or when I was out in the workshop with my head under a car fixing this or fixing that. You think what happened back then has something to do with where she is now?"

"It's possible," I tell him.

"Anyway, like I said, I haven't gotten to the weird part."

"No?"

"No. These two men from twelve years ago, I see them from time to time. They ain't stopped off for gas since then, but they sure drive by once or twice every year. Want to ask me when the last time was I saw them?"

"When was the last time you saw them?"

"Well, they were here about a month ago. Again, they couldn't have stayed in town for much more than a half-hour or so. The second to last time was last week," he says, and he watches as I draw a conclusion from that, and then, to be sure, he tells me what I've already figured out. "How long you think

Alyssa's been missing this time?"

"She was reported missing on Thursday."

"Well now, ain't that a coincidence? Those two fellers, they came through here Wednesday night."

"Jesus," I say.

"I still haven't answered your question," he says.

"Which one?"

"About the last time I saw them."

"Last week wasn't the last time?"

He looks at his watch. "They came by four hours ago. I was working on the lights when they drove by, and was still working on them when they came back. Musta been all of twenty minutes. Thing is, as you know ten minutes only gets you halfway there."

Ten minutes. It doesn't get you into town.

But it does get you to the Kelly farm.

Thirty-seven

It's a tradition of Earl's to always have cars he's finished repairing facing the road, even when they're in the shop. People can come in and drive right out the door and onto the highway. Cars still needing work always face away from the road. Earl always jokes that way the cars don't get jealous of other cars they see go by.

The pickup is facing the shop. That means there are things on it that still need work. It's an old faded red Ford, so old that Cain could have fled Eden in it, with scratches and dents reading like Morse code. Earl wasn't kidding about it needing new tires — they're so badly frayed they look like they've been stuffed with straw. I sit in it with the engine warming up and the window down thinking I'd be happy to never see another pickup again.

"You need anything else?"

I want to tell him I need a different car. "Two things," I say.

"Shoot."

"Call me if you see them again."

He nods. "And the second?"

"Don't tell anybody I was here," I say, "and when I say anybody, I really mean anybody. This conversation, it didn't happen, okay?"

"You sure you've taken care of my light problem for me?"

"You've got nothing to worry about."

"Then nor do you, Deputy," he says, even though he knows I'm no longer a deputy. Still, I can't deny it sounds good. "Good luck with whatever it is you're doing." He pats the pickup on the roof. "And try to bring her back in one piece."

I give him my number and he doesn't need to write it down.

I back out onto the highway. First gear grinds and then slips into place, but not as loudly as second gear, third and fourth. The purple that leaked out of the sky last night before it turned black is leaking its way back in. The night is deathly still. The pickup's suspension is stiff and every little bump is magnified.

I get the car up to pace, and a little over ten minutes later I turn off at the Kelly farm. Out here, where neighbors are miles apart, it's no surprise nobody called the fire department. It would have lit up the sky, but nobody would have been looking, and nobody was close enough to hear. I find my shoes where they'd slipped off my feet earlier. I carry them around the building, thinking it's a miracle the fields themselves didn't catch fire, but the weeds are so thick and nasty they're probably fireproof. The shell of the house is still

241

standing, it's black and smoking and there's still heat coming off it. The kitchen table is fairly unscathed, and one end of a couch has turned to ash and the other is perfectly intact. Some walls have gone, part of the roof has collapsed. It's hard to tell which room is which. The basement is buried under the rubble of burned wood and roof tiles. With the house hidden behind the oak trees from the road, it could go unnoticed for a while. The shed has survived, the hay bales and the car and the tractors no worse for wear.

There's an old wooden swing hanging in the oak trees. I apply some weight and it creaks but doesn't break. I sit on it and hold the ropes and stare at the house. Yesterday morning I thought the house looked like it was begging to be put down. If so, it got its wish. I'm exhausted. If I closed my eyes I might not be able to open them for a week. I take off the dead man's shoes and am almost too frightened to look at my feet. They're bruised and torn up and the cut I got earlier in the evening is bigger for all the pounding it's taken. My pants are still damp. I strip down and limp over closer to the house where it's still warm and lay them on the ground to dry off. I keep the Acacia Pines t-shirt on. I grab a blanket from the back of the pickup and carry it into the shed, throwing the t-shirts I'd used as shoes into the burned-out building, along with the dead man's shoes, on the way. They start to smoke.

I pull apart one of the old hay bales in the shed and kick it around, making a sort of mattress to put the blanket over. I lie on half of the blanket and wrap the other half over me. Red is being added to the purple sky and it's beautiful. The paddocks stretch out miles, but beyond them The Pines is pushing back, blurring the boundaries between the farm and the forest. The top of the trees catch the early morning light and look like they're on fire. Before we were married, I'd go camping with Maggie out in those forests. We'd scale one of the many peaks and we'd watch the sun set and the following morning we'd watch it rise. We used to go a lot back then. I wonder if she ever went with Stephen.

This is where the two men came that Earl saw earlier. It's where they've come every other time. Twelve years ago they didn't turn around and leave town because they forgot something, they came here for Alyssa, only Alyssa was gone. I'd found her before they got here. Over the years they've come here to get others. But who are they picking up? And who are they picking them up *from*?

The sun breaks through and hits my face. It makes my eyes water. I roll away from the sun and take out my broken cellphone and the cellphone I took from Anderson and I switch my SIM card over. The phone is over half charged. I set the alarm to give myself four hours of sleep.

Twelve years ago if I hadn't beaten a location out of Conrad Haggerty, the two men who came here would have gotten here first. It may have been wrong, what I did, and I may have beaten the wrong guy, but that beating saved Alyssa. Then last night those two men came here looking for me. They knew I was at the Kelly farm. If Good Morning knew where I was, then others know too. They came and saw the fire and turned around and left. They have no reason to come back, at least not this morning. I prop my head on my elbow and, with the sun hitting my back, I close my eyes. I fall asleep knowing Stephen and his friends coming to get me last night may very well have saved my life.

Thirty-eight

After four hours of solid sleep, I wake up wondering what I could have done different. Last night, all fired up on adrenaline and a sense of justice, any sense of guilt at killing four men wasn't even on the horizon. Now I can see each of their faces in their moments of death, I can see their pain, their regret at leaving a world in which there are still things they wanted to accomplish. I took that from them. I took their lives. I ended them. I changed the path of those who loved them. It's like the world has shifted off its axis — yesterday I was trying to help convince a girl to come back home, today I'm a killer. And others . . . the world has shifted for them too, for Maggie, for her children, and they don't even know it.

I have to tell Drew.

Drew might forgive me, but Maggie won't.

If I had listened to Maggie, none of last night would have happened.

I get to my feet, feeling unsteady. The sun is no longer

coming into the shed. I try to identify any part of my body that doesn't hurt, and come up with nothing. Ligaments stretch and muscles twitch when I step outside. The sun beats on my body. My pants and underwear are so dry they feel brittle. The t-shirts and shoes I threw into the house last night have turned to ash, and my own shoes hurt when I pull them on. I start the pickup. There's a thin layer of ash on the windscreen. The window wipers clear two arcs through it.

It's ten-thirty when I get into town. It's going to be a long day, most of it spent at the police station talking to Drew, maybe some at the quarry where I show him how it all played out, maybe some behind bars. Best not to be doing all that on an empty stomach. I go to the same diner I ate at yesterday, and I order the same breakfast from the same waitress and get the same coffee too. The diner only has a handful of people in it. The waitress does the bare minimum to acknowledge my existence, almost jumping back the moment she's taken my order, perhaps scared whatever got me looking this way is contagious.

I use the bathroom to clean up. The blood and dirt mostly got washed away from my swim, and my pants got a bit of a clean too, but there are spots of blood on my new t-shirt from where I got scratched up running through the trees, and there are pine needles in my hair and my face still hasn't healed from the kicking I took two days ago and the bruises from last night have added to the old ones. I wash my face and tidy my hair and it's not a big thing but I feel better for it. I can feel my foot bleeding. I wad up tissue paper and stuff it under the cut, so the shoe feels lumpy when I walk on it.

My breakfast is ready when I get back. When I go to eat, I find I can't. I have no appetite. I swirl things around on my plate and take a few bites but nothing more. I drink the coffee, and it provides a sense of calm that won't last long. I leave a fifty percent tip to convince the waitress not to leave her job. I drive to the police station and park up across the road in the shade. I head inside and the air conditioning is still messed up, the only progress being there are now four people working on it instead of two.

I walk into Drew's office and he does a double take. I slump down in the chair opposite him. He looks genuinely concerned. "What in the hell happened?"

I go to answer him, and end up saying nothing. Will Drew see my actions as self-defense? Or will he and his colleagues head out there and weigh up all the angles and conclude not only did I bring this on myself, but it's what I wanted? Even if Drew does believe me, Old Man Haggerty won't. I don't know how much influence he really has, but he'll certainly try throwing his weight around. He'll say I was trying to do the same shit I did twelve years ago with his son, only worse. There'll be a trial. My fate will hang in the balance against twelve people who weren't running for their lives.

Maggie will never talk to me again. I could be behind bars for twenty years because four assholes figured they'd get a hoot by killing me. How does me going to jail benefit society?

I can't tell Drew. Which means I also can't tell him about the car I found in the quarry last night.

"Hey, Noah, you fall asleep?"

"I'm sorry," I say. "I zoned out. You have any luck convincing Alyssa to come back?"

"Back up a moment," he says. "Tell me what happened."

"I walked into a door," I say.

"Jesus, Noah, what happened?"

"Nothing worth talking about."

He throws his hands into the air. "Fine," he says.

"Is Alyssa coming back?"

"She says she's considering it."

"I'm gonna need her phone number again," I say. "My phone died and I lost it."

He looks at something on his computer and then writes it down for me. "You want mine too?"

"Yeah. Maggie's also," I tell him.

"Wasn't Maggie who did that to you?" he asks. "That why you don't want to tell me about it?"

"No."

"Stephen?"

"It wasn't Stephen," I say. "You gonna talk to him?"

"When he gets back. I spoke to Maggie. She said him and some buddies are hunting and they'll be a few days at least. My advice to you is to stay away from him while you're here. Best-case scenario is he stays out there shooting at trees and getting drunk until after you've gone. Wasn't Old Man Haggerty, was it?"

"No. Why haven't you done more to help Maggie?"

He looks like I've just hit him.

"I'm sorry," I say.

"She's refused our help," he says. He leans forward. "Damn it, Noah, I'm keeping an eye on that situation as best as I can, but without her wanting to press charges or make any kind of statement, my hands are tied. You know what that's like. I don't know if he hits her or the kids or if the black eyes and broken bones really are accidents." He leans back. "Like I said, I'll have a word to him. Thinking and knowing are two different things, Noah. Isn't that why you're still in town? To prove that?"

"Needs to be more than just having a word with him," I say. "You need to throw his ass in jail."

"Let's hope it works out that way." He writes down the phone numbers on a piece of paper and slides it over the desk for me. "What will it take for you to tell me what happened?"

"I will soon, I promise."

"This have anything to do with what you were asking yesterday?"

"I'll tell you everything soon."

"If Old Man Haggerty were still in charge, he'd arrest you, you know that, right? I should arrest you for your own good before you get yourself killed."

"I'm fine. Trust me, I'm fine."

"For now," he says.

I shrug. I don't say anything.

"Fine," he says. "It's your funeral. And, speaking of funerals, Father Frank's is on Thursday. If you're still alive then, you'll come to it?"

"You think Stephen and his buddies will be back by then?"

"I don't know. My guess is they'll be out there till the weekend. If you're lucky maybe they'll get lost out there. They wouldn't be the first."

"I'll be there."

As I walk out, the four guys working on the air conditioning are swearing. They sound like a barbershop quartet all out of time. When I get back to the car I put the numbers into my new phone and I think about calling Maggie, but don't. I can't tell her what happened, and I can't lie to her. She thinks her husband is out hunting, which I guess he was, and it's only a matter of time before people start to question when they're coming back, and that's when Drew will think on all my cuts and bruises and figure those two things are related. By then I want to be long gone. I call Alyssa and she doesn't answer, and I leave a message.

I drive to a store I haven't been to since I was kid, called Acacia Sporting Supplies, a name both simple and accurate and one that as kids we used to shorten to *ASS*. The place still smells the same — leather, rubber, maple, ash and hickory — otherwise seven-year-old me wouldn't recognize the place. There are posters of athletes all over the walls, posters of sporting equipment and brands with clever logos. Technology has advanced sport products a long way, with equipment performing faster and better and for longer, all while looking cooler doing it. I pick up a snorkeling mask and add a pair of flippers and take them up to the counter. The same woman who used to serve me back as a kid serves me now. Her glasses are so thick everybody must look the same to her.

"Found everything you're looking for, honey?" she asks.

"Don't suppose you have any scuba gear?"

She shakes her head. "That kind of thing is special order."

"How about climbing rope?"

"Sure do," she says, and she points me in the right direction. I grab some nylon stuff that's bright red and a hundred feet long.

"Anything else?" she asks.

"You have any fishing buoys?"

"We got a couple," she says.

I grab a red one, and she inflates it for me while I add a pair of blue swimming shorts to the mix along with a pair of hiking shoes since my ones have blood soaking into them. I buy a few pairs of socks too. I add a pocket knife to the collection and Cliff pays for half of everything and Anderson pays for the rest. I scoop everything up and toss it into the pickup. I head into a convenience store and buy some bottles of water and some sunblock and a pair of cheap sunglasses since my other ones are trapped somewhere in Father Frank's car. I get some antiseptic cream and gauze and Band-Aids and bandaging and a cheap pair of flip-flops. Then I head into a hardware store and buy a prybar the length of my arm and two cinderblocks that each weigh thirty pounds. I pick up a waterproof flashlight, one more powerful than Father Frank's. It has a wrist strap. I toss those into the cab too and drive out of town, over the bridge where the two old guys are fishing again, past the small farms and the big farms and Earl's, Earl watching me as I go by. I drive all my new goodies out to the quarry. The biggest problem I'm worried about is running into other people out here, cranes and bulldozers and diggers, and I can hear them, but they're way off to the right and I'm heading way off to the left.

I get the coordinates from the screenshot I took last night, and use the GPS to cover the same three miles I walked. The sound of the machinery dies away, until all I can hear out here are the birds and the wind. The sun is climbing high, and the higher it gets the hotter it gets. The sky is nothing but blue in every direction. I find where the road faces the pit. I take the corner and pull over, the trees to my left, the lake to my right. I take off my shoes and put on the flip-flops. I walk to the edge and look down. I can't see the cars. Can't see any bodies. The only thing I can see are the beer cans, floating. The pickup engine is pinging and I can feel heat coming from the engine bay. I load up on sunblock and I sit in the shade and unspool the rope and tie knots in it every five feet. I use the pocket knife to cut a couple of yards from one end and put it aside, and with the rest I tie one end to one of the cinderblocks and the other end to the buoy. I tie the prybar to the buoy too. I may not need the prybar, but better to have it and not need it than the other way around. I head back to the edge and I visualize everything the way I saw it last night, then I swing the cinderblock and the rope and the buoy out over the pit where I think Father Frank's car is, and gravity takes care of the rest.

I change into my swimming shorts and take the road that

goes down into the water. I take off my flip-flops and sunglasses and make a small pile with my t-shirt at the bottom. I wet the snorkeling goggles and spit into them and clean them a little before putting them on, and then I pull on the flippers, which hurts my battered feet, and I strap the flashlight to my wrist. I swim steadily with the cliff on my right, until I reach the buoy, only a few feet away from the wall of the pit. The water is warm. I pull up the rope, counting the knots, until I feel the weight of the cinderblock. I do the math. The bottom is roughly at thirty feet.

I tie off the slack. I release the prybar from the buoy, adjust my goggles, and look down into the water. There is no current, no sense of the water moving at all. I still can't see the cars. I can't see anything. I shine the light into the water and can see the wall of the pit ahead of me, but nothing else. I put visibility at ten feet. I let go of the prybar and watch it disappear. I steady my breathing, exhale quickly a few times, suck in a deep breath, grab the rope, and pull myself down.

Thirty-nine

I find Stephen at fifteen feet. He's become neutrally buoyant, hanging halfway between the bottom and the surface, like God hasn't decided yet which way he ought to be heading. My chest is tight, but it's not uncomfortable. I kick with my flippers and I pull at the rope. It gets darker as I go deeper. Colder too. At twenty-five feet I can make out two boxy shapes below. My chest is still okay. I keep going. The flippers make moving around under the water quick work. The shapes become cars. The bottom of the lake looks like the surface of the moon. No life, just a barren of concave gouges where diggers have cut into the ground, stone and grit stretching out of sight to the left and right, and ahead of me the wall. There's another shape ten feet away. I swim over to it. It's the pickup. Good Morning is still in it. He's behind the wheel, the limp airbag floating around him. Cliff must be around here somewhere too.

I make my way back up to the surface. It's easy work, but

I'm heaving for air when I break the surface. I take the snorkel off and lie on my back in the sun and slowly kick my way back to the buoy. I take a few minutes to get my breath and then I head back down. I get to the bottom and I pick up the prybar and swim to Father Frank's car. It's still on its side, leaning up against the mystery car. I reach in and pop the trunk of Frank's car, ready to use the prybar in case it's gotten jammed in the impact, but it opens easily. My bag falls out. I take it over to the cinderblock, then pull myself up to the surface for air. I lie on my back for a couple more minutes, holding on to the buoy, letting the sun beat down on me, and I stay this way getting my breath back until I think about the dead men below me, about them reaching up for me. I roll over to look down, but of course they're not there.

I get my breathing under control. This would be easier with scuba equipment. I exhale quickly a few times, draw in a deep breath, and make my way to the bottom again. I check out the mystery car. There's nobody inside. Because the car is upside down, the trunk release is up. I find it, pull it, and feel it release. I have to apply some weight to get it to open all the way.

A suitcase tumbles out. Next to it a purse. I hook the purse over my shoulder and push off hard from the lake floor and swim to the surface.

I tie the purse off next to the buoy. I give it a few minutes and then head back down, first cutting away the slack from the rope I wound up earlier to take with me. On my way down I tie the rope around Stephen's waist, and when I get to the bottom I brace myself against the car and pull. He comes down easier than I would have thought, and when I get him down I maneuver him into the trunk of Father Frank's car and get it closed.

I go back to the surface. I need a break.

I swim with the purse over to the road. I put my flip-flops on and grab my sunglasses and head up to the pickup. By the time I get there I've mostly dried off.

I lay the blanket I slept on last night out on the ground. I drink a bottle of water and open the purse and lay everything out. There's a set of keys, a hairbrush, lipstick, a wallet, chewing gum, a cellphone, a mirror, some loose change, some hair ties, dental floss, sunglasses, a bunch of receipts now unreadable, a pen, lip balm, a mush of tissues, movie ticket stubs that are also unreadable, tampons swollen to twice their size, another pen, a small pocket knife, and a pair of nail clippers. I open the wallet. There's money, credit cards, more receipts, a driver's license, a discount card for a local coffee shop. I hold the driver's license for a while, turning it in my fingers, looking at the photograph and studying it from every angle.

The car, the purse, everything scattered across the blanket — it confirms all of my fears. All this stuff, it belongs to Alyssa Stone.

Forty

I lay on the blanket getting my strength back. The shadows that were on the left of the car when I arrived are now on the right. I think about what comes next. About bringing Drew in on this. Alyssa was taken. Maybe she was held at the Kelly farm first, just like she was all those years ago, and those two men came and took her. Could be one of them dumped the car, could be the car was dumped before they got here by whoever chained Alyssa up. Problem is, the only way to convince Drew that Alyssa is in trouble is to tell him about the car, which is a conversation that starts out with good intentions and ends with him throwing me in jail for murder. I can't tell him. I can't tell anybody. I'm in this alone. After twenty minutes of repeating that thought process and seeing no way out of it, I walk back down to the water. I make the same pile of flip-flops and sunglasses and I put the flippers and snorkeling mask back on and swim out to the buoy.

I swim back down to the bottom and check out the

suitcase, and sure enough, it's full of clothes. Whoever took Alyssa wanted it to look like she'd packed in a hurry and left. I go over to the pickup, pointing the flashlight in all directions, looking for Cliff. There's no current, so he should be nearby. I find him on my way back up to the surface, neutrally buoyant, just like Stephen was.

I cut the buoy free, and use the rope to pull myself back down. I swim over to Cliff and tie the rope around his waist and pull him down further and wrestle him into the trunk of Father Frank's car. I grab my bag and head for the surface. I push the buoy ahead of me and swim back to the road.

I open my bag and wring out my clothes and lay them out flat in the cab of the pickup so they can dry. My foot is raw and seeping blood. It needs stitches, and when there's more time I'll go and get some. For now I apply the antiseptic cream, then put gauze over the wound and bandage it up. I change out of my swimming shorts and into the clothes I came out here in, along with the new shoes. I head into the trees. It doesn't take long to find the series of broken branches and busted-up fronds from last night, and then to find Anderson Veich. He smells. I get him in a fireman's carry and haul him out of the forest. His arm dangles against me and it feels like he's trying to get his money back.

It's hard work carrying him to the pickup. I tie the remaining cinderblock to his feet nice and tight. I drag him to the edge and send him down into the water to do what I didn't do last night — and that's reunite the four of them.

My clothes haven't dried out yet, but I stuff them back into the damp bag and throw it onto the passenger seat. I do the same with Alyssa's purse. I fold the blanket up and drive out of the quarry. I pass the two sawmills and Earl's and the Kelly farm. Big farms become small farms. Small farms become—

My phone rings. I must have hit cellphone range. It's Maggie. The feelings I had earlier today all rush back, the guilt, a queasy feeling flooding my system, my legs feeling week. *You're a killer. More specifically, you killed Maggie's husband. You killed the father of her children.*

I pull over and answer it.

"Hey," Maggie says.

"Hey," I say. "Look, I'm sorry about yesterday," I say, sorry for a lot of things, most of which she doesn't know about yet.

"So am I," she says. "Everything you said, I know you're right, I really do, but what you need to realize is that what you say is only right in theory. In reality it doesn't work that way."

"I know. I overreacted. I just . . . I just couldn't help myself. The idea of him hurting you made me ill." I look down at my feet, one resting gently on the clutch, the other off to the side of the accelerator. I tighten my grip on the steering wheel, white-knuckling it. "How are you? How are the kids?"

"We're fine," she says. "We're staying at Victoria's. Stephen has gone camping and drinking with his buddies. He told me that you attacked him, that he didn't see it coming. Is that true?"

I picture him bleeding out. Going over the edge. I hear the splash. For a moment, a very brief moment, I think, how does she know about that? But no, she's talking about yesterday afternoon. "No," I say. "He came at me with a tire iron. All I did was defend myself."

"You should be careful of him," she says.

"I will be. Have you heard from him?" I ask, and I wince as those words come out. I wonder if lying gets easier. Small lies become big lies, and those who are the best at it become serial killers or go into politics.

"No," she says. "Not since he left."

"And when he gets back? What are you going to do?"

It takes her a while to answer, like it's a question that's been stuck on repeat in her thoughts since yesterday. I keep staring at my feet, at my new shoes, misted by quarry dust. "I don't know," she says. "We have the kids to think about. Children need their father."

"Children don't need that kind of a father."

"I should go," she says.

"I'm sorry. I shouldn't have said that."

She sighs. "Yes, you should. I know you care, but you're telling me things I already know that hurt to hear. Are you going to be here for Father Frank's funeral?"

"Yes."

"Is Alyssa coming?"

"I don't think she is," I say. *Not because she doesn't want to.*

"You've spoken to her?"

"Not since before Father Frank passed away."

"I hope she comes," she says.

"I hope so too. Let me ask you something — do you have any idea at all who Alyssa was seeing?"

"None," she says. "I thought you didn't think it was so important."

"It may not be," I say. Or it might be. Getting pregnant could be what's led to her being kidnapped again twelve years later. Or not. I don't know.

"Ask Father Barrett. He might have seen her with somebody. Or some of her friends might know. I really do have to go," she says. "Noah . . .I know you think I should leave Stephen, and the thing is, I'm just . . . I'm so embarrassed by it all, if that makes sense. I can't imagine what you must think of me."

"Embarrassment is the last thing you should be feeling. You're a strong person, just one who needs help, and there's no shame in asking for help. You have people in your life who love you and care about you and want the best for you."

"Despite everything, I still love him," she says. "How messed up is that?"

Before I can answer she hangs up, and I'm left listening to an empty line.

Forty-one

I pull into the parking lot behind Saint John's. Father Barrett comes wandering out.

We shake hands, and he says, "You look like shit." I had figured if one person in Acacia Pines wasn't going to say that, it would be the Catholic priest — and if I'm wrong about that, then I might as easily be wrong about everything. "Something wrong with your foot?" he asks.

"I cut it."

"What happened to Frank's car? You trade up?"

"I'm not sure I'd call it that."

"You've spoken to Alyssa?" he asks.

"Not since Frank died. I'm here to ask you if I can look through her stuff."

"Why?"

"Because Father Frank was right. Alyssa didn't just up and leave. Something happened to her."

"How do you know this?"

"I just do."

"And what does Drew say?"

"I haven't told him."

He looks confused.

"I can't tell him," I say, "for reasons I can't get into. Think of it as like breaking the confessional seal," I say, which this is nothing like, but hopefully he'll like the analogy.

"You're saying she's in trouble?"

"That's exactly what I'm saying."

"Then you need to talk to Drew."

"Like I said, I can't. Not yet. So let me ask you again, can I look through Alyssa's things?"

"If you think it will help," he says. We walk to the house. "If it looks like somebody's already been through it, it's because somebody has. The police looked through her stuff when she was reported missing and didn't find anything to suggest anything nefarious happened."

We reach the porch. The angle of the sun now means the verandah offers us some shade. The floorboards aren't straining so hard to stay in shape.

"Alyssa was seeing somebody. Do you have any idea who?"

He gives me a stern look. "I'm not a gossip," he says.

"So you have seen her with somebody."

"I didn't say that."

"I wouldn't be asking if I didn't think it was important."

"You think this person has done something to her?"

"I think this person has forced her to leave Acacia Pines, and she's in trouble, yes."

"You spoke to her," he says. "She said she was okay."

"I think she was lying. So, again, I ask you, do you know who she was seeing?"

He shakes his head. "She never brought any boys by."

"Anybody confess something that might help?"

"You know better than to ask me that."

"Can't blame me for trying."

He doesn't say anything.

"How long have you been here?"

"Almost six months," he says.

"In that time, as far as you know, has anybody ever up and disappeared?"

"You mean like Alyssa?"

"Maybe like Alyssa, maybe not. Just, you know, just disappeared."

He thinks about it. "Nothing," he says.

"Ever heard any stories about people vanishing?"

"What are you getting at, Noah? What have you found?"

"Have you?" I insist.

"As far as I know nobody has ever disappeared. Have you asked Drew?"

"He said the same thing."

"So maybe nobody has disappeared."

The water. The mattress. The chains. The two men.

I thank him for his time, and he makes me promise to keep him updated on anything I hear, which is a nice irony. I head into the house and it's become different over the last day. The air isn't as thick and the house is able to breathe. I go into Frank's room. There are photographs of him, of Alyssa, of Alyssa's parents, of people I don't know. I pick up a photo of Frank and Alyssa. She can't be much older than ten. They're camping. She has a big grin on her face and Father Frank has a big grin on his. They've staked out a tent somewhere in The Pines, no doubt near a river because there are fishing rods on the ground. I take the photograph out of the frame and tuck it into my pocket. I search the room for notes, for a journal, for anything to tell me who might have confessed to him and what, but there's nothing. Of course there's nothing. Priests aren't psychiatrists — they don't take notes.

In Alyssa's room there are more photographs. Some in frames, some pinned to a corkboard on the wall, others taped to the edge of a mirror, plenty with her and her friends in them. There's one of her sitting on the front of her car. She's giving a thumbs up. It looks clean. It could be the day she bought it. It's a dark blue Honda Accord. I can see the last three numbers of the license plate. It's the car in the quarry. I pick up the photo and I look closely at Alyssa. She's grown up, but I can still see the seven-year-old girl. There's another photograph next to it. Her and Father Barrett, standing outside the church. She has an arm around him and she's taking a selfie, holding the camera at arm's length. She's smiling, but Father Barrett looks put out, like the kind of guy who thinks selfies are for a much younger generation.

I tip up drawers to see if anything has been taped beneath them. I check behind the mirror, under furniture, in the back of her wardrobe, all the places I imagine Drew checked.

I don't find any answers. I put some of the photographs of Alyssa and her friends into my pocket. I add the one of her and Father Barrett.

I head into the church. Father Barrett is in his office. He leans back and looks at me and drops his pen onto a notepad he's scrawling on. He's working on what to say at Frank's funeral. I show him the photographs I took from Alyssa's room. He picks up the one of him and Alyssa and frowns. "Where did you find this?" he asks.

"Pinned to her wall. You guys were close?" I ask.

"As her father became sicker, I ended up helping more and more, but no, we weren't close. We were friendly, but I must admit I never really knew that much about her. This," he says, looking down at the photograph, "her smiling like this, that's a rarity. Of course she hasn't had a lot to smile about as of late. If she was seeing somebody," he says, "then I don't know who."

I hand him the other photographs. "Do you know who any of these people are?"

"You want to tell me what's going on here? You want to tell me why you have all those cuts and bruises and why you're no longer driving Frank's car? You're different today. I can see that as clearly as I can see you standing here. Something has happened and it's not sitting with you well. People don't say confession is good for the soul simply to hear themselves rattling off a cliché, Noah. It's true. Whatever you're going through, you can tell me. I can help you."

"You can help me by taking a look at the photographs."

He sighs. He can tell I'm not going to open up to him. He goes through the photographs. He stops on one where there's a blonde girl holding her fingers together to make the shape of a heart for the camera. She's in several of the photos. She has a big smile and big blue eyes. Father Barrett drums his fingers against the table. "I've seen her here a couple of times," he says. "I think they're best friends."

"You know her name?"

"Charlotte," he says. "I don't remember her last name."

"You know anything about her?"

"Not really. If she's the girl I'm thinking of, she's hoping to be an actress, and it's only a matter of time before she leaves town — she used to say that a lot."

"Charlotte Bauer?"

"That's her. You know her?"

She's the girl who babysits for Drew and Leigh. "I went to school with her dad."

"I'd say it's a small world," he says, "but that means nothing in a town this size."

I straighten the photographs up and slip them into my pocket. "You know where I can find her?"

He pulls a phonebook out from a desk drawer. "Parents?"

"Her dad is Antony."

He looks down the list. "There are a couple of possibilities," he says.

I write them down.

"One more thing," I tell him. "Father Frank used to take Alyssa camping. Any idea where he keeps his tent?"

"It'll be in the church basement."

"You mind if I borrow it?"

"Is the same thing going to happen to it that happened to his car?"

"I hope not."

"But it's possible," he says.

"Have a little faith, Father."

Forty-two

I get the tent loaded into the pickup. I grab a mat to sleep on, and a hammer to bang pegs into the ground, then drive to my favorite diner. The place is full, mostly with men and women in boots and fluorescent vests who look like they've all come in from the sawmill and the quarries. I'm about to head back out and look for somewhere else when a booth becomes free. I take it. The sun still has some height behind it, good for another hour and a half maybe. Shopkeepers pull merchandise inside. Lights are flicked off and doors are locked. The streets start to empty.

The burger and fries I had last night were so damn good I order them again. I sip at a soda while waiting for my food and look at the photographs I collected from Father Frank's house. In the camping picture Alyssa looks like a happy and healthy and normal ten- or twelve-year-old kid, the horror of her earlier childhood behind her. In others she's goofing around with her friends, enjoying life the way teenagers can when they have nothing to worry about. I stack the photographs into a pile with the one of Alyssa and Father Barrett on top and tap the edges against the table to square them up when my food arrives. I try not to wolf it down, but it's a struggle. I'm still hungry when I finish and order another burger to go.

I head out to the pickup. It's eight o'clock. The sun is dipping behind the storefronts. The streetlights are on and neons light up bars promising live bands and best beers. The streets that were emptying earlier are filling back up. Bars have tables outside, people sitting around smoking and laughing and flirting and drinking.

I tuck the photograph of Alyssa and Frank into the sun visor so I can keep looking at it, and I start calling the numbers on the list Father Barrett gave me. I hit pay dirt with the first one I try when the guy answering the phone introduces himself as Antony.

"I'm hoping I can speak with Charlotte," I say.

"She's not here," he says, "but I can take a message."

"Does she have a cellphone number?"

"That depends," he says, "on who's calling."

"It's Noah Harper," I say.

"Noah Harper," he says, saying it slowly, then he repeats it a second time, but quicker. "I heard you were back in town. How the hell have you been?" he asks, as if we were friends at school, which we weren't, or as if we know each other, which we don't.

"I've been better," I say.

"Man, what's it been? I haven't seen you since school."

"It's been a while," I tell him.

"Didn't you use to be a deputy or something?"

"Something like that."

"Then you beat the shit out of Conrad Haggerty, right?"

"I just need Charlotte's number," I say.

"Man, that guy always was an asshole, and like — you know — some things never change."

"Ain't that the truth."

"Didn't he use to date your wife? Back before she became your wife?"

"No," I say. "Listen, Antony, you'd really be helping me out if you could give me Charlotte's number. I wouldn't be asking if it weren't important."

"What kind of important?" he asks.

"It's a private matter," I tell him.

"And Charlotte's a nineteen-year-old girl and you're in your forties," he says, his tone changing. "More importantly, she's my daughter. So let me ask you again, why do you need her number?"

"You know why I'm back?"

"Something to do with Father Frank, isn't it?"

"It's to do with his daughter, Alyssa. He asked me to find her."

"I heard she skipped town. Broke up with her boyfriend or something."

"You happen to know who that boyfriend was?"

"No idea," he says. "You know what teenagers are like."

"In what way?"

"In the same way we were when we were teenagers."

"Please, Antony, it's important. I think she can help me."

He says nothing for a few seconds, and then, "She's babysitting tonight, but I'll tell you what, you give me your number and I'll get her to call you back. How's that sound?"

I tell him that sounds fine. We hang up. The light has gone now. It's dark out. I'm tired and still have to set the tent up, but there's somewhere else I want to go first.

Forty-three

I drive past Old Man Haggerty's house and there are lights on inside. He's in there alternating between sucking oxygen from his mask and sucking smoke from his cigarette. I pull over half a block away and am drumming my fingers against the wheel trying to figure out how I can get him out of the house when the solution presents itself — Old Man Haggerty getting into his SUV and backing down the driveway. I slink down in the seat and I don't get back up until he's well past. There's no way of knowing how long he's going to be out, but I do know I won't need long.

I head straight for the woodpile and climb up to the roof. The office window is open an inch, and I widen it the rest of the way and climb through. The lights are still on downstairs, but not upstairs, so I close the curtains so I can switch on my flashlight without anybody seeing. I open the wardrobe, pop open the panel and the box I saw yesterday is still there. I sit it on the desk and the light to the office is switched on and my heart stops and I look up to see Haggerty standing in the doorway pointing his gun at me, his left arm hanging by his side.

"You always were predictable," he says. "I take it that was you here yesterday?"

"You were waiting for me?"

"All day," he says. "That thing you're driving, that's Earl's old piece of junk, isn't it?"

"It is."

"Thought you were driving Father Frank's car."

"It died."

"Symmetry," he says. "Gotta love it."

"You going to shoot me?"

"It'd be a clean shoot. A pensioner comes home to find a guy breaking into his house. The guy threatens him, tries to jump him, but this pensioner isn't like most old men because this pensioner has a gun. He uses it to defend himself. Case closed."

"You do that, and you don't get to hear what I have to say."

"And what is that, Noah? I mean, you found the girl, right? She's okay, so why are you here?"

"She's not okay," I tell him.

"No?"

"No. And something isn't right here." I tap the box. "I suspect you know that already. Only question is, what side of it are you on?"

"What in the hell are you talking about?"

"How many people have gone missing in the twelve years

since I've been gone?"

He looks confused. "What do you mean, missing?"

"One day they were here and the next day they were gone and you never figured out where they went."

"None," he says. "I know you have a pretty low opinion of me, Noah, but if people were going missing, I'd notice."

"I think you did notice. I think you've known something isn't right here for some time."

He sighs loudly, tucks his gun into the front of his pants, then reaches for his mask that's hanging over his shoulder and takes a hit. "Bring the box."

He disappears from the doorway. I grab the box and he's still making his way down the stairs carrying his oxygen tank when I catch up to him. The lounge is full of dull colors and old photographs, one wall mostly taken up with a TV that's too big. He tells me to put the box on the coffee table, then he grabs a couple of glasses from the kitchen and a bottle of bourbon. Turns out his left arm does work, just not very well, but he gets the bottle open. I've never liked bourbon and he knows that, but he goes ahead and pours us a drink each. We sit opposite each other on couches from a long-ago era and he puts the gun on the couch next to him.

"First off, nobody has gone missing," he says. "Whatever you think is going on here, it ain't that."

"So what is it?"

"Tell me what you have," he says.

"Nothing concrete."

"Well, that's not a good start now, Noah, is it?"

"Did you take photos at the Kelly farm twelve years ago?"

"Of course I did."

"Are they in that box?"

"They are."

"Can I look at them?"

"Once you've told me what's going on."

"Why didn't you come after me twelve years ago? I mean, not as an angry father, but as a policeman who could have arrested me?"

"That's a conversation you should have with your ex-wife."

"What does Maggie have to do with this?"

"She's a good lawyer," he says. "She made a convincing argument for Conrad to drop the charges."

"Which was?"

He takes a drink, then he gets out a cigarette and pops it into his mouth but doesn't light it. "She told me what Conrad did to her, back when you were all in school. She said if I didn't shut my son down she'd go to the papers and tell them what happened. She told me there'd be others out there that he'd done the same thing to. She had no proof, mind, but once it was out there, it would snowball. Headlines — *Sheriff's son's a rapist* — they'd ruin my reputation."

I feel sick thinking about what happened in high school. She told me about it six months later. We weren't dating back then, but we were friends. Close friends. I wanted her to tell Sheriff Haggerty, but she said it would only make things worse. It would get around the school, only the story would change. She knew what the other students would call her. She made me promise to do nothing, and it took a lot of strength to do as she asked.

He sips at his drink. "I didn't take a lot of convincing. That boy . . . he's always been trouble, and he's a big part of why my wife walked out on us, and the truth is I can't rightly blame her for it. But Noah, you have to understand that I truly didn't know. If she or anybody had come to me back then I would have done something about it, regardless of the fact he's my son. And if you'd come to me twelve years ago, I'd have done the right thing back then too. You should have trusted me."

"I couldn't."

"You could, but you took the opportunity to hand out some justice. What you did to Conrad . . . you went too far, Noah. Way too far. He's a messed-up kid, but he's still my son."

"He kidnapped a girl," I tell him. "He might have killed her."

"He didn't kidnap her," he says. "And I think now you're figuring that out."

"It still doesn't explain how he knew where she was," I say, "and don't give me that bullshit about him overhearing two rescue workers at a bar."

"My son is too stupid to kidnap somebody," he says.

"Yet he knew where she was."

"No. He didn't know. You were beating on him, you'd shot him, and you were threatening to kill him if he didn't give you a location. He had one shot at survival, and that was to send you away and hope like hell Drew would be able to free him."

He drinks more of his drink. I haven't touched mine. "Jesus, Noah, he made a guess. That's all it was, but even then it wasn't about guessing a location, it was about giving you somewhere to go. The Kelly farm had been abandoned for — what? Two years by then? Three? He didn't send you there to find the girl, he sent you there to get rid of you. Fact is, even we should have thought to look there back then, because when you think about it, it's an obvious place to go. It's why Conrad came up with it. You finding her, that was shit luck for him because it made him look guilty, but that's all it was — shit luck."

"Not for Alyssa," I say.

"No. Not for Alyssa," he says. "In a way he saved her life."

In a way, he's right.

If what he's saying is true.

"I struggled to believe it myself," he goes on. "I mean, it's some coincidence, right? So I went out there. I wouldn't let anybody else go in. I know it was a conflict of interest, but Conrad is my son, my boy, no matter how useless he might be. I printed that place by the book. I did everything right, and I didn't find a single shred of evidence to say he'd ever been there. But you want to know what else I didn't find?"

"What's that?"

"Your fingerprints. Or any fingerprints on any door handles. Everything had been wiped clean. Between the time you found the girl, and the time I got out there the following day, somebody else came in and tidied up. That's why I believe my son, Noah, when he says he didn't do it."

"You print the chain?"

"The chain you left in your car? No, because it wasn't there when I went to get it."

"The two men took it," I say. "They wiped the house clean."

"There were no two men at a bar," he says. "Conrad told me that. He said he made that up."

"That's not what I mean," I say. "Earl Winters says two men came into town the same evening I found her. He says they were in town for an hour. My guess is they came in to get Alyssa, but when they found she was gone, they stayed to clean up."

"That's exactly what happened," he says.

"What?

"At least that's my take on it too." He takes another drink. "I know all about the two men. I don't know who they are, but I know they're trouble on a scale like you or I have never seen."

"And what? You let the investigation go? You didn't try to figure out who they were? You know they came here to get Alyssa, right?"

"Open the box," he says.

The way he says it, the way he looks at me, it's unnerving.

"Open the box, son."

I open the box.

Forty-four

There are folders stacked on top of one another, a thick layer of dust on them, some stained with rings from a coffee cup. I pick up the top one. There are photographs in here and an envelope. I spread them across the coffee table. There are six pictures, all of them of Alyssa Stone back when she was a child, two of them taken outside her home at the church, two of them outside her school, and the remaining two of her at a candy store with a girl who might be Charlotte Bauer. The temperature in the room drops. Despite that, Haggerty gets up and moves over to the fridge.

"I need some ice," he says. He opens the freezer while I look at the photographs. There's a crunch as he twists the ice tray. He drops a couple into his drink.

I pick up the envelope. There's no writing anywhere on it.

"It was slid under my front door," he says. The ice cubes rattle in Haggerty's glass as he sits back down. I open the envelope. There's a single piece of paper in it. I pull it out and unfold it. Scrawled on it are eleven words.

> *Look for us and she dies.*
> *Do nothing and everyone lives.*

I read it a second time. Then a third. I look up at Haggerty. He's sipping at his drink. It's been topped up. His hand is no longer near his gun.

"I believed them," he says. "The way they framed my son, the way they cleaned up the crime scene, the way they delivered these photographs — this wasn't some small-time crook. I've never backed down from anything in my life, and when I got those pictures, it made me mad, made me madder than I've ever been before in my life," he says, but he doesn't look mad, he looks resigned to the decision he made and can't take back. "I vowed I would find the men who had done this. I'd already spoken to Earl. He told me everything he told you. I wasn't going to let it go, but then . . . well, things changed. Open the next folder."

I open the next folder. More photographs and another blank envelope. I look at the pictures. It's been a long time since I saw the woman that's in them.

"Your wife," I say.

He nods. I keep looking. There's a photograph of Alyssa coming out of the hospital, her little hand inside Father Frank's. And there are photos of other children too. A dozen different ones, some teenagers, some as young as five.

"They're all local," he says.

I open the envelope. The letter has two words.

Final Warning

"You ask why I let it go? That's why I let it go. I wanted to protect Alyssa. I wanted to protect my ex-wife. I wanted to protect the other children in these pictures. It might have been a bluff, but it sure felt real. I had a choice to make. If I did nothing, we'd never find the men who took her, we'd never understand why they chose her. But if I did nothing then she would be okay. All these people, they'd be okay. I could protect her — of course I could. I could watch her every day, but for how long? A week? A month? A year? But I couldn't watch them all. These guys could get to me, or her, and anybody else at any time they wanted."

I keep looking at the photographs. I keep thinking about what I would have done in his situation.

"They took Alyssa," he says, "but they didn't kill her. She was okay. Nobody died. It was an awful crime, Noah, but nobody died."

I say nothing.

"I had to make a choice whether or not to open Pandora's box. Do nothing and she lived. Do nothing and everything would be okay. Do something and Acacia Pines would have monsters to deal with, and even if by some chance I found those two men, there would be others like them. Men like that, there are always others. The thing is, everything has been okay. No other children have been hurt. And despite what you think, Noah, nobody else has gone missing."

Never Conrad.

"You're the one who confessed to Father Frank. You told him everything, didn't you?"

He slowly nods. "I had to," he says. "I had to stop him from asking what had happened."

"All these years, he's known Conrad was innocent, and these last few days, he's known what happened twelve years ago is happening again."

"We don't know that," he says.

"Others have gone missing."

"No," he says. "These guys, they kept their word. Nobody has gone missing, and Alyssa wasn't taken again, she left. She left on her own terms."

"Earl says they were back last Wednesday night. Alyssa was reported missing on the Thursday."

"Alyssa is fine," he says. "Drew tracked her down, and even you spoke to her."

"I found her car," I tell him. "At the bottom of one of the lakes out at the quarry."

Haggerty's eyes narrow.

"These men, they have her," I tell him, "and they're forcing her to tell us what we want to hear. I'm sure she isn't the first."

"Why do you keep saying that? What is it you know that I don't?"

I tell him what I found at the Kelly farm. The mattress. The chain. The empty bottles of water and the expiry dates on them. Halfway through he gets up and pours himself another drink. He's gone pale. His cigarette remains unlit.

"You've spoken to Drew about this?"

"Not yet. Father Frank, he told me that anybody I involved would be in danger."

"Father Frank was right. You bring Drew into this, and you bring his family into it too. How'd you find the car?"

"It's a long story."

"Tell me everything," he says.

I tell him everything. I tell him about the fire, about the quarry, about being pushed off the edge in Father Frank's car. I tell him the fate of the four men who did that to me. When I'm done telling him he just sits there slowly shaking his head.

"What happened to you, Noah?" he asks.

"I just told you," I say.

"I don't mean that. What happened to you to make you this kind of a person? You sit here and tell me like it's no big deal, but you murdered four men, Noah."

"Technically I only killed three. Stephen was shot by his friend, and the other three were all self-defense," I say, which is true . . . to a point. I don't tell him about Cliff, who I rolled off the edge with my foot. Instead I tell him he went over the edge during the fight. "It was them or me. It wasn't murder. You ask what kind of man I am? I'm the kind who does what it takes to survive. What was the alternative? Stay in the car?"

He takes a packet of cigarettes out from his pocket and then realizes he still has one in his mouth, the same one he's been taking out so he can get to his drink. He puts it back in and this time he lights it. I wait for the room to blow up.

"That's why you haven't told Drew," he says. "You're worried you'll end up in jail."

I don't say anything.

"What in the hell am I supposed to do with this information?"

I still don't say anything.

"You know I have to tell Drew, right? If not now, then at least when this is over."

"You're focusing on the wrong thing," I tell him. "You're thinking about these four assholes who tried to kill me, when you should be thinking about Alyssa's car at the bottom of that quarry."

"You're sure they had nothing to do with that?"

"I'm positive. I think when it comes to finding somewhere to dump a car, the quarry is a good fit. Could be if you went out there and drained all those lakes you might find a dozen or so more."

"Of all the people that you think have been going missing."

"Yes."

I go through the box. There's an evidence bag in there that contains Alyssa's headband, the one we found in Conrad's car. Looking at it makes me wonder why I beat the shit out of somebody over such a small thing. I set it aside. Cigarette smoke starts filling the lounge. Next folder has photographs from the scene. They cover different angles of the basement. Dozens of them. Of the house too. The feeling I missed something that night comes back to me.

"These two men, you think they know you're looking into

what happened?"

"Without a doubt," I say. "They came for me last night, only I wasn't there."

I tell him how Stephen and his friends dragging me out to the quarry meant I wasn't at the farm when the two men came for me. They sure would have done a better job of finishing me off than Stephen did.

"Men like this," he says, "they're not going to stop coming back till they've done what they wanted done."

"I know."

"Men like this," he says, "they're going to kill anybody who gets in their way."

I know that too.

Forty-five

Old Man Haggerty agrees to help me. He agrees to keep my secrets, and we both agree that if he were to phone the hotels to lift the ban he put on me that it'd look suspicious. We need to keep up the appearance that he'd be willing to shoot me if he saw me crossing the street. The only thing we don't agree on is him giving me a gun. He says it's too dangerous. He says I've killed four people already. I point out technically it's only three. It doesn't change his mind.

He walks me to the door.

"Let me ask you one more thing," I say. "You said earlier you were worried if people found out what kind of man Conrad was, it would ruin your reputation. Was your reputation really more important than the women he had hurt?" He says nothing for a few moments, just stares at me. "There's a reason me and my son haven't spoken much since then. I told him if he ever did something like that again, I'd put him in the ground."

"Would you really have done that?"

"Good night, Noah," he says, and he closes the door.

I carry the folder of photographs from the Kelly farm out to the pickup. It's getting up toward ten-thirty as I drive through town. Most of the bars have closed and the neon is cold. Shops become houses become farms become forests. A few miles short of Earl's Gas Station I take the turnoff out to the hiking and camping trails. It's a straight shingle road with a dogleg at the end that opens into a large lot made up of hard-packed dirt and more gravel. There's a ranger station that is often unoccupied, but has a facility for hikers to sign in and out of and file a plan. This time of year I'd expect to see a half-dozen cars at most out here, but a quick count shows there are twenty.

I stuff the folder of crime scene shots into the backpack, along with some of the other supplies, and the extra burger I bought, and strap it to my back. Two more cars arrive. The moon is full and lights up the parking lot with pale blue light and reflects off all the chrome and glass and smooth paintwork. There are tents on the edge of the parking lot. There are folks sitting in camping chairs and drinking beer while they talk, their voices low. Some acknowledge me as I walk past.

I carry my tent into the trees. I pass other tents. A lot of them have lanterns glowing inside. All these cars, all these people, it suggests some kind of event. Maybe tomorrow morning they're all going to wake up at 5am and hike a hundred miles. My guess is an orienteering competition of some type.

I find a clearing where the ground is flat, a good fifty yards from anybody else. I get the tent out of its case and immediately wish I'd practiced putting this thing up earlier. It's a two-person tent that needs to be put up by ten. I consider putting down the sleeping mat and draping the tent over me as a blanket, but I persevere, and it pays off thirty minutes later when I get it standing. I sit cross-legged on the mat and eat my cold burger and get out the folder and look at the photographs of the scene from twelve years ago. It looks incredibly similar to how it looked a few nights ago.

There are photos of the basement. There are pictures of the mattress that Alyssa got to lie on, and it's the same mattress that's still there now. Or was, until it burned up. There's a photograph of the wall where the chain was attached, of the four bolts I had to fight with. There are no water bottles, and I can't remember if there were any there that night or not. There are exterior photos of the building, of tire tracks found outside, of the door I kicked in. Haggerty has taken pictures of every room in the house, and I study each one and they look the same as those rooms did before Stephen and his friends came along. When the two men drove there after I had rescued Alyssa and cleaned up, all they did was wipe down the surfaces of things they touched — it would have been easier for them to burn the place down, but they didn't. They must have known they were going to continue to use the farm until it eventually sold. My eyes are getting heavy and the images blurry. I bunch the photographs up and put them into the folder and I lie on my back and turn out the lamp.

The tent walls glow, lit up by the moonlight seeping between the trees. I have so much stuff racing through my mind that it's not as easy to fall asleep as I thought it'd be. Plus, even though I have a mat, the ground is uncomfortable. My foot is throbbing. I close my eyes and try to let my mind empty.

I'm almost asleep when it hits me, a final image that flashes through my head. I reach for the light and switch it on and it hurts my eyes. I flick through the photographs looking for the one I want, looking for the thing that's been bugging me all these years. I find it, the one with the bolts. I hold it by the light and look at it closely.

The bolts are old and even a little rusted. So was the bracket and chain. Hell, I even remember wiping my hand on my pants at the hospital to wipe the grime off from dealing with it. There are marks on the edges where I undid them. Those marks are shiny and fresh, the marks on the opposite edges made when the bolts were tightened are old.

I lie back down and think it through. I can hear the occasional breaking twig as somebody out there walks near me. I hear another car arrive, and soon after that stakes being banged into the ground as another tent goes up.

I think of Alyssa. The chains. The bolts. The mattress. The shackle.

This is what I haven't been able to see. The set-up in the basement, it wasn't there for Alyssa. It was used on her, but it wasn't installed for her. Alyssa wasn't the first person to be held captive down there.

I hear voices, I hear the wind, I hear nature and, after staring at the darkness for some time, I hear nothing.

Forty-six

And then I do hear something. Lots of voices. Then those voices fall away, replaced by one that's much louder. I drag myself out of the tent. There is enough light coming from the parking lot that I don't need my flashlight. I can see the reds and blues and greens of tents pitched in all directions. I look at my watch. It's two minutes short of midnight. I've slept twenty minutes, and I feel worse for it. I stumble through the woods to the parking lot. There are sixty people here. Maybe seventy. They're holding candles. Behind them six cars have been put into a semicircle and the headlights are on to light up the scene. At the front of it all a bald guy in his late fifties is standing on a picnic table. He's looking out into the crowd with his head lowered but at the moment he isn't talking. Nobody is talking. All the voices that woke me have been silenced. There's something eerily creepy about this, about walking into a group of so many silent people. Some of them are crying. A lot of people have

292

arms around each other. Some are looking at the ground, some are staring into the candles. I've seen this before. Many times.

It's a midnight vigil for a missing hiker.

I stand in the crowd and I stay silent. Another minute goes by, and then the man on the picnic table straightens and looks into the crowd.

"I know my Jennifer is out here somewhere," he says. "I know she's safe, I know that if anybody can survive out here it's her. It's you, Jennifer," he says, and then he calls out into the woods. "Wherever you are, Jennifer, I want you to know that we all love you. We're all here waiting for you. Please . . ." he says, and his voice catches then and a few people in the crowd start to sob. "Please come home," he says. "We miss you. We . . . we miss you so damn much."

He climbs down and into the embrace of a woman waiting for him. Nobody takes his place. Everywhere in the crowd people are talking, but they're keeping their voices low. Jennifer is out there, missing, and these people all have hope in their hearts, but in their minds they know the reality.

I turn to a couple standing next to me, both in their early thirties, the woman with a ponytail and sunglasses pushed up over her forehead, the guy with a beard and hair up in a man bun. They have an arm around each other, holding on tight.

"I'm Noah," I say, and I put my hand out.

"Danny," the guy says, and shakes my hand. "This is my girlfriend Gina."

"Gina," I say, and I shake her hand too. "Look, at the risk

293

of sounding insensitive, can you tell me what happened to Jennifer?"

Both of them look uncertain.

"I was camping out here anyway," I say. "I heard the crowd. I didn't know about the vigil until I walked right into it. I didn't know anybody had gone missing. I'm sorry, I don't mean to intrude, but maybe I can help, you know, if I see something."

"Oh," Gina says. "Well, Jennifer . . . Jennifer went missing out here."

"A month ago," Danny says, and he reaches into his jacket pocket, first the left side, then the right, but doesn't find what he's looking for. "I have a thing here somewhere," he says, then pats down his pants.

"She . . . was . . . I mean, she is an avid hiker. She—" Gina says.

"Should never have come out here alone," Danny says. "I mean, what kind of person does that?"

"Danny," Gina says. "You know—"

"I know," he says, and now he's starting to cry. "Where's the—"

Gina hands me an 8x11 photocopy of a black-and-white photo of Jennifer Ferguson, smiling at the camera, dark hair tucked behind her ears, backpack straps over her shoulders. There are details of when she went missing, along with a phone number and the promise of a reward. "Jennifer is Danny's sister," Gina says, "and he goes from being destroyed by what's happened to being real angry about it."

"She shouldn't have come out here alone," he says again.

"Did the search turn up anything?" I ask.

"Search and rescue didn't find any trace of her," Gina says.

"She file a plan?"

"Of course she filed a plan," Danny says, and then his voice softens. "It's just that there's no way of knowing how long she stuck to it. The thing is, Jennifer . . . Jennifer is a free spirit. It's possible she changed her mind, it's possible she teamed up with somebody else and went off with them . . . we don't know. All we know is it's been a month and if she were able, if she were okay, she would have let us know."

"And her car? Her car was found out here in the parking lot?"

"It was," Danny says. "Though the local police had it towed into town when search and rescue stopped looking for her. She's out there somewhere. That I'm sure of."

The mattress. The chain. The bottles of water.

Earl told me the two men came to town a month ago.

The same time Jennifer went missing.

I've been thinking about this all wrong. Drew, Old Man Haggerty, even Father Barrett — they were right when they said nobody has gone missing — and that's because nobody has. Not from Acacia Pines.

But people come to these hiking trails from all across the country, and sometimes they go missing.

They fall into the Green Hole and nobody ever sees them again.

Forty-seven

Danny and Gina tell me about Jennifer. Today she turns twenty-five. It's why they're having the vigil. They've had them before — they came out here to help in the search when she first went missing, and a week into it they had a vigil and a week after that they had another. Jennifer is a dentist. They say that she was constantly on their case to stop drinking soda drinks. They say she's the kind of person who can talk to anybody. She has a calming personality. She can make people laugh and she can comfort people and she always knows the right thing to say. Children who are afraid of drills and needles are putty in her hands. She loves a lot of people and a lot of people love her. Hiking and camping is her passion. She's hiked all over the country. She'll go away for a few days or a week at a time. Gina laughs when she tells me about the time she went with Jennifer and only lasted two hours.

"It was everything I knew it would be," Gina says, "which convinced me to never go again."

Four weekends ago she came out here. It was a Saturday. It was a three-hour drive from home, which means most of the people here for the vigil have driven the same. She filed her proposed plan with the ranger station, took her tent and food and water and enough clothing to get her through any problems. She took a fishing rod and a gas cooker. She took a GPS unit that blinked out of existence just like Jennifer did. Search and rescue think the GPS unit stopped working when she fell into whatever ravine or when whichever river swept her away.

"She knew what she was doing," Danny says. "She was an experienced hiker but, like I said, she was a free spirit too. Filing a plan and . . . and shit," he says. "Shit. I don't mean to refer to her in the past tense. That makes it sound like she's dead, when she's *not*."

Gina puts her arm around him. "A couple of years ago she did this trip and we all thought she was lost, but she'd just changed her mind," she says. "She'd filed a plan and search and rescue got involved and found her the first day they went looking."

"Boy, were they pissed off," Danny says. "It's a lot of time and effort and money getting those crews together," he says, "and . . . and we'd give anything for that to be the case now. If you see her when you're out there make sure you tell her to get her ass back here, okay? Even if you have to drag her back, you make sure she comes home."

"I will," I tell him, but she's not out there. She was, a month ago, but not now.

When I get back to the tent my mind is racing. How many Jennifers have spent time at the Kelly farm? And the Kelly farm is just a waypoint, but one to where?

I end up tossing and turning and staring at the dark. I can't get comfortable. I can't switch my mind off. I picture happy smiley Jennifer from the 8x11. How far did she make it before she went missing? Did they take her the moment she stepped out of her car? Or did she make it a day or two in, until somebody dragged her from her tent to the basement of the Kelly farm before two men came to town to get her?

Forty-eight

It's almost nine o'clock when I wake up. I feel like I've hardly slept. I roll over and feel every year of my age, and every year of Old Man Haggerty's age too. Something in my back pops when I straighten and something in my knee pops too. I pack my bag and leave the tent set up, figuring I may need it again tonight. The sun is over the trees, but the angle is still low and there isn't much heat in it. That will change. There are thirty cars in the parking lot. People are hustling and bustling their way around portable barbecues making breakfast. Some or all of them are going into The Pines today to look for Jennifer. I can't tell them they're wasting their time.

I get into town and park near the diner and the waitress asks me if I'd like the usual, and I tell her I would, and she jokes that if I spend much more time here they're going to have to charge me rent. She seems happier than yesterday, which must mean I look less scary. I go to check my phone for messages, but it's flat. Fifteen minutes later I'm eating, and fifteen minutes after that I'm trapping notes beneath the salt shaker and waving goodbye. There's an electronics store in the next block. The guy behind the counter barely looks up from his cellphone to make the effort to sell me a charger for mine.

The main library is another block down, a two-story brownstone with a flat roof that extends a few feet over every edge, making the building look like it's wearing a hat. I park in the lot in what, for now, is shade. Last time I was here I was still in school. Back then it smelled of old books. You could see dust trapped in the air, and you'd never run your hand under any of the tables for fear of it getting caught in chewing gum. Now there are floor-to-ceiling windows, tinted to protect the books from the sun, air conditioning, posters on the walls, a kid-zone, computers, newer shelves and newer books, beanbags by the windows and tables with chairs on rollers. But at ten-thirty in the morning it's completely dead, which makes me being here somewhat of a novelty for the librarian. She tells me this, and tells me parents generally bring their kids in from around eleven, and older folks come in not long after that. "Mostly for the air conditioning," she says. "So, what can I help you with?"

The librarian has dark hair that hangs past her shoulders. Every few seconds she has to keep tucking one side of it behind her ear. She's late thirties and looks like she could outrun or outswim me in a competition. When she smiles at me, I can't help but smile back. She's wearing a name badge. *Rochelle*. She looks familiar. I think she was a couple of years below me at high school. I think her dad is Doctor Jackson, the dentist my parents used to take me to.

"Actually, I was wondering if you could plug this in for me and let it charge while I'm here," I say, and I hold up the cellphone.

She looks at it, and suddenly I think she's going to say *That's my boyfriend's phone* or *That's my brother's phone*, but she smiles and says, "Sure thing. Anything else?"

"Well, I guess things would go much easier if you could help me out with something. I'm doing some research."

She smiles. "You've come to the right place," she says. "What kind of research?"

I could have gone to the ranger station today. I could have spoken to whoever works there, but whoever is taking these people most likely has access to the plans they're filing. I don't want to tip anybody off to what I'm looking for. Except, maybe, Rochelle. "On hikers who have gone missing over the years. All that stuff will be in the newspapers and online, right?"

"It will be," she says. "How far back do you want to go?"

"As far as we can."

She stands up. "I guess you want to start with the woman who went missing last month? Jeanette or something, right?"

"Jennifer Ferguson," I say, "and yes."

"Jennifer. I remember now." She crouches behind her desk and plugs the phone in, and then walks me over to the computers. The computers are all modern with wireless keyboards and wireless mice, and I wonder what stops them from going missing. "It'll be easier if I do this," she says, and she sits in front of one of the computers and I angle a chair to sit next to her. "Rather than surfing all over the Internet, we can look through only newspaper articles."

She uses the mouse to access a database. I notice a tattoo on her ring finger. It's a smiley face that looks like it was drawn by a child. She types in *Jennifer Ferguson*, *Missing*, *Hiker*, and *Acacia Pines Forest*, and a list of articles comes up.

"Here," she says, "you take over."

She gets up and I take her seat, but instead of leaving she uses the computer next to me to carry on looking for other stories. I click on the articles. They cover what I learned last night. Jennifer was an experienced hiker who went missing. Teams searched for two weeks. There were dozens of people and dogs and helicopters and no result. I remember what that's like. Every direction you turned you'd hope would be the right one. Sometimes it was, and you'd find the missing hiker huddled in their tent afraid and running out of supplies, or maybe they wouldn't have a tent because they only went out for a day's hike. Other times they've taken a fall, or been stung by something or bitten by something or eaten something they shouldn't have. There were occasions we'd get to them in time, and occasions when we wouldn't. Every summer we'd come across it at least once, sometimes two or three times. Once we had to organize a search party to find a previous search party. When Old Man Haggerty was Sheriff Haggerty, he used to say we should put a chain across the road to stop people from going.

Then there's the flipside. During summer hikers will

come to our town, they'll spend money at our restaurants and drink at our bars and they'll stock up on provisions for the trip, maybe spend a night or two in one of the hotels before or after. Over a season The Pines can see upwards of a thousand people out there, and they're just the ones who file plans. During the height of the summer the ranger station will be manned, staff giving out all kinds of advice. The Pines are great for hiking, they're great for camping, and they also have the most beautiful lakes and rivers this country has to offer. People will spend days looking out over the water, or swimming, or fishing, and you can't blame them. There are sunsets across those lakes that will take your breath away, vistas so stunning they can make you cry. The views out there are like drugs, you want more and more, with each scene more jaw-dropping than the last — and that's why people go off the beaten path. It's why they stray from the plan. It all looks so beautiful, and it is, and it all looks so safe, which it is . . . just not all of the time.

I read through the rest of the articles. Jennifer had done what many others do, she had come into town and stocked up on camping supplies and eaten a good lunch and left, and had filed a plan at the station, which was unmanned. There's a consistent theme to the articles — after she walked out of the ranger station, she disappeared. The plan she filed was useless.

Nobody could tell if she went west like her plan said, or east or north or south. It's like she stepped into the forest and fell into a giant hole.

Forty-nine

I carry on with the articles. In the beginning, the tone is hopeful, as are the rescue teams searching for her. She's experienced. She knows how to stay alive. There's only so far she could have gone. Hopeful, yes, but with a sense that this may end badly. A week in and the tone changes. Jennifer is experienced, but experience doesn't count for much if you're taken by a bear, or fall off a cliff. She would have run out of food. She might have run into the wrong kind of people. It's no longer about search and rescue, it's about search and recovery. The articles get less frequent. There hasn't been one for ten days.

Rochelle puts her hand on my shoulder and I jump.

"Sorry," she says, "you were so focused you didn't hear me."

"Have you found something?"

"There's a lot here," she says. "It's no secret people go missing out there a lot, but you can see here the articles are pretty small for those they find."

"And for those they don't?"

"They get bigger."

"How many so far?"

"I've gone back five years and I have four people who died out there," she says, "and another four people who disappeared and never showed up."

We switch computers again. People are filtering into the library. Children are chattering and parents are telling them to keep it down. I look through the articles Rochelle has found for me, and I read about the people who died. One of them was a suicide. An old guy who had lost his wife a month earlier drove out there and hiked to the same lake where he had proposed forty-five years earlier. He took with him a photograph of his wife and a bottle of sleeping pills. A guy in his twenties went out there with a camera and fell to his death trying to take a selfie on the edge of a sheer drop. The other two were a couple, they'd gone out there and the weather had changed, a storm had rolled in and the temperature dropped. The rescue teams found them, but not in time.

Rochelle is back at her desk talking to some folks checking out some books. She's been joined by a second librarian. The library has filled up a little. Parents are reading books to kids who can't do much more than point and smile and laugh. People are scanning through shelves and opening books and sitting in chairs and reading. Rochelle sees me looking at her and smiles at me. I smile back.

Prior to Jennifer, the last people to go missing out on the trail were Adam Schultz and Antoinette Berger. Adam was a pilot and Antoinette a flight attendant and they'd been dating for three years. Antoinette had grown up camping and this was Adam's first time. They were both a year short of turning thirty. They were both adventurous. They had seen the world. They drove to Acacia Pines one Friday afternoon and picked up some supplies before heading out to The Pines. They filed a plan. Search and rescue followed their route and found their tent near one of the lakes. Backpacks, food, clothes, a gas cooker, all of it there. They'd gone swimming and run into trouble. Maybe one had dived in after the other to help, maybe they'd both cramped at the same time, nobody will ever know, but the conclusion was that Adam and Antoinette had drowned. The lake was a hundred square miles. They dragged it and found nothing.

"You hungry?"

Rochelle's holding up a couple of sandwiches and a couple of juice boxes.

"I got bacon and egg, and I got a B.L.T. Which would you prefer?"

I look at my watch. It's one o'clock. I tap it. "Is this thing right?"

"You've been here over two hours," she says.

"You're kidding."

"You don't know about the rule?" she asks.

"What rule?"

"That librarians aren't allowed to kid." She smiles at me, and I laugh. "You look like a B.L.T. guy," she says, and hands it to me along with one of the juices.

"Thanks," I say. She sits down next to me. The library has cleared out, parents taking the kids away to give them lunch. The other librarian, a guy wearing a shirt and tie who must be in his sixties, sits behind the counter reading a newspaper.

"Are you finding what you're after?" Rochelle asks.

"I am."

"And what exactly is that?"

"I'm not sure." I nod at her hand. "So, what's the story with the tattoo?"

She looks at her finger, and then blushes. "I got it when I was twelve," she says.

"Twelve? You're kidding."

"You've already forgotten the rule," she says.

"Librarians don't kid," I say. "Got it. So what's the deal? You were in a street gang? You don't seem the street gang type."

"No? And what type do I seem like?"

"The helpful type," I say, holding up my sandwich. "So what happened?"

"It was my sister. She's a couple of years older than me. She borrowed a tattoo gun from her friend — the friend's dad is a tattoo artist. She wanted to try it out, and she convinced me to let her try it on me. Mom and Dad freaked when they saw it, and we both got in so much trouble. Instead of getting it removed, they made me keep it as a reminder not to be so stupid, although they also made me wear a Band-Aid over it at school so nobody could see it. As I got older it became part of me. I still smile when I think about it. You have any tattoos?"

"None," I say.

She smiles. "I could ask my sister to give you one, if you'd like. I'm sure she wouldn't mind."

"Another smiley face?"

"She can do sad faces too."

We eat our sandwiches for a bit. Then she says, "I recognize you, by the way. It's Noah, right?"

"Right," I say. "I recognize you too. From school."

She looks happy that I know who she is. "You . . . you helped me once. Back when we were kids."

"I did?"

"Yeah. It was after school, and these other kids . . . they, you know, they were giving me a hard time. They were teasing me because of my braces. They took my bag and wouldn't give it back, and they were going to throw it into the creek that ran behind the school, you remember the one?"

"I remember it."

"You came running along, like . . . like a knight in shining armor," she says. "You demanded the bag back, and one of the guys punched you, you remember that?"

"Really hard in the face."

"You fell down," she says, "and they laughed at you, and I was crying and asking them to leave us alone, and then you got back up and when the guy tried to hit you again, you hit him first. You fought them both off."

I remember it all clearly. The two boys were from another school, and I'd seen them around before. Rochelle is being kind when she says I fought them off. The truth is after we'd all hit each other it became a standoff. We stood looking at each other, then one of them said that this was a waste of their time, and they threw the bag into the creek and ran away.

"I got your bag out of the water," I say. "You opened it and everything was wet."

"I cried at that. I'd just used my pocket money to buy two new *Star Trek* novels, and they were ruined. The next day you found me at school. You'd bought me new copies of those same books. I hugged you when you gave them to me. Do you remember that?"

I remember it. I used to deliver papers in the morning before school, and those books cost me an entire week's pay, but it had seemed the right thing to do. I also remember her dad offering me free dental care for life after that.

"Do you remember what you said to me?"

"Something about keeping them dry?"

She laughs again. I love hearing it. "No. You said *Star Trek* can show us who we can be. You said the boys who threw my bag into the water could one day be better too, if we let them."

"I said that?"

"Yes. Do you still think that way?"

I think of Stephen and his friends. "It's getting harder to keep believing it."

"You were so nice to me," she says, "and . . . and I had such a crush on you after that," she adds.

"I haven't thought about that in a long time," I say.

"I have," she says. "Every now and then. It didn't surprise me when you became a cop. I used to see you around, and . .

. and back then I used to dream up ways that I could get you to save me again." She laughs. She looks embarrassed. "Stupid kid stuff," she says.

"No, it's sweet," I tell her, because I'm not sure what else to say.

She takes another bite of her sandwich, probably to stop herself from saying anything more. I take a bite of mine too. It's good. I didn't realize how hungry I was until that first bite a few minutes ago. I ought to carry around a backpack full of food.

"Are you back for good?" she asks.

"No," I tell her.

"That's a shame," she says. "So . . . why are you back? To find missing hikers?"

"Something like that."

She finishes her sandwich and she stands up and looks around the library for a few moments then sits back down. "I still have some time," she says. "I'll go back another five years, okay?"

"You sure?"

"I figure I still owe you for those books," she says.

I finish my sandwich and drink my juice. Rochelle comes up with more articles while I carry on reading the ones she's already found for me. Jennifer, the couple who drowned, and before them another woman who went missing, a nature photographer who planned on being away five nights. Her tent and equipment were found, but there was no sign of her or her camera. The theory is she hiked away from her tent to take some photographs, perhaps with the intention of going only fifty yards, or a hundred, perhaps to chase something beautiful, or to chase the lighting, but once you lose a line of sight with something out there you can lose yourself. Her name was Elizabeth Blake. She was twenty-seven.

We switch computers again. Rochelle has gone back five more years and pulled up more stories.

I go through the five years of death and disappearances. A boyfriend who killed his girlfriend during an argument. A fitness fanatic who, at the age of twenty-six, had a heart attack while running one of the trails. Two others who, like the two I read about earlier, died from exposure when the weather changed. A couple who couldn't save their six-year-old son from drowning.

Then there's a story similar to Elizabeth Blake's. Marcy Greer's. Marcy was twenty-nine years old and had broken up with her husband two months earlier and had the romantic notion of writing the great self-help book. She was going to become one with nature and the entire experience was going to make her stronger, and she was going to write all of it. But the experience had her fall into the same deep hole that Jennifer fell in, that Elizabeth fell in, that Adam and Antoinette fell in.

I keep reading.

There are two more people who were never found. A husband and wife on their honeymoon. No trace of them, or of their tents, they hadn't filed a plan and nobody knew they were missing for a week, and a week out there is a long time.

A week can lead you a long way from anywhere, it can get you lost in a cave, down a ravine, over an edge. I read about Trevor Hughes. He was twenty-eight. He went out there with a tent and a mountain bike and The Pines swallowed him up.

On the other computer Rochelle has finished pulling up articles. She's gone back another ten years. "I can't believe it's this many," she says.

We switch computers so I can look at the disappearances between ten and twenty years ago. Some of the articles I read are cases I remember. We're in the time frame where I was one of the people out there searching. I remember coordinated efforts, and helicopters overhead, and dogs on leashes leading the way. Joy, jubilation, fear, heartbreak — we had it all. In that ten-year period eight people died out there and there were another five we never found. One story here from eighteen years ago was the first one I ever worked. It was a guy in his early thirties. Martin Clark. He was suffering from depression. He'd lost his job and lost his wife and was out there taking stock of his life. I wonder if what happened to him was the result of a bad decision, a bad turn, a bad piece of luck, or if he got chained in the basement of the Kelly farm. Back then we figured there was a good chance it was suicide.

Twenty years' worth of articles.

Thirteen disappearances going back over eighteen years. Seven women and six men. All of them under thirty.

And possibly all of them victims of somebody sick and twisted who's been stalking those woods for the last two decades.

Yet their fates and Alyssa's fate are different. That's why her car is out in the quarry, and other cars aren't — the cars of those other victims were left at the parking lot by the trails. They had to be, because people missing out on the trails wouldn't have missing cars too. Somehow Alyssa's world intersected with that world twelve years ago, and intersected again last week. How?

I pace around the tables the computers are on. It's mid-afternoon and I've been sitting reading for over four hours. My body feels the same way it felt this morning when I climbed out of the tent — like somebody tucked me into bed the night before with a sledgehammer. The library is filling back up. Soon school kids are going to start arriving. Another librarian has joined the team.

"There are more here," Rochelle says. "Not as many over the previous ten years."

"How many?"

"Five," she says, "of people who died, but nobody who disappeared. Want me to keep looking?"

"Go back another five years," I say. "That is, if you have time."

"It won't take long," she says, and it doesn't. The search string that has given us so many articles gives no more. It started with Martin Clark and ended with Jennifer Ferguson.

"That's a lot of people," she says.

"I know."

"This isn't just research, is it?" she asks. "All these people, they match a certain profile, right? Young and fit."

"Yes," I say.

"The fact you came here to look for all of this, it means you already suspected, right?"

"Something like that," I say. "Just . . . just not on this scale."

"Somebody has been hurting these people," she says.

"I think so."

"Somebody from Acacia."

"I'm not sure."

"How come nobody has seen this before?"

"Because they're all from different places," I say. "Nothing links them. People going missing in forests isn't anything new. It happens in forests all across the country, all across the world. There's no pattern because nobody ever thought to look for one."

"It's home time," she says. "We take turns at finishing at three o'clock, and today is my day."

"Nobody wants to work past three?"

"You'll see why soon. If you want, I can stay and help you."

"I'll be okay," I tell her, and she looks disappointed.

"I just have to grab my stuff," she says. "I'll come back in a minute and say bye."

I sit back down in front of the computer. I go back twelve years, to the time Alyssa went missing. Back then a hiker by the name of Debra Olsen went missing. She was eighteen years old. She was taking the summer off between high school and university. She had camped The Pines in the past with her dad, but her dad had died the year before in a car accident and she was coming out here to say goodbye to that part of her life.

She came into town and stocked up on supplies and nobody ever saw her again.

Debra Olsen went missing one week before Alyssa went missing.

I remember being pulled off the search team when Alyssa disappeared. For me, Debra Olsen drifted into the past as my focus turned to finding a seven-year-old girl. After we did find her, and after I was kicked out of town, I don't think I ever thought of Debra again.

The two people Conrad pretended to have overheard, he said they were search and rescue. The hiker he implied they were looking for was Debra.

"Hey," Rochelle says.

"I think I've covered everything I can." I stand up. "I appreciate your help. Everything you've done today, it's been really important stuff, but I'm going to ask you to do me a favor."

"Anything."

"Don't tell anybody about what we found here."

"Okay," she says, without any hesitation. "You want me to print out these articles?"

"Please. Not all of them. Maybe just one for each person."

She clicks a few options and then a printer behind the desk whirrs and starts printing. There's enough here that neither Old Man Haggerty nor Drew can dismiss what I'm saying. The last of the articles comes through the printer and Rochelle picks them up and taps them against the counter to straighten all the edges. She hands them to me. The school crowd is filtering in.

She walks me to the door.

"Umm . . . do you want to have a proper lunch with me?" she asks. "I mean, if you've got no plans and all. We could discuss the case," she says.

I look at my watch. It's a little after three. The effects of the B.L.T. have faded, and I'm going to need to fuel up.

"Or we can meet later on for dinner if you like," she says.

"Lunch sounds good," I tell her. "But it'll have to be somewhere close by. I still have a lot to work on."

She looks like she was expecting me to say no, and her expression is blank for a second, and then she smiles. "I know just the place," she says. "We'll be able to order right away. It'll be . . ." She doesn't say what. I think she was about to say *It'll be fun*, but then remembered all the people that have gone missing and those who died. She shrugs.

"Oh, your phone!"

I'd completely forgotten about it. She goes back behind the counter and the two librarians say something to her, and they all look in my direction and smile. She grabs my phone and the charger. The school kids in here are starting to take up a lot of real estate, with their bags and books spread out over tables. Some of them read quietly and some talk loudly and a couple of them who walk past me smell of cigarette smoke. Two kids are having a tug-of-war with a bag and another kid throws a pen at somebody else and I can see why the staff take turns at not being here after three. Rochelle comes over and hands me the charger and the phone. They're both warm.

I switch on the phone and it beeps. I have voicemail.

"Just give me a second," I say.

I check the messages. I'm expecting to hear Charlotte Bauer, but instead it's Earl Winters. *Those two men I've been telling you about, they just drove past here*, he says. *They're heading into town. I'll call you when they come back.*

The message came in at eleven o'clock last night. I was on my way out to the hiking trails at that time, and my phone might have been flat by then anyway. There's a second message an hour later. It's Earl telling me that the two men have driven back out of town.

They came here again last night looking for me.

Fifty

"I'm going to need to take a rain check on that lunch," I say.

"Oh," Rochelle says, and she sounds disappointed. I'm disappointed too.

"If you give me your number I can call you later," I say. "If there's time we can grab dinner, and if not we can try again tomorrow."

She smiles. "Sounds great," she says.

In the parking lot out back the bike stands are overflowing with bikes, and others are leaning against the walls of the adjoining buildings. Rochelle's car and my pickup are the only two cars out here. The other librarians either walked or got dropped off. Rochelle looks at my pickup and I get the feeling she's thinking she just dodged a bullet. A vehicle like this, the guy driving it must be into self-harming.

"It's a loan car," I tell her.

"I didn't say anything," she says, and she laughs. "Till next time," she says, and she kisses me on the cheek and climbs into her car.

I've left the windows down on the pickup, and thank God I did, otherwise I wouldn't be able to climb in this thing until winter. The crime scene photos from the Kelly farm are still on the passenger seat. Of course they are. Nobody looks at this pickup and thinks there might be something in it worth stealing. The photographs I took from Alyssa's bedroom are on the front seat too, and the one of her and Father Frank is still tucked into the sun visor from last night. I take it out and tuck it into my pocket along with the most current picture of her, the one where she has her arm around Father Barrett.

The roads are full of kids on bikes carrying school bags. SUVs with kids strapped into the back clog the roads. A yellow school bus is making a turn at the next intersection, children moving around in there so much it's rocking on its axles. It takes me twenty-five minutes to get to Old Man Haggerty's house because of the traffic. I park up the driveway behind his car and carry the printouts from the library up to the house.

He doesn't answer when I knock. He could be off buying cigarettes or he could have an appointment with Doctor Osborne . . . but if that's the case, why is his car still parked up his driveway? I don't have his phone number. I knock on the door again, and then I try it. It's unlocked. I open it.

It's the smell that hits me first. Raw, like meat gone bad in the sun, which in a way is exactly what it is. Haggerty is lying on the floor in the lounge, his oxygen machine tipped over beside him. I drop the papers on the floor and crouch next to him. There's no point in checking for a pulse. My guess is he's been dead all day. His eyes are wide open. It wasn't a heart attack that did this, or another stroke. His oxygen cord has been wrapped around his neck. His fingers are clutching at it. The Pandora's box he thought he had prevented me from opening was open the whole time. The monsters he thought he had kept at bay have been coming and going all these years, and last night they weren't coming into town for me, but for him. They came here, did this, then left. Haggerty was a good man. People respected him. This town, for a long time, was his town, and his death will be the town's loss.

I hold my nose to try and block the smell. Haggerty's gun is on the couch where he had it last night when we were talking. Other than his body, and the tipped-over oxygen machine, there's no sign of a struggle. I think about him trying to get his fingers under the oxygen hose. I think about the world fading, him dropping to his knees as it fades some more. He'd have known he was going to die and he'd have known the secret he kept for so long was the reason why. The men who killed him, who else are they going to target? Old Man Haggerty isn't the only person in town who's been helping me. There's Maggie, there's Father Barrett, there's Drew, and there's Rochelle. Are they in danger too? Or did they come here to put an end to a loose thread?

I go into the kitchen where the smell isn't as bad and open a window. I pull my phone out of my pocket to call Drew when Conrad steps through the front door. He stands motionless looking at his dad, and for a moment I'm not even sure he's seen me, but then he looks toward me, his face clouding over and going red.

"It's not what you think," I tell him.

His expression keeps changing. His face is still red, but the anger is gone. He smiles, and at the same time he steps forward and picks his father's gun up off the couch. He points it at me. He has me dead to rights.

"In a way you've done me a favour," he says. "I never liked him."

"I didn't kill him," I say.

"Sure looks that way."

"He was like this when I found him. Surely the smell can tell you that."

"The thing is, Noah, sometimes things look a certain way when they're not, you know what I mean?"

I don't answer him.

"And when that happens, it doesn't matter what the person being accused is saying, it only matters what the accuser is thinking. You can stand there and tell me a hundred different ways that you didn't kill my dad, but here we are, you in his house, an unwelcome guest, my dad dead on the floor. I can see there could be a couple of reasons for things being different from how it looks, the smell being one of them, but you know what? I'm going to choose you did this. That means you're guilty. You know what it's like to make those decisions, right? To be judge and jury?"

"I'm sorry about what happened all those years ago," I say. "I know you were framed. I'm trying to find the person who did that to you."

"You did that to me," he says. "You framed me. You ruined

my life. Now, back up a bit."

I don't move.

"I mean it, Noah, you back up a bit or I'm going to shoot you dead."

I take a few paces back into the kitchen. I have my arms up, like I'm a hostage in a bank robbery.

Conrad opens a cabinet drawer in the lounge, and I hear the rattle of something I haven't heard in a long time — handcuffs. He tosses them to me. I let them bounce off my chest onto the floor.

"Pick them up," he says.

I don't move.

"Seriously, Noah, I don't think you understand how much I'm itching to shoot you right now. You have a choice. You stand there like an idiot and I shoot you, or you pick up the handcuffs and see where this goes."

"You shoot me and your life is over. Drew will arrest you."

"Maybe," he says. "Or maybe I'll shoot him too. He let you pull that shit twelve years ago. The way I see it, you're both guilty. You at least had the decency to leave town, but I see that asshole out and about all the damn time."

I pick up the handcuffs.

"Put one on," he says.

I put one on.

"Nice and tight," he says.

I tighten it.

"Now put your hands behind your back and put the other one on," he says.

"Let's talk about this," I say. "You're not thinking straight. You're too caught up in what happened twelve years ago. You're in shock at what's happened to your dad."

"Too caught up? Too caught up? My leg still hurts, man. I limp in cold weather. The pain, the pain is chronic. I have to take painkillers. There are days I can't work. I lost my job out at the sawmill, and I loved that job. I was good at it too, but when you can't walk for a year it's not a job you can keep. Too caught up? You're a piece of shit, Noah. Now do what I ask or I'll shoot you right now."

I do what he asks.

"Turn around so I can see you've done it right."

I turn around. I face the window I opened. I tighten my jaw and I tense my body and I close my eyes because I know what's coming, and I know there's no way to avoid it. He steps in behind me, and in one of the windows I can see the reflection of his arm moving up into the air, and then moving back down. The gun hits me hard in the back of the head.

Fifty-one

I'm aware of a few things that happen then, but not in any great detail, and certainly not in a way that enables me to do anything about it. Conrad puts the gun down and drags me through the lounge, past his dead father's body, to the front door. He gets me outside and it hurts being pulled off the porch and over the yard and partway down the driveway, my spine raking over the edges of the steps, my head bouncing off every surface. He drags me feet first, so my shirt rides up and skin is torn from my arms and hands that are still cuffed behind me. He gets me to his car and this time there's no Father Barrett to save me. The same neighbors who never saw me breaking into Haggerty's house now don't see me being stuffed into the trunk. Conrad gets me in and it's uncomfortable with my arms behind me and something is going to break, but I can't do much about it. He leans in and puts duct tape over my mouth. He closes the trunk and starts the car and it's hot in here, really hot, and cramped. I pass out as we drive.

Every time I come to, the trunk is hotter than the last time. I pull at the cuffs but it's a pointless exercise. I try to hook my legs through my arms so I can get my hands out front, but there's not enough room in here to do that. My shoulders are cramping. I'm no longer passing in and out. I'm completely aware. The side of my body is numb. My wrists are screaming. My neck hurts. I can't see a thing. The temperature climbs. It climbs some more. I try shifting my weight. I try getting onto my other side. I can't. I'm still in the same position he put me in. I can't feel my arms. The phone in my pocket is digging into my hip. The temperature climbs again. I kick at the car. Confined in the trunk, it sounds like a gunshot. I kick some more. The car doesn't slow down. Conrad doesn't do anything but drive. We keep motoring along. Still the temperature climbs. I'm breathing heavily, and it adds to the heat. I pull at the handcuffs again. I try to roll. My keys dig into me. The air gets thicker. I can smell gas. I can smell grease. I can smell his dead father on my clothes. I've been in here five minutes. Five hours. Five days. This is torture. This is hell. It's so hot in here I want to die. I want Conrad to crash the car or, at the very least, drive it into the quarry and send me to the bottom of the lake with those other assholes and let me drown in the cool water. Perhaps this is karma for killing those men. I have to be punished somehow, don't I?

We pull over. Conrad gets out and he pops the trunk. The sun is behind him shining right into my eyes. It blinds me. I turn my head to look away. My neck hurts. I have a headache. My brain is pulsing.

"We have to be patient," he says. "Where we're going, we can't go yet." He looks at his watch. "We're going to wait here for two hours. I suggest you relax," he says, and he slams the trunk closed.

I want to scream. I can't. I can't do anything. I'd be better off if he clubbed me with the gun and knocked me out. I try to calm my mind. I can't. I count my breaths. It doesn't work. The temperature climbs. I kick at the side of the car. I pull at the handcuffs. Another five hours go by. Another five days. I keep kicking at the car. I can feel blood seeping into my shoe from the cut on my foot. I keep a constant rhythm going, and after a minute Conrad comes and opens the trunk.

"What?"

I mumble into the duct tape. He reaches in and pulls it away. I take a deep breath.

"Whatever you have planned," I say, "it ain't going to work if I cook to death."

He goes to say something, and thinks better of it. He knows I'm right. He has something he wants to do that doesn't involve me accidentally dying along the way. "Fine," he says, and he slams the trunk closed and starts the car and we drive for ten seconds until he pulls over again. He pops the trunk open. "Better?"

We're in the shade of some big trees. I have no idea where we are. A farm, probably. Or a rest stop on the highway.

"Whatever it is you—"

"I don't want to hear it," he says, and he reaches in and puts a fresh piece of duct tape over my mouth.

To his credit, when he closes the trunk, he doesn't close it all the way, letting it stay open a couple of inches, and those two inches are the difference between me living and dying. All I can see through the gap are the trees. I don't even know where Conrad is, or what he's doing. A car goes by in the distance. I can't see it. Then another. I count to sixty in my head. I figure if I can do that a hundred times, then we'll be getting close to the two hours he said. More cars go by. The work day is ending. Traffic increases. Then it decreases. Then there are no cars. Conrad opens the trunk.

"Here," he says, and he takes the duct tape off my mouth and tilts my head so he can get the top of a water bottle against my mouth. I drink it quickly. "Slowly," he says. "I don't want you choking to death."

I drink it slowly. When I've had enough he pulls it away.

"Thank you," I say. "We don't have—"

"Save it," he says, and he puts the duct tape back over my mouth.

He shuts the trunk. He starts the car. We drive. I can hear my breathing and I can hear the engine and I can hear the road beneath us. The road goes forever. The temperature climbs again. The air is on fire. I can't do this. I can't survive this. We've been driving a week now. A month. The pressure on my shoulders and wrists is immense.

Eventually the car slows. The brake lights come on and the trunk glows red, then goes dark again as we go from a sealed road to a shingle road. Stones ping up against the undercarriage. I can visualize them. They're inches from

327

hitting my face. We're on another endless road. Then we slow down. We come to a stop. The engine dies and the door opens and there are footsteps across the gravel and they disappear. I don't know for how long. Five minutes. Or ten. I kick at the wall of the car and try to twist my body but it's all for nothing. The footsteps come back. Conrad pops the trunk. The hot air inside escapes. The hot air from outside comes in. It circulates around me. Conrad reaches in. He grabs me by my shirt and he pulls forward.

"Work with me here," he says, "or I'll lock you back in there and we can try this again tomorrow."

I work with him. He gets me sitting up. He keeps pulling. My weight shifts over the edge of the trunk, then gravity kicks in and I spill the rest of the way. My shoulder takes most of the impact. I'm left staring at the wheels of the car and the shingle road. Conrad grabs the back of my shirt and pulls.

"On your feet," he says.

I get to my feet. I struggle to stay balanced. He turns me around to face where he's brought me, and now I can see why we had to pull over and wait for a couple of hours. He was waiting for the workers to finish for the day.

Conrad has brought me out to the sawmill where I beat him all those years ago.

Fifty-two

Conrad prods me in the back with the gun. I struggle to walk because my legs are numb and my shoulders are tight and my foot is aching. I can feel it squishing around in blood. I manage to get one foot in front of the other. I know where this is going and, in a way, I can't blame him for it. How can I? I did this to him twelve years ago — doesn't that entitle him to do the same?

There are truck-sized doors to enter the factory, but within one of those is a normal-size door that Conrad has already opened. Maybe he kept the key for this place all these years hoping for this moment.

Things have changed since the last time I was at the sawmill. Back then the surrounding area was in an early stage of regrowth. Now the trees are back and I imagine it won't be long until they're logged again — that's one thing about the sawmill, there's never been a shortage of trees. There's been a whole swath of renovations, some sections being rebuilt, others repainted, and there's even an extension out to the side, but those renovations are already looking old. Usually I'd expect to see piles of logs, saws with blades bigger than a car, logging trucks and diggers and bulldozers in every direction, but all that stuff is gone to the new location, leaving big empty patches of flattened land with oil stains and cracked pavement.

We step inside. The trees are blocking the sun, and the windows are so thick with sawdust and dust that light struggles to get through. We go past empty shelves in the process of being dismantled, and steel columns reaching up to the ceiling. We walk the two hundred yards to the office. The rail I handcuffed Drew to now has a sign hanging from it that says *240 days without an accident.* I wonder if they'll change that in a couple of days to *1 day without a beating.* That is if it's a beating. Maybe it'll have to say *murder.*

Conrad turns on the light in the office. Everything that was old has been replaced with everything that was new ten years ago, but has become old again. Perhaps the last office has been buried as a time capsule for future scholars. There's a chair behind the desk and two chairs on this side of it. Conrad tells me to take the closest chair. It's a normal office chair. Four metal legs welded to a metal frame, a plywood bottom and back wrapped in foam and fake leather. He keeps the gun pointed at me as I sit down. He's taking no chances. Because I've been ahead of him this entire time, I haven't noticed until now that he's holding a rope. He moves behind me and loops the rope over me and I think about trying to stand, maybe trying to run or hit him somehow, kick him or kick the chair at him, but I can't see any of those things working. He throws loops of rope over me, pulling it tight against my body and my legs and my ankles. He ties it off.

"Did you think this day would come?" he asks. He drags the chair from behind the desk so he can sit facing me. He looks pleased with himself. His chair is on rollers and is padded and a beating in that chair would be a more comfortable experience. "Shit, what am I thinking?" he says, and he leans forward and tugs at the duct tape.

"Think about what you're doing, Conrad," I say.

He laughs at that. I'm not sure what's so funny.

"Oh, I am thinking about it," he says. "I've thought about little else over the years. I kid you not, Noah, but every single morning I wake up and pray that somehow today will be the day where I get you back for what you did to me. Then this week my prayers were answered. If I'd known what it took to get you back here, I'd have made sure Alyssa went missing years ago."

"You know where she is?"

"No, and I don't care. I had nothing to do with her back then, and nothing to do with her leaving now."

"What I did to you was wrong," I tell him. "What you're doing now is wrong."

"And yet it feels so right."

I'm not going to get through to him — there are too many years of anger to break down, but I have to try. "Listen to me, Conrad, I know you're angry, and you have every right to be, but if you do this you're letting the person who abducted

Alyssa get away with it. There are others involved — they've abducted others over the years. Your dad . . . your dad was helping me."

"And this affects me how?"

"Like I said, people are being abducted."

"You think I care?"

I shouldn't be shocked by his lack of empathy, but I am. How can he be so different from his father? "You always were an asshole, Conrad. Your world doesn't extend beyond you, does it?"

"It's extending to you right now," he says.

"I didn't kill your father," I say.

"You think any of this is about that? My father was a loser. I hated him. If anything, all of this would end up going a little easier on you if I really thought you killed him."

"Somebody killed him," I say.

"Then I'll buy that person a drink. You know what he used to say? He used to say, *Conrad, why can't you be more like Noah? That kid, he's taking responsibility for his life. He's becoming somebody. He wants to help people.* I got that all the time. And you know what? After you beat the shit of me, he never took any of that back. Not once did he go, *Hey, Conrad? I was wrong about that Noah. He's a son of a bitch. He should be in jail.*"

"He didn't say that because he knows what you did to Maggie. He knows what you've done to other women."

"She was up for it," he says. "She always was, Noah, and it used to make all of us laugh that you were the only one who couldn't see it."

332

"Bullshit."

"The stuff she was into still makes me blush when I think back on what we had. We hooked up plenty of times. She couldn't get enough of me."

I don't pull at the ropes or the handcuffs. It's pointless. I have to stay calm. Have to stay thinking. But mentally I'm pulling his arms out of their sockets. "You can say what you want, Conrad, I know you're full of shit."

"You don't believe me? The same way you didn't believe me last time we were in this office?"

He has me there.

"You can tell yourself what you want to, Noah, but I'm telling you, your wife . . . I mean your ex-wife, she's a good liar. Perhaps the best liar. You ever figure that out?"

"She's not a liar."

"No? You don't think she's ever lied to you?"

She lied to me in the car two days ago when she said she didn't know why the charges against me were dropped. "No."

"You know what they say about lawyers and actors, right?"

"What?"

"That it's almost the same thing. People go into one profession and become the other. Being a lawyer, that's acting, and an actor's job is to lie to you and make it real. Your wife, she's a good lawyer, but an even better actor. It's all about performing."

"You drugged her and you raped her."

He laughs. "Only the first time."

"You're sick," I tell him.

"What you did to me back then, that was you being jealous. You can't stand the fact that I had her first."

Stay calm. Keep your strength.

"Why were you even at your dad's today?" I ask, wanting to change the subject.

The change in direction confuses him for a few seconds. "He called me last night," he says. "Said he'd been thinking about things. Said he knew he was running out of time because of his stroke, and he wanted to put the past behind us. Said he wanted us to have some kind of relationship. He asked me to come around this morning, and I told him I would, only I didn't. I had a hangover. But you know, I figured, why not go and see the old coot? Make nice with him. Make sure I get the house after he dies. I have no idea whether I'm going to get it now."

"Even if you do, you won't get to appreciate it from jail."

"Me going there today at the same time you were there, that's fate, right?"

"Not fate," I tell him. "Just the world messing with me."

He laughs. "I like that," he says. "The thing I like the most about it is how you think the world is messing with you, how you think you're the victim, when you're the bad guy here. You're the one who tortured me."

"Whatever you're going to do," I say, "just get it done."

"Okay." He stands up, puts the gun on the desk and stretches his arms and his fingers and there's nothing I can do but watch. He rolls his shoulders and loosens his neck. "I remember it all," he says. "Every blow. Every punch. I remember the order it all came in. You started here," he says, and he taps the side of his jaw, "and you ended it here," he says, and he taps his leg. "You look worried, Noah. You look like a man who thinks I'm about to kill him. But you're wrong. I'm only going to do to you what you did to me. Everything, in exactly the same order. That should give you some comfort, right?"

I tighten my muscles. I hold my head up high and look at him. "You don't have to—"

"I'm not interested in talking anymore," he says, and his fist flies in and cracks me in the side of the jaw, and it's the first punch of many.

Fifty-three

I try to remember the order of events from that night twelve years ago. But I can't — and, even if I could, I don't really see how it can help knowing which direction the punch is coming from, or for what body part. Conrad has to stop often to shake out his hand. I broke two fingers that night, and I suspect he's done the same. Fireworks go off inside my head, skyrockets and comets and Roman candles ignite from every corner. There comes a point where I don't feel the blows as much. The view of the office becomes dim. My left eye is swelling shut.

I lose track of time. The punches keep coming. I look up at him between blows. I try to remain strong and try to look defiant. I didn't hit him this many times, did I? Then all that strength, all that defiance, it drains away. I lose count of the amount of shots I take. There's blood all over my shirt and my pants. I'm broken inside. My teeth are loose. I think my jaw might be broken. Same goes for my nose. Same goes for my everything.

"Ooohwee," Conrad says, and he stands back and laughs. I look up at him but can barely see him. He's puffing, and I'm puffing too. "That sure was a lot of work. I guess I never got an appreciation of what you had to go through when our places were reversed."

I try to say something but can't. I don't even know what I want to say.

"By my reckoning," he says, "we're done here. Well, almost done," he says, and he picks up the gun. "I ought to shoot you in the head and throw you into the woods, but in the spirit of fairness, since you didn't do that to me, I'm not going to do that to you. Now," he says, and he pushes the muzzle of the gun into my leg, "I think around about here looks right. I should warn you, this is going to hurt. You think the other stuff was painful? That ain't nothing compared to this."

I look up at him. All I can see is a blur.

"Bullet hit my bone and broke into a few pieces," he says. "I don't know if I can replicate that exactly, but let's give it the old college try, huh? You ready?"

I glare at him. I want to kill him.

"You look ready," he says

I move my jaw. It's not broken.

He smiles. "Tell you what, Noah, something tells me that you're a man of your word. Am I right?"

I don't say anything.

"How about this, and this is a one-time offer," he says. "You keep your mouth shut about what happened here tonight, and maybe I won't shoot you like I was planning. That sound good? That way I avoid jail, you avoid a lifetime limp. I know it's not exactly even-steven, but you've given me enough joy here this evening that I can live with that. You gotta promise me, though, that I walk out of here and it ends. You don't come for me. On that I want your word."

I cough up a wad of snot and blood forms in my mouth and I have to spit it out. I don't see it hit the floor, but I hear it, all wet and all loud and all bloody. My nose isn't broken after all, because I can talk properly. "Okay," I say, because what other option is there really?

My vision is starting to focus. He takes the gun away and wipes his hands on his shirt. "You won't tell anybody about tonight?"

"No."

"You won't come after me?"

"No."

"So we're square?"

"We're square."

"I have your word on that?"

"Yes."

He thinks on that for a few moments. "You remember how you didn't believe me when you had me tied into the chair?"

"I believed you. In. The end," I tell him. "That's why. I left."

"You believed me after I lied to you," he says. "You wouldn't believe the truth, but you believed the lie."

"I'm not lying to you. You walk away. You . . . you walk right now and we're square. Either that, or you kill me right now. So make yourself a decision, Conrad. You shoot me, and

Drew will figure out right quick it was you. You want to end up in jail the rest of your life? You've gotten your revenge," I say. "I'll take your deal and I'll stand by it."

"Okay," he says, and he turns the gun around so he can use it as a club. "This wasn't just about having fun, Noah, but this evening has also been cathartic for me. This, this was important. You know you had this coming, right?"

"I know."

"Then I think I can finally move on."

He swings the gun down and clubs me in the head.

Fifty-four

When I come to, I'm lying on the floor of the office. There's a shrill ringing in my head. My hands are no longer cuffed. I roll onto my back and look up at the ceiling and something in my head wobbles and sways, and I have to roll back onto my side so I can throw up. There's blood all around me. I reach up and touch my face and it's puffy and tender and parts of it are bigger than they ought to be, and everything beneath the surface throbs. I blow clots of blood out of my nose.

I prop myself against the desk. I rest a few beats, then hoist myself into the seat Conrad was sitting in earlier. I'm able to wheel myself to the other side of the desk. I rummage through the drawers and find some aspirin. I get some saliva going that tastes like blood and swallow three of them down, one at a time, the third one getting stuck at the back of my mouth where it dissolves, tasting like death.

I give it ten minutes. The pills don't help. I touch my

swollen eye and the fireworks have a second showing. I get my phone out of my pocket and there's no reception, and one day Acacia is going to have to do something about that, like build some goddamn cellphone towers out this way.

I have to call Drew. I promised Conrad I wouldn't talk about what happened here, but one look at me and one look at where he's picking me up from, and Drew will connect the dots. I have to call him. I have to bring him in on everything that's happened, and everything I've learned. I can't do this alone any longer. I'm going to break my promise to Conrad, but I'm sure that won't keep me awake at night. I'm going to break my promise to Father Frank too.

I get Drew's number from my phone, and use the office phone to call him.

"Noah," he says, once I tell him who's calling. "This isn't a good time."

"I need your help."

"I can't," he says. "Not right now."

"Can you come and pick me up?"

"Hang on a second," he says, and the voices I can hear in the background disappear. "What's happened?"

"Actually, quite a lot," I tell him. "Can you come and meet me?"

"Come where?"

"I'm out at the sawmill. The original one."

"What the hell are you doing out there?"

"It's a long story, but one I'll tell you about when you get here."

"The sawmill," he says, and I know what he's thinking — he's thinking about the last time we were there together. "Please don't tell me you've got somebody tied up out there?"

"Nothing like that," I tell him. "Please, Drew, it's important."

"Look, Noah, I got my hands full right now."

"With what?" I ask, and I know what the answer is going to be even before he says it. He's busy with Old Man Haggerty.

"Look, whatever it is, it's going to need to wait, okay? Gimme a couple of hours and I'll call you back."

"Drew—"

"Damn it, Noah, I'm not your goddamn chauffeur, okay? Are you in immediate danger? Is somebody about to cut your damn head off, or shoot you?"

"What's going on, Drew?"

"I have to go," he says.

"Is this about Old Man Haggerty?" I ask.

"Now why in the hell would you ask me that?"

"Is it?"

"No, it isn't."

Shit. Is it Stephen? Have Stephen and his friends been found? "What is it you're not telling me, Drew?" I ask. "What has you so riled up?"

"We have a missing person report," he says.

"Who?" I ask.

"Where were you last night, Noah?"

"Are you kidding me?"

"Where were you?"

My alibi sounds like shit, but I go with it. "I was camping."

"Camping?"

"I had to stay somewhere," I say. "Why are you asking me this?"

"Because your name has come up," he says. "Why didn't you stay back out at the Kelly farm? I thought you liked it there."

"How did my name come up?"

"Let me ask you again, Noah, why didn't you stay back out at the Kelly farm?"

"It burned down."

"What? What the hell are you telling me?"

"It's all part of the long story I'll tell you when you get here."

"Where were you camping?"

"Out on the trails."

"Where'd you get the camping equipment?"

"It belonged to Father Frank."

"You realize how thin this sounds?"

"That's where I was, and I spoke to a few people out there — they're probably still out there and can back me up. I was there all night. They'd have heard me if I'd tried to leave."

"What time did you get there?"

"Around eleven."

"And before then?"

I don't answer him.

"Where the hell were you before then, Noah?"

"What's going on?" I ask. "Who is missing? Am I a suspect?"

"Just answer the question."

"I was at Old Man Haggerty's place."

"You were what?"

"I was at his place."

"Dammit, you go there to take a beating?"

"He was helping me with something."

"And if I call him right now, he'll confirm that?"

"What?"

"If I call him right now," he says, "he'll tell me the same thing you've told me?"

"You don't know . . .?"

"Know what?" he asks.

"Nothing."

"Goddamn it, Noah. Maybe I should come get you, just to arrest you for being so goddamn difficult. I honestly don't know what to say to you right now."

"Look, Drew, I had dinner in town, and got to Haggerty's place around nine, and I would have been out at the trails by eleven or so. It took me ages to put up the tent, and plenty of people would have seen me lugging it out of the pickup. Why don't you tell me what's going on? Who's missing?"

"What pickup? I thought you were driving Father Frank's car?"

"It died."

"It died? Okay, okay, let's back up a bit. So, eight o'clock, that's around the time you called Antony Bauer, wanting to speak to his daughter."

"He wouldn't give me her number," I say, "but he . . ." And

it comes to me then what he's saying. I was wrong when I thought the two men came for me last night, and wrong to think they only came to finish off Old Man Haggerty. They came here for somebody else. "It's Charlotte Bauer that's missing?"

"She didn't make it home after her babysitting job last night," he says.

"Was she babysitting for you?"

"For one of our neighbors. She was there until midnight, and then she left, and nobody's seen her since."

"I had nothing to do with any of that," I say.

"Why were you calling her?"

"I was calling her to talk about Alyssa."

"Alyssa? Why?"

"They were best friends," I say. "I figured that if anybody could get Alyssa to come back for her father's funeral, it'd be Charlotte."

"That's it?"

"That's it."

"Nothing else? No other reason you needed to talk to her?"

"No," I say, lying to my friend. "That was it."

"That was a good idea," he says, and the tension between us breaks. "I should have thought of doing that. So she didn't call you back?"

"No," I say. "I was going to try calling her again tonight."

"You have her number?"

"No, but I was going to call Antony and ask him for it."

"Okay, Noah. Well, you do none of that now, okay? I don't

want you poking your nose into this."

"Okay," I tell him, "but I still need you to come and get me."

"Is Charlotte out there?"

"No."

"So me coming out there to get you is going to help me find her?"

"Yes."

He doesn't react right away to that. He asked the question thinking he was going to hear one thing, and ended up hearing another. "You say yes?"

"Come to the sawmill," I tell him. "There's a lot more going on here than you think. This is a lot bigger than Charlotte."

"Bigger how?"

"Come to the sawmill. Trust me, you're going to want to hear this."

"You better not be jerking my chain here, Noah, because if you are I'm going to lock you up. I'm not kidding. As it stands, I might be locking you up anyway."

"I'm not jerking your chain," I tell him.

"Twenty minutes," he says.

Fifty-five

I look through the office for something strong to drink, and come up empty. I'm unlucky, because I know for a fact many of the tenants of this office over the years have had something stashed away. I stay at the seat behind the desk. I think about my dad, and how he got fired from here and begged for his job back, only to get fired all over again six months later. He was near the end then.

I feel like I'm at the end now.

It can't be a coincidence that Charlotte has gone missing the same night I tried contacting her. Her disappearance is something I put into motion. The only person who knew I was calling her was her father, and unless we're dealing with the kind of guy willing to dispose of his daughter to keep some kind of secret, then . . .

No. Antony wasn't the only person to know I was going to try and contact Charlotte. I reach into my pocket. The two photographs I tucked in there earlier are still there. I put the one of Alyssa and Father Barrett on the desk and stare at it. I think about our conversation yesterday, how he changed the subject when I asked him who the girls in those photographs were.

I dial Antony on the office phone. I'm getting ready to hang up when somebody picks it up. There's some puffing, and then, "Charlotte?"

"It's Noah," I say.

"Noah? Where the hell is my daughter?" Antony asks.

"I don't know where your daughter is," I tell him.

"The hell you don't. You were looking for her."

"And I'm still looking for her. She never called me back. Did you give her the message?"

"What?"

"The message. Did you give her the message?"

"Charlotte is missing, and you want to know if I gave her a goddamn message?"

"It's important," I say. "It could have something to do with where she is."

"What the hell are you talking about? Where is she, Noah? What the hell have you done with her?"

I stare out the window. It's dark out there. All I can see is my reflection, and it isn't pretty. "Do you know Father Barrett?"

"I've seen him around."

"Does Charlotte ever talk about him? Or Alyssa?"

"No," he says. "What are you getting at? Do you know where Charlotte is?"

"No," I say, and the conversation is making my head hurt. I look away from the window. "But I'm going to help Sheriff Brooks find her."

"You don't know? You really don't?"

"No," I say.

He's quiet for a few moments. I can hear him fighting back tears. "We just want her back," he says, his voice softening. "We want her back safe."

"I know you do, but I need to know, did you give her the message?"

"I did," he says.

"When?"

"Last night."

"When last night?"

"I called her right after you called. I told her it was about Alyssa, and . . ."

He stops talking. He's having the same kind of moment I had on the phone to Drew, where he's making a connection. "Alyssa," he says. "Oh my God, you think Alyssa went missing too?"

"Yes."

"And now the same thing has happened to Charlotte."

"Father Frank asked me to look for Alyssa. It's why I'm here."

"But you haven't found her," he says, "because she didn't go missing, she left, right? She up and left town."

"I'm not so sure." I keep looking at the photograph. It's possible Father Barrett accidentally put this into motion by mentioning it to somebody. I wasn't confessing anything to him, and he had no reason to stay silent. He might have been trying to help. I need to call him. However, the timeline suggests there's another possibility.

"Where is she, Noah?" Antony asks yet again. "Where in the hell is my daughter?"

"I don't know, but I'm going to find out."

I hang up. I called Antony around eight o'clock last night, and right away he called his daughter. Three hours after that, Earl called me to tell me the two men he's seen before he's seen again. Who did Charlotte talk to?

What did she say that made those two men come for her?

Fifty-six

I call Father Barrett. He doesn't answer. I try a few more times for the same result. Twenty minutes later Drew arrives. I lose sight of the car as it swings near the entrance to the mill. I don't hear anything else, until a couple of minutes later when the stairs leading up to the office creak. Drew is out there moving slowly.

"Don't shoot," I say. "I'm alone."

I see his gun before I see him. He has it pointing ahead of him, his arms bent so it's close to his chest. He flinches when he sees me — or, more accurately, when he sees my face. He looks around the office. He keeps hold of the gun. He looks desperate to use it, hopefully not on me. He looks disappointed I don't have Charlotte here, or the men who took her.

"You can lower the gun," I tell him. "What happened here is over."

He holsters the gun. "What happened to you?"

"Some good old-fashioned payback," I tell him.

351

He takes it all in. The chair in the middle of the room, rope still caught up in the legs of it. Blood on it, on the floor, on my clothes, all over my face. He looks at my swollen eye and battered face. He nods. He gets it. He looks as mad as hell. He clenches his fists and tightens his jaw.

"Let it go," I tell him.

"That prick did this to you?"

"It's okay," I say. "Honestly, it's okay."

"You and me, Noah, we have a very different definition of what *okay* is. I'm going to drop you off at the hospital, and then I'm going to go and arrest the son of a bitch, and if Old Man Haggerty has a problem with that, then I'll arrest him too."

"I didn't call you out here to arrest him," I say. "I called you out here so you could give me a lift back into town, and to tell you what I've found."

"About Charlotte?"

"I'll tell you everything I know on the way."

I get to my feet. The room spins and I lose balance and have to sit back down.

"I should call an ambulance," he says.

"I'll be okay," I say.

I get my arm over his shoulder and he gets his arm around me and he helps me to the office door. The effort has me breathing hard. My face hurts. It feels hot and puffy and they ought to put a disclaimer on the side of aspirin bottles that says *Won't help after a beating*. My foot hurts to stand on.

"You're not going to make it down the stairs," Drew says.

"I will."

"We should sit you down and you can tell me what you need to tell me and I'll send an ambulance out."

"Let's just get to your car," I say.

"Jesus, Noah, this isn't about you, okay? This is about finding Charlotte. Tell me what you know."

"I will," I say. "On the way back into town."

"You really are one stubborn son of a bitch."

"Let's get this done," I say.

We get through the office door. I keep one arm around him and one on the handrail of the stairs, and each step downward is agony. We make it to the bottom and the walls stop swaying and the floor levels out.

Coming in here earlier, the factory was two hundred yards long. Walking it now with Drew, it's two miles. It takes five minutes to get to the doors. Drew has parked right outside. He helps me into the passenger seat and it's a relief to be sitting back down. My face is hurting worse, but I'm far more balanced. It's an effort reaching for my seatbelt. Drew gets behind the wheel and we drive.

"Shit, not so fast," I say, as the car moves over the gravel road, every bump sending another firework off in my head.

He slows down. It helps, but not as much as I'd have liked. We reach the highway. "Tell me," he says. "Not the Conrad shit, that stuff I can figure out for myself, and I'm not making you any promises that I'm not going to arrest the son of a bitch, but Charlotte. You know where she is?"

I look over at the dash. It takes a second for things to

come into focus. I can see a yellow petrol light. I can see we're travelling at forty miles an hour. "Slower," I say. "Please."

He slows down to twenty. I want to ask him to slow down even further, but I know he won't. "I don't know where Charlotte is," I say, "but I know two men came here last night and took her."

"Two men? What two men?"

"The same two men who came here the night we found Alyssa twelve years ago. The same two men who came a week ago when Alyssa disappeared again. Did you ever find out who she was seeing?"

"What the hell are you talking about? Alyssa didn't disappear. I've spoken to her. Hell, so have you."

"I found her car," I say, knowing what this confession means for my future. Or, more specifically, for my freedom.

"What do you mean, you found her car?"

"It's out at the quarry," I tell him. "About thirty feet underwater."

"What?"

"It's down there," I tell him. "It's her car. I searched it. I found her purse. It has her ID in there, a whole bunch of her stuff."

"I . . . what?" He slows down further so he can look at me. "You're not making any sense."

"Somebody drove her car out to the quarry and dumped it in one of the lakes."

"Bullshit," he says. The pace we're going, he can afford to take his eyes off the road. "I mean . . . that has to be bullshit, right? All that shit Conrad did to you, you're not thinking straight."

"I saw it, Drew. I was there. It was her car. It was her purse. I still have it. I have all her stuff. I can show you, and I can take you to the car."

He looks back at the road. I watch his face. What I'm telling him makes about as much sense as me telling him I was chased through the quarry by a dinosaur. He can't process it.

"Okay," he says. "Okay, so let's say I believe you, how in the hell did you find her car? What led you out there?"

"It's a long story," I say.

"So tell me."

"Focus on Alyssa for the moment," I tell him. "Nobody who leaves voluntarily dumps their car and their purse and their suitcase in the quarry on their way out of town. Whatever she's saying to us on the phone she's being forced to say. Did you figure out who she was seeing?"

"No."

I realize I've left the photograph of Alyssa and Father Barrett in the office back at the sawmill. I think of the way she had her arm around him. "Is it possible she was seeing Father Barrett?" I ask, and I remember how evasive he was yesterday when I asked him if he knew if she was seeing somebody, if he knew who her friends were in the photograph. Does he fit into this somehow?

"You're kidding, right?" Drew asks.

"He's the one who gave me Charlotte's details last night," I say, "and she went missing not long after."

"Come on, Noah, you're not thinking straight. Nobody would be after the beating you took."

"Remember I asked you if people were disappearing?"

"Jesus, that again? I'd know if that were true. We'd all know. They'd be screaming it from the rooftops. It'd be on the town sign — *Welcome to Acacia Pines, population dwindling.*"

"But they have," I tell him. "A lot. Thirteen times over the last eighteen years."

"Thirteen times? Geez, Noah, now I *know* you're rambling. Conrad must have done you some real damage. We have to get you to the hospital, because if you ain't seriously deranged, then I'm the worst sheriff in the world."

"Hikers," I tell him, "and campers."

"What?"

"They're who have gone missing. Hikers and campers. Thirteen of them went out there and were never seen again."

"Hikers and campers go missing all the time out here," he says. "The Pines are notorious for it. It's like the Bermuda Triangle out there. Hell, somebody even went missing a month ago."

"Jennifer Ferguson."

"That's her," he says.

"She didn't go missing," I tell him. "She was taken, the same way the others were taken."

"Taken?"

The highway ahead brightens. Earl's Gas Station is coming up, all lit up and visible from outer space. "Pull in here," I tell him.

He looks at his dashboard, at the yellow fuel light. "We've got enough to get back," he says.

"It's not about that," I tell him. "Pull in, it'll help."

"What will help?"

"Trust me," I say. "It'll take five minutes."

We pull into the gas station and Earl wanders out to greet us.

Fifty-seven

The gas station lights highlight every speck of dirt on the patrol car, every nick, every scratch. Moths the size of golf balls hover near the bulbs, some bouncing into them, some bouncing into each other.

"Noah," Earl says, nodding at me. "You look like shit. Sheriff," he says, nodding at Drew. "Want me to fill her up?"

"Sure," Drew says.

Earl moves around to the pump. He pulls up the nozzle and pops the cap on the side of the car and jams it in. The machine starts pumping.

"What are we doing here, Noah?" Drew asks.

"Tell us about the two men," I say to Earl.

He looks up from the car. "The two men from last night?"

"Yes."

"They came by here around eleven o'clock," he says. "I called you and left a message. Then about two hours later they left."

"What the hell is this, Noah?" Drew asks. "Who are these two men you keep talking about?"

I ignore Drew. "Tell us when you saw those two men last time," I say to Earl.

"The night before," he says. "They passed by, and twenty minutes later they came back."

"And before then?"

"Well, that would be a week ago," he says. "Last Wednesday night."

"Around the time Alyssa went missing," I say.

"Is this—"

I put my hand up to interrupt Drew. "When did you see them prior to Alyssa going missing?"

"Would be a month or so ago, I reckon," Earl says.

"Can you narrow it down?" I ask.

"I suppose I could, if I think on it some more."

"Would you do that? Think on it some?"

"Okay, okay, sure," he says, and he tilts his head slightly and he stares up at the moon as if that's where the answers are. Drew looks impatient and goes to say something, but I put my hand up again for him to wait. The machine keeps pumping petrol. Earl says nothing for a bit. Just keeps thinking. I bat away a moth. Then the machine stops pumping and Earl takes the nozzle out and hangs it up and locks the gas cover back into place on the patrol car. "Was a Sunday night," he says. "Four weeks ago last Sunday. I remember because I was watching the game. Out here I can hear a car coming from a mile away. The shop looks right out over the highway."

"Noah . . ." Drew says, groaning my name.

I put my hand up again and Drew stops and I ask Earl to carry on.

"Often I hear a car coming by, I'll keep an eye out, you know? In case it's somebody about to pull in, or in case it's some asshole getting ready to take a shot at my lights. That's the catch," he says. "I light up the highway so I can see who's shooting at me, they shoot out the lights and drive past in complete darkness. I do that a lot, you know, watch whoever goes by because there ain't much else to do out here in the evenings. So I hear the car, and it's these same two guys again. They come in around eleven at night, and unless you're the assholes shooting at my lights, then you're gonna get lit up on your way past, and these two boys got lit up both on the way into town and on the way back out. That time, they were probably in town no more than half an hour."

"Okay," I say, "now this is important. What else happened that day?"

"What do you mean?"

"What else happened that day, or around that day. What was in the news?"

"The news?"

"Yeah. What do you remember about the news?"

"Lots of things," he says. "There's always lots of things, and most of them bad."

"What was happening in town? You remember anything that stands out?"

"Noah . . ." Drew says, groaning my name again.

"Well," Earl says, and then he frowns a little, "well, I guess this would be around the time that girl went missing, the hiker. Search and rescue and the police drove past a lot around then. She was in the news — at least not that day, but she was a day or two later on account of her not coming back out of the Green Hole. I remember her because she'd come in here for gas on her way into town. She was nice. Real friendly like. Came here to hit the trails, and I warned her, like I do when people tell me that, that you gotta be careful, and I tell them I don't just mean careful, but careful careful, because folks misjudge The Pines all the time, and then she went and misjudged them. It was a real shame."

"And before that?" I ask. "Before Alyssa and before the girl who went missing a month ago, can you think of when you last saw these two men?"

"I get the point," Drew says.

"Well, I'd have to think on that," Earl says, "but I reckon I can come up with a date. Would be last summer."

"Okay, okay," Drew says. "I said I get the point. You ever speak to these two guys?" he asks Earl.

Earl tells him that he has. Tells him about that night twelve years ago. Tells him about the other times he's seen them. Goes on to say he reported it to Sheriff Haggerty.

"Haggerty knew about it," I tell him. "He told me as much."

"We need to talk to him," Drew says. "There might be other stuff he hasn't told us."

"We can't," I say.

"Why not?"

361

"Those two men, they came here last night and killed him."

Nobody says anything. Drew looks like he could put his fist through the fuel pump. Earl takes it in his stride, like it's something he expects to hear every day. Drew looks up at the sky, and then he looks back at me, and he says, "You have got to be kidding me."

"I bet if we could narrow it down," I say, "you'd find the dates these two men come to town line up with when people go missing on those trails."

Drew is shaking his head. "I can't believe you. Because if you're right, then it means all these times we went out there searching, we were looking for people who weren't even out there. That's something, well, that's something I don't want to consider."

"You have to consider it," I tell him, "because that's exactly what happened."

"Damn it, Noah, I know, okay? I get it. I believe you . . . I just . . . I just don't want to. And Haggerty . . . he's dead? He's really dead?"

"Will that be cash or card?" Earl asks, and the question seems to confuse Drew even more, and then he catches on.

"Card," he says.

Earl heads inside. Drew follows him, and I follow them too, mostly to get away from the bugs. I'm steadier on my feet now. There's a drinks cabinet I remember seeing the other night that I want to crawl inside and consume all the contents. I find it, and next to it is a freezer with ice creams in it. There are also bags of ice. I tear one open and grab a handful and hold it against my face. Drew digs his wallet out of his pocket and Earl rings up the sale. The flat-screen behind the counter is showing the news. It's local. There's an anchorwoman standing outside a house with police cars parked outside. The banner across the bottom of the screen says *Local Girl Missing*. It's Charlotte Bauer. Drew hands his credit card over and I watch the screen while the ice starts to melt in my hand and onto my swollen eye.

A photograph of Charlotte comes on the screen. There's an information hotline beneath it. The photograph is a headshot. I remember Leigh telling me that Charlotte wanted to be an actor, or a model, and how she was a real heartbreaker. She wasn't kidding. I can imagine casting agents all over the country wanting to take a look at this girl. I want to get her back. I want her to be okay so she can live out those dreams.

The anchorwoman keeps talking. I'm guessing she's already covered the parts about Charlotte not having been seen since yesterday. She's covered the details, and now she's talking about Charlotte as a person, because here's the profile photo, and now here comes one of her audition videos.

"This was Charlotte one month ago," the anchorwoman says, "filming an audition for an agent she was hoping to meet in Los Angeles later next month."

Charlotte smiles at the camera, and before the audition starts, she introduces herself.

My name is Charlotte Bauer, she says. *I'm nineteen years old and from Acacia Pines, and today I'm going to read a scene from one of my favorite movies.*

I look at Drew. He has his back to me, but he's completely tensed up. His shoulders have climbed up around his ears and his arms have gone still, and I've tensed up too, my own shoulders climbing up around my own ears. He doesn't move and I don't move and Charlotte carries on talking to the camera and Earl keeps ringing up the sale.

Then, slowly, Drew turns away from Earl to face me. I can't hide what I'm thinking, because it's all just slotted into place. He can see it all over my face the same way I can see the shame all over his. Not just shame, but disappointment. He's wishing the TV hadn't been on. He's wishing I hadn't made the connection. I'm wishing I could have hidden the realization that he's been lying to me from the beginning.

Sheriff Drew Brooks, the guy who was my best friend growing up, looks like a man whose world is ending.

"Don't," I say, as he reaches for his gun.

Charlotte Bauer keeps talking into the camera, her voice filling the gas station, and as she talks it confirms what I figured out the moment I heard her introduce herself on the audition tape.

It was never Alyssa I spoke to on the phone two days ago.

It was Charlotte.

Fifty-eight

"Goddamn it," Drew says, spitting out the word. "Goddamn it, Earl, why'd you have to have the TV on?"

Drew is pointing his gun at me. I stand with my hands up. The ice falls to the floor. Charlotte is still talking. She's doing a scene from *Pretty Woman*.

"It doesn't have to go like this," I say.

"What in the hell are you boys doing?" Earl says.

Drew turns and shoots him. Shoots him right in the chest and the old guy doesn't even know what's hit him. I don't see what happens to him, how long he stays on his feet before falling, because in that moment I duck behind the row of car batteries, the motion enough to make my head spin. I suck in a couple of fast breaths and stay balanced.

"Look what you made me do, Noah. I really liked Earl. He didn't deserve that," he says, and his voice is high and whiny and reminds me of the guy who robbed the bar the other night. "That's on you for not keeping your goddamn nose out of our business."

His voice is coming from the counter. I can't hear any footsteps. My bet is he's standing there panning the room with his gun.

"If you'd kept yourself to yourself none of this would have happened."

To my left are the drink counters. Behind me the window that looks out over the forecourt. The door out there is too far away, but to my right, back toward Drew, is a door that goes through to the workshop. It's open, but it's dark in there. It'll be like running into a cave.

I pick a battery up off the shelf. It's heavy. I throw it at the window that overlooks the forecourt. It hits the glass but, surprisingly, doesn't break it. It bounces off with a heavy thud. What does break the window is the gunshot that comes a moment later as Drew shoots in that direction. By then I'm already running for the door to the workshop. A bullet hits the frame behind me as I pass through it. I trip on something heavy enough that it doesn't even budge. I land on the floor as a bullet hits a car in front of me. The wheels have been removed, and it's up on axle stands. I can see a little bit because of the light coming through the door. I roll beneath the car and come out the other side. I can see Drew's feet in the doorway of the shop. I end up beside a range of box wrenches on the floor. I launch them one at a time over the top of the car toward Drew. They must look like throwing stars coming out of the dark and the first one hits him in the arm and the second one goes over his head. He fires a shot in my direction but I've already ducked back down, the bullet hitting a wall lined with tools further behind me. He doesn't keep firing. He's hanging on to his ammo for when he has a better shot.

I look back under the car and see that Drew is being cautious. He's taken a step back toward the shop. There's not enough light coming in for me to get a good look at my options. Between me and the wall is another car, this one not up on stands. There are sockets and spanners on the floor around me. To my left, toward the road, there's a large rollup door with a chain hanging from it that has to be pulled over and over to get the door to open. No way I can get it open quick enough.

"There's no way out," Drew says.

"So what? You want me to come out and make it easy for you?"

"It *will* be easier for you," he says. "You have to believe me, Noah, I didn't want it to come to this. You only have yourself to blame."

"You're the one who was seeing Alyssa," I say, and as soon as I say it I realize even her being pregnant is probably a lie. "Was she pregnant?"

"No," he says.

"You were seeing her?"

"No," he says.

"You were seeing Charlotte," I say.

"You saw her," he says. "What red-blooded man wouldn't want to have her?"

Have her. Like she's an object to possess.

"You're the reason Charlotte disappeared?"

"No," he says. "You're the reason. She called me last night and said you were trying to get hold of her. I couldn't let that happen."

"The two men who came here, you called them."

"I gotta say, Noah, I'm impressed you put that together. Not just that, but the rest of it. All these years and nobody ever saw it. Even Old Man Haggerty couldn't get there."

"It was always you? Over the last twenty years? You're the one who abducted Alyssa twelve years ago and framed Conrad?"

"This isn't twenty questions, Noah, but I'll tell you what, you step out and I'll answer everything you want to know. That way you at least won't die wondering."

"Why don't you come in here and we'll discuss it."

"There are only so many tools you can throw before you run out," he says.

"I only need one to hit you."

It's a difficult decision for him. He has a gun, but he knows that one lucky shot from me with a flying wrench and he could be out for the count. Then again, he can't wait me out. Somebody might stop by for gas.

He doesn't answer me. I keep looking under the car. I can't see him. I can hear him moving out in the shop. I head for the chains. I can barely see them. I reach them and pull on them and in the quiet of the night they're as loud as gunfire. The way they're geared, I have to pull a few times just to get the door to raise an inch at a time. I figure opening and closing this door was Earl's exercise regime. The harsh lights from Earl's forecourt shine into the workshop. The door is a couple of inches higher when I hear movement behind me. I don't turn toward it, instead I duck down as Drew fires another shot, this one punching a small hole into the door that light spills through. I move across the front of the workshop, glancing at the two-inch gap to freedom. With the door open slightly, I can see a lot better, but with the door open and a flashlight, Drew can see a whole lot better than I can. I need to get back into the shadows before he circles around and shoots me, but even that isn't much of a solution. The two cars are between us, the one on axle stands, and the one that isn't. The one that isn't is facing the road.

Facing the road . . .

If Earl has been sticking with tradition, then whatever was wrong with this car has been taken care of.

I swing the door open and jump behind the wheel. I hear Drew yell something, but I don't hear what, and the keys are in the ignition like I hoped they would be and the car starts on the first try like I hoped it would, and Drew fires a couple of shots through the back windscreen like I knew he would. I've ducked down and the shots go over my head. The car is an automatic. I slip it into reverse and back up as far as I can, and then slip it into drive and go forward as fast as I can. The side window explodes as Drew fires a shot into it, and then he fires a shot into the door, the bullet punching into the dashboard.

The car hits the roller door. It grinds and squeaks and rattles and it sounds like a hurricane, but the damn thing doesn't break. I slam the car into reverse and back up and I don't know what Drew is doing because I stay low. I jam it into drive again and go forward and crunch into the door. It grinds and squeaks and rattles and dents a whole lot more but still doesn't give way, but there's a gap of a foot to the left where the side has twisted away. Light floods through it.

I put the car into reverse. Drew fires another shot at me, this one smashing the front windscreen. I can see him in the side mirror. He's standing on the other side of the other car where he won't get run over. I punch the accelerator and the car goes back, only it doesn't go back as far this time because the wheel has turned and the angle has changed, so it bangs into the other car instead. I get it into drive and ram it into the door, and the door grinds and squeaks and rattles and dents and tears and the one-foot gap out to the left becomes two. Something pulls at the front bumper when I put the car into reverse and holds me in place, until I gun the engine enough to make the tires spin, and then the car shoots back and I don't wait around, I put the car back into drive and this time the impact shears the door out of its tracks on the left. The car carries on, the door bending up and dragging heavily over the bonnet and the roof. I straighten up and look in the mirrors. The forecourt lights are flooding the workshop. The other car I ran into it earlier has been knocked off its axle stands.

And Drew is pinned to the ground beneath it.

Fifty-nine

My nose is bleeding. All the jarring and the impacts of driving into the door have loosened up more clots. I tear off the bottom of my shirt and roll up small balls of material and jam them into my nostrils. I take the car around the corner of the workshop and walk back on foot. I get to the edge of the twisted door and peek around the corner. I don't want to make a target of myself. So I jog around the back of the building, where there are wooden crates and barrels and dumpsters and beyond all that the edge of The Pines. I circle around to the forecourt and come in through the door to the shop. I check on Earl. He no longer has to worry about arthritis or getting old. I close his eyes and put my hand on his shoulder for a few moments and tell him I'm sorry things went this way. Then I rummage around behind the counter. There's a cavity under the till where he keeps his .22 caliber rifle. He always had it here in case he was ever held up, but he never needed it — at least not until today, and today he was

371

dead before he even knew he needed it. It's old and scarred and has a faded strap running from the end of the barrel to halfway down the stock. I check to make sure it's loaded. It is. Then I point it at the door to the workshop and walk toward it. I peer around the corner. First thing I see is Drew. He's lined right up with the doorway. His left leg is caught under the car just above his ankle. The car fell off the axle stands when I reversed into it, and with the wheels having been removed the bottom of the car is almost flush with the disks that remain, meaning the car is fully pressed into Drew. He's unlucky. The two axle stands on this side have gone up into the cavity of the wheel wells, and the two on the other side have been spat out.

He hears me. His gun is on the ground a foot away from him and he reaches for it.

"Don't," I tell him, and it's the first time I've said that recently where somebody actually listens. He goes back to pulling at his leg. The weight on it must be considerable. He can pull at it all day long and it's not going to budge. His face is red. Veins are standing out in his neck and forehead.

I keep the rifle trained on him. I walk over and kick his gun further away. There's nothing else nearby he can reach.

"So now what, you're going to shoot me?" He seethes when he talks. Spittle sprays out. This isn't Drew. I don't know who this man is.

"You think you deserve anything less?"

He pulls at his leg again, then his body slumps. He puts his hands back to brace himself so he can look up at me. "I guess not," he says, calmer now. "How did it get to this?"

"I don't know, Drew, how *did* it get to this?"

"I can't feel my leg," he says, and he caresses his lower shin. "It doesn't hurt. It doesn't do anything. Just nothing."

"Where is Alyssa?" I ask him.

"I'm probably going to lose my foot," he says.

"I think your foot is the least of your worries. Where is Alyssa?"

"What's your play here, Noah? You going to shoot me? You going to do what you did to Conrad all those years ago?"

"Not if you tell me what I want to know."

"I don't know where she is."

"But you know who took her."

"Yes."

"The two men."

"Get this car off me and we can talk."

"We're talking now," I tell him. "The two men, did they take her?"

"Yes."

"And Charlotte? The others? All the people who went missing out in The Pines?"

"They took Charlotte," he says. "Not all the others. There are people who do genuinely go missing out there — but yeah, a few of them."

"A few?"

"Most," he says. "Nearly all of them."

I have so many questions. I start with the most important one. "Where are they now?"

"I don't know. Honestly, I don't know where they go once

they take them away."

"You had Charlotte taken so I couldn't talk to her," I say, "but what about Alyssa? Why was she taken?"

"Alyssa knew we were having an affair," he says. "Charlotte told her. Teenage girls," he says, and he shakes his head, "they can't keep a goddamn secret."

"You didn't think of that when you got into this?"

"Alyssa . . . she phoned me. She told me I had to stop seeing Charlotte. Told me if I didn't stop, she'd tell my wife. The balls on her, I couldn't believe it. She had to go, Noah, I couldn't risk Leigh finding out. This girl . . . Charlotte, seriously, Noah, you wouldn't be thinking straight either if you saw her."

"Let me guess," I say. "You kept telling Charlotte you were going to leave your wife for her?"

"Something like that."

"When did you become such a cliché?" I asked.

"You son of a bitch, you don't know what it's like to live here. Sure, you did for a while, but then you pissed off. Acacia Pines is the most boring place in the goddamn world. I wanted to leave too, only . . . only I can't. I'm locked in. I can never leave. Charlotte was a distraction from my god-awful life."

"You talk like leaving was impossible. You could have loaded up your car and driven out of there. I did it, you could have done it too, with or without your family."

"You don't get it," he says.

"What don't I get?"

"There's no leaving. Not for me. They'd come for me."

"The two men?"

374

"Yes. Or others like them."

"The girls, are they still alive?"

"Maybe. I'm sorry, Noah, I really am. I never wanted things to be like this."

"I don't give a damn about your apology. Tell me about Alyssa. What happened?"

"Like I said, she phoned me. I asked if we could meet, and she agreed. I told her she should come into the station later in the evening, and she said she would. I told her I was embarrassed, and not to come in, that I'd come meet her out in the parking lot by the fire exit. We agreed to meet at ten. I stayed late, and sent the others away. She showed up right on time. Her face," he says, and takes a deep breath. "I can still see it, the way she looked at me when they put her in the trunk of their car. It haunts me, Noah. You might not think it does, but it haunts me. One drove their car, one drove hers, and after that . . . after that I don't know. The men snuck into her room and took her clothes and a suitcase so it'd look like she left town."

I feel like lifting the car back up and putting his other leg under there too. "How'd you get Charlotte to pretend to be Alyssa on the phone? Why'd she go along with it?"

"That abortion bullshit, she believed that too. The thing is, when Alyssa found out about us, she fought with Charlotte. So I told Charlotte that Alyssa had been seeing somebody, and left town for an abortion and wasn't coming back, that their fight had been the final straw. I told her Father Frank was paranoid because of what happened years ago, and refused to believe

375

Alyssa was okay. So Charlotte agreed to tell you what you needed to hear in order to convince Father Frank that Alyssa was safe. She lied to help bring him closure before he died."

"She was convincing," I say.

"She's an actor," he says, which reminds me of what Conrad said earlier, how actors are good at lying. Lawyers too.

"And the others? The people from the trails?"

"I've told you everything I want to tell you," he says. "Just know that whatever you do here, these guys are going to come for you. Whether you shoot me or turn me in, you're done."

I move around to the front of the car. I rock the suspension and the chassis bites down harder on his leg and he screams.

"You use your access to the plans that hikers and campers log," I tell him. "You go out there and find them and bring them back to the Kelly farm and then your friends come and take them away. What do they do with them?"

"They sell them," he says. "For parts."

I feel my blood run cold.

He carries on. "It's why they take both men and women. These people, they're given up for dead. The world thinks they're out in the woods and gone forever. It's perfect."

"Perfect? For who? The people getting murdered?"

He doesn't say anything.

"Tell me about Alyssa."

"I already did."

"No. Tell me about Alyssa twelve years ago. You took her, right?"

"Yes."

"It was not long after another camper went missing. Debra Olsen."

"Yes."

"What happened?"

"What happened is we were unlucky," he says. "Debra was young, she was eighteen," he says. "I got her back to—"

"You subdued them out on the trail."

"Yes."

"How?"

"I'd see them come into town and have lunch or load up on supplies, and then I'd head out to the car park by the trails and wait for them. It was always easier that way. Go to shake their hands and taser them instead. Sure as hell beat carrying them out of the forest. I'd get them back to the Kelly farm and make the call. Nobody ever goes to the farm. It's the perfect location."

He has access to the keys since it's his wife's listing. He'd know if anybody was coming to take a look — which nobody ever did.

"Most of the time they'd be there for a night at the most, but sometimes it'd be three or four. After I got them back there, I'd head back to the trails and scatter their equipment out there somewhere, maybe set up their tents. You need to know that if I didn't do what they were asking, they would kill me. They said they would cut Leigh open and feed her to the rats. The thing is, Noah, the thing is, they meant it. They really meant it. I didn't want to do those things but I didn't have a choice."

377

"You had a choice," I say.

"You don't get it," he says. "These guys, you don't get it. When I say they'll never let me leave town, I'm not kidding. When I say you're done for as well, I really mean you're done for."

"So tell me," I say.

And he does.

Sixty

It started eighteen years ago, but not with Drew. For Drew, it started fifteen years ago. For him it started the same year the Kellys died out on their farm.

But eighteen years ago Jasmine Kelly was dying. She was fifteen years old. We knew Jasmine was ill, but we didn't know the Grim Reaper was looking up her address. Also looking up her address were two men. They were from out of town. They'd heard about Jasmine, they said, and they believed they could help her. She was on a recipient list. She needed a heart transplant. They explained to the Kellys what they already knew — explained the laws of supply and demand, and that lists were long. Jasmine was on the list, but so were a lot of other people, people who died every day because they couldn't get help in time.

These two men, they could help. They could get Jasmine a new heart. What was the cost? Well, the cost was going to be high, but you'd pay anything, wouldn't you? To take the pain away from your daughter? To give her life? The price was murder. The two men, they told Ed and Leah Kelly that people go hiking in the forests around them all the time, and the thing about people who go into forests is this — sometimes they don't come back out. They would save Jasmine's life today, but tomorrow, or the next week, or the following month, they would want that favor returned — they would want somebody taken from those forests and delivered to them, so they could save somebody else's life. They would pay it forward.

Ed told them to get lost. So they got lost, leaving a card with a number on it, and they knew, as perhaps even the Kellys knew in that moment, that the Kellys would call. People think one way until they're forced to think another. There are things people will never do until that's the only option. They called that number twenty-four hours later. Could they choose the hiker? Could it be somebody they didn't like? Sure, if that made it easier — as long as the hiker was fit, healthy and fell into the age range they specified.

The Kellys agreed to the deal. The following day the men came and took Jasmine and her parents away. That night Jasmine was operated on. The surgery went well. Jasmine was going to be okay. A week later they returned to the farm. Two months after that the Kellys got a call saying it was time to pay up.

They didn't pay up. Not at first. Not until one morning they woke up to find their daughter missing. They got a call. They were told by the caller that he wasn't unsympathetic to their plight. He said this was a common reaction. He said he didn't take it personally, and would give them a second chance and, when they had what he wanted, they would get Jasmine back. If they didn't do what he wanted, they would get her back — but with her old decayed heart instead of the new one.

That morning Ed Kelly drove out to the hiking trails.

That afternoon, he called the number. He had somebody. He'd been lucky. He'd gone out there and he'd found a guy sitting on the side of the lake with a gun in his mouth. It was Martin Clark — the first missing person I ever looked for out in The Pines. He'd talked to the guy. He was depressed. Ed Kelly talked him out of doing anything stupid. Talked him into going back to the parking lot with him. Hit him over the head with a branch and took him back to the farm. It was easy to justify. The guy was going to die anyway, why not die for the greater good? The guy came to and struggled and they had to tie him up, and the following day the two men took him away and suggested they put some chains in the basement.

For next time, they told them, and what was supposed to be a one-time thing was a one-time thing no more. The Kellys were in for the long haul. That night Jasmine came home, and for a while everything was okay.

Until it wasn't.

They got another call.

Everything Drew tells me matches up with the timeline of what I learned at the library. The Kellys would get a call, and Ed Kelly would go out into The Pines and he'd find somebody. The calls always came during the summer. That's when there'd always be somebody out there. For three summers he went out there and chose his victims, and it never got easier, but he did it, until he couldn't do it anymore. Jasmine was oblivious to what was going on. On the day she'd been taken, she'd been drugged, and she had no idea she'd even gone anywhere. She was in the recovery phase of her treatment then and spent a lot of time drifting in and out of consciousness. On the days when Ed would go out into The Pines, Leah would drug their daughter. When she was eighteen years old they encouraged her to leave Acacia. They wanted her to see the world. They wanted her to go to college in a big city, and they were lucky because she wanted that too. When the phone rang again that summer, they didn't answer it. They had sent three people to their deaths. They wouldn't send any more.

It was the same summer Drew got sick. He'd been looking ill for a while. He got diagnosed with a kidney disease. Both kidneys were failing. He had to stop working. He had to go into hospital three times a week and park up next to a dialysis machine for hours on end. Then two men came to his house one night and made him a deal. I remember him telling us that his uncle had been tested and it was a match. His uncle lived in San Diego. That's where the operation would be performed. He'd have both his kidneys removed and he'd get one from his uncle because people functioned okay on one kidney.

It wasn't his uncle. He made the same deal with the two men as the Kellys had made, and he didn't get one kidney, but two. He wanted to live. He would do what it took. Two months later he was back at work. I remember him getting better. That summer he got the first call. He told the two men to go screw themselves.

"That's when things started showing up in the mail," he tells me.

"Photographs," I say.

He shakes his head. He wipes away some tears. "Over the course," he says, and he squeezes his eyes shut and looks up at the ceiling. "Over the course of that summer I had every single body part of Jasmine Kelly mailed to me," he says, "all except her kidneys, because I already had those."

He had freaked out. He didn't know what to do. He tried telling me, he tried telling Sheriff Haggerty, but he couldn't. He was in deep. He'd known somebody was going to die so he could live, and he'd made the decision to be okay with that, and by the time he wasn't okay with it, it was too late. The last part of Jasmine Kelly came with a note, telling him to head out to the farm. He had gone out there and knocked on their door and over the next thirty minutes Ed and Leah told him everything, and he told them everything.

That was the night they killed themselves.

He knew the Kellys were dead. Knew it from the moment he walked away from their house. Either they would do it, or the two men would do it, and he went back out there the next day to check if it was so, and it was, and the following week he told a story of having gotten a call from Jasmine saying she was worried she hadn't heard from them. All the contact with her since, that was him. He told us how angry she was when he gave her the news her parents had killed themselves. He told us that she would never forgive them, that she wouldn't come back for the funeral, that she never wanted anything to do with Acacia Pines ever again. Nobody questioned it. Why would we? Not in a thousand years would any of us have guessed Jasmine was dead too.

Drew came to an understanding with the two men. If given enough notice, he could use his position to plan better. Where they had only given the Kellys a day or two to act, they gave Drew two weeks. They told him the time and the date they would show up expecting a delivery, and he'd have the person there waiting for them.

"Ten people," I tell him. "You sent ten people to their deaths, and then there's Alyssa and Charlotte too."

"I had no choice," he says. "Don't you see that? I had no choice."

"You could have died," I tell him. "That was a choice."

"Yeah? You try making that choice when you're staring down the barrel of a gun."

"I'd have chosen death," I tell him.

"Easy to say," he says, "not so easy to do, especially when you know they'll kill your family too."

"What happened with Debra Olsen?"

What happened is Drew had locked her up in the basement, and when he'd gone back the next day she was dead. She'd had a heart attack or died from fright. He didn't know. What he did know is the men would be angry. He rang them. It was like they told the Kellys — they weren't unsympathetic to his cause. These things happened. The trick, they said, was to make sure they didn't happen again. Then they told him that they needed a girl. Somebody much younger. Ten years old at the most. They needed her urgently, and his failure meant they needed him to step up and do this for them. They told him what would happen if he came up empty-handed. They gave him the rat scenario. They'd gut Leigh like a fish and make him watch her being eaten alive. They'd do the same to Glen, who was only a toddler. Then they'd do the same to him. They told him if he arrested them, there would be others. They told him if he killed them, there would be others. And he believed them. These were bad people. He stresses it over and over, and I believe him. Good people don't cut up innocent people and send them in the mail. Good people don't have rat scenarios.

He took Alyssa. It wasn't personal. He took her because he had to take somebody. He hated himself for doing it. He planted her school bag in Conrad's car. He was the one who found Alyssa's headband and ran it for prints. He was hoping I'd put a bullet into Conrad and end him, and the case would be closed. He knew I'd be itching to do just that. Part of him was relieved when I found her. But he was scared too. If I hadn't taken his gun off him after handcuffing him to the rail, he would have shot me once Conrad gave up the Kelly farm location. He would have shot Conrad too. He'd have made up a story and the two men could have taken Alyssa.

He knew they wouldn't be happy that I had found her.

He was right.

They didn't come for him right away. A month went by. He thought about chaining a couple of hikers up in the basement

385

of the Kelly farm and offering them as an apology. He thought about taking his family and running. By then I was gone. I'd been run out of Dodge. Not that it mattered — he could never have come to me with what had happened. He couldn't go to anybody about it. He did nothing. He knew they would come, and he knew the best thing he could do was wait.

They had him raped in front of Leigh. They pointed a gun at him and at her and they made her watch while the baby screamed and cried from the corner of the room. Leigh screamed and cried too and there was nothing she could do for him. They had brought two other men along to do it. They told him he got off easy. They told him if he reported it, they would do the same to her. They didn't tell her anything else. Leigh had bought into the same lie the rest of us had, that his kidney had come from his uncle.

When they were gone she went for the phone. He told her not to. She took some convincing. He asked, if it had been her, would she want the town to know? Because that's what would happen. Something like that in a town like this, the story would spread like wildfire. She didn't know why it had happened, only that it had. She helped him into the shower. He curled up on the floor and let the water wash their DNA away.

They changed the locks on the doors and for the next three months she could barely look at him, and for the next five years they slept in different beds and he'd hear her crying herself to sleep at night. She got better, and they got better, and they carried on making a family — but sometimes she would look at him the way she looked at him that night the men hurt him. He'd been humiliated in front of her. Emasculated. He needed to get back the power he had lost. He found that power with other women. Charlotte wasn't the first woman he had cheated with.

"That night, when I beat Conrad, why did you stop me from killing him?"

"You beating the shit out of him, I didn't know you were going to do that. I had to distance myself from what you were going to do. I couldn't afford to lose my job. If I did . . . there'd be a price to pay. That's why I stopped you, and asked for a word outside. I knew you'd do something, and you did. You handcuffed me to the rail. I was grateful, but then he told you to try the Kelly farm . . . I . . . I couldn't believe it. The stupid shit picks a place out of thin air, and it changes everything. I rang the two men and they were already on their way."

"They came and cleaned up your mess."

"They did."

"You played me."

"I had to."

"Alyssa said the person who took her wore a ski mask. I used to think that meant she was going to survive, and that the person who took her didn't want her identifying him. Everything you've said, she was going to die, wasn't she, so why wear the mask?"

"What does it matter?" he asks.

"I'm curious."

"I couldn't have her look at me. What I did to her, I hated

it. I still hate it now. This . . . this isn't who I was meant to be. Back then, I . . . I just couldn't face her. I couldn't have her look at me."

"Yet you can look at me, even though you sent those men to kill me two nights ago."

He doesn't say anything.

"That's what you did, right?"

"I had no choice. When they said you weren't at the farm, that the house had burned down, part of me was relieved."

"I don't believe you. When you came to pick me up at the sawmill earlier, when I told you what I knew, were you going to kill me?"

"What does it matter?"

"It matters to me," I tell him. "Were you?"

"Whatever you're going to do, Noah, just do it."

"You didn't shoot me out there, because you wanted to know what I knew. You figured the best way to do that was to let me talk. We weren't heading back into town, were we? You weren't taking me to the hospital. Where were you going to do it? The Kelly farm? Were you going to suggest we stop in there?"

"Shooting you would have been a favor. You don't see that yet, but you will. Once these guys track you down, you'll wish I'd killed you. You've doomed yourself. You've doomed everybody you know."

"No," I say. "What I'm doing is putting an end to this, the same way you should have ended it."

"Why did you burn down the Kelly farm? What happened?"

"Stephen happened. Him and his buddies happened. They burned the place down and tried to drown me out in one of the lakes at the quarry."

His mouth hangs open as I tell him that. He's trying to make it make sense. Then it does. "That's how you found Alyssa's car," he says.

"Yes."

"And why you were so beaten up yesterday morning."

Now something makes sense to me. "When I came to your office, you thought it was the two men who had done that to me."

He nods.

"That's why you didn't push for an answer. You must have figured they'd come for me, and somehow I'd killed them."

"Part of me was hoping that's what had happened. If you'd dealt with them, then maybe the others would need to regroup before two more men came along. Maybe I wouldn't have to hurt anybody for a bit. Where's Stephen now?"

"He's still out at the quarry."

"You killed him? You killed all four of them?"

"Yes."

"I should have dealt with him years ago."

"Yeah, you should have, and if you had, Maggie would have fewer bruises and I'd be getting cut open for parts. Did you know those men were going to come here last night and kill Haggerty?"

He doesn't answer. He looks defeated.

"Jesus," I say. "That was you?"

"Yes."

It's why there was no sign of a forced entry. It's why Haggerty didn't have his gun on him. A wave of nausea runs through me. I need to sit down, but instead I lean against the car and Drew winces as it shifts. "Let me guess, you had no choice."

"He called me right after you left. Said he was on to something. I went around there and he told me what you guys had been talking about. I know you think I had a choice, but I didn't. You've already killed me, Noah. You turn me in, and they'll kill Leigh, and the kids, and then they'll kill you and everybody close to you. You need to know that. You need to believe that. I'm dead either way, as are you, but you put a bullet in me and my family has a chance. I need you to shoot me, Noah. I mean it."

I think of the guy I tipped over the edge of the quarry. I remember the internal debate. Good versus evil. That man's future over the future of others he might hurt.

"Seriously, Noah, if my family is to have any chance of surviving, you need to do it. I'm asking you, please, do it."

"That thing you said in the church the other day, did you mean it?" I ask.

"What thing?"

"About thinking we can all be forgiven. Do you really think that way?"

He looks down at his hands and thinks long and hard, and I wait for him. We have time. Then he looks up, and he says, "No, I don't suppose I do."

390

"Over the years, did it get any easier? Killing these people?"

"I wasn't the one who killed them."

"Yes you were," I say. "Maybe not directly, but you were still killing them. So? Did it get easier?"

He looks down at his hands again and he doesn't look back up when he says, "Yes. Yes, it did."

I decide to give him what he's asking for.

Sixty-one

Only I can't. I point the gun at Drew and I think about the things he's done, the people that have died. I could put a bullet in him. I could put a bullet in him for every one of those people who went out into The Pines only to end up in the basement out at the Kelly farm. I think of the fear each of them felt, beaten and chained, sedated and cut into. I think of Jennifer, of her brother Danny, of Gina and the others out at the vigil, of Jennifer's father calling into the woods for her to hear that they all loved her. So much pain and misery, the epicenter this small town in the middle of nowhere, the pain spreading out like tentacles across the country, reaching family and friends and changing their lives. I picture Drew approaching hikers and campers, all smiles, all *How's it going there*, and then the horror. I go through it all the same way I went through it with Cliff the other night, picturing the good and the bad.

I think about my friendship with Drew. Our days at

school. Days in the pool competing. Drew getting married, his fears at being a bad father when he found out Leigh was pregnant, him getting sick, then getting better. Drew always wanting to help people, Drew always the nice guy, Drew my partner on the force.

Drew, my best friend.

I lower the gun. Some of that old Drew has to be in there, doesn't it?

"What are you waiting for?" he asks.

"I'm taking you in," I say.

He shakes his head. "You do that, and you sign a lot of death warrants. I'm not messing with you, Noah. You take me in and I'm dead, you're dead, everybody we know is dead."

"I'm not going to shoot you."

"Then hand me my gun and let me do it."

"No," I tell him.

"You have—"

"Goddamn it, Drew, can't you just shut up for a moment and let me think?"

He shuts up.

I can hear the buzzing of the fluorescent lights. I can hear bugs flying through the air. The breeze through the trees outside. I can feel the night pressing in all around us, miles and miles of forest making me feel claustrophobic.

I look for a jack to lift the car, but the problem is the car is only the width of Drew's shin above the ground, and I can't fit a jack under it. There are several prybars in the workshop, one almost as tall as me, and I use it to try and budge the car but I can't get enough weight into it, and all I do is rock the car slightly which makes Drew scream. I leave half the prybar under the car, and put the jack under the other half where I have more room. It slips on the first effort, but the second time it bites into the bar and starts to lift. It only needs to go up an inch, and then Drew is able to slide his foot out, which he does just as the prybar slips on the jack again, crashing the car to the ground.

Drew brings his knee up to his chest and wraps his hands around his ankle. When he straightens up he has a snub-nosed pistol in his hand that must have been in an ankle holster he couldn't get to earlier. I kick the jack and it hits him in his wounded leg and the gun goes off, the bullet punching the side of the car. I'm already lowering myself back down and reaching for the rifle when he takes another shot, this one going above me. My hand finds the strap, I pull the rifle toward me as I continue to roll, get it into my hands, and pull the trigger.

"Why did you have to do that?" I say, when I stand over him a moment later. The gunshots have my ears ringing. There's a neat hole in his cheek, not at all that big, and a thin line of blood running down from it. His eyes are wide open, but he can't see anything. "It didn't have to go like this."

He doesn't answer. He can't. If he could, perhaps he'd tell me it was always going to go like this. From the moment his doctor told him his kidneys were failing, he was never getting out of this alive.

I close his eyes. I take his phone out of his pocket. Last

night, because he was pressed for time, he wasn't able to take Charlotte out to the Kelly farm like he did with Alyssa. He gave the two men the details of when she would finish babysitting for his neighbor, along with a photograph identifying their target, and they came and got her right after she stepped outside to walk home. I use his thumb to unlock the phone. I scroll through the messages. Like he told me, he'd deleted their messages right away. I go through his contacts and search for *Jasmine Kelly*, the name he saved the two men under.

I go into the settings and turn off the prompt that asks for a passcode or for a thumbprint every time the phone is turned on, then drop the phone into my pocket. I head into the shop and turn off the lights for the forecourt. The highway goes dark. I shut off the shop lights and pull down on the twisted roller door and get it looking as straight as I can. I use the flashlight Drew was using earlier to look around the workshop and find some tow rope. I take it, along with Earl's rifle, the two handguns and a bottle of water, out to Drew's car. The keys are in the ignition. I pull the wadded-up bits of shirt out of my nose and dump them on the ground.

I pull the car as close as I can to the door and pop the trunk. I rummage around and find what I'm looking for. Then I go back inside and drag Drew out. I bundle him into the trunk and head for town.

When I'm close enough to town, I call Maggie. She answers after half a dozen rings. "It's late," she says.

"Are you home? Or at your sister's?"

"My sister's," she says. "What's happened?"

"Drew's dead," I tell her, and then I tell her the rest. Not all of it. I don't tell her about her husband, or the cars out at the quarry, or that Drew's in the trunk of the car. I tell her about Conrad taking me out to the sawmill. I tell her about Charlotte, about hearing her voice at the gas station, about Drew shooting Earl and then trying to shoot me. I tell her everything Drew told me, about the Kellys, about Jasmine needing a new heart, about him needing a new kidney. I tell her about the vigil, about the missing hikers, about Drew killing Sheriff Haggerty, and by the time I tell her all of this I've arrived outside her sister's house.

She comes outside to meet me. She looks me up and down, and at my injuries that are going to hurt more tomorrow once the adrenaline has worn off. I tell her what I need from her. Why I came here.

"You have to be kidding."

"It's the only way."

"That's what you thought twelve years ago," she says. "And you were wrong then."

"I'm not wrong this time. This is the only way of getting Charlotte back alive, and Alyssa too, if we're not too late. We do it your way, and they disappear forever."

"It's the same damn thing," she says. "Only this time you're asking me to help."

"Will you? Will you help those girls?"

She tells me she will.

She goes inside and gets her keys and jacket and tells

her sister she's going out. Then we drive to the Kelly farm in separate cars. We park behind the trees and stand in front of the burned shell of a house with my headlights pointing at us, the rope in my hands. The bruise on the side of Maggie's face is yellow and shiny.

"You want to tell me what happened out here?" she asks, taking in the burned house. Between yesterday morning when I left here, and today, another section of it has fallen in on itself.

"Not really," I say.

"That's what I thought."

Maggie sits on the ground. I wrap the rope around her legs and her arms and let the rest trail off behind her. I use Drew's phone to take the photo. I point the phone at Maggie and she turns her face slightly to hide her features. I frame the shot. I get her bruise in there but she's unidentifiable. I get the rope in there, and the burned-down house.

"Done," I say.

We walk to her car, and we drive to Earl's. We get out and she stands by the driver's door and I move around and stand in front of her.

"Part of me never stopped loving you," I tell her.

"I know," she says.

"You know?"

"Yes, because it was the same for me. I wish . . . I wish I'd dealt with things better back then. I wish I'd come with you."

"I'm sorry I messed up," I tell her.

"You did what you thought you had to do."

I lean in and hug her and she hugs me back. We hold on to each other tight. I don't want to let go, but I have to.

"Bring them back," she says.

"I will," I say.

"No matter what it takes?"

"No matter what it takes."

I watch her drive off. I take a couple more aspirin. I swallow them down with water and watch her taillights get smaller. Then I go into the gas station and find Earl's keys and take Earl's car, a ten-year-old Ford F-150 painted silver. I top it up with gas then drive the pickup toward town until signal bars pop up on Drew's phone. I text the photograph of Maggie to the two men. I tell them I have one more woman I need them to take care of.

Thirty seconds later they text back.

They tell me they're on their way.

I turn the Ford around and drive back toward the farm, pulling over half a mile short and parking it behind trees. I walk the rest of the way, the big open sky above me, a pool of black ink dotted with specks of light as far as the eye can see.

Sixty-two

I spend the first hour propped up on the hood of Drew's police car, leaning against the windscreen. There's blood on my hands. I wipe them on my shirt. My feet scuff the front of the hood but at this stage in the game I figure Drew's got other things to worry about. I stare up at the sky and look at the stars and wonder how long this world will last, how long it will be before we pollute it so much we'll be looking at these stars from a new home on a new planet. It's so breathtakingly beautiful. The Kellys used to say this land was cursed, and I see no reason to deny it. The warm wind carries the smell of smoke from the remains of the farmhouse. There is a sense of peace that won't last.

After another hour I begin to think they're not coming. I remind myself they're coming from a long way out of town, that they have to be, otherwise every time Drew or Ed Kelly took somebody from The Pines, they'd have driven them to their final location. The fact they were using the Kelly farm means these men aren't coming in from a neighboring town.

Another hour goes by. Last night, when I called for Charlotte, her dad would have called her, she would have called Drew, and he would have called the two men. I made the call around eight o'clock. Earl called me at eleven. If the men left right away, that puts the journey around three hours. Give or take.

Which turns out to be what this journey takes them too. Because five minutes after reminding myself about all that, I hear it long before I see it, a solitary car on the highway that sounds like any other.

I climb down and get into position near Drew's body. The car slows for the turnoff to the farm, and then I hear wheels on gravel and the low hum of the engine as it comes down the road to the farmhouse. I see headlights through the trees between the house and the highway, and a moment later the car comes around them. The moon is throwing out enough light that I can see both men clearly. The car slows down. The two men who have in the past cut women into pieces and mailed them look confused because they can see Drew's police car, but they can't see Drew. They can't see anybody. They look at each other as the car slows even more. The passenger gets out his cellphone.

I take the shot before the headlights hit the trees. A hole appears in the center of the windscreen. The car comes to a stop and I take the second shot, this one into the engine bay. By now both doors are open. I stay low and get moving, gunfire returned in the direction I just fired from. I know there's no way they can see me from where they are, and there's no way they can hear me over their car or the gunfire. I get behind the burned-out shell of the house and put more distance between me and the two men, heading out into the thistle and gorse and weeds, all the time staying low. When the gunfire stops, I turn, drop to my stomach, and watch through a pair of binoculars I took from Drew's trunk. My heart is hammering. My arms and legs are itching from the weeds.

It doesn't take the men long to find Drew. He's lying on the ground between two of the trees, his gun in his hand. It looks like he's the one who opened fire on them. At least that's how I'm hoping it looks. He opened fire, and they shot back and hit him. They turn and look out into the night, looking if anybody else is here, each of them poised to return fire if it comes. Which it doesn't. I keep watching. They turn back toward Drew.

This is the moment of truth.

There's a bullet hole in his head. But there's also blood all over his face. A couple of hours ago I dug into Drew's back with a knife and squeezed a few ounces of blood from him into a drink bottle. I drained that bottle over his face when I heard their car approaching. Now his face is messy red rather than mottled gray. The night is still warm and his body temperature hasn't dropped much, though some rigor mortis has crept in. They seem to be discussing their options. Do they know he was already dead? Or do they think they shot him when they returned fire? I'm hoping for the latter, but it could go either way. If it's the former then I'll open fire and take my chances, hopefully killing one and wounding the other and getting him to talk.

Their car engine hiccups a few times, a result of the gunshot, then dies. One of the men disappears and one waits with Drew until his partner returns. He returns with a gas container. They pour some over Drew and set him on fire. My stomach turns and I have to look away. I can hear him burning. I can smell him. It makes me think of the barbecue we had the other night.

The men back away. They go to their car, but it won't start. I stay where I am. Soon there's a glow from the other side of the house. They've set their car on fire. Then there's the sound of an engine coming to life. Drew's car. I left the keys in the ignition for them. Soon I can see the car out on the highway, two red taillights getting smaller, and I stay where I am until they're gone.

Sixty-three

And then I wait some more. I don't move for another twenty minutes in case one of the two men is also here, the leaving car a simple subterfuge to draw me out. Then I get to my feet and brush myself down and walk out of the thistle and gorse hoping twenty-five minutes wasn't the cut-off time. I keep the rifle pointing ahead and I reach the house and I peer around corners and through missing walls. There's black furniture and black carpets and black paintings hanging on black walls. If I sneezed some of it would fall. I don't see anybody. Drew's body is no longer burning. Nor is the car.

I walk down the driveway, casually at first, then I break into a jog, but the jogging has my feet impacting harder onto the ground, which in turn jars my legs, which jars my body, all of it accumulating in my head. So I don't jog. I walk at a brisk pace, covering the distance back to Earl's Ford in a little over five minutes. I climb inside and switch on the GPS unit on the passenger seat and it takes a minute to get a signal, and a few moments later I'm looking at a red dot moving across a map. That red dot is a signal from the GPS unit I found in the trunk of Drew's car earlier, an upgrade of the units we used to use years ago when we were out looking for missing folks out on the trails. I switched it on earlier and hid it in a cavity beneath the rear seat and carried the receiver back down to Earl's F-150 earlier.

The dot is a half-hour ahead of me.

I start the car. I follow the only road away from town. I pass Earl's Gas Station, the lights off, the door twisted, and Earl's body cooling on the floor inside. No reason for the two men to pull in there since Drew's car is flush with gas. I pass the sawmill, the road leading into darkness, my blood on the floor of the office inside. I pass the quarry, four dead men out in the water.

I keep driving. A three-hour plus change trip to the Kelly farm means a three-hour plus change trip back to wherever they came from. I reach the point on the map where I first saw the red dot. There's still nothing but trees and mountains and sky. Three o'clock comes and goes. My back is getting sore. I shuffle a little in the seat and straighten up. Another twenty minutes and there are other roads, lefts and rights that the guys ahead of me don't take. I go faster than the limit, knowing the two men will be doing the limit or just under, not wanting to risk being pulled over in a police car. I close the distance to twenty minutes. Then to fifteen.

We pass turnoffs to smaller towns. We pass big intersections with long sweeping bends, not a lot of traffic, a few trucks on the interstate from point A to point B, headlights bright, strips of light along the edges of the trailers.

We pass turnoffs for bigger towns. Highways to cities. More trucks. More traffic. The distance between me and the dot gets to within five minutes. It keeps moving west, out toward the coast, chasing the night. The men have been on the road for two hours. Still one more to go. Give or take. It depends what speed they drove out at. It depends on whether they're going to stop at a roadside diner, or if they're going to go to where the women are being held, or go home first, or perhaps to pick up other victims. Maybe they're staying at a motel somewhere.

The interstate snakes on and on. I shuffle some more in my seat. I open the window to let the breeze hit my face. Every now and then my eyes will pop open wide with the realization I was almost asleep. Five miles up and there's a roadside diner. The dot keeps moving, but I pull in. I go inside and order a coffee to go. The waitress doesn't comment on my busted-up features. Maybe she sees people like this every day. I use the bathroom and splash water on my face and avoid looking in the mirror.

I get back out to the car. I drink the coffee and the dot is ten minutes ahead, then nine, then eight, and I bring it down to two. The coffee tastes great. Or maybe that's because I'm tired. Either way, right now it's the best coffee in the world. We keep driving west. More turnoffs. More sweeping bends and snaking highways, more trucks and more traffic, so much light pollution the inky black sky now only has a handful of stars.

It's 5am. We're closing in on three hours. We're closing in on the North Pacific Ocean, up ahead miles and miles of coastland, small towns and large towns, the ocean connecting all of it, small islands and inlets and ports. We pass strip malls and motels, gas stations and diners. Closer to the ocean big roads become small roads. Buildings become empty lots, and empty lots become trees. There are no other cars. It's like we're driving to the edge of the world. New becomes old and shiny becomes gritty, right up to where we reach the coast, where all that lies beyond is miles and miles of water and trees.

The dot stops moving. I stop moving. I kill the engine. I sit in the car and listen as it pings and cools. There's half a mile between me and that dot. Maybe half a mile between me and Alyssa.

Half a mile between me keeping the promise I made her all those years ago.

I get out of the car, grab Earl's rifle, and start walking.

Sixty-four

My eyes adjust to the dark. The road up ahead is littered with potholes. To the left empty lots of concrete, weeds pushing up through the cracks, to the right a guardrail and on the other side of it trees that look tired and old, like they grew up wanting to be trees but became bitter and twisted knots of wood. Half a mile up there's a T intersection, the top part of the T a left and right leading to buildings that look like they have the same cancer that got Father Frank, abandoned warehouses with boarded-up windows and boarded-up doors, a combination of fire hazards and health hazards, all of them looking like perfect hideaways for serial killers and sociopaths. Beyond them all the Pacific keeps rolling in, out on the horizon lights of ships passing in the night, closer the waves slap up against a concrete stone wall that drops away into the water. There's a guardrail a foot high running the length of the narrow road to stop people falling in.

I go right. I follow the dot. I wonder what used to be out

407

here, why this place was built, whether it got used or was left from day one to fall apart. The wind coming off the ocean is cold. Being in Acacia Pines for the week, I'd forgotten what cold could feel like. I check my phone, expecting there to be no signal, but there is. Two bars. I send a message to Maggie with the location. I tell her I've tracked the men here, and that I'll call her soon with an update. I put the phone on silent and carry on walking.

Most of the buildings join each other, cinderblock walls separating one space from another, the roofs thirty feet high, the occasional dumpster and sunken-in doorway for me to take cover behind, wooden pallets rotting in the wind and rain and sun and leaning against walls, bird shit and dust and decay and graffiti in all directions. I can hear rats keeping pace with me as they run through weeds that have broken through the concrete.

I crouch behind the first dumpster and use the binoculars. There's an SUV parked a hundred yards away, facing me as if for a quick getaway. There's no sign of Drew's car, but the dot tells me it's down there, either driven into the ocean or into one of the buildings. It's too dark to see if the car up ahead is empty.

I move slowly forward, checking the windows of every building I pass, looking for signs of life and not seeing any. I scan the walls for security cameras but don't see any. I get to within thirty yards of the SUV. I look at it through the binoculars. It's empty.

I reach the edge of the warehouse. There's no noise coming

from it, no light either, the windows having been blocked up. There's a big roller door like the type at Earl's Gas Station, and past it a normal-sized door. Maybe it's unlocked.

I head toward it, and almost have my hand on the handle when the sound of chains being pulled and metal vibrating along rollers breaks through the sounds of the waves hitting the wall. There are no dumpsters or doorways nearby, and I can't stay hidden against the walls.

I run toward the SUV and duck down on the other side of it. I look beneath it, waiting for feet to come into view, only they don't. Instead a car comes from the direction I just came from. A dark SUV. Which is a problem, because it would have driven past Earl's F-150. More light spills out across the road as the door to the warehouse gets higher.

The SUV turns into it, coming to a stop next to Drew's patrol car parked inside. The driver gets out and opens the back door, and then he and a man in a suit help a woman climb out. They get her into the wheelchair. She's somewhere in her fifties, her skin pale with a yellow tinge, thin hair and dark bags beneath her eyes, looking all kinds of unhealthy. They wheel her deeper into the warehouse where plastic sheeting is hanging from rails, forming a square in the middle of the room. The warehouse door starts to vibrate again and the chains rattle as a guy to the left of the door pulls on them — one of the two men from the Kelly farm. The door is halfway down when I see her, Charlotte, being pushed toward those sheets of plastic. She's crying.

The door closes.

I do the addition. People killed for body parts. A sick person showing up at a warehouse. Only it's not going to be just a warehouse. Those sheets of plastic are the walls of a sterile operating room. There will be doctors and nurses and expensive equipment that beeps and monitors and saves some lives while ending others. The woman in the wheelchair is going to be getting a new body part and Charlotte is going to be losing one. I grab my phone. I figure the police could be here in twenty minutes, assuming I can convince them I'm not some crank. Maybe I should call the FBI. Only Charlotte might not have twenty minutes. Could be she doesn't even have five.

I have to do both. Call for help, and find a way in there. Or at least slow them down. Distract them somehow. Fire a few shots with the rifle and run.

I dial 911. A voice comes on the line. At the same time the smaller of the two doors opens. The two men I saw earlier come out. They're carrying guns. The driver or the sick woman must have told them about my car. They stand back to back, each peering in different directions along the length of the warehouses.

The woman on the phone is asking me if I'm there. If I shot both of these men, what would happen? How many more people with guns are inside? None? Five? A hundred?

I'm about to be exposed, and there's nowhere to hide.

Except for the wall behind me that drops off into the ocean.

I stay low and run toward it, the height of the SUV keeping

me covered. The water is six feet below, slapping against the stone walls, looking dark and cold. I hang the rifle over my back with the strap and slip under the guardrail then lower myself down. My feet digging into the stonework take a lot of my weight, one hand taking the rest while still holding on to the phone.

"My name is Noah Harper," I say into the phone. "I used to be a police officer," I say, but I can't hold on to the phone anymore, not if I don't want to fall into the water. I tuck it into my pocket but don't hang up. I hug the wall then peer above it. One of the two men is walking toward me, while the other is climbing into the SUV. My forearms are burning. I can hear the woman on the phone, but can't make out what she's saying. The man starts the SUV. I can hear the other one approaching.

I can't hold on any longer.

I let go, and the ocean swallows me up.

Sixty-five

I hit the water. It's cold. I sink fast. My feet hit the bottom, and I push off a smooth slippery boulder. I kick for the surface and get there quickly, the water turning me and throwing me against the wall, the rifle slung over my back taking the impact, and then I'm going under again. The strap on the rifle snaps. I kick for the surface and swim away from the wall, ten feet, twenty, thirty, out past the breaking waves. I turn and look toward the warehouses. They're black holes against a sky that is starting to lighten. I look left and right. There's nobody looking back. The wall travels the coast in each direction, I can't tell how far. I don't have time to swim it, and I can't scale the wall, not with the water coming in hard like this.

A ladder. There will have to be a ladder somewhere. There has to be some way of getting out of the water for when people have jumped or fallen in. It's just a matter of finding it.

I let the next wave take me in, then swim at right angles to it, more comfortable in the water now, working with the ocean

412

rather than against it. I get to the wall and push myself off from it, going beneath the waves when they come in, moving further along, back in the direction I came from, thinking there won't be just one ladder leading into the water, but several. After a minute I'm thinking the opposite. There aren't several, there isn't even one, and I'm running out of time.

I don't see the ladder, instead I swim into it, my hand hitting one of the rungs hard, my wrist flaring with pain. I grab hold of the rails and get my breath and then slowly climb, the entire thing shaking violently and threatening to come away from the wall. I get to the top and can't see any signs of life. I'm back at the T intersection. I roll under the rail and onto the road and get to my feet and run toward the buildings, hunkering down behind the first dumpster I find. I grab my phone from my pocket knowing it'll be dead, and it is, dead probably within the first few seconds of getting wet.

The SUV from earlier is nowhere to be seen. My guess is they've gone out to take a look at my car to decide if it's a threat. They'll have parked next to it, one of them will have put a hand on the hood to see if the engine is still warm, and that will have told them they were followed. It will tell them what happened out at the Kelly farm isn't the same thing they thought happened. My name will come up. They'll suspect it could be me, but at the same time it could just be somebody lost, or somebody broken down. They'll be checking police scanners and listening for traffic and they're going to get nothing. Which means now they're on their way back. It means they've phoned others still inside the warehouse and

413

soon there will be more people with guns.

I check my pocket for the snub-nosed pistol I took from Drew. It's still there. I drain the water out of it but there's no need to dry it off. A quick dip in the ocean won't stop it from working. There are four bullets left. Drew's phone is in the F-150. I left the vehicle unlocked, the keys inside. I have to get to it. I get to my feet and pause at the edge of the building and slowly peer around the corner and down the road leading to the T. The sky is still lightening, and it's because of that that I see the car moving toward me slowly, the lights off. I step back behind the corner, and lean back around, the revolver steady as I brace myself against the wall. The SUV is fifty yards away. Thirty. Fifteen. And now I can see it's two vehicles, Earl's F-150 leading the way, the SUV behind it.

When the F-150 gets to within ten yards, I shoot the driver in the head. He slumps forward against the horn and the engine revs and the car shoots toward the water. The SUV behind brakes fast and the driver dips down beneath the windscreen as I fire a shot into it. Behind me the F-150 hits the metal barrier. The engine keeps revving. I glance back in time to see one side of the metal barrier give way in slow motion, the car inching forward, screeching against the edges of the metal and then disappearing into the water.

The SUV's headlights come on, set to full beam, blinding me. I hear the car door open. I have two shots left, and the second of the two men knows where I am. Behind me the area outside the warehouse lights up, spotlights bolted to the front of it all coming to life. They've heard the gunshot and the F-150 crashing. I've managed the distraction part, but not the part where I call for help.

I grab my cellphone. I angle the screen so I can see the reflection of the car around the corner. There are two bright orbs and not a lot else. If I step out I'm a sitting duck, and the guy out there waiting knows it. I picture him hunkered down behind an open door, or leaning over the hood. He can wait there all day, and the people in the warehouse can wait there too, knowing I'm pinned between them.

Only I can't wait.

I tuck the gun back into my pocket, move along the buildings, run across the road and dive feet first back into the water.

Sixty-six

The water isn't as cold this time. I kick my way to the surface and take a beat to get my bearings and then swim toward the ladder. Only the ladder isn't there anymore, it's been removed by the F-150, the back half of which is sticking out of the water. The lights are on, and the front half of the vehicle is wedged against rocks buried beneath the water.

I get into the bed of the pickup. It's like climbing a ramp soaked in butter. I slip a few times but get there. The waves vibrate through it, but the F-150 feels solid. I hoist myself up onto the tailgate and stand on it, the taillights on either side of me glowing. I'm still a couple of feet short of the top of the wall. Part of the guardrail has been pulled down with the F-150, it's twisted and tangled and I'm able to grab on to it to hoist myself higher, my feet finding purchase on the stonework, my hands getting to the top, and then I pull myself up and look out.

The SUV is still pointing toward the corner of the building.

The driver is kneeling behind the open door and looking through the open window, his gun trained on the spot where I was standing. With his free hand he reaches into his pocket and pulls out a phone and starts fiddling with it.

I drain the water out of the gun again. Then I shoot him in the stomach. He jerks toward me, trying to figure where the shot came from, the motion banging his gun into the window frame of the door and making him drop it. He drops the phone too.

I have one shot left.

I take it.

This one gets him in the elbow.

He drops to the ground. I'm already on my feet and covering the distance fast, sea water flicking off me with every step. He has to move around the car door to reach the gun, and I get there at the same time he does. I stomp on his hand and kick his elbow and he screams and tries sliding himself backward. To where, I don't know. Maybe back out toward the road. Maybe he thinks he'll be safe out there. I pick up his gun and shoot him in the other elbow. His arm falls to his side. He looks up at me. There isn't a lot of expression. He seems to be taking it all in his stride. I was expecting two young vibrant men, with bulging biceps and thick necks, but these two guys are in their early fifties. They're dressed like travelling salesmen, with cheap suits and cheap ties.

"Where's Alyssa?" I ask. "Is she in there too?"

"You can't save them all," he tells me. He sounds calm. Resigned. Like he's been through this before, and one day he'll go through it again. Only he won't. This is the end of the line. Blood is leaking out of him at a pretty good clip.

I kick him in the elbow. He cringes but doesn't scream.

"There's nothing you can do to me you haven't already done," he says. "In two minutes I'll be dead anyway. Maybe less."

"I can make those two minutes hell for you," I tell him. "Or you can do something right for the first time in your life and tell me where Alyssa is. Is she in there?"

"Why don't you kiss my ass?"

"How many others like you are in there?"

"You've killed yourself," he says. "You've killed everybody you love."

"How many are there?" I ask.

"Too many," he says. "You think we're it? There are lots of us. There are others who know who you are, Noah. We know everything about you."

"Then I'll hunt down every one of you."

He laughs. "You're too late for Alyssa, parts of her are in there, parts of her are elsewhere, parts of her are out there," he says, nodding toward the water, "submerged in barrels." And he looks me up and down. "Maybe you noticed them when you were in there."

My body goes tight. My stomach rolls and I take a small step backward. I want to be sick. He notices all of this, and he starts to laugh. I struggle to hold on to the gun. Struggle not to collapse. I look out at the water. That's what the F-150 got stuck on. Not rocks, but barrels that have been tossed over

418

the edge into the rocks and weighted down. It's also what I pushed off from when I first went into the water. Not a slippery boulder, but the side of a barrel. How many are littered along the bottom of the wall? How is it nobody has ever spotted them?

"You're lying," I tell him.

"I've no reason to lie."

I put my foot onto his elbow. I crush it into the ground. He fights with the pain, and then can't fight anymore, breaking for the first time. "Okay, okay," he says.

I lighten the pressure. "Where is she?"

"There's this thing they're going to do to you," he says. "They're going to feed everybody you know to these rats they have."

"I have nobody you can threaten."

"There's always somebody."

I point the gun at him. I choose a spot. His knee. "Where is she?"

"I told you already."

I shoot him in the knee. He screams. His eyes bug out and cords of sinew and thin muscle stand out on his neck. "Where is she?"

"You're a dead man," he says.

I shoot him in the shoulder. "Stop lying. Where is she?"

"They'll come for you," he says.

I shoot him in the other knee.

I shoot him in the first elbow I shot him in earlier. "Where is she?"

He doesn't answer. He can't. He's gone. I shoot him again anyway. I shoot him for Alyssa, for Charlotte, for all the others out there in barrels, twenty years' worth of them, more maybe, some from Acacia Pines, some from other parts of the country, piling up in the water and stretching along the base of the stone wall.

When I asked Drew earlier if killing people got easier, he said yes.

He was right.

Sixty-seven

I check the dead man's phone. He didn't complete the call he was about to make. I tuck it into my pocket. The lights are still on outside the warehouse, but there's no movement down there. I'm suspecting now there aren't many armed guys like this in there because they'd have come out by now. There'll be some, but not many. My binoculars are long gone, somewhere in the water. I keep watching that direction for a minute then turn my attention to the dead man. There's blood all over his clothes. I figure guys like this, all the travel they do, all the situations they get into, they're going to keep changes of clothes in the car. Which they do. There's a small suitcase in the back. I check the contents. Same suit, same tie, same jacket.

I strip down and dress in his clothes before getting him into the SUV. I prop him up in the passenger seat and put on his seatbelt. I check the gun. It's a black Colt 1911. These things have been killing people since before World War One, and I can't imagine that ever changing. I check the magazine. It's empty. I go through his pockets, finding a spare magazine in the inside pocket of his jacket. I slide the bullets out to check how many are in there, then slide them back in. Eight.

I check the SUV for more handguns, more ammunition, more weapons, and find nothing. I guess these guys figured a gun each and a couple of spare magazines between them was all they ever needed. I figure they were one hundred percent right on every other occasion, and one hundred percent wrong on this one. I use his thumb to unlock the phone, then use the Internet to search for a phone number to contact the FBI. I call it, knowing I'll be put through to the nearest field office, but not knowing where that is.

I identify myself as Deputy Noah Harper and I ask to speak to somebody with an expertise in organ trafficking. You ring anywhere other than the FBI with that question and they'll hang up on you. I get put on hold listening to classical music, and as I listen to it I look at the dead man in the car, and the warehouse, and the edge of the road where the F-150 went over into the barrels. The music doesn't go with what I'm looking at. I don't know what music would. But not this. A woman answers the phone. She identifies herself as Special Agent Belinda Watkins, and asks what she can do for me.

I don't have time to explain in detail, but I figure I'll give it sixty seconds. I cover the fact I'm a deputy with the Acacia Pines police department, and that an investigation has led me to follow two men to a location where organ transplants are being made, the organs having come from missing hikers. I can't tell if Watkins at any point thinks I'm bullshitting her. The sixty seconds go by and I figure I can give her another sixty, but no more. I tell her about Alyssa. About Drew. About the warehouses. That an operation is currently about to take place. She doesn't say anything. The only reason I know she's still there is occasionally I'll hear her shuffle around in her seat or slide something across her desk.

"How quickly can you get here?"

"If what you're saying is true," she says, "we can have people leave here within minutes. Comes down to where you are. Which is where, exactly?"

"Can you give me your cellphone number?" I ask.

She gives it to me. I use a map on the phone then screenshot my location, and text it through to her. I can hear her phone beep as it arrives.

"Twenty minutes," she says.

"Charlotte may not have twenty minutes."

"That makes me think you're about to go in there," she says, "which would be a very foolish thing to do. Wait for us, Mr. Harper."

"I have to go," I say.

"Wait . . ." she says.

But I don't wait. I hang up. I toss the phone onto the passenger seat. I wipe my hands through the dead man's blood and smear it over my face and through my hair. It makes me feel sick, but I do it, covering myself as best I can. I start the car, hold my hand on the horn, and drive toward the warehouse.

Sixty-eight

I take my hand off the horn when I get closer, then press it again, on and off, on and off, here I am and things are urgent. Which is how I want it to sound. Which is exactly how it must sound to the people inside too, because the side door opens. My headlights are pointing at it. A guy peers around the edge, shielding his eyes. I hang my arm out the window and twirl my finger in what must be a universal way of telling him to open the door. He sees me and thinks I'm somebody he knows, and he sees his dead buddy and thinks he's the other guy he knows. He's fifty percent right. He closes the door and starts yanking on the chain to open the big door, a line of light spilling out along the bottom, the line getting taller as the door gets higher, a guy to the side working away on the chain, hand over hand over hand. They should have got an automatic door.

People start rushing over. A guy in jeans and a flannel shirt, plus the guy in the suit I saw earlier, and the driver of the car, and another guy with a suit and a gun. Five men, including the guy working the chains. Maybe the folks in the killing and harvesting business don't like hiring women. But then a couple of women — doctors or nurses, dressed in green scrubs with green hats and hospital masks over their faces — push through the plastic curtains as the man in the suit starts yelling at them. There's nobody else. I figure this would be an all-hands-on-deck situation, and these are all the hands.

I slump against the wheel. I'm too wounded to go any further. The first guy in the suit stands watching as the guy in the flannel shirt and the second guy in the suit come toward me, followed by the two women. The two guys reach the car, one on each side. I stay slumped against the wheel as they open the doors. The guy in the suit starts yelling something, but what that something is gets cut off by gunfire as I fire two shots into the guy opening the door next to me, and two more shots into the guy opposite. That leaves four shots.

I sit up and rest the gun between my legs and take my foot off the brake and punch the accelerator. The two women figure out what's happening quick enough to jump to the side, but the guy working the chains doesn't, and I hit him with the SUV, the angle not sharp enough and the speed not fast enough to send him up and over, instead he lands on his back and his head smacks the ground and then four thousand pounds of metal roll over him as I drive further into the warehouse, past Drew's patrol car, gunfire erupting and the back windscreen of my SUV exploding into tiny cubes of glass. I keep going, hanging a left and driving behind the operating theater, a plastic sheeted room with walls thirty feet wide. The warehouse must be ten thousand square feet. Opposite me is a wall full of rooms, all with doors closed and small windows inset at head height, faces pressed up against the glass, other people with compatible blood types and organs.

I don't stop. I can't, because there might be other shooters I don't know about. Instead I keep driving, circling the operating theater in the center, pulling hard on the wheel. More rooms to the side, bigger windows going into offices. There are blue barrels stacked against a wall, and I think for a second how miserable it must be, how frightening, for the captives to watch out their small windows as others like them are operated on before being stuffed into one of those metal coffins. There are more SUVs, four of them, a woman and a man wearing white medical jackets are climbing into one, and then I'm coming back around the theater and facing the entrance to the warehouse. The driver of the other car that showed up with the sick woman in the back has hunkered down against it, his hands up above his head, trying to sink into the ground. The guy in the suit is standing on the other side of the SUV reaching over the roof to point his gun at me.

A hole appears in the windscreen, the bullet smacking into the seat next to me. I stay low and aim for the SUV. The driver rolls out of the way as I crash into it. The airbag goes off and smacks me in the face and I can't see a thing as I come to a stop, and then I'm battling with the airbag as it deflates, getting it out of my way. I get my seatbelt off and get the door open and get out as the SUV with the doctors goes speeding by. The gun is on the floor by the pedals and I reach in and grab it. The SUV I hit has been shunted back. The driver is a few yards away but he's kneeling with his hands up in the air. I point the gun at him and move around him to bring the other side of the SUV into view, where the guy in the suit is lying on his back reaching for his gun, thrown there from the impact.

"Don't," I say.

And he does. So I fire a shot into his hand, severing one of his fingers. He stops reaching for the gun.

"How many others are here?" I ask.

"There's nobody else," he says. "Just . . . just doctors." But the doctors and the nurses have all hightailed it out of here, including the two that dived out of the way a minute ago.

"Get up," I say. "Both of you."

They get up. They don't complain. I pick his gun up and walk with them over to the doors with the windows and the faces. There are ten doors. Four are locked, six aren't.

"Strip," I say.

"What?"

"You heard me."

They strip, any concealed weapons they may have had piled up in their clothes. Then I tell them to go into one of the rooms.

"You're making a big mistake," the guy who was in the suit says.

"I get told that a lot," I tell him.

I close the door on them and slide the deadbolt across and I make my way over to the other doors, unbolting them one at a time. Two men and two women come out, each of them trying to hug me, each of them scared and thankful. Alyssa isn't here, but Jennifer is, the girl whose vigil I attended. They all look pale, but healthy enough — I imagine they've all been well fed — the last thing their captives needed was for the merchandise to get sick. I think about handing one of them the second gun, but figure they all might be prone to shoot whatever they see move. They ask me questions and I tell them everything is going to be okay, to stay calm, that help is on the way.

They follow me cautiously as I make my way over to the theater. As I get closer I can hear beeping from a machine. I pull one of the plastic sheets aside. There are no doctors, but there are two people inside, the woman I saw being driven here earlier, and Charlotte. Each of them has been sedated. I walk over to Charlotte. She's naked. Dotted lines have been drawn over her body, like patterns a tailor would make before cutting. I take the sheet off the older woman and place it over Charlotte, and then I step back out of the operating theater and wait for the FBI to arrive.

Sixty-nine

Two minutes into that waiting, the four people I've saved come to a collective decision they don't want to wait around. I can't blame them, and I'm not going to stop them, so they pile into Drew's car. There's a bottle of water in the backseat that I grab. I tell them to pull over when they see cars with flashing lights coming toward them, and if they don't see them, then to drive to the FBI field office, or to the first police station they come across. Of the four of them, Jennifer has been here the longest. I tell her about the vigil, how her family haven't given up hope. She tells me others like her have come and gone. She tells me there were two weeks when nobody was operated on, a week where one person was, and this week there have been three already, with tonight's being the fourth. Other people have come in after her and have left, somebody else was here for three weeks, and the new girl, Charlotte, has been here only a day.

"I guess it comes down to people's schedules," she says.

"Or who needs what and when." She's sitting in the backseat with the door open. I can sense how restless they are to leave.

"There was another girl," I tell her. I have the photograph in my pocket of Alyssa camping with Father Frank. It's wet and close to tearing when I pull it out. "Have you seen her?"

She looks at the photo and doesn't say anything.

"Have you?"

"Maybe," she says. "I can't be sure it's her."

"Can't be sure it's who?"

"There was a girl, she came in a week ago. They drove her in here and they got her out of the car and she did what I was too scared to do — she put up a fight. She punched one of the men and ran, only she didn't get far. This guy . . . this guy chased her down, and he hit her hard, really hard, and she just collapsed in a heap. I don't know if she was dead or what. They picked her up and they took her through there," she says, nodding toward a door near the office. "There are others in there too."

"Other men with guns?"

She shakes her head. "Other girls, like the one you're looking for. Young and pretty. Some even younger. They go in there and they come back out days later and are driven away. Sometimes . . . sometimes I wonder if what's in there is worse than what's out here."

I watch them drive off. I walk to the big door and watch the taillights get smaller, then watch them take the corner of the T and disappear. I open the bottle of water and drain it through my hair and over my face, washing away the blood I smeared there earlier, then drying it off with the jacket. I head back inside, the gun still in my hand, and take the door Jennifer pointed out. The door opens into a corridor. There are empty rooms with cots and lockers inside, a couple of offices, none of the doors with locks on them, places for doctors without boundaries and bad guys with guns to sleep. I reach the end and around the corner there are two more rooms, each with bolts to lock them.

The bolt of the first door is unlocked. I open it. There's nobody inside, but the room has been done up, the walls painted pink, with teddy bears on the bed, and a security camera above the door. My stomach turns. I close the door and walk to the second one. The bolt slides open. My breath catches in my throat as I swing it open.

My stomach stops turning.

Seventy

I travel back in time to the night I found her at the Kelly farm. Only Alyssa is older now, all grown up but made to look young, dressed in a tight school uniform, her hair in pigtails.

"Deputy Harper?" She gets up off the bed and comes forward and wraps her arms around me. I've never had anybody hug me so tight. She starts crying. She sobs hard into my shoulder. After a minute I'm almost as wet as I was when I came out of the water earlier.

She pulls back. She looks at me. She takes a breath to calm herself down. "How'd you find me? Did Dad call you?"

"He did," I say.

She smiles. She nods. She wipes fingers at her tears. "And you came."

"I did."

"Because you promised me you'd protect me from The Bad Man."

"I did. How about we get out of here?"

432

"In a moment," she says, and she hugs me for another ten seconds as tight as she can, and then she takes my hand in hers and we walk out of the room the same way we walked out of the basement twelve years ago. We go down the corridor and into the warehouse. She looks at the dead men and doesn't say anything. She looks at the operating theater, and I tell her Charlotte is okay, and she tells me she didn't even know Charlotte was here. I wonder how many people died in there, how many were saved.

We walk across the road toward the water and we sit on the guardrail and look out over the ocean. There's a ladder here, it's newer and more secure than the other one, so maybe people came here by boat too. Alyssa asks me about Father Frank, and I tell her he died peacefully and she cries again. I hold on to her, her body racking as she sobs.

We hear the helicopter well before we see it. It's been right on fifteen minutes since I made the call. It comes in from the north and circles the warehouse. A spotlight sweeps over us. We shield our eyes from it. I suspect there are a couple of guns trained on me. The helicopter lands and the motor winds down and the lights stay on. Six people come toward us. Four of them are in tactical gear. Two point their guns into the warehouse, the other two point theirs at me. The other two people are in suits. A woman and a man. The woman is tall and lean and the man is short and wide. We get up off the guardrail and move toward them. The woman introduces herself. She's Special Agent Belinda Watkins. She doesn't introduce me to the man she's with, but he pats me down looking for weapons while I hold my hands in the air. Then he pats Alyssa down too, looking uncomfortable as he does it. Even though I'm the one who made the call, I was expecting this kind of response. I'm guessing they looked me up to find I'm no longer a deputy. There are dead men scattered around, and the one who phoned them has been caught in a lie, and is battered and bruised and oozing blood. He goes through my pockets and doesn't find anything of interest. He handcuffs me, and then they separate us, Alyssa following the man to the left where they start talking. Satisfied I'm no longer a threat, the four agents in tactical gear start moving through the warehouse. I warn them about the two men locked up.

"Looks like you didn't take my advice and wait," Watkins says.

"I did what I had to do."

"Want to know what we found out when we looked you up, Deputy?"

A string of dark SUVs come out of the T intersection toward us, blue and red lights flashing, but sirens off.

"You found I wasn't a deputy anymore."

"Exactly. You stopped being a deputy around the same time Alyssa Stone went missing the first time. Here's what I'm going to need you to do, Mr. Harper. I'm going to need you to explain everything to me, starting with what happened twelve years ago, right up until two minutes ago when we arrived here."

"It's a long story."

"Good. You can start telling me on the flight back."

She leads me to the helicopter. We get in, along with her partner and two other agents in tactical gear, while agents start spilling out of the SUVs. Alyssa is sitting in the back of one of them. She waves at me and I can't wave back because of the handcuffs.

The helicopter fires up. I've been in them before, back when we'd be scouring the Green Hole. This one is newer but isn't any quieter. It looks complicated to fly. I sit between Watkins and her partner and two guys in tactical gear sit opposite. We get up into the air and I look down at the coastline, unable to see the barrels through the murky water. We wear headsets so we can hear each other, but nobody talks. Watkins must have changed her mind about when the long story will start. We fly for fifteen minutes. The warehouses become oceans become forests and then the forests become buildings and lights and streets and the houses of a big city, all of it lit up now as morning takes hold. We land on the rooftop of a tall building surrounded by other tall buildings. Out here, the sky isn't so big. It isn't so pretty.

We take an elevator down to the sixth floor where Watkins leads me into a room with no window and no color and no comfort. There's a table with two chairs opposite each other.

"Try to get comfortable," she says.

"Handcuffs?"

"Not yet," she says.

I take a seat. I can't get comfortable.

"Let's hear that long story of yours," she says.

I tell her the long story. Most of it. I don't tell her about the quarry and the dead men out there. If they're ever found, I'll say I don't know anything about it. I'll say they must have run into the men who took Alyssa and Charlotte. There's nobody left alive to know anything different. She makes notes and says nothing. When she's done she taps her pen against the table a few times.

"Question," she says. "Why didn't you call us before you left Acacia Pines?"

I don't have a good answer, so I don't say anything.

"You could have called us at any time, instead you take photographs of your ex-wife pretending to be tied up to draw the two men out to you so you could follow them here. Seems to me that gives you a lot of time for getting help."

"I did call you," I say.

"By my calculations, about seven hours after you should have. What else aren't you telling me?"

"That's everything," I say.

"Uh huh," she says. She undoes my handcuffs, gets up and walks out, closing the door behind her.

There's a camera up in the corner of the room watching me. I sit patiently at the table and stare at the door waiting for her to come back. That waiting takes an hour. They're trying to figure out what to do with me. When she comes back in her attitude has softened. I can tell because she's brought some coffee. She has one for herself too.

"Thanks," I say.

"I got you these as well," she says, and hands me a couple of painkillers.

"This mean you're warming up to me?" I ask.

"No."

She doesn't sit down. She isn't staying. She gets to the door.

"How's Charlotte?" I ask. "And the others?"

"They're all fine," she says. "Charlotte and Alyssa will be taken back home today."

"You've seen this before, haven't you?" I ask. She leans against the doorframe. "When I called earlier, I asked to talk to somebody with a knowledge in organ trafficking, and I got put through to you. That means you know what's going on. It means everything I'm telling you you've heard before."

"You mean have we seen rogue ex-deputies out of their league screw everything up while stumbling blindly forward?"

"You know that's not what I mean."

She sighs. She sips her coffee. For the first time I think that maybe she had to drag herself out of bed a few hours ago to answer my phone call. I think about the personal life she's put on hold to be here right now, and how difficult her job must be. I think about the things she's seen, and the things she knows are out there that she hasn't seen yet.

"They call them farms," she says.

"What?"

"The place you found. The men who run them call them farms. They put people into pens, they cut them up like butchers, they harvest organs. They farm people. Organ recipient lists are long," she says. "Twenty people a day die waiting. It's a question of supply and demand. When demand exceeds supply, that's when organized crime syndicates step in. Every hour of every day, somebody is selling or buying an organ on the black market. It's one of the biggest illegal trades in the world. Kidneys, lungs, hearts — these things can sell for one hundred and fifty thousand dollars, sometimes more. We've all heard the urban legends about people waking up in bathtubs full of ice with a kidney gone, but it's worse than that. People are found in alleyways with their eyes missing. Children," she says, "small children are found abandoned, dead, with lungs or hearts or kidneys removed, all so wealthy people can stay healthy. We estimate that up to twenty percent of kidneys transplanted in hospitals are trafficked illegally. The doctors and hospitals don't know. Some don't want to know. Sometimes organs are taken from funeral homes, with consent forms forged and signed, but other times, as you know, it's far more nefarious, with them coming from farms like the one you found. The trade in black market organs is worth billions. What you did was find yourself smack bang in the middle of a small-time crime syndicate supplying organs and brokering deals."

"Small-time?"

"Small-time," she says. "Don't get me wrong. These are very bad people, but they're still small-time compared to some of the bigger groups we see in the U.S., who themselves are often small-time compared to what we see in Europe or Asia. This group you found, they weren't just dealing in organs."

I think of the room I found Alyssa in, and the one next to it, painted to look pretty, to look young, to appeal to kids. I think of people being kept in rooms, like animals in pens. I think calling these places *farms* is both horrible and accurate.

"They were auctioning her off," she says, almost reading my mind. "She isn't the first and she won't be the last."

"How do they choose?" I ask. "Why auction Alyssa off, and not Charlotte?"

"Alyssa is a virgin, and Charlotte isn't. It's that simple. Charlotte was worth more in parts."

I don't say anything.

"But we have somebody we can question now, and we have their computer and cellphones, and we'll track down more, and this small-time farm might lead us to bigger farms. We already found the doctors and nurses you were telling me about earlier, and they'll talk." She pushes herself off from the doorframe. "Between you and me, you did good, Noah. It's not the way I would have liked it done, but you did good."

"What happens now?"

"Now?"

"With me."

"It's simple. We're not going to mention to the media that you were even there. We're not going to mention you in any way. Last night the FBI took down a crime syndicate, and you had nothing to do with it. Aside from Alyssa and Charlotte, the people you saved, they don't know who you are, and we'll tell them you were one of us. We get the credit, and you go free. You blab about it, or go to the media, then I'll come after you. You might think that the media will call you a hero, and there'll be a public outcry if we arrest you, but that won't stop me from throwing your ass in jail. You go back to being a bartender and you stay off the radar and we never want to hear anything about you again."

"What about Drew's family? These guys are going to go after them."

"We'll look after them. So we have a deal then?"

"Yes."

"Good. I'll get you a ride back into Acacia Pines later this morning."

Seventy-one

They drive me to a hospital not long after that. My cuts are treated and my foot is stitched up and I'm given pills to bring the swelling in my face down. If I'm lucky, within a week most of the bruising will be gone and I'll be back to normal. I'm given a hospital breakfast that's on par with the airport breakfast I had at the beginning of the week.

After I've eaten, a nurse checks over my wounds again. I'm given pills to take away with me, and some painkillers, and then an FBI agent hands me a fresh set of clothes before he takes the role of taxi driver and drives me back to Acacia Pines, a trip that takes us four hours, neither of us talking much. We pass the quarry, then the sawmill and the new sawmill. We pass Earl's Gas Station, where patrol cars from Acacia are parked out front, and Earl inside, probably uncomfortable about all the attention he's getting even in death. There are a couple of media vans too. We pass the Kelly farm where there's another patrol car and more media. When we get into

441

town the driver asks where to drop me off and I tell him Saint John's. The parking lot is full, and there are no spaces on the road outside. Father Frank's funeral must be taking place. There are media vans out front. The FBI driver drops me off at the curb. The church is so full of people that there are some that haven't made it inside. They're standing as close as they can to the door. I walk around the church and sit on the porch of Father Frank's home.

I end up waiting for an hour. The service ends and people flood out into the parking lot. Father Barrett comes out of the church and smiles and nods in my direction, and I smile and nod back, feeling ashamed that there was a moment last night where I thought the worst of him. People stand outside talking for a while, before disappearing in pairs or in small groups. Reporters approach some of them looking for statements. This morning the town has woken up to the news that Sheriff Drew Brooks was a killer. They've woken up to the news that Old Man Haggerty and Earl Winters are dead. They've woken up to the news that Alyssa is safe and so is Charlotte. I imagine they don't rightly know what to do with all that information. I'm surprised the funeral wasn't postponed. Maggie comes out of the church. She's wearing sunglasses and she's alone. I wave to her and she sees me and comes over.

"You're okay," she says, and she leans in and hugs me. She feels good to hold on to. We let go.

"I'm okay."

"And the girls, they're okay too. Thanks to you."

"Thanks to Father Frank," I say. "He was the one who convinced me to keep looking."

"I'm leaving Stephen," she says. "I'm taking the kids, and we're going to leave Acacia. The FBI are going to help us. I don't know where we're going to go, but I want to get away from here. I want a fresh start."

"That's good," I tell her.

"We're going to leave today, before he gets back. I know he won't be happy, but I'll let the lawyers deal with it."

"Isn't that kidnapping?"

She looks out into the thinning crowd of people. "I haven't heard from him," she says. "I always hear from him several times a day, not because he wants to let me know how he is, but because he wants to know what I'm doing. He's always checking in with me. It's like having a boss."

"You know what it's like out in The Pines. There's zero cellphone reception."

"He's not hunting," she says. "All his hunting gear is still at home. He'd never go out there without it, which means he's somewhere else. And aside from that, he wasn't going hunting."

"Drew told me you said he was."

"I lied."

"Why?"

"To cover for you."

I don't say anything.

"He was so angry," she says. "I spoke to him on the phone. If I'd spoken to him in person I think he would have killed

443

me. I know he would have. He said he was going to let off some steam and he'd come and see me in the morning. He never did. My sister saw you the following morning at the diner. You didn't see her, but she saw you. She said you were all beaten up. He came looking for you, didn't he?"

"Let me ask you something. Whose idea was it to call me to come and look for Alyssa? Was it Father Frank's? Or was it yours?"

"Why does it matter?"

"It matters to me."

She's no longer looking out over the parking lot. Now she's looking at me. "It was mine."

"When you came back to see me at the church that first day, you had your son with you."

"Damian," she says.

"Damian. You must have known he would tell his dad about me. You must have known it would upset him, and that he would take it out on you. You must have known where that simple meeting was going to lead. From the moment you decided to call me to come back to Acacia to help, you must have known where this was going to go. When I came to your house after he'd beaten you, and you begged me not to confront him, you didn't mean any of it, did you? You wanted me to go and see him."

"Did you kill my husband?"

"Did you want me to?"

"That's not an answer," she says.

"Nor was yours."

444

"It's possible," she says, "that Stephen ran into the same men you ran into."

"More than possible," I say. "I'd say it was likely. Good luck, Maggie, wherever it is that you're going."

"Same to you," she says.

We don't hug goodbye. It won't feel as good as it did a few minutes ago. Drew wasn't the man I used to know, and the same thing has happened to Maggie. Or maybe they were always like that, and I just couldn't see it. I don't know. All I know is that Acacia Pines changes people. I watch her walk over to her car. She doesn't look back as she drives away.

Epilogue

Three months later

The bar is full. There's a bachelor party in one corner and a bachelorette party in another. They're different parties, but after a while the two groups merge and more drinks are bought and everybody gets louder. In another corner a couple of guys are playing pool, one of them useless, the other one worse. There are a few people at the bar by themselves, mostly older guys nursing the hard stuff. There are three TVs on the wall behind me showing three different games — tennis on one, baseball on another, soccer on the third.

A woman from the bachelorette party comes up to me. She has a big smile. She orders a drink and asks if she can order me one too. I tell her I can't drink, that I'm working, and she shows me a mock sad face and tells me that's a shame. Then she tells us they're moving on soon, and that I should close up the bar and join them. I tell her that's tempting, but I can't, I have a lot of work to do.

The bachelor and bachelorette party move on. They make a lot of noise as they exit the bar, leaving behind a vacuum of sound that is soon filled with clicking pool balls and glasses being put down on tables. An old guy at the bar asks if I can turn the volume up on the TV, and I ask him which one, and he says it doesn't matter, just any one. I pick the baseball.

The two guys playing pool stop playing. It's after eleven o'clock and I signal last drinks. The pool guys leave, and the half a dozen people remaining all order another drink. I watch the clock. I want to get home. Want to sleep. Want to get home and question why I'm here, why I don't move back to Acacia and try to start another life there. I miss it. I think Lego would like it there. I could apply for the police force. Nobody really knows what I did out there three months ago, so I'd have a good chance of being accepted.

One by one the guys at the bar leave, leaving just the one, the one who asked me to turn the volume up. He picks up on the fact he's keeping me from going home. He stands up and pushes himself away from the bar. He looks like he could fall over.

"You okay?" I ask.

"I'm fine," he says, and he must take my question as some kind of challenge, because he picks up the rest of his drink and knocks it back in one shot. He puts his jacket on and heads for the door and I follow him so I can lock it behind him.

"I left you a tip," he says, and he salutes me and walks out into the night. I lock the door and head back to the bar.

There's a box on the seat next to where he was sitting.

Something in my stomach turns.

The box is three inches square. Like a box that would contain jewelry. It's plain cardboard. It has a bow around it. I pour myself a drink and knock it back.

I think about what Drew told me about getting Jasmine Kelly sent to him in the mail, and about what the man I shot out at the warehouse told me, how there were more like him, how they'd kill everybody I ever loved. Drew said the same thing.

I pull the ends of the bow and it opens.

Inside is a finger. It's surrounded by cotton wool to absorb the blood. I look away from it, and when I look back, that's when I see it, the tattoo. It's a crudely drawn smiley face. I stare at it, and I wonder what part of Rochelle they're going to send to me next.

Acknowledgments

W*hatever it Takes* was a whole lot of fun to write. It came about when an author I really like and all round cool person — Joshua Hood — got hold of me to tell me a real life story. It was a crazy story, but not one either of us would base a novel on – it wasn't "in his lane" as he puts it, as he writes explosions and action and military thrillers, and I never write anything based on something inspired by a real life story. But it was a crazy story to listen to, and at the end of it we were shooting the breeze a little, and then he said something that stuck with me. He said he wondered what it would take to get a character to come back to town after leaving and swearing they would never return.

It was a good question, and one I had an answer for two seconds later. For me, that character would need to be in law enforcement. He or she would be run out of town for beating a confession out of the sheriff's son (at the time I imagined that would be with a phonebook). He or she would save the girl, and ten years later they'd need to save that girl again by returning to the place they were no longer welcome. I love it when ideas come this way — somebody will utter one line, or ask a question, and bang — within seconds a novel is created, the beginning of it mapped out. Then it's a matter of putting in the hard yards and getting that idea to work on paper.

So, first of all I want to say thanks to Josh — the novel didn't start with the story he was telling me, but started with the musing at the end of it, with the 'what would it take', which, two years later, has become *Whatever it Takes*.

Then came the big decision — could I get a novel like this to work in Christchurch like all the others? Even two and a half years after writing that first draft, it's a question I was still asking myself, but no matter what angle I looked at it from, *Whatever it Takes* couldn't be set there. It needed a small town dynamic. It needed an isolated police force. So I ventured away from what I know and love, and created Acacia Pines, and immediately it felt like a second home for me. I've put down roots in this fictional town, and am going to write another book or two from there. I'll get back to Christchurch, I promise — just give me a year or two.

As with every other book, there's a bunch of folks involved after you've finished that first draft — friends and editors who tell you what works and what doesn't. The first to read it was David Batterbury — he's always the first. Sometimes he's reading them before I've even finished the manuscript. We play tennis every Friday and it's not just tennis balls we're hitting back and forth, but ideas too, as I tell him what I'm working on next. Next was Fiona Cummins — a fantastic crime writer whose books I admire. She gave me a bunch of notes that I took into my second draft.

Around the same time another friend of mine who is also a fantastic editor, Rebecca Farrell, gave me a whole bunch of more notes — notes that, along with Fiona's, made a significant impact on how the story plays out. While all this was happening, Kevin Chapman, my New Zealand publisher and friend and fellow gin connoisseur, was also reading it. Kevin has always been a huge supporter of the books, and I'm grateful he's given them a home here in New Zealand. He's often the first to hear about my ideas, usually over a drink or two in a bar in another city or in another country, where he generously picks up the tab while being a sounding board for what ails my serial killers. Then came the next round of editing, for which I want to thank Mary Sandys and Stephanie Adie, who put the final touches on the manuscript and turned it into the version it became. Thanks to Nicole Helfrich, my Evil Twin, for spotting one of the best typos I've ever made, and to Ceren Kumova, for reading the manuscript and chatting with me about what makes people tick.

Thanks to Sahar Ben Hazem, who read the novel and offered half a dozen title ideas — including the very title this book would become. And thanks to my French translator, Fabrice Pointeau, who went above and beyond when it came to weeding out the final few mistakes.

So, thanks guys, for all the hard work. Thanks to Kevin and the team at Upstart Press: Warren Adler, Gemma Finlay and Craig Violich.

And, like I have in the past, let me sign off once again by thanking you — the reader. You guys have been great, and have given me the opportunity to keep doing what I love to do — and that's make bad things happen . . .

Paul Cleave
Christchurch
May 2019